CANARY

DUANE SWIERCZYNSKI

MULHOLLAND
BOOKS
HODDER

First published in Great Britain in 2015 by Mulholland Books
An imprint of Hodder & Stoughton
An Hachette UK company

1

A CIP catalogue record for this title is available from the British Library

Trade Paperback ISBN 978 1 444 75418 6
eBook ISBN 978 1 444 75419 3

Printed and bound by Clays Ltd, St Ives Plc

Hodder & Stoughton policy is to use papers that are natural, renewable
and recyclable products and made from wood grown in sustainable forests.
The logging and manufacturing processes are expected to conform
to the environmental regulations of the country of origin.

Hodder & Stoughton Ltd
338 Euston Road
London NW1 3BH

www.hodder.co.uk

For Parker and Sarah

I CAN FEEL THE HEAT
CLOSING IN

November 27

Hi, Mom. Last night I got arrested. (Sort of.)

I'm writing this so I can sort out the details, just like Dad taught me. He always said things have a weird way of making sense once you write them down. Putting this on physical paper (and not the laptop) for a number of reasons:

1. These days you have to assume that anything you type on a computer or cell phone can be read by some random geek anywhere in the world
2. Nobody can ever see this, and I don't want some random geek trolling for revenge porn yanking it off my laptop
3. Paper burns

I'm addressing this to you because you always said I could tell you anything, no matter how awful. Which brings me back to the (sort of) arrest…

So last night I'm at an off-campus party where everybody's getting wasted because it's their last chance to get wasted before returning home for the long holiday weekend. Pretty much the kind of party you used to warn me about. But don't worry, there are no orgies, no needle-sharing, no Satan worship. Just a bunch of us freshman honors geeks blowing off steam before the last two grueling weeks of final papers (next week) and final

3

exams (the following). Beers and shots, loud rap music, that kind of thing. But I can't blow off anything because I have to go pick up Dad at this god-awful hour of the morning.

Fortunately, I know how to make a single beer stretch. You'd be proud of me. The past two months of college life have given me the chance to perfect my technique. You simply

1. Take shallow micro-sips
2. Opt for cans over see-through bottles
3. Occasionally fill can with tap water from bathroom sink

Nobody's ever given me shit about being a lightweight. Hey, I've always got a (nearly) full beer in my hand!

Anyway, I'm on a crowded couch when a glass bong starts making the rounds. The couch frame is broken and the cushions have sunk so deep that one good sneeze and I'd knee myself in the face. The dude sitting next to me takes the bong with his two hamburger-patty hands, huffs it, and immediately, chivalrously, offers it to me. He's pretty insistent, like take it, take it, take it. The only thing a happy, stoned drunk wants is to make sure everyone in the immediate vicinity is also happy and stoned and drunk. Nothing against the marah-ju-wanna politically, personally, medicinally. You know Dad's always saying: You want to try something, just bring it home and we'll try it together. (Like that will ever happen.) No, I just hate losing 20 to 30 IQ points in a single puff. Weed is not for me, and I'm not just saying that for your benefit.

Good thing I have strategies for pot, too:

1. Suck in your cheeks to feign inhalation
2. Seal off your windpipe at the same moment

3. Hack, hack, hack like a newbie, complete with slightly bulged eyes that indicate to those around you that you're doing it right/wrong, and you're well on your way to baked-land.

But the strangest thing happens. When the bong comes my way, and I take it in my hands, and all of these eyes are on me, I hear this voice in my head. It tells me that I'm wound up so tight all the gray matter's going to pop out of my skull. I'm supposed to be here partying, and what am I doing? Faking like I'm having a good time. Shit, I'm not even supposed to be here in Philadelphia. I should be fake-getting-high in California. So I press my lips to the opening and when I inhale, I do it for real.

Of course I cough like a newbie; got that part down right. Classmates who hardly ever look at me slap me on the back and shoulders, laughing and yelling their astonishment. I can almost hear them gossiping this coming Monday: Dude, she got sooooo high. And you know what, Mom? Maybe I am, just a little. My skin feels pleasantly warm. The tight little ball in the back of my brain seems to unclench a little. Even my internal give-a-shit-o-meter ticks down a few degrees.

I'm proud of myself. I even follow up with a congratulatory real sip of piss-warm beer.

That's when I notice D. staring at me.

(Not giving his full name here, for reasons that will soon become obvious. No, not because I'm afraid you're going to have him tracked down and killed, Mom. Though if anyone could make that happen, it'd be you.)

Apparently D. caught the whole thing. He nods and gives me a lazy, proud smile. I cough again and try to smile back.

D. weaves his way across the crowded living room, which is when I notice his pants: bright red chinos, topped off with a striped sweater that clings tight to his lanky torso. Few men can pull off red pants; D. is one of those men. Then there's the hat—a 1950s-style Stetson that he doffs as he crouches down. He presses two fingertips against the can like he's taking the beer's temperature and says,

—Sarie Holland, I had no idea you were a nursing major.

I stick out my tongue. But like a stupid schoolgirl I'm thinking, Wow, he actually knows my name. (He even pronounces it the right way.) I cough again.

D. smiles, leans into me.

—Let me get you a cold one. Beer this shitty has to be enjoyed at a certain temperature.

D. tries to grab the can but I lean back and move it just out of reach.

—No, I'm okay, seriously. My dad's plane gets in at 6:30 a.m., which means I have to leave pretty soon anyway.

—Text him now, have him call a car.

—What? No. I'm not making my dad take a cab on Thanksgiving.

—Not a taxi. One of those private cars. Plush leather, wet bar. Let your old man kick back with a bourbon highball!

—What exactly do you think my dad does for a living? Anyway, I've gotta pick up my brother, too.

We have one of those weird moments of silence where the person who breaks it first loses. Surprise, surprise, it's me.

—So are you going home?

—What?

—Are you going home. For Thanksgiving.

—I'm supposed to go upstate to see my mom, then over

to some gated fortress in Jersey to see my asshole dad, but whatever. I'll get there when I get there. Where's your dad flying back from?

—California. Business stuff.

Just speaking aloud the name of the state makes me think about how sunny and eye-poppingly gorgeous Southern California probably is right now, even in the depths of November. Dad has been there since Sunday, another consulting trip— third one this fall. (He's really trying, Mom.) Anyway, Dad traveling means I always have to be home for Marty. But tonight he was invited to a sleepover, leaving me free until the morning. Dad and I made a deal: I could go to the party as long as I didn't get drunk (ha-ha, he knows I've never been drunk) or high (ha-ha…oh shit) and was willing to pick him up from the airport at crazy o'clock in the morning.

—Well…I should go…

—Wait, are you okay to drive?

—I think I'm the only sober one here.

—Hah, you can't fool me, I saw you blowin' it up over there.

—I just did one hit! I'm totally fine. I look fine, right?

D. smiles wide. His eyes are kind of swimmy.

—I'm just fucking with you.

—Asshole.

But I'm smiling too. Like a dork. Another awkward moment of silence as D. seems to roll something over in his mind, rubbing his hands on his thighs.

—Hey.

—What?

—Can I ask you a favor?

Now it's been a long, stressful day in an even longer, stupid-stressful week. I've been up since 4:30 a.m. force-feeding facts to my eyeballs, processing them, scribbling down neatly ordered sentences that may eventually turn into a coherent paper. (Even my eidetic memory only goes so far.) The half beer I've nursed along with that half-hearted puff from the bong have taken their toll. All I want now is sleep. Sweet, sweet sleep. Just a few hours before I'll have to shower and wash the smoke out of my hair and pull on some clean clothes, then make the drive to the airport.

D. senses none of this. Or if he does, he doesn't care.

—Well, here's the thing, I need to pick up a book from a friend of mine. He's just a couple of blocks from Pat's. Could I maybe get a lift? I'll buy you a cheesesteak for your trouble.

My mind unpacks this favor in pieces. He wants me to

1. Drive him (because I'm obviously sober, and no one else is, least of all D.)
2. Somewhere near Pat's Steaks (which is all the way down in South Philly, while we're currently standing in an off-campus house way up in North Philly)
3. To get a book (never mind that tomorrow's Thanksgiving break, and he'll have all weekend to pick up said book)
4. And my reward is a big greasy cheesesteak (even though I'm vegan)

All of it, I see now, through the golden glow of hindsight, is seven kinds of sketchy. Mom, I'll admit it: In the moment, all I can see is his strong, limber frame beneath his shirt and those goofy red pants.

—Okay, sure, I'll drive you.

Before I know it we're both in the Civic hugging a tight curve on the Schuylkill Expressway as the twinkling skyscrapers of Center City emerge on the horizon. So beautiful this late at night. So weird, having D. in my car. Philly may always be Hostile City to me, but downtown isn't so bad, to be honest. I should hang out down here more. The first month of school it seemed like every other day someone in my nerd herd was making an excuse to take the subway down to Old City or South Street—even though everyone told us that South Street's heyday had come and gone before we were all born. I guess if I'm stuck in this city I might as well make the most of it.

(Sorry, Mom. I swear, I'm over it.)

D. opens my glove box, starts rummaging through the cassette tapes.

—Holy shit, I can't believe you have these! You're into the Clash?

—Uh, yeah.

—That's so fucking cool. Hey, you've even got *Sandinista!* Tell me you have a tape deck in your car…

—Right there.

—Fuck yeah motherfucker!

D. slams in reel one and after a few seconds of awkward tape hiss, "Magnificent Seven" comes on.

Of course the cassette tapes are Dad's. I found them in a plastic container of his old crap and have been listening to them all semester. The Clash, Talking Heads, Television, Lou Reed, the Velvet Underground, the Cure (all of the stuff you used to hate!), and a whole bunch of mix tapes with no liners, so I have no idea what's on them. Some of it I like, some of it sucks. But if D. here wants to mistake me for cool, who am I to stop him? And huge props to you, Mom, for ordering the last Honda Civic that ever came with a cassette player.

—So who do you have for the triple? The three Cs or KGB?

—The three Cs.

The three Cs of the honors freshman triple: Calkins (history), Curnow (philosophy), and Chaykin (lit). The first C is friendly but a tough grader; the second C is incomprehensible but an easy grader; the third C is cryptic and fast-talking and funny and a sadistic grader. I might be looking at my first B. Ever.

—That's really funny you have Chaykin. Is he doing the Lost Generation or the Beats this semester?

—The Beats.

—Have fun with *Naked Lunch.*

—I'm supposed to start reading it over the weekend.

—Ha-ha, you're fuckin' dooooomed.

(D. curses a lot, if you haven't noticed, Mom. With the cute ones, you tend to forgive a foul mouth.)

I steer the Civic to 676, cutting through the guts of the city, whiz under the Ben Franklin Bridge and ride I-95 for literally ten seconds before exiting on Columbus Boulevard, then hang a right on Christian Street. Welcome to South Philly. The streets down here still confuse me, especially the streets around Pat's. D. tells me to just keep going until Ninth. Then a right turn. Then he looks at me. My eyes are focused on the street, but I can feel his stare. I turn down the Clash.

—Well, here's Ninth…

—Hey, look, thanks so much for this, Sarie. I really, really appreciate it. I'll be, like, two seconds.

—Good, because I'll be timing you.

(This is my version of flirting. I flirt about as well as I drink and smoke.)

D. points to a row house that looks way too nice to be a

South Philly crash pad for a bunch of college guys. Maybe they're Penn students or something, with rich parents. Either way, cars are jammed up and down the block, with no visible spaces.

—Where should I park?

—See that valet? Just pull up there and tell him you're waiting for a friend of Chuckie. He'll let you sit, no worries.

At first I think D. is making a reference to some mob movie I've never seen, *The Friends of Chuckie* or some such shit. Takes me a full second before I realize he's serious.

—Wait…who?

—That's my buddy. Chuckie. He's worked out a deal with the guy. You can sit there and not have to pay anything. Two seconds! I swear!

D. jumps out of the car and slams the door so hard it makes me flinch. Hate that. After a moment of stunned silence, I steer the Civic a quarter block up and pull over into the valet line, which is busy. A second later I realize I am accidentally cutting into the line. The valet guy in the bow tie and vest sweeps his arm in a sarcastic "after you, ma'am" gesture. I lower my window and feel the tiniest bit absurd asking:

—My friend's a friend of Chuckie?

Astonishingly, dude loses the attitude instantly. He nods and moves on to the next car.

The digital clock on the dash says ten past midnight. It's freezing and crazy windy. At this moment Dad's red-eye has already lifted off, slinging him from lush California back to the grisly East Coast. I have to be at Terminal C in less than six hours. And D. is definitely taking longer than two seconds.

The valet guy, although busy with customers, finds the time to gawk at me, giving me an oh-so-charming smile that showcases the shiny black tooth in his upper jaw. (I know how to attract the lookers, right, Mom?) I turn my head and watch customers drift in and out of an old-school Italian restaurant on the corner, which apparently is the reason for all of this traffic. Now, mixed breeds such as myself should not cast ethnic aspersions, but damn, it's like Goombah Fest up in here. Gold chains, blown-dry 'dos, older dudes with dates who could be their granddaughters, town cars and Caddies, the whole nine. Tammy would appreciate this. We should come back sometime just to people watch. (Who I really need to call this weekend. It's getting ridiculous already. I haven't talked to her since Halloween.)

The minutes tick by and, yes, Mom, I know I'm screwed. Another hour for the sandwiches; another thirty minutes back north to campus. I'm not getting home until 2:00 a.m. at least. All for a boy.

I met D. the first week of school, at some honors program social in some pseudo-nightclub on the first floor of the union building. Later I heard that the social was referred to as "Trader Ho's" by the upperclassmen. All of us fresh young geeks on display, ripe for the picking. Turnout for the social was predictably huge. D. was different, though; he kind of just joked around, inviting a group of us over to his off-campus house for some beer — my first ever, by the way. (Dad would be proud.) Some of the other girls from my honors triple, who bragged about drinking beer since sophomore year of high school, were more into the shots of Jack.

D. just smiled at them all, flirted with them equally, including me. Apparently he liked to date freshman girls who had their own cars. To D., the ability to go off campus at will was a magical thing. Word around the honors nerds was that he'd gotten in some serious DUI trouble in high school and pretty much wouldn't be driving until the end of the second Obama administration.

Not that a carless D. is a bad thing. The dude clearly drinks a lot and smoked his fair share of the wacky weed. The idea of him behind a 2,700-pound motor vehicle frightens me.

After a few more minutes of awkward waiting with the Valet to the Friend of Chuckie, watching sketchy-ass characters come and go, along with the Goodfellas parade up the street, my mind goes back to D., and cars, and weed. Wait wait. What if he's not here picking up a book? Of course he's not here for a book.

This is probably the place where D. scores his weed.

Party's running low, so they ask D. to conjure up some more. He doesn't have a car of his own (and shouldn't be driving anyway) so he finds the only sober person with a car in the general vicinity.

Me.

I feel like a world-class idiot.

So Thanksgiving Eve, as my drug counselor Dad is boarding a plane in California, I'm in South Philly on a drug run.

Happy Thanksgiving, right?

Undercover narcotics officer Benjamin F. Wildey, 32, seated behind the wheel of his unmarked car, maintains a laserlike focus on the front door of the row house. Feels like the city's one big freezer tonight. Not much warmer in this piece of junk hooptie, either. The whole day's been an icy raw mess with rain and sleet and Wildey out on the street for most of it. He glances at his watch. Look at that. Thanksgiving, as of three minutes ago. Time flies when you're posted in your car doing surveillance based on a tip from a couple of desperate snitches.

At first glance there's nothing about the place on South Ninth Street that screams "drug house." Clean unmarred sidewalk, freshly painted window frames, refaced brickwork. This was the kind of South Philly row home that immigrants struggled to buy for $4,000 back in the day and now could easily fetch $400,000.

But a snitch swore that a guy at this address is doing a lot of slinging with college kids. Word is he's a midlevel dealer who calls himself "Chuckie Morphine" and specializes in small-time trappers who work the universities, sometimes doing direct sales to kids who are leery of driving to the Badlands or Pill Hill. Years ago this whole neighborhood—Passyunk—used to be solid working class, maybe a little sketchy in places. Wildey remembers those days. But now it has gastropubs and consignment shops and pop-up restaurants and all that other hipster catnip. Kids feel safe popping down here.

If the past few hours are any indication, it's clear *something's* going on inside this house on South Ninth. Lots of visitors. Could be a pre-Thanksgiving party, sure, but why is everybody staying for only a few minutes at a time? With no music? No noise of any kind?

What Wildey needs is a legal way inside the house. One that won't raise any objections from the Man in the Widener Building. Doing narcotics work these days, you've got to be careful. Knuckleheads, perverts, and money grubbers in the department have made the job difficult of late. Take the guys whose blazing stupidity got them featured in a Pulitzer Prize–winning series a bunch of years back.

Yeah. *That* Pulitzer. A narcotics squad in the Badlands came up with the brilliant idea of busting neighborhood bodegas for selling small plastic baggies. Questionable at best. But that wasn't the stupid part. Once inside the bodegas, the narcs helped themselves to hoagies, Tastykakes, batteries, milk, loose cash, whatever. You know, because Tastykakes and hoagies are so expensive.

Now, skimming from a dealer is a time-honored Philadelphia law enforcement tradition. But the thing with skimming from a dealer is, you have to actually skim from the dealer—the *perp*. You don't steal from the frightened immigrant couple selling plastic baggies that, the last time Wildey checked, were not illegal. So these idiots sold out the department for a bunch of Tastykakes. Bravo.

Following the Tastykake Takedown, there seemed to be new scandals popping up all the damn time. A local reporter crunched some numbers and realized that, over the last four years, a Philly police officer was charged with a crime something like every three weeks. Not just narcotics, of course. But those were the ones that seemed to stick in citizens' minds. Perhaps the most notorious being the cop who shook down a junkie, making her strip naked before jacking off on her jeans. "He was too disgusted to touch me, but he wasn't too disgusted to touch himself and ejaculate on my seventy-dollar friggin' pants," the junkie told a federal judge. The cop gave her six dollars for cigarettes and told her to get dressed and scram. The local tabloid had a field day: THOUGHT YOU GOT OFF, EH? And a new phrase entered the local legal lexicon: "the masturbation civil rights violation."

All of this culminated in a full-scale clusterfuck that closed an entire field unit, saw five hundred drug cases tossed, and sent a bunch of cops to desk duty or early retirement. As a result, the D.A.—most likely sowing his mayoral oats—declared war on the entire narcotics division from his office in the Widener Building.

So Wildey knows to be super-careful. The old ways don't fly anymore—"old" meaning as of six months ago. Last spring he could have braced any one of these college kids and ordered them up against a wall, pockets out. Boom, probable cause. A ticket to the show.

But Wildey can't stop any of them. Not without a solid, defensible-in-court reason. In the wake of all this departmental chaos, defense lawyers would knock the whole thing down without so much as a *thanks for nothing*. Chuckie Morphine himself was too smart to be caught in the open. The name on the lease of the property is a corporation, probably a shell. Nobody knows Chuckie's real name, or even what he looks like. Wildey has yet to snatch a glimpse of him.

But he's exactly the kind of guy Wildey's dying to bust. Nobody else in his unit's even heard of this guy, which means he's relatively new.

So Wildey keeps an eye on the place, waiting for an opening. This is only one of a half-dozen leads he kept tabs on, but this is the fattest— a bloated tick ready to pop. Lots of traffic. And a pusher with an irritating nickname. Man would Wildey *love* to be the guy who busted Chuckie Fucking Morphine. Idiot should serve time just for that name.

There is also the little matter that Morphine is almost certainly a white dude. Now, Wildey isn't racist. But a few months before he was recruited to the newly formed Narcotics Field Unit-Central South (NFU-CS for short, as in Nobody Fucks with us) he read a study from the ACLU that said the majority of people arrested for pot were black. Yet whites bought and smoked more dope than anybody else. In Philly, something like 80 percent of the marijuana arrests were of blacks. Wildey had arrested his fair share in the Badlands, though he tried to be an equal opportunity cop, busting black, brown, and white alike. Still, it would be nice to get those percentages down.

Lieutenant Katrina "Kaz" Mahoney told him the day she hired him: Find me the cases others have missed. Forget the street corner busts. Bring me big cases. I don't care who's paying who or what's happened before today. The rules are different now.

So sorry, rich white drug lords. A brother has to start his career somewhere.

And here's hoping it starts with Chuckie Morphine.

But of course . . . done right.

In the words of his superior: "Imagine the Man in the Widener Building is wedged up your ass at all times, watching everything you do, second-guessing every thought in your head. You take a leak, imagine him complaining you're taking too long and massaging your prostate to get things moving."

Ten minutes after midnight Wildey perks up when he sees a silver Honda Civic glide into the usual spot—up near the corner, where the valet guy lets all of Chuckie's (alleged) customers idle for a bit. Breaking no laws.

Wildey actually likes this setup. Makes it easier to keep tabs on the customer base. A hat-wearing hipster, about twenty or twenty-one, bright red pants, green backpack slung over his shoulder—yo slick, Christmas ain't for another month yet—launches himself out of the passenger seat, clears the sidewalk in a few long strides, then jogs up the short stoop to the front door. Knocks three times. Door opens. Red Pants slips inside. Say yo to Chuckie for me.

He picks up his notebook, scribbles quickly:

0044 Sub 1—W/F, driving Honda Civic
0045 Sub 2—W/M, passenger, 6'2" skinny build, green backpack over
shoulder, bright red pants, navy windbreaker
0046 S2 approaches target house, unknown male lets him in. S1 stays in
car in valet spot

Once the guy goes into Chuckie's place, Wildey turns his attention to the driver. The girl. Maybe eighteen or nineteen? Latino? Italian? Hard to tell in this light. Her hair's up, held in place by some kind of silver piece. She's doing the awkward *idling-in-the-valet-area* thing. Looking around, body language nervous, shoulders fidgety. An older cop told him most times you don't need a confession. Just watch the body; it'll tell the whole story. Clearly this girl doesn't want to be here. Is she here against her will? Wildey writes down the Civic's plates to look up later. There's no laptop to run a search. All he has is a notebook, pen, badge, gun, and a portable dashboard lights/

screamer that plugs into the cigarette lighter. You know, just in case this gets real.

Wildey's hoping this is the case. *C'mon, girlie, gimme a little reasonable suspicion.* He's been watching Chuckie's pad off and on for almost a week now with no luck.

After quite a long while Big Red pops out of the house, tattered green backpack still slung over his shoulder. What you got there? He trots back down the stoop, crosses Ninth, not even really looking, and opens the passenger door. Taillights blink. They're pulling out. Come on, Wildey thinks, give me *something.* Some reason to pull this car over. A twitchy taillight? Any reason to believe her inspection's past due? Somebody cut the tags off her license? Wildey knows cops who would do that. Instant probable cause. Can't do that anymore, though. The D.A. is probably right now sitting on the edge of his bed, nursing a glass of pinot noir, just *waiting* for someone to call to tell him that narcotics cops have fucked up again.

The Civic continues up Ninth—she's almost to the stop sign. Wildey rolls the dice in his head. How do we feel about this one? Do we follow and hope? Or do we stay put in our stuffy car and wait for the next one?

Wildey has four such cars situated around Philly, each within visual range of a suspected baby kingpin's house. The lieutenant had encouraged them to think outside the box. Well, this is what Wildey came up with. Just take a car from the impound lot, something boring that runs. Slap some city council tags on it so the parking authority leaves it alone. Take turns inside each car, watching the customers bounce in and out. See something you think might be good, give up that precious parking spot and you pursue. But do so with caution. Parking spots are tough to find—especially down here. Wildey spent a lot of time fighting for the four spots he has. For him to pull out, this Civic's got to be worth it.

That green bag, though. Wildey's feeling good about that green bag.

He puts his car in drive and slides out of a parking space that will be occupied within seconds, guaranteed.

Just one bust. A Chuckie Morphine–sized bust. That's what Wildey needs to put his name out there. The scumbags he'd really love to bust are elsewhere in the city and virtually untouchable by departmental degree. But things change. Wildey scores enough Chuckies, he can touch the untouchables. Which is what this whole thing is about. And maybe it starts now.

D. heaves himself into the passenger seat so hard the suspension rocks. I'll bet his mom yells at him for stomping up stairs and slamming doors. He's like a goofy puppy who has no idea of his own size.

—Still up for that cheesesteak, Sarie?

I can't help it. My eyes are drawn to the grubby green North Face backpack now on the floor between his legs.

—Uh, sure.

When I met D. at that mixer I thought it was sort of cute that he was a stoner nerd guy. He talks about pot like some guys talk about craft beers. "Dankness" is one of his favorite words. D. is the kind of boy who would annoy Dad for any number of reasons, mostly because Dad was probably a lot like D. back when he was a teenager. At least based on the stories you told me.

But now I see Dad is probably right. Because now I'm just the silly girl who has a car, takes him on drug runs.

The blocks surrounding Pat's are swarming with drunks and roving packs of hungry carnivores looking for a fix of greasy meat and processed cheese before gorging on turkey and stuffing tomorrow. Thanksgiving Eve is a well-known national drinking holiday, the night everybody goes out, front-loading for the family holiday ahead. So there are no empty parking spots. Maybe we would have been better off telling the valet we were really, really good friends of Chuckie's—and hey, would you mind darting over a few blocks and scoring a cheesesteak for us? Calm as I can, taking a deep, soothing breath before opening my mouth, I ask where we might park. I try to stop staring at that green backpack. How much does he have in there? A little baggie? Or like a few *Midnight Express*-sized bricks? Meanwhile D. is tugging off his jacket and nearly elbows the side of my head. I flinch and jerk back just in time. Navy jacket fabric brushes my nose.

—What's that?

—I said where am I supposed to park?

Jacket finally peeled off, D. bunches it up into a loose ball and gently lowers it into the backseat with a mumbled "hang on" before turning back around and squinting out of the windshield. He half-heartedly points out spots that aren't legal spaces by any stretch of the imagination. I suspect he isn't really trying to help; he's trying to exhaust the conversation so I'd agree to circle the block while he picks up his food. Which is what I eventually agree to do. Of course.

—I'll be two seconds.

D. kicks open the passenger door, offers to bring me back something. I decline, telling him I don't like to eat this late. Not worth getting into the whole vegan thing with the requisite lecturing about how I'm gonna fucking starve or something because I don't eat animal flesh. He nods. I notice his green backpack in the foot well of the passenger seat. You know, the one probably containing illegal substances.

—Wait! Hey!

—What?

—Don't you want to take your bag with you?

—Why? I'll be right back.

—No, seriously, I'd feel better if you took it with you.

D. blinks in confusion.

—Why?

—Please just take it!

After a few seconds of a dumbstruck stare, D. opens the door, picks up his backpack, slings it over his shoulder. He seems like he's about to say something mean, but instead he just smiles and slams the door shut. I flinch like a dumbass.

A minute later I join the Cheesesteak Merry-Go-Round. Up Ninth Street one block. Right on Wharton. Right on Eighth. Right on Reed. Right on Ninth, and so on, and so on, and so on, and if you look out the window, you can see poor Sisyphus with his rock following the same route. The crowds and cars make it extra-slow going, but I press on like a good drug-running accomplice. Which, by the way, is a one-and-done deal for me. Yep, my intention is to go to drop off D. and go home and consider myself Scared Straight.

Which of course is when I turn right onto Eighth for the eighth or ninth time and hear a loud shriek from hell.

Mom, I swear, I had no idea what was going on. Did I make an illegal right-hand turn? Cut someone off? Hit an elderly nun in slow motion? No. I may be many things, but I am an insanely safe driver. I do not screw around behind the wheel. What is going on?

Then I remember there is a chance I might have a wee slight high going on. And this is on top of that single warm beer swimming around my bloodstream. Shit, why did I do that bong hit! Did I weave or something? Give some other kind of tell? My heart is racing. Shit, shit, shit.

I flip on the right blinker and look for a spot along Reed. There are none, of course, so I settle for a half-spot near the corner, which means my front end is sticking out a little. I check the rearview. The car following me is not a standard police vehicle; it's a normal car with one of those domes you slap on top. Shit, shit, shit. Why is an unmarked cop car pulling me over? It slides into a spot in front of a driveway. Guess cops in unmarked cars can do that.

A thought chills me. What if this particular unmarked car has been following me for a while? Since, say, D.'s buddy's place on Ninth Street?

I will myself to stay perfectly still. If I wiggle around, it's going to look like I'm hiding something. Or reaching for a sawed-off shotgun. So I keep my paws on the wheel at perfect 10 and 2, though I allow myself a quick check of my eyes in the rearview. Thank God. Not too bloodshot.

In the side view, the cop climbs out of his car. The guy is huge. Not fat; more tall and broad than anything else. Great. Somehow I've attracted the biggest, baddest cop in Philadelphia. He clears the distance between us in an easy three strides. Then he's looking down at me through the driver's-side window, flashlight the size of a Sharpie in his hands. I can't see him too well, but I can tell he's African-American, and in plainclothes. He's got a badge attached to a chain around his neck, hanging midchest. Shiny. Real, as far as my untrained eye can tell.

—You lost, honey? Looking for somebody? You've been around this block a couple of times.

—I was?

—Yeah, you were. And you know what? You were breaking cruising laws.

—Huh?

I'm not playing dumb; I have no idea what he is talking about.

The cop helpfully points to a rusty metal sign bolted to a metal post across the street: NO CRUISING ZONE. It's partially obscured by a small tree or steroidal weed that had punched through the sidewalk.

—Three times around the same block in one hour is technically cruising.

—Oh shit. I didn't know.

—Didn't think so. Which is why I asked you if you were lost. Maybe I can help.

By this point some faint alarm bells are going off in my head. Why would a plainclothes cop in an unmarked police car just pull me over, completely out of the blue, because he thought I was lost? Considering I was an accomplice on a drug run, I knew it was best to say as little as possible. So, come on, think of a lie. Tell him why you're circling the block. Come on, now. Quick. He's *staring* at you.

I come up with absolutely nothing. Zilch.

—Let me see your license and registration.

This snaps me out of it. I try to keep my head straight, my voice calm and confident. There are YouTube videos that tell you what to do if you're pulled over, and I'm pretty sure calmly asking for a reason is an excellent strategy.

—Why did you pull me over, Officer?

—License and registration, please.

—Officer, am I under arrest?

—Do you want to be?

Undercover cop: 1. Sarie Holland: 0.

I dig my license out of the plastic compartment in my wallet, pop the glove box, retrieve the registration, hand both out the window. The cop scans them with his flashlight. The light in his fist, shining back down into my face, makes it tough to see his expression.

—Who's Laura Holland?

The question catches me off guard. Just hearing your name can still jolt me.

—My mom.

—She know you have her car?

I tell him the truth, that you died last year, that this is my car, but my dad hasn't changed the registration yet.

—What are you doing down here?

—Just went for a drive. To clear my mind. Got a lot of papers to write this weekend. They're all due next week.

His tone softens a little. Maybe he's commiserating, maybe it's the mention of you.

—Oh yeah? They don't even give you a break for Thanksgiving weekend? That's a shame. Where you goin' to school?

—St. Jude's.

—The college? Up there in Olney?

He pronounces it like a real Philadelphian: oll-o-knee.

—Yeah.

Then I add, as if it will earn me points or something:

—I'm in the honors program.

—Honors? In college? Isn't that a high school thing?

—No, they've got an honors program. I have the triple. Which means three honors classes this semester.

I didn't want to tell him it's the freshman-year triple because the license I just handed him alleges that I'm twenty-one years old. Which of course, as you know, I am not. Not even close. The cop, though, is too busy mulling over the whole honors thing.

—So you want to graduate with honors, is that it?

—I guess?

—Whatcha studying?

—I'm undecided.

—Undecided, huh. Aren't you a little old to be undecided?

I say nothing.

—Okay, fine. Mind if I take a look inside your vehicle?

My stomach unclenches a little as I thank the gods I made D. take his stupid green backpack with him. I could imagine the cop training his flashlight on the ratty bag, reaching in, zipping it open, and, like, the light from heaven shining down, illuminating a brick of Hawaiian Gold or whatever D. was always talking about. There's nothing in my car except a brown paper bag on the backseat, the contents of which will probably make this cop laugh, if he pops the tape off the folded top and takes a look inside.

    —Sure. Go ahead.

Wildey shines his Maglite in the back. Then he pops open a back door and reaches in, feels around. Nothing back here but a navy windbreaker. He pulls it out. Feels heavy. He puts the flashlight in his pocket and pats the windbreaker. Heavier on one side. He unzips a pocket and reaches inside.

This pocket contains a big Ziploc bag stuffed with three smaller Ziplocs stuffed with pills. Most likely Oxys, Mollies, and stop signs — suboxys. A nice fat re-up for the holiday weekend. And more importantly, the beginning of the end for Chuckie Morphine. Wildey could make a little dotted line of pills leading to the house on South Ninth, easy enough for the D.A. to follow.

The only thing missing: the owner of this navy windbreaker.

Big Red.

But if he keeps her talking, Wildey is sure he'll be back soon. Better get out of sight, keep the element of surprise.

Mom, he found pills in a baggie.

    Correction: lots of multicolored, oddly shaped pills in a medium-sized Ziploc baggie. Like nothing I've ever seen before. Not even when you were sick and taking all kinds of painkillers.

    The cop's talking but I can barely understand the words through the icy numb shock. It's like a blood vessel has burst in my brain.

    This isn't just weed. This is pills! I didn't know what they were aside from bad fucking news. So D. is a pill dealer. Even though I've known D. for three months, it's clear I don't know him at all.

The cop heaves his large frame into my backseat, closes the door behind him. For what? So I can drive myself to the booking station? I feel like I should say something, start explaining. The cop exhales and a chill runs down my spine. Fuck if I'm not brought right back to high school, stammering in front of a nun.

—Take it easy, Honors Girl. What's your boyfriend's name?

—I don't have a boyfriend. (Truth.)

—C'mon, don't play me like that. You know I'm talking about the young male who exited the passenger side of your car. The dude gettin' his cheesesteak on right now. The one who's probably waiting for you to pick him up right now. I'm interested in him, not you.

—I told you, I don't have a boyfriend.

—Okay, fine. Your special guy pal, whatever. You did have a passenger in your car just a few minutes ago, did you not?

Ice stabs me in the base of my brain. So this cop was watching us. He followed us! From the drug house on Ninth Street! I force a shrug. Inside I want to cry. The cop in the backseat counters my shrug with a soft series of chuckles. Which worries me. What does he know? What's he laughing about?

—He at least bringing you back a steak?

—No.

—No?

—I'm vegan.

So weird, the feeling that washes over me, like I *did* take drugs or something, because I'm hyper-alert, so much so I'm practically having an out-of-body experience. Which is probably why I notice D. ambling down Passyunk with a wrapped-up cheesesteak in his hand, completely fucking oblivious, happy in the moment, raindrops falling on his head and shit, probably thinking about nothing but eating his greasy bun full of meat and cheese on the ride back to campus then maybe trying to peel my clothes off for a little pre-Turkey Day action. *Found the wishbone!* D. is still living in the old universe, where a cop wasn't watching us, and didn't just pull me over, and didn't just find a lot of pills in his jacket.

—But your boyfriend, he ain't vegan is he? You know how many times I've seen this, a guy comes down here to score AND get his cheesesteak on?

—I don't have a boyfriend.

—Male friend, whatever. We're just going to sit here and wait for him, see who these pills belong to. How about that?

How about we're totally fucked. And D. has no idea. But with all of this hyper-clarity comes a thought. Yeah, D. lied to me. Yeah, he put me at risk here. But that wasn't his intention. He just needed a ride. Am I really going to be the one who helps send him to jail? I'm the one who let the cop search my car. This is just as much my fault. I can't do this to him.

You understand Mom, right? Tell me that if you were in my shoes you wouldn't do the same thing.

I place two fingers on the turn signal lever then hook my right arm over the seat and turn to face the cop and tell him, okay, okay.

—Okay what?

—I think I know what happened.

A smile now.

—What's that, Honors Girl?

—Okay, obviously someone used my car as a place to stash some drugs. As you probably know St. Jude's is in a not-so-great neighborhood.

—Uh-huh.

Flick flick. Flick flick.

—Can you, like, run windbreakers for DNA or something?

27

The cop stares at me a moment before breaking into an amused chuckle.

—DNA? Are you serious? Do you really think we need to get all *CSI* on this?

Flick flick. Flick flick. Come on, D.! Look up!

—I'm pretty sure you know the owner of this windbreaker. Tall skinny guy, bright red pants?

Yeah. I know him, and I wish he'd clue the fuck in. I keep working the lever: Flick flick. Flick flick. High beams. Universal highway code for A COP IS WATCHING! Sure, it's out of context, but, considering the circumstances, it's the best I can do. I try to send a psychic message to D. but the cop in the backseat seems to pick up on it instead. Suddenly he shifts in his seat, leans forward.

—The fuck are you doing with the lights?

Two desperate flicks of the high beams later, the cop gets it, curses, kicks open the back door, heaves himself out of the car. The suspension rocks.

—Shit.

I look out the front windshield. D., at long last, has finally received the message. He drops the Pat's and darts across Ninth Street. I've never seen D. move so fast. It's like a gazelle bolting away from a predator.

Wildey is halfway across the street when the entire world slips out from under him. Skinny Boy's body hits the chain-link fence across the street with a metallic *ching* that echoes off the nearby walls. Wildey's body weight is momentarily supported by his left knee before momentum carries his body the rest of the way and his right side slams into the asphalt. Brakes squeal—headlights splash over him. Wildey is confused. What the fuck he just slip in? As he scrambles to his feet, he smells it, then visually confirms it a second later: a burst-open Pat's cheesesteak, grease and cheese and onions smeared over the blacktop like it had committed suicide from the roof of a nearby row house. The driver of the car who almost turned him into creamed corn glances down, sees the badge dangling from the chain, and immediately stops his cursing. Wildey gives him a hard look anyway.

Meanwhile Big Red goes *ching-ching-ching* up the fence and over it.

Wildey sucks in air and launches himself toward the fence, hooks his fingers into the fence, and pulls himself. He's over in six, maybe seven, seconds. But the perp has a serious lead on him—he's already halfway across the field. Wildey pumps his legs, run-limping like he's suddenly developed a tumor in his left knee.

"Freeze! Police!" he yells, huffing way too much to sound authoritative.

The perp either doesn't hear him or doesn't give a shit. He moves like a streak, kicking up dust from the field like a cartoon character zipping across the desert.

I'm thrilled for a few seconds to see D. escape until I remember that the cop is going to be crazy pissed. And then he's going to come back for me. I sit behind the steering wheel contemplating my options. Just pull away, some meek little voice tells me. Put the car into drive and pull out into the street and go right home and pick up your dad in the morning and then your brother and eat Thanksgiving dinner and hope this just all goes away...

But that would be stupid. The cop has my license, my registration, my whole fucking life in his hands.

I feel weird about rooting for D. now. It would honestly be easier for me if poor D. came back in cuffs, and I got tagged as an accessory or some such shit. Granted, Dad would go nuclear, but it wouldn't be as bad as taking this one alone. Just a case of wrong girl at the wrong place at the wrong time. I'd recover...right? Because what did this cop really have on me? Someone—anyone— could have put a jacket stuffed with drugs in my backseat, right? And yeah, that crap might work, if not for the fact that this cop saw me drive up with D., saw D. go up to that house, saw me pull away.

After a small eternity the cop returns, limping, out of breath, looking like a bull that ran through a red cape. I steel myself.

—Get out of the car and put your hands on the hood.

My mind goes numb. I try to remember more from those YouTube videos about getting pulled over but my mind goes blank, like someone's cut the Wi-Fi.

—Out of the car. Now.

I unbuckle my seat belt, open the door. A gush of cold air, chilled by the nearby river, hits my body just as I take a step out. Guys in oversized coats watch me from across the street. I don't know where to put my hands. Should I be standing in the street along- side the car, or in front of it? Someone catcalls.

—Hey, honey, you holding?

The cop yells back.

—Shut the fuck up and move along.

The cop directs me to the front of my car, tells me to put my bare hands on the hood. The metal is warm from the engine but as I press my hands down the heat vanishes instantly. I hear a car door slam and realize it's my own door, which I'd forgotten to close. I hate it when real life supplies you with a super on-the-nose metaphor for how badly things are fucked.

Lieutenant Kaz is in the hallway when Wildey returns to headquarters, leading Honors Girl by the arm. The poor thing refuses to make eye contact the whole walk up here, as if keeping her gaze fixed to the floor will make this all go away. Sorry, honey, you're caught now. You should have listened to your teachers in school. Be Smart, Don't Start.

"Well, if it isn't my Wild Child!" Kaz calls out.

Wildey tries to keep his face appropriately stern. "Hey, Loot."

Lieutenant Katrina Mahoney's unit knows to never, *ever* call her "Lieutenant Mahoney." It's either "Lieutenant" or "Loot" or, if they're feeling unusually chummy, "Kaz." That's because Mahoney is the name of her ex, who is also on the force, and they hate each other with the fury of a thousand blazing suns. After the divorce everybody expected her to change the name, but she kept it just to spite his cheating ass. (Another pro tip: Married to a cop? Don't cheat on her with another cop.) A few years after their scorched-earth divorce the ex ended up in Internal Affairs, Kaz in Narcotics, and the whole recent D.A. probe made it so that the two collided on a regular basis. It was ugly for a real long while.

But strangely, the situation was a boon to her career. The fact that the ex *didn't* bust her made it clear that Kaz was in fact clean beyond all doubt. If she had so much as a friggin' recycling violation, the ex would have crucified her naked on the top of the Art Museum steps and hired little kids to throw rocks at her all day. After the public scandals of the past year, the mayor himself appointed Kaz head of NFU-CS, with carte blanche to clean house and set things back on course.

Kaz appraises the girl, shoes to head. "What, did you catch her copping some Adderall?"

"A little more than that, Loot. I'll fill you in."

"You're liking them younger and younger."

"Nah, you know I'm into the older women. Keep hoping to catch myself a Betty White type hooked on smack."

Wildey has an uneasy relationship with Kaz. She likes to goof around with him, calling him "Wild Child" even though his name was pronounced *will-dee* and was not supposed to rhyme with *wild*. And he jokes back most times, which is good. In building the ranks of her newly formed Narcotics Field Unit-Central South, she was careful to pull guys from all over the city to bust up any existing allegiances. But she could be frustratingly cryptic and hard to read. Frankly, Wildey never quite knew where he stood with her.

At first she told Wildey he was the perfect fit for the unit. Wildey was fresh off a commendation for his role in taking back the notorious McPherson Square Park from drug dealers last year. For three decades "Needle Park" had been littered with syringes and gun casings and junkies dozing on benches. When the Twenty-fourth District decided to take it back, Wildey was one of the bicycle cops who was racking up steady and constant arrests. Which was impressive alone, considering his size. (He dropped twenty pounds riding that damn bike.) Somehow, word of his exploits found their way to Kaz. She liked that he was a lone wolf with no wife, no kids, not much of a life outside the job. But all of his work so far seems to have vaguely disappointed her. "Keep digging" is a common refrain. No leads excite her. Sometimes, Wildey thinks he'd be better off on his bike, picking off street dealers one at a time.

Wildey puts Serafina Holland, a.k.a. Honors Girl, in one of their birdcages—what they call their meeting rooms—then returns to brief his boss. "I'm making some real progress on Chuckie Morphine," he says.

"Who's this now?" Kaz asks.

"The guy I think's dealing to college kids, high school kids, based out of the house on Ninth—you remember. His name kept coming up in September. A couple of my CIs came up with an address and I've been watching it."

"So this girl is one of his dealers?"

"No—her boyfriend is."

"Where's he?"

"Probably still running through South Philly."

"So what did you catch her with?"

Wildey tells her: Oxys, Mollies, stop signs. Kaz nods appreciatively.

"That's a fairly solid haul. You sure she's not the dealer?"

"Positive."

Kaz nods for a good half minute then looks steadily, calmly into Wildey's eyes.

"Let's do this."

I've never been inside a police station before but this looks like no police station I've ever seen. I'm pretty sure most police stations don't smell like cheese curls, chalk, and bleach. Or have black-boards.

Maybe it's just late and I'm working on no sleep, but the whole building looks like a former school. The cop who arrested me—I don't even know his name at this point—leads me down a cramped hallway until he makes a sharp turn into a tiny room, pointing to a chair where I'm supposed to sit. Nothing else in the room but a dented metal folding table and gunmetal gray shelves lining the walls. I'm guessing this used to be the school library. Too bad there are no law books in here.

The advice from every cop movie and show ever: Ask for a lawyer then STFU. But as smart as that advice seems in the ab-stract, I can't bring myself to do it. Calling a lawyer makes all of this irrevocably real. Calling a lawyer means Dad will find out. There's no way I can do that to him. Not after this past year. No offense, Mom.

On the way in, the cop tells me if I'm smart there'll be a way to straighten this out. I keep seeing those bags of pills. The cop, bouncing them in his oversized hand, smirking, proud of his catch.

So I sit at the table, hunched forward slightly, palms down on the surface. The room is small, airless, windowless, stripped of all decoration. There isn't even one of those obvious one-way mirrors you see on the cop shows. I'm wired but exhausted. The two sensations play tug-of-war with my nervous system. I'm tempted to start pacing or put my head down on the table but I do neither. Years of Catholic school have trained me for this. I so, so badly want to blink and wake up and realize this was just my brain playing a cruel little scared-straight nightmare.

The wait is long. For all I know the sun is already up and Dad is at the airport, pissed.

There is no clock and I don't have my phone, so I can only guess at the time when the two cops finally, at long last, enter the room. I try to look as innocent as possible. After all, I am (basically) a good girl in a bad situation.

The cop who arrested me casually tosses two objects on the table in front of me: D.'s fedora. And D.'s navy windbreaker. He introduces himself and his partner—who I later learn is actually his boss.

—I'm Officer Ben Wildey, this is Lieutenant Katrina Mahoney.

Officer Wildey's smiling like we're old pals. His boss, though, gives me eye daggers. There's a smile on her lips, too, but not one of those warm, reassuring ones. It's the I'm-gonna-fuck-you-up kind. Introductions made, they sit down across the table from me. Officer Wildey looks at me head-on, while Lieutenant Mahoney is half turned, like she's not ready to make the full commitment. When she speaks it's with a Russian accent.

—You like the pancakes and syrup?

I blink. Are they offering me breakfast? I know it's probably close to dawn, but what the hell?

—You must like pancakes and syrup a lot. I mean, considering what Officer Wildey found in your car. You must have had a real big weekend planned.

I seriously have no idea what she's talking about. Officer Wildey chuckles.

—You don't know what she's talking about, do you.

Lieutenant Mahoney makes a tut-tut sound.

—Oh, she knows. Look at her.

—No, I don't think her boyfriend was into the breakfast treats, probably just slinging 'em.

—Uh, what are you guys talking about?

Pancakes and syrup, he explains, is a mix of Xanax and codeine cough syrup. Something kids like if you don't want to mess around with heroin. The high is similar. I start to stammer, telling them that not only have I not heard of pancakes or syrup, I don't know anyone who has. This is all news to me. This is a mistake that I'm here at all. Somebody stashed some stuff in my car without me seeing and now...

—Easy, now.

Officer Wildey reaches across the table and touches my hand. His skin is rough.

—There are exactly two ways this can go.

The lieutenant, meanwhile, is busy flicking something from one of her nails.

—We charge you with possession and intent to sell. You receive serious jail time—five years, mandatory. This is not us being hard-asses. These are federal guidelines, and we can't do a blessed thing about them. You won't be finishing your senior year until you're in your midtwenties. Doubt the honors program's gonna take you back then.

I take this in. Not all the way in. More like inside the vestibule of my mind, where it can be quickly kicked out the front door again. This first way? Shit, this was no way at all. *Going to jail?* No. That would ruin my life. Kill Dad. Probably ruin Marty's life, too. Dead mother, crazy father, jailbird sister. Good luck, kid.

Wildey pats my hand reassuringly.

—Now let me remind you that this can all go away. You can walk out of here tonight in, like, just five minutes…if you tell me the name of the guy in the red pants who I chased all the hell over South Philly.

I almost blurt it out. Instead I imagine steel rods emerging from my teeth and locking in on the opposite side and clamping my jaw shut. If I speak that name out loud, all of this falls on his head. And I can't do that. Yeah, he shouldn't have taken me on a drug run. But I was the one who got pulled over. I was the dumbass who said sure, search the car. If D. had somebody else drive him, that somebody else would have been smarter about cruising laws and unmarked cars and all of that. All D. wanted was a cheesesteak. I tell myself: Don't pussy out now.

I tell them, slowly and confidently:

—I don't know any guy in red pants.

Officer Wildey and Lieutenant Mahoney exchange glances. She smirks.

—No guy, huh.

—No.

—So the drugs in that car were yours.

—No! They're not!

Officer Wildey turns to face me again, sighs.

—Okay, then there's the other way this can go. We can't just let you walk out of here, not with what you had in your car. The good news is, you can work off the charges. Work hard enough, as a matter of fact, and it's like this never happened.

—What, do you mean, like, intern with the police?

Both cops turn to smirk at each other, not even trying to hide it. I feel my cheeks burn. Fuck you both.

—No, not an intern, Honors Girl. You can help us another way.

—How?

—You can become a confidential informant, and help us catch the scuzbags who sell drugs to your classmates.

—A confidential what?

They explain it to me. They want me to become a CI—a confidential informant. Only Wildey and his boss would know my identity. In short, they're asking me to be a snitch. In Philadelphia. Where snitches are killed on a regular basis.

—But I don't know anything. I'm telling you, I'd be the worst snitch ever.

Lieutenant Mahoney stands up and leans over the table, gives me the eye daggers so hard I twitch.

—Guess you're going to have to learn. Otherwise we're forced to go with the first option.

The lieutenant's office used to be the principal's office. There's not much of Kaz in here except a dying cactus ("to remind me not to get too close to pricks") and a small boom box, which almost never plays music, only AM radio news. Once in a while Wildey will hear Kaz playing crap like Billy Joel and REO Speedwagon and it cracks him up.

Wildey stays on his feet while Kaz stands behind her desk, tapping an index finger on the track pad of her laptop. She never seems to sit. Wildey knows he won't be here very long.

"Looks like she'll be CI one thirty-seven," Kaz tells him. "The important thing is to keep on her constantly. Keep pressure building. You need to be this unrelenting hard-ass who will not go away. Ten bucks she cracks by Black Friday."

"She's just a kid."

"She's the kid standing in the way of your case. You want to help her, get her talking, then get her out of the way."

"Okay. Gonna drop her back at her car, then I'm out. I'll keep you posted."

"You're a sweetheart, Wild Child."

"Happy Thanksgiving, Loot."

Even though tomorrow is not really a holiday for either of them. There is no overtime in the NFU-CS, not anymore—that gravy train has long left the station. But Kaz expects the same hours and unflagging devotion to the task. Wildey agreed to this when he signed up for the unit. Doesn't matter to him, as he doesn't have much to do outside the unit anyway. He can catch up on video games and cable shows and movies when he retires.

Wildey shows me where I can wash my face, then returns my purse, hairpin (after all, it could be a deadly weapon), and cell and gives me a ride back to my car on Reed Street. The sun isn't up yet and the wind is howling. The cold sinks deep into my bones. I don't know if I'm shivering because I'm still scared or because it's like negative twenty out. I check the time. If I haul ass I can still make it down I-95 in time for Dad's flight. There's an awkward moment when, if this were a date, a fumbling first kiss would be attempted. But this is very much not a date.

Officer Wildey looks at me.

—You all set now?

—Yes. I mean…no. Not really.

—No?

—I have no idea how this works.

—Damn, and here I thought you were an honors student.

—But I don't know what you want from me because I don't know anything. Is there a rule book or, like, instructions?

Wildey chuckles.

—Couldn't be simpler. You're an informant. You give me information. I follow up on it.

—I'm not a drug dealer and I don't know any drug dealers. At school, or anywhere else.

—Yeah, yeah, and those bags of pills just magically ended up in your car.

—Exactly!

—Cut the shit, honey. Why are you protecting him? Has he ever hurt you? Are you afraid he might hurt you? Because we can do something about that. I can do something.

Again I almost say something dumb like, No he wouldn't hurt me, he barely knows me. Then I remember: There is no him. I can never admit there ever was a him. Stick to the story—weird as it is—that I was alone in my car tonight, driving around, looking for a place to park so I could pick up a cheesesteak for my little brother at home. I have no idea how that jacket or those pills ended up in the back-seat of my Civic. Maybe some junkie near St. Jude's used my car as a stash spot.

But I know Wildey must have seen me and D. together. The cop saw me warn him off. It's all gonna unravel on you, so you'd better keep your mouth shut. There's a way out of this you're not consid-ering.

—Is that what's going on? He like to hit you?

—No.

—So there is a he?

—No, there's not.

Wildey exhales like a steam train ready to pull out of the station. I look around the quiet freezing streets and a thought hits me.

—Look, can't I just work this off another way?

The cop seems genuinely mystified.

—What do you mean?

—I mean, can't you give me a lead or something, and I'll follow up on it? I'm great at research. I can help you that way.

Wildey smiles.

—That's cute, Honors Girl. But that's not how it works. You're supposed to bring me the leads. You're the informant. And you'd better have something for me soon, because informants who don't inform are of no use. You know what happens to those informants, right? You're a bright girl. You'll figure it out.

—Right.

—Now listen.

—Yeah?

—I know you're probably going to want to tell your pops about this, and that's perfectly natural. But let me tell you why this is a bad idea. The moment Pops hears about this, he's gonna call a lawyer. And the moment we hear from a lawyer, our deal with you goes up in smoke. You're going to have to do some jail time, no matter what he says. And there's nothing I'll be able to do about that. You understand?

—I understand.

Wildey gives me a cheap pre-paid phone—a pay-by-the-minutes deal already loaded with his number. He calls it "the burner." Wildey tells me he'll never answer; just leave a voicemail or a text and he'll get back to me. I have to keep this cheap phone on me at all times. No matter what. Then he hands my iPhone back.

—Here's yours. I have your number. You don't get back to me on the ditch phone, I call this. You understand me?

I reach for it but he teases me, refusing to let go.

—You're smart, Honors Girl. I know you'll do the right thing.

POLICE ON MY BACK

PHILADELPHIA INTERNATIONAL AIRPORT

November 28

Kevin Holland startles awake, surprised to find himself back in Philadelphia. When had he drifted off? That almost never happens to him on planes. He's usually awake for every cramped, dim, agonizing twilight moment. What's more bizarre is that he slept through the landing, too. Only the final *bing* of the overhead seat belt indicator roused him from slumber.

Then again, this is what happens when you drink a little too much at an airport bar and then basically pour yourself into your window seat.

The tear started the way it usually does. *Used to;* he doesn't do this anymore, it's just an aberration, he tells himself. He had one beer to calm his nerves, maybe help him sleep on the flight even though he knows he never sleeps on flights. Second beer in, he's primed up for one Jack on the rocks, just one, you know, to calm his nerves on the flight, even though he's never been a nervous flier. One Jack becomes three and Kevin knows that's enough, more than enough, but one more and maybe he really could sleep on the plane, because tomorrow's Thanksgiving and there'll be so much to do, so much he can't even keep it all straight in his head. But the bartender, a blonde with purple streaks and some hard living on her face, was his buddy by now and poured him a double, no extra charge. And then it was a rush to grab his bag and settle up and dart to the men's room for an epic piss and wash his face and look in the mirror to see Old Kev staring back at him. Hey, where you been, poser?

What worries Kevin is the utter lack of hangover, which means he's still drunk this morning. He turns on his phone and texts Sarie. She texts back a nanosecond later, from the cell phone lot. Rock-solid dependable as always, his daughter. "Strong like bull," he used to joke in a grunting voice when she was younger, and it remains true. He's relieved as hell she agreed to pick him up this morning. Two trains all the way to the Northeast on Thanksgiving morning would be depressing. Kevin doesn't drive, not since he lost his license in high school in the worst way you could lose it. Even though he was allowed to drive again, he refused. Kevin never wanted to be back in that kind of situation ever again. Laura always drove. Then Sarie took over. Kevin is the eternal passenger.

Kevin makes a detour into a terminal men's room to splash some cold water on his face and check on the condition of his eyes. They don't call it a red-eye for nothing, but there's plane red-eye and still-drunk-and-unfocused red-eye. Sarie and Marty know the difference. The cold water feels good on his skin, and the busy thrum of holiday travelers all around him is somehow reassuring. Life resumes. You're going to be okay.

As long as you maintain The Fiction, Mr. Holland.

The Fiction is the defense mechanism he came up with over the summer. He knows it won't work forever, but that doesn't matter; it's working okay now. A blend of his own counseling training and his imagination, The Fiction is a state of mind designed to help him deal with the awful new realities of his life one day at a time. Yeah, same basic thing he's been telling his patients for years. Don't think about never having a drink again for the rest of your life—that's too much weight to carry. Just avoid taking a drink today. Don't think about how you'll never lose yourself in that high; just avoid sticking the needle in your arm today.

The Fiction is: Don't think about the fact that Laura is gone forever. That you're never going to feel her fingertips running up and down your forearm, because she knows it relaxes you—she knows all the places that relax you. You're never going to kiss someone whose lips taste like a blend of cinnamon and strawberries. That the intangible, wonderful, fragile, beautiful, difficult thing you shared can never be replicated, and was gone for good. That is too much for anyone to bear.

So: She's only gone *today*.

According to The Fiction, Laura Gutierrez Holland is merely in Guadalajara taking care of her mother after hip surgery. She'll be gone a few weeks, maybe a little more. She doesn't call or email because the connections down there are so unreliable, but she's thinking of him all the time, and she misses the kids so very much.

It doesn't matter that Kevin knows The Fiction is exactly that. Kevin's never even met Laura's mother, nor will he ever. He has no idea about the condition of the woman's hips. And the real Laura would never go a day without hearing the voices of her children. She never could understand how Kevin could travel for days at a time and seem to be okay without hopping on the phone on a regular basis. Laura never traveled alone, and even if she did, she wouldn't let many hours pass without hearing from her babies.

So today is Thanksgiving and Laura isn't here because she's taking care of her mother in Guadalajara. They're going to have a small meal together because they don't do Thanksgiving in Mexico—Laura always thought the holiday was bizarre anyway.

Sober up, Kevin, you're on duty this holiday.

Kevin exits the men's room, pulling his roller bag behind him.

Sarie pulls up to the crowded curb looking happy to see him. Behind the open trunk Kevin hugs his daughter tightly, hoping the five mints he chewed and the cold morning air are enough to mask the lovely *eau de Daniels* that he's sure is oozing from his pores.

"How was the party?" he asks.

"You know, pretty much what I expected," Sarie says. "How was San Diego?"

"They kept me busy pretty much the entire time. Though I did manage to sneak off to the Gaslamp to walk around a little."

Kevin told his kids he was visiting his ex-colleagues at the retreat for a couple of days. Which was true. But he didn't tell them he was up for a job at the retreat. And he wouldn't—not until he was sure the job was his and the contracts were signed.

"No La Jolla?" Sarie asks.

"Why would I do that?" Kevin says sharply, and just like that, the awkward silence is back. La Jolla. Why did she bring that up? Of course to her it's a happy memory; to Kevin, it's a brutal reminder that The Fiction is Fiction. He does a forensic analysis in his head and realizes he may have snapped at his daughter. Fuck.

"Did you end up driving Tammy home last night?" he asks, as Sarie merges onto I-95. Planes scream overhead. Everybody's coming in for a landing on the busiest travel day of the year.

"No. She didn't show."

"Seriously? That whore!"

Sarie giggles. "Yeah, well."

"So you were there alone?"

"I knew some people from the triple, so that was fine. And before you ask, I limited myself to one can of beer, nursed lovingly over a period of four hours."

How much did you limit yourself to, Kevin?

"I think you can handle more than one beer, Sarie. You could have had a little, I don't know, fun?"

"The beer wasn't very good. Anyway, I don't have any of the sides ready yet. And I didn't start the stuffing, either. By the time I got home I was exhausted and just crashed and then I got up to pick you up and—"

"Don't worry. We've got all day. Seriously."

The Civic speeds past some of the most depressing vistas Philadelphia has to offer. Abandoned fields of industrial muck and a few struggling refineries. Burst of fire in the distance. Smoke. Weedy swamps and dump sites. Must be a shock to tourists when they land and hail a cab to the City of Brotherly Love and feel like they're pulling into the set of *Blade Runner.*

"Dad?"

"Yeah?"

"You told me to always tell you when something happens, no matter what, right? And you won't freak out?"

Kevin's stomach sinks. Sure, he probably meant the words when he spoke them. Doesn't mean he actually wants to hear the words that will follow. Instantly his mind sprints to dark places. Roofies, and grabby hands, and worse. He glances over at his daughter. She's seemingly no worse for wear, no visible bruises. But Kevin knows that doesn't mean anything, which takes him to an even darker place.

"You can tell me anything."

The moments between that last word and the next are excruciatingly long, giving Kevin's brain plenty of time to invent new awful scenarios.

"Somebody was passing around a bong."

"And...?"

Sarie turns for a second to lock eyes with her father. "And what?"

"And how was it?"

Sarie turns her attention back to the highway for a second to make sure the Civic isn't about to slam into anything, then locks eyes again.

"I didn't try it, I *swear,* I sort of just…faked it and passed it down the line. Why would you think I'd try it?"

"It's okay, just asking. Watch the road."

"I swear, I didn't know they'd have pot at the party."

"Seriously, it's okay. And I appreciate you telling me."

"Why *wouldn't* I tell you?"

The implication being, *I tell you everything, Daddy.* And that makes Kevin more relieved than anyone could possibly know. Despite all they've lost this year, he hasn't lost her.

I'm almost to the Bridge Street exit when my heart starts buzzing. Takes me a second to realize it's the super-secret snitch hotline—the phone Wildey gave me. Already? I know I have five minutes to respond, and it's like a digital clock comes to life inside my brain. I'm not proud of this, Mom, but I play the only card we ladies have sometimes.

—Uh, Dad…?

—Yeah?

—Sorry to do this, but I have to stop to use the bathroom.

—We'll be home in fifteen minutes. Can it wait?

—It really can't. You know. Girl stuff.

—Oh. Okay. I really don't know where we can—

But I've already spotted it: off the highway, in the distance, the reassuring red glow of a Wawa sign. Dad told me you made fun of them when you first moved here from California—"Wha-what?" The rest of the country has 7-Elevens; we have Wawas. Hoagies, sodas, Tastykakes, all your Philly essentials. But most importantly: bathrooms. Doesn't matter if this one is clean or not, because I'm not really going to be using it.

The burner buzzes again. Problem is, I'm all the way over in the left-hand lane, and the exit's coming up, and I'm going to have to pull some breakneck maneuvering right now.

—Easy, Sarie...

I check the rearview. Clear, but there's a truck racing up the lane trying to close the gap. I slide into the right lane, then into the next right lane. Someone honks at me. Fuck you, you were nowhere near me.

—Sarie!

Then the far right lane, and then the exit ramp, which shares lanes with the on-ramp, with cars rushing up from the right, forcing cars to do this polite crisscross dance. I have no time to be polite. I signal and turn the wheel and there's a huge chorus of horns to my back and right, so loud it's as if they're in the backseat...

—Sarie, for fuck's sake!

But I hammer the accelerator and I'm all the way over now, and cars whiz past the Civic, and I see an old lady—seriously, she looks fucking ninety—giving me a bony, crooked finger as she passes. I gently press down on the brakes as I approach the light at Aramingo Avenue. Dad's giving me this what-the-hell look. The phone buzzes again.

With that screeching halt Kevin Holland has been slammed back into vivid sobriety; adrenaline has burned off the remaining booze buzz. His heart is slamming inside his chest, and all he can think of is Marty waking up at his friend's house to the news that his sister and father both died in an accident on I-95. This is why he loses control. Or so he explains to himself in the moments after he yells at Sarie so loudly and borderline incoherently that she runs from the car and into the Wawa almost shaking. Forget The Fiction. He's been slammed back into Fact. And the fact is, he can't control himself. He can't control anything anymore. He's an asshole and a horrible father and he's the only thing his kids have left. God took the wrong one.

Transcription of text messages between Officer Benjamin F. Wildey and CI #137.

WILDEY: You there

WILDEY: Let me know

WILDEY: You didn't lose this phone already Honors Girl, did you

WILDEY: Times almost up

CI #137: I'm here!

WILDEY: Hey

WILDEY: Just wanted to make sure you got home okay

CI #137: Had to p/u my dad

WILDEY: ok

WILDEY: where was he?

CI #137: business trip

CI #137: gotta go dad is waiting in the car

CI #137: you still there?

CI #137: is it okay if I go???

CI #137: going now

WILDEY: keep your phone close honors girl

WILDEY: happy thanksgiving

Wildey feels like a massive dick, doing this to a college girl. But Kaz is right—this is the only way she's going to crack. She's not like the other CIs he deals with. She doesn't need to be courted or threatened. She just needs to feel the full-on pressure of that Monday morning deadline all weekend long. Kaz seems to think she'll crack long before then. "Give her a good night's sleep, she'll come to her senses. No guy is worth throwing away your life for. Believe me." Wildey hopes she's right. He doesn't want to keep this up all weekend long. *Excuse me, Auntie M.—I need to go torment this little girl for a minute. Enjoy your turkey roll.*

Wildey drives his unmarked car back to Ninth Street and of course there's a car squeezed into his former space. He pulls into another spot around the corner, then hustles back to the alleged Chuckie Morphine house. The air is freezing this morning, which is good. Nothing better to wake you up. He's been up for what…a full day and a half now? He tells himself he's just going to take a look, satisfy his curiosity, then head home for a few hours' sleep before the family dinner.

There are wooden shutters covering the first-floor window. The front door has a diamond of cloudy glass set in the upper middle, impossible to see through. Wildey walks around the block, counting houses as he goes. Around back there's an alley, and he counts them down until he finds the right house. There's a six-foot wooden fence, but the lock is simply a hook-and-eye latch, and Wildey uses a pen to unhook it and opens the fence door a few inches. The yard is overgrown but otherwise clean. No sign of lights or life up in the windows. Guess everyone's sleeping it off after a big night of sales.

Go home, Wildey. Get your rest.

One minute, one minute.

The D.A. in his head keeps after him.

You got probable cause here, Officer Wildey?

Probably, Mr. D.A.

That's no answer, Officer.

Best you're going to get.

Because Wildey *has* to look. He's already opened the door. It'd be a waste not to step inside. He creeps through the tall grass, keeping one eye on the back door and windows and the other on potential hazards in the yard. Stash guns, tripwire, dog shit.

The back stairs are wooden and creaky. Wildey eases up them, scanning the other yards for curious neighbors. He always forgets he's not in uniform, and a black man trespassing in a yard is the kind of thing that might get some jittery people in this neighborhood calling 911.

The back door is solid, no windows, but the blinds are up a little in the back windows. Wildey holds the post, leans over, takes a look inside. The kitchen is stripped, empty. Remodeled and painted, but there is no fridge, no oven, just the places where the appliances would go. What the fuck was this? Did he count houses wrong? No. This was it. He sees through the front of the house, and there's the same diamond-cut window in the door, the shutters closed. This house is empty. Then why were people coming and going all night last night? An open house? No. You don't just duck into an open house for five minutes. Besides, college kids like Skinny Boy aren't in the market to buy houses. There's no real estate signage. This house is just a shell. Unless he somehow spooked them last night. Maybe Skinny Boy called and warned them, and they cleared out quick.

Sorry, Honors Girl. You're going to have to help me find them.

I drive us home in silence. I know Dad feels like shit about yelling at me, and I know he has a point with that crazy exit I made, but I've been through the worst night of my life and the outburst from my dad is one thing too many. I pay attention to the road, coming to full stops at every stop sign, accelerating as gently as possible after every light. I avoid Roosevelt Boulevard—which is crazy enough even on a good day. I am the perfect driver, following the letter of the law.

We pick up Marty, who's still laughing about some shared joke with his friend. Dad and I try to fake it but we're both still pissed and rattled and Marty notices it, too, so he lapses into confused silence. He wants to ask what's wrong but knows better. There's so much to do to get dinner ready, but I don't want to deal with anything right now, so I go up to my room and slam the door and collapse on my bed, exactly where I should have been eight hours ago.

Marty Holland's mom is sort of buried in the basement.

She thought burials were the most horrible thing ever and made

Dad swear that, in the unlikely event of her death, her body would be cremated and not injected with chemicals and then locked in a box six feet below the surface of the earth. Dad would smile and deflect Mom's death wish with statistics about how husbands usually died before their wives. But Dad turned out to be wrong.

A month after the funeral her ashes had been spread near Coronado Island, one of her favorite places.

What's half-buried in the basement are Mom's belongings, in a dozen plastic containers that have a harsh chemical smell. It clings to your hands even after a good washing or two. Dad couldn't stomach the idea of throwing her stuff away, but he didn't want to stare at it every day, either. So down into the family den/laundry room it went. The containers—purchased and packed by Dad in a frenzy one humid Sunday afternoon in early June—sat in the corner where a television and cable box might go.

Marty started spending a lot of time down there after that. Cooler in the summer, sort of warm in the winter, with the space heater going. Dad leaves him alone, like he usually does. Sometimes he just needs to open a container and pull out one of his mom's sweaters—she was always cold—just to make sure her scent is still there, and not over-whelmed by the plastic smell. He knows that every time he opens a container a little more of her disappears. But Marty can't help himself. It's like he has to reassure himself that she was real, after all.

For the millionth time, he wishes she were here now.

Not just because it's Thanksgiving. But because Mom was always the one who explained things to him. Not the case with Dad...or, now, Sarie. Ask Dad a question, almost any question, and you'll most likely hear a brush-off. *Don't worry about it. Wasn't talking to you, Marty. Nothing to do with you, Marty, don't worry.*

Yeah. Don't worry. Sure, Dad.

Sarie used to be like Mom, the kind of older sister who didn't (usually) think he was a jerk face and would take her time talking to him. Ever since she started college, though, she was acting more like Dad. *Don't worry, don't worry.* The constant refrain. Which is why Marty knows it's useless to ask either one what happened between them this morning, because he would be told it was none of his business and not to worry about it. Something was clearly wrong, though. He'd have to figure it out for himself.

He opens a container, reaches in, touches one of his mom's old sweaters. Wishes for a moment, then tells himself to stop being such a baby.

Wildey lives alone in a bad neighborhood.

He used to date someone who lived in a much better neighborhood, and for a while he considered moving. They seemed to be on the same page right up until she turned to the kid page, and Wildey realized he had no choice but to close the book. For a while he tried to talk himself into it, but he knew himself too well. He knew what he wanted, and kids didn't figure into that. Wildey's not about to leave this neighborhood. Not before he has the chance to save it.

So this Thanksgiving evening he's off to pick up the one member of his family still alive and at liberty: his great Auntie M. The M is for "Margaret." She doesn't remember her name most times, nor does she know who Wildey is. Sometimes there's a glimmer of recognition, but there's never much follow-through. Wildey can't blame her. Auntie M. turned a hundred over the summer—they showed her grainy photo on the *Today* show and everything. She's survived improbable odds. Wildey just wishes she was one of those centenarians who remembered every blessed detail of their lives, down to what they ate for breakfast on the first day of kindergarten.

"Hi, Auntie M.," he says in the lobby of the retirement home in Germantown, about twenty minutes away from his house.

She looks at him and smiles but it's pretty clear she has no fucking idea who he is. Her mind constantly reboots itself. To Auntie M., Wildey is just someone who's going to wheel her somewhere for a warm meal. Maybe down the hall. Maybe somewhere outside. Can happen either way. It's just nice to move somewhere different. She isn't very hungry.

This is fortunate. Wildey is not much of a cook.

Somewhere hidden in the shadows and mists and cul-de-sacs of Auntie M.'s mind is a past Wildey would very much like to recover. Her older brother was John Quincy Wildey—his great-grandpops and a hero cop, working the tough, booze-soaked streets of the 1920s. There weren't many black cops working then; the trade was dominated by the Irish. But John Quincy managed to stand out, and was even once commended by the public safety director—a marine general and war hero—for his efforts battling bootleggers, pimps, and racketeers. Wildey didn't hear the first glimmer of these stories until a year after he joined the force, when some oldhead asked for his name again. *Wildey, huh? Any relation to John Q.?*

That offhand question sent Wildey to the central branch of the Free Library on Vine Street, where he dug up old newspaper clips from 1924, the year his great-grandpa joined the force. He spent the better part of a weekend pumping quarters into the microfiche machines, the homeless guys slumming around the tables, pretending to read the *Daily News* for the tenth time just to stay warm. Wildey printed out everything he could but still wanted more. So he bought an old bound volume of the *Philadelphia Record* on eBay, just to get a feel for the times—the old ads, the weird little stories, even the weather reports. The enormous slab of yellowed newsprint was already crumbling into fragile little flakes when it arrived. Turning the pages was an exercise in frustration. The past quite literally crumbled under his touch. Wildey had to Shop-Vac the floor under his kitchen table three times a day.

It all turned out to be true: Great-grandpops John Quincy Wildey was a goddamned police hero. Back then all the bad stuff happened in a downtown neighborhood called the Tenderloin, and John Q. worked its notorious Eighth District, which was corrupt as hell until that marine general hit town to clean things up. Wildey read the clips with a dizzy fascination. How did he not know this? Why didn't anyone ever tell him this shit? Granted, only one article mentioned his great-grandpops by name (and probably grudgingly, because, you know: black folk). But there were plenty of stories about the Eighth, and Wildey knew his own blood was mixing it up in those streets back then.

Until he started researching, all Wildey knew was that his grandfather, George Wildey, had been a cop until the mid-1960s, when he was gunned down in the line of duty. He left behind a boy, George Wildey Jr.—Wildey's own father. Whose name had made the papers, too. For all the wrong reasons.

Knowing that John Q. existed changed everything for Wildey. Before him came two hero cops and one bad egg. That tipped the scales considerably.

So Wildey made sure to have meals with Auntie M. as often as possible, hoping that something would break loose in her mind and she'd be flooded with memories of her much older brother, cleaning up town when she was just a twelve-year-old black girl growing up in the slums of South Street.

"I remember this house," Auntie M. says now, as her great-grand-nephew wheels her up the cracked sidewalk toward his concrete front stoop, which has partially sunk into the sidewalk.

"Do you, Auntie M.?"

"My bedroom was in the back."

Wildey smiles. Her bedroom was most definitely not in the back. She has never lived here. Wildey bought this place three years ago—

cash. Cost less than a used car. He almost didn't want to bring Auntie M. here—she shouldn't have to deal with a block as grim as this on Thanksgiving. But her retirement home didn't have a kitchen, and spending Thanksgiving in a restaurant just wasn't the way it was done. You have to cook at home.

Dinner tonight is a turkey breast roll, closer to lunch meat than actual roast bird. Stuffing comes from a box, which Wildey screws up anyway. Yams from a can. Green beans from a can. Cranberry sauce from a can. Olives from a can. The olives are the appetizers. Olives and crackers, which come from a box. They're not very good, and Auntie M. wisely avoids them. Maybe the gourmet part of her brain is still functional, as she instinctively seems to know to avoid processed food.

"Want some wine, Auntie M.?"

"That would be lovely."

The funny thing about Auntie M. is that she isn't one of those out-to-space centenarians. Her eyes are young and fix on you like tractor beams. She's aware of everything that's unfolding around her. She just can't access the memories anymore. As if her brain sealed off those old rooms and passages, convincing her she didn't need them anymore, that it was enough just to keep a handful of rooms in the house warm and lit.

"Tell me about your older brother again," Wildey says, handing her a glass of pinot noir he picked up on the sale rack at the state store. Somebody told him that if you paid more than eight dollars for a bottle of wine you were a fool. Most of the people who bought pricier vintages lacked the capacity to taste the ultra-subtle differences. Wildey didn't care either way. He only bought the wine because of the holiday.

"Who?" Auntie M. asks.

"John Quincy," Wildey says. "Your older brother."

"Oh, my John."

The way she says it, it's like great-grandpa is standing in the room with them. She's addressing him, not summoning a memory.

Can she see ghosts? Wildey sometimes thinks so. (Hopes so.) But whenever he tries to play that angle, like he's talking to a medium or something, Auntie M. looks at him with these big, accusing eyes. *No, you're not going to get me to do that.*

"He was a police officer, like me," Wildey says.

"Oh, John. He was so handsome."

"Tell me about him."

"Oh, John," she repeats, as if trying to conjure him up. If this is the case, she fails. And then forgets.

A few long moments pass before Wildey says it's time to check on the turkey.

WILDEY: hey

WILDEY: hope you got some sleep and time to think things over

WILDEY: worried about you text back, ok

CI #137: I'm here, almost dinner time

CI #137: why are you worried

WILDEY: Thought about something

WILDEY: Your boyfriend probably knows you were picked up

WILDEY: He's not gonna try to hurt you is he

CI #137: I don't have a boyfriend

CI #137: Seriously

CI #137: Are you there? I have to go we're eating now

CI #137: please dont text now going to the table

WILDEY: happy thanksgiving honors girl

Something in Sarie's jacket buzzes. Dad is still in the backyard so he doesn't hear it. Sarie's head, though, whips around like she's a police dog who just caught a sniff of a bad guy. She takes a step closer to the living room, where her jacket is slung over the couch. There's another buzz. She looks at Marty and tells him to keep an eye on the carrots, then hurries into the room. What the hell? Marty wonders.

He stirs the carrots a few times, then moves to the doorway. Sarie's back is to him, but her body language makes it look like she's texting. Clearly hiding it. She texts all the time, though. Why be so secretive about it?

Marty is clear of the doorway before she turns around. He slides across the kitchen linoleum in his socks, making no sound, and gives the carrots a few more stirs before realizing there's something missing. The brown sugar, like Mom always used to add. Maybe they're eating healthier now. When Sarie returns Marty tells her to watch the carrots—he has to go to the bathroom. He expects her to say *thanks for sharing* or something wiseass—the kind of thing they usually say to each other. But she seems preoccupied, says nothing.

Of course Marty doesn't go to the bathroom. He slips his hand into Sarie's jacket pocket expecting to feel the familiar contours of her iPhone. Instead he pulls out a cheap flip phone.

After dropping Auntie M. off at the retirement home with plenty of leftovers, Wildey retraces his route, taking Germantown Avenue, which slashes across North Philly, until Lehigh. There he hangs a left, heading toward Kensington Avenue—the heart of the so-called Badlands. Wildey's three-bedroom row home is here, on Hope Street.

Yeah, yeah, he heard it from everybody when he first moved there. Hope, in the most hopeless area in the city. There's even an Obama mural on a wall to drive the irony home—though some idiot did spray BONER over the one-word slogan beneath the portrait of the president.

When Wildey let his new address slip one day a couple of years back, his buddies back in the Twenty-fourth told them he was fucking nuts. *Why the fuck you living there? Don't you know you don't shit where you po-*

lice? All Wildey would do is smile and give them a line about its being cheap. *It'd better be fuckin' cheap, Wildey. Shit, man, they should be paying you to live there.* But Wildey had his reasons, and he thought it was better to keep them to himself.

The Badlands *are* a strange choice for a cop to live.

For decades now its streets had been the biggest open-air drug market on the East Coast. And in recent years, it's only gotten worse, because word got out: You want the purest, most potent heroin available? Head to Philly's Badlands. It's coming straight from the Mexican cartels, and they don't mess around! Junk fiends have been known to drive from as far away as Florida and Maine to score, but mostly it's junkies from other (better) neighborhoods or the burbs, near and far. And during the years Wildey worked those streets, he saw an increasing number of white people from the burbs. Not just kids, either. Middle-aged professors. Accountants. Soccer moms and so on.

Wildey quickly figured how it happened. Most well-off white kids don't drive to a dangerous and heavily policed neighborhood just for the hell of it. They usually start out copping Oxys from friends, then scoring some from a small-time dealer near home. But a few years ago they changed up the Oxys, made it harder to get high on them. So white people had no choice but to go with heroin. The dope they could get in their neighborhoods and towns didn't quite do the trick. As a general rule: The farther you got away from the city, the weaker and more expensive the dope. The joke going around was that suburban dope has been stepped on so many times, all you smell is sneaker.

No, they wanted the real deal, and it was no mystery where to get it. So they started cruising the strip between K&A—the Kensington and Allegheny El stop—and the next stop on the line, at Kensington and Somerset. Black dealers work one side of the avenue, Latinos the other.

Most of Wildey's time with the Twenty-fourth was spent in an endless cat-and-mouse thing. You had your cops in uniform (like Wildey).

You had uncover guys. You had your junkie CIs, trying like hell to work off their own shit. All three would triangulate on buyers. Some of them, commuting in from the burbs, would try to go for a package deal, buying sixty bags at a time—sometimes even selling it off back at home. The more they carried, the harder they fell. Most times, though, it was small-time, and you might bust a so-called caseworker (corner dealer), but rarely a midlevel player. They were too smart for that.

So on and on it went, the PD more or less fine with the casual deterrent of arrests, the city doing nothing about the endless abandoned houses that served as shooting galleries—"abandominiums," they called them, turf wars breaking out on hot summer nights, legit business owners saying fuck it and moving out, scared residents with no means to get out sleeping in their bathtubs because they're seriously afraid a bullet's gonna come punching through the walls of their house overnight.

So why live here?

Because Ben Wildey wants to be the man who finally cleans it all up.

Not now, but someday. He doesn't have the political muscle or the career busts right now. But he's read enough and talked enough to know how it could work.

Why does he want to clean it up so badly? Plenty of reasons. But most of all it's because his great-grandpops helped clean up the Tenderloin. And now Wildey wants to do the same with the Badlands. Carry on the Wildey family business.

The more Wildey reads, the more he realizes his neighborhood *is* the modern Tenderloin. Same shit, different decade. Just like it was ninety years ago, it's pretty much hands-off. No pretense is made to clean it up unless someone decides to do it through sheer force of will.

Wildey takes a spin down the ave., just to see what's what on this fine, brisk holiday evening.

There is the usual assortment of junkies hawking clean works and Subs from their bags. A buck for a needle, $10 for a Sub, $5 more to point you in the direction of the corners with the best stuff.

Some cars with out-of-state plates, a dead giveaway. If Wildey were still with the Twenty-fourth, that would be probable cause to pull a car over. Nicer cars, too, and there are plenty on the road tonight. It's a long holiday weekend, and people need their dope. Let 'em go for it. For now. Wildey will be back for them soon enough.

He takes Lehigh again and turns right onto hopelessly narrow Hope Street. These blocks were built long before the dawn of the automobile, and there is literally no space to park unless you run up onto the sidewalk. Which some people do. Wildey parks his current peep car in the empty lot next to his house. Someone tries to steal the car? Whatever, Wildey will get another one. But no one does, and nobody messes with his house, either. He made sure the word spread: The po-po live here. Yeah, he has bars on the windows, but that wouldn't stop most housebreakers. No, the thing that gives them pause is that they know how much a cop makes. It ain't worth the bars.

Still, the previous tenant of his current abode was selling wet—cigarettes dipped in PCP. From time to time, junkies would knock on Wildey's door and get the surprise of their lives when he would answer it in uniform. "What, you change your mind?" he asked, barely able to contain his laughter as they went booking down the narrow street.

As he drives back to Hope Street Wildey thinks about Batman and Robin.

Robin, especially.

When Wildey was coming up in the late 1990s in the Badlands, Batman and Robin were the two busiest narcotics cops working the streets. Both black guys in their late twenties, afraid of nothing. They'd swoop in with little warning, prompting cries from lookouts— "Yo, here come Batman and Robin!" Their real names didn't matter to anybody, and they didn't seek out publicity. Local papers caught on anyway and did a big story on them.

But back then Wildey wasn't reading newspapers. Wildey was keeping himself indoors those days, but he liked when Batman and Robin would make an appearance because you could step outside and not feel like something was going to happen to you. He especially liked Robin, because he'd slip fifteen-year-old Wildey comic books, ask him, "What's the word on the street, youngblood?" Not asking for real info, just making conversation.

A short while after the profiles appeared, a drug gang put a $5,000 hit on the heads of Batman and Robin. The small-time wannabe Tony Montanas were quickly rounded up—you don't threaten a cop in Philadelphia and expect to be walking around for long. Batman and Robin shrugged it off.

Robin was the reason Wildey joined the force five years later. Yeah, he knew about his cop-grandfather, but he never met the man. Robin, though, was the real deal. To Wildey, Robin was how to be a black police officer in Philadelphia. When Wildey finally joined the force, he reached out to Robin to thank him. Robin said that he didn't remember him but was proud of him anyway. "Still reading comics?" Wildey asked him. Robin just laughed. "I never read them. Those were for you youngbloods, calling me Robin and shit." Yeah, Robin was his hero.

Until this year, that is.

In this bad, crazy year, Batman was one of the "tainted six" shuffled out of his NFU. And Robin . . .

Oh, Robin.

In late May, Robin was arrested while stealing drugs and money from a dealer in Southwest Philly. The FBI set up a sting with the help of a CI. Robin, a twenty-four-year vet, caught with $15 in his pocket and five pounds of pot in his jacket pocket. The feds had Robin on a wire, talking about all the dirt he'd done over the years. Even the police union didn't want to bother with him. Wildey—now reading the papers—stared at Robin's puffy face staring back at him. *Sorry to let you down, youngblood. But the streets got to me. They'll get to you, too.*

The scandal sent Wildey into a mental tailspin, one that lasted all the way through Memorial Day weekend, which was strangely cold and rainy. *Would the streets get to me, too? Am I staying good just till the right bribe comes along?*

Then came Monday, and the mayor and commissioner are naming Kaz Mahoney to head up a new "untouchable" narcotics field unit, and Wildey decides that no, the streets would not win.

Mom, you're not missing much this Thanksgiving.

Strange to think that a year ago I was sitting at this very kitchen table, filling out the early admission forms for UCLA, still buzzing from our trip to L.A. the month before. Remember the four of us, walking around Westwood in the warm California sunshine? Me, finding it hard to believe this could be my new life? I kept glancing at your faces, bracing myself for one (or both) of you to tell me, Sorry honey, we can't do this. But you and Dad were strangely quiet, taking in the sights, holding hands. At the time I thought it was weird but cool. The other weird thing was the headache that you couldn't seem to shake. It was just the flight, you told me.

On the last morning of our trip Dad suggested an impromptu drive down to La Jolla. You dismissed it, saying it was close to three hours down, then three hours back, and then we all had a red-eye to deal with. Dad just smiled, told you the kids should see the smelly seals. Me and Marty looked at each other—seals? What was so special about seals? And why did they smell? Dad continued to press his case, and you gave in and made the drive, despite the headache.

So you drove down Highway 5 all the way to La Jolla, a hilly, pretty beach town totally unlike the Jersey Shore, which is the only beach I remember. Dad swears we were here once before, when I was three, to look at the seals. Nothing rings a bell but I instantly love the vibe of the place. The harsh salt of the ocean, the wet stairway leading to a little promenade where you could watch the seals laze about in a little sandy cove. The creatures were adorable but they also reeked, as promised. It was beautiful and gag-inducing, like so many things in life.

It's also the last happy "normal" memory I have of us as a family.

Because four weeks later, at the pre-Thanksgiving table, I ask you for your social. You don't hear me. You're darting between oven and counter and fridge and stovetop like a hummingbird, feverishly trying to get dinner together. I repeat the question, Mom, what's your social, and I know I sound irritated, which is what probably catches your attention. The look in your eyes startles me. Halfway through dinner you excuse herself. You almost make it to the first-floor bathroom, but then you don't. I don't understand until after dinner, when you and Dad tell me to wait a minute, you have something you need to tell me. And the floor of the world drops out from beneath my feet.

Don't tell Marty, you say. So I don't.

Twelve months later, I'm the one darting around the kitchen, with Marty at the table on his iPod. The thing's practically glued to his hands these days, just as you predicted. Dad's out in the backyard, even though it's freezing, because he has this idea about grilling the small turkey I picked up two days ago. I don't eat meat, but Dad jokes that I might change my mind once he gets this sucker grilling. I tell Dad I doubt it.

This isn't the way it was supposed to be. I was the one who should have been flying home from California this morning. If I'd been in California, none of this would have happened. I wouldn't be a snitch, facing jail unless I do something I know I can never do.

Fuck, the most I should be worrying about right now is how I'm going to finish Kant's *Critique of Pure Reason* in time to make it down to Venice Beach with my friends. Or grappling with the tough Friday night decision of hanging out in Westwood vs. driving over to Los Feliz to go to that cool indie bookstore you and I found last year. (Do you remember that place, Mom? Skylight? Remember me promising you that, yes, we'd always go back whenever you visited?)

I stare at Dad's back thinking I should tell him. Not everything, but enough. There's a version I've worked up in my mind. A version that doesn't implicate D., because that would be as bad as narking him out to Wildey. You know Dad. Dad would hit poor D. with the double-barreled shotgun blast of "You so much as look at my daughter again and I'll rip out your heart" (concerned father) and "Hey, buddy, I'm going to help you beat this thing" (concerned drug and alcohol counselor).

So maybe I tell him I'm doing extra credit by volunteering with the police department. Observing for a paper, maybe? No, that won't fly. I'm not taking any criminal justice classes and Dad knows it. None of my freshman triple classes (The Beats, The Greek Way) fit, either.

So…no. I can't bring it up. I can't even hint at it. Talking to you like this is one thing; talking to Dad is another. Dad is still uncannily sharp about these things, despite the events of the past year. For the past four years our relationship feels like that of an ex-con and parole officer, where the P.O. is basically a decent guy who genuinely wants the best for you. But he's still going to crack down hard on your ass if you so much as think about stepping out of line.

Now Dad has the turkey in a disposable aluminum pan. He picks it up and turns with an excited look on his face.

—Want to get the back door for me?

—You're really going to do this?

—I told you, unless it snows, I'm grilling this sucker.

—You're hard-core, Old Man.

—Right on, Sarie Canary.

In the days immediately following Mom's death, Dad and I tried to keep up the old routine. The banter, the puns. You always said I had inherited Dad's weird sense of humor. But we quickly noticed that without you, there was a vital piece missing: our audience. Without you giggling or rolling your eyes, there was no reason for the puns or the banter. It sounded hollow. We stopped. It was bull-shit anyway.

Now Dad's out back trying to make the grill thing work, but it's not the same. I miss you two out there, standing around the grill, sipping iced tea and laughing. I miss Marty waging action figure spy wars near the edge of the woods. I miss pretending to read, but mostly listening to you and Dad goof around. I miss the smell of the burning coals and wood chips. After you died, Mom, the whole backyard routine died, too. If me or Marty asked about cooking out, an awful look washed over his face. Kind of like guilt mixed with sorrow mixed with a bit of anger for even bringing it up in the first place.

Then school resumed and Dad inexplicably rekindled his love for the backyard. I arrived home one day to find him scrubbing the grime off the Weber with a wire brush and a hose. That night, he'd started small—spiral-cut hot dogs for the boys and marinated tofu for me. Dad continued to expand his repertoire, coming up with a surprising number of vegetable dishes. Last week he announced that he would be grilling the Thanksgiving turkey.

I want to tell him, No thanks, Dad—the police already grilled me down at the station.

I want to tell him, Dad I'm in serious fucking trouble and there you are playing around in the backyard. Your wife is dead and your daughter's probably going to jail on a drug charge.

I want to tell him so much, but for the past year I've found it impossible to tell him anything. Why start now?

FRANKFORD

NOVEMBER 29

At approximately 1:30 in the morning, Confidential Informant #69, a twenty-six-year-old junkie whore, hears a noise.

CI #69 isn't stupid; she suspects the cops assigned her that number on purpose. I mean, for fuck's sake, can you be more obvious? But let them laugh all they want. She's just received a letter from her friend down in Naples, Florida. She says that her back room is cleaned out and that she can come down and spend Christmas there, with good chances for a job if she can clean up. CI #69 knows she can. All she needs is to be out of the cold and dark under the fucking El and be on a beach with warm sun and the clean fresh sand all around her. She's young. She'll rebound. This city and all of its sickness will be just a bad dream.

The El; she won't miss the relentless rumbling of the El, just a block away from the place she's been bedding down lately.

But wait.

It's not the El she hears now.

It's the cracking of wood.

Oh fuck, someone's breaking in. CI #69 isn't the legal owner of this row home on Darrah Street—that's some dealer who was sent up earlier this year. But she considers it her squat, man. She's been taking care of it. Practicing for when she's a guest in her friend's place down in Naples. She grew up dusting and vacuuming and generally slaving away for her bitch stepmom; she knows what to do.

CI #69 isn't so much frightened by the intrusion as annoyed. In a few minutes the burglars are going to see she owns nothing worth carrying out of here. And she'll have to figure a way to secure the back door again.

"You picked the wrong house, assholes," she calls down the staircase. "Ain't got nothing worth stealin'!"

The voice that responds frightens her. Not because it is inherently menacing or sinister-sounding, but because CI #69 knows a cop when she hears one.

"We're not here for your stuff," the voice says. "We're here for you."

And with that CI #69 grabs her bag and is out the back window. Which is why she chose to bed down in the back bedroom—just in case she had to leave in a hurry. It's a quick hop down to the roof outside the rear room of the house, then another hop to the small fenced yard. But from here, there are three ways out: left or right down a weeded alley, the left leading to Herbert Street, the right leading to another alley that took you to Darrah or Salem, take your pick. Because the cops came in the front, it was likely their cruiser was out on Darrah, so Salem seemed to be her best bet.

If these guys are cops, though, why didn't they identify themselves? Cops can be dicks, but they all tell you what's what first.

Maybe these aren't cops?

CI #69 lands in the backyard and is preparing to sprint to the gate when a voice behind her commands her to freeze.

He's not in uniform but he is holding a police gun, and the steely look on his face is definitely a cop's. He's black and clean-shaven and has the demeanor of someone who is used to having his commands followed.

"What do you want?"

"Yo, she's back here."

Calling to his partner inside—a mean-looking chick with dark hair and eyes that seem almost black. And when she emerges, CI #69 knows that she is seriously fucked, because these are not cops and this is not a break-in. She's survived this long because she knows how to read faces. Nothing fancy. Just little cues she picked up from her asshole step-mom. She just knows what someone looks like when they're willing to hurt you.

This bitch, the one who's just stepped out of the back of her house? She looks more than happy to hurt someone.

So CI #69 bolts.

The chase doesn't last very long. They catch up with her before she can even see the street lamps on Salem Street. The beating is mercifully brief but severe; she loses consciousness. She's been beaten before but not like this. When she wakes up she's tied to a chair and apparently she's in the middle of a torture session whose beginning she cannot recall.

"You were saying," someone tells her, but CI #69 has no idea what she was saying. She could have been saying anything. There's a weird burning in her blood, and sweat trickles down from her hairline. They stick something in her arm and then it comes back to her. She *was* talking. She was talking a lot. She was talking about the stuff she usually talks about with Wildey and *only* Wildey, and suddenly she knows what this is about, just as she knows that she's never going to see Naples or feel the sun or smell the sand. She's a silly junkie whore to have thought otherwise.

The police call her Confidential Informant #69, but her real name is Megan Stefanich. Within twenty-four hours her corpse will be underwater.

JOAN OF NARC

November 29

Well, Mom, if I'm a snitch, I guess I'd better learn how to be one. BTW, I hate the word snitch. I check the Internet for synonyms and they're all horrible:

Narc

Fink

Rat

Rat Fink

Deep throat

Turncoat

Weasel

Squealer

Stoolie

Stool pigeon

The only one that isn't completely awful is canary, which will probably make you laugh. Remember Dad and his stupid songs about my name? Sarie Canary, who's she gonna marry? Okay, so I'm a canary. I can deal with canary. Better than being a snitch-ass motherfucker.

(Sorry. Guess D. is rubbing off on me.)

Online I find a PDF organizational chart for the whole Philadelphia Police Department. Wildey's team seems to fall under the category of special investigations, which itself breaks down into two categories: narcotics and major crimes. Drugs and Serious-Ass Shit, in other words.

Under narcotics there are narcotics field units (presumably like Wildey's Nobody Fucks With Us unit), a narcotics strike force (presumably a Nobody Really Better Fuck With Us, Because We Will Fuck Your Shit Up But Good unit), and then a third division called Intensive Drug Investigations, just in case the first two categories didn't automatically make you wet your pants.

So they're real, at least.

Apparently the whole confidential informant thing is governed by Police Directive 15—a rule book for how cops deal with their snitches. To wit: "Police personnel will maintain professional objectivity in dealing with informants. No personal relationships will jeopardize the objectivity of the informant or the integrity of the department."

You hear that, Officer Wildey? I'll be keeping my eye on you.

Can't find any pieces online about Wildey, but his superior is another story. She's apparently Super Hot Shit in the department. According to one article, she's in line to be the city's next drug czar. Though in the comments section on the newspaper website, jerks make fun of her Russian accent:

—What are they gonna do, bust Rocky the Flying Squirrel?

—More like drug czarina

—Kill moose and squirrel and take their crack!

Why am I researching this? I have real stuff to research. Namely Goethe's *The Sorrows of Young Werther* as a Reflection of the Paradigmatic System of German Culture.

Can't help it.

Monday there was apparently this big citywide drug bust and they caught this doctor in South Philly writing phony prescriptions. Cops busted into some row house (wonder if Wildey was among them) and found the sixty-one-year-old doc sitting at the kitchen table, calm as can be, writing those scripts. Guess he was trying to beat the Thanksgiving rush? He also had $740 worth of weed and $425 worth of pills on hand.

The pills remind me of D., of course, but he hasn't texted or called. I know he fled from the police, but you'd think he'd give me a yell, if for no other reason than to inquire about his missing hat, missing windbreaker, missing Ziploc baggie full of illegal narcotics.

Tammy isn't returning my calls, either. What the hell? Is it something I did?

The only person I'm hearing from is Officer Wildey.

WILDEY: You there
CI #137: I'm here
WILDEY: Thought of something
WILDEY: Your boyfriend doesn't know I picked you up. For all he knows you still have his stuff
WILDEY: So you should reach out to him and tell him that you have his stuff and want to give it back
WILDEY: You follow me?
CI #137: I can't do that because there is no boyfriend!
WILDEY: Whatever you call him, doesn't matter to me.
WILDEY: Look, it's the easiest way. Just agree on a meet location and I'll be there to scoop him up.
WILDEY: Hey, you there
WILDEY: Get back to me
WILDEY: Guess I'll have to call you
CI #137: I can't set up someone who doesn't exist!

Mom, I swear, once you start looking, you can't stop.

Just read a story about a Philly college student named Tracey, sweet-looking hippie chick based on her online photo (and stuff on Facebook) who bought some LSD online and made the mistake of selling some to some people back home, one of whom was an undercover state cop. Busted, just like me. The way she describes it, the cop was all sweet and shit, even brought her coffee. (Take some notes, Officer Wildey!) But then they put her to work, forced her to bust somebody at Drexel, her own school, in exchange for having her own charges dropped. Her identity was supposed to be sealed and secret (just like me! again!), but the drug world is apparently a small world, at least on campus, and people found out pretty quick. Everybody turned on her. Seriously—everyone. Tracey was big with campus activist groups and they all dropped her. Now she's pet-sitting and whatever, struggling to make ends meet, and her life sounds pretty fucking miserable. So I suppose I have that to look forward to.

Then there was the story about a dude on some photo-sharing site calling himself rat215. In addition to posting weird porn selfies, guns, and his headless self flashing gang signs, he also put up photos and court documents that outed a witness to two drug killings. EXPOSE ALL RATS, the caption read. Rat215 turned out to be a high school kid, and nobody has any idea how he found the docs and photos—they were supposed to be sealed, grand jury–style shit. (What was it that Wildey and his boss said about my identity never being revealed?)

And I wish I could erase from my memory the *New Yorker* piece I just skimmed. The one where this sweet girl named Rachel gets busted for having a little weed in her apartment and then all of a sudden they're sending her to buy serious drugs and a gun from this psycho crime family in the middle of Florida. They put a surveillance device in her purse, but it doesn't matter because the psycho crime family is tipped off. They pump the purse, drag Rachel away. All the cops find at first is a flip-flop.

They found her body hours later, shot up with the gun she was supposed to buy.

Still no word from Tammy. Her mom says she's around, but...well, that's Tammy these past few months. Always around, but never really around. I'm guessing it's a new boyfriend. I'm sure I'll hear all about him one of these years. Not that it matters. I'm sure he'll be a charming loser, just like the others. You know Tammy, Mom. Her taste in men is as predictable as the tides.

Also: Not even a goddamned text from D.

Isn't he wondering about his cornucopia of missing pills?

I need to shower and stop thinking about this.

The moment Sarie steps into the shower, Marty takes her keys from the plastic hook on the side of the fridge and sneaks outside to her Honda Civic. Looks up and down the block. Too cold for anyone to be out walking around or putting up Christmas decorations, which is good. Not that Marty is overly worried about a potential witness; he could just be running out to his sister's car to grab a book or something else she forgot. No, his biggest worry is that Sarie or Dad will take a look out a front window while he's in the driver's seat, turning the ignition key. How would he explain that?

Fortunately, he doesn't have to send power to the engine—just supply enough power to the car so he can read the odometer and jot down the digits.

This wouldn't work were it not for his older sister's anal habits. Whenever she sits behind the wheel of her car (actually, their mom's old car), she hits the NEW TRIP button, setting the mileage to zero. Every time, without fail.

Miles (50.2) entered into a notebook app on his iPod, Marty turns off the power, pulls the key, steps out of the car, and closes the door as silently as possible. Sarie is still in the shower when he slips into his room, opens up Google Maps, and does some math. He's good at it. What he discovers doesn't surprise him.

Sarie lied about where she went last night.

Is that why Dad's angry?

Marty knows that Dad checks his iPod for messages and notes and emails and stuff, and that's fine. Dad gave him the same speech he gave Sarie last year on Christmas: "These devices don't belong to you, they belong to us, you're just borrowing them, meaning that we can look through them at any time. And we will." Mom was too sick to say much but she nodded her agreement. And even though Dad kind of zoned out for a lot of spring and summer, he was back to checking the iPod again, which was obvious because of the way he would bring up things supposedly at random ("Hey, what's new with Adam? You two still hanging out?"). But ultimately technology is the friend of Marty's generation, not Dad's.

Marty opens up his favorite game, Diggit, a world-building app. You can use it to create more or less anything; for the past few weeks Marty has been obsessed with making his own MI6 building, Babylon on the Thames. In a secret torture room Marty lifts up the floor and opens a password-protecting text file. For Dad to get in here, he's going to have to somehow make it past Britain's top spies *and* a flock of mutated sheep with laser eyes (Marty's personal addition to the facility) *and* this new password. Marty is pretty sure Dad wouldn't even be able to find *London* in Diggit.

Marty thumbs in what he knows so far:

Facts:

My sister has a burner phone

She lied about where she was the night before Thanksgiving

She looks exhausted

She is short-tempered and stressed even more than usual

Dad was angry with her but seems okay now

Questions:

Did she lie to Dad to get out of something?

Is my sister dealing drugs?

FRANKFORD

SATURDAY, NOVEMBER 30

Wildey inhales a bowl of Sugar Pops and pulls his unmarked car out of the weedy lot next to his house. He makes his way to Kensington Avenue and follows the shadowy underbelly of the El all the way through Frankford—another down-on-its-ass neighborhood with more than its share of shootings and drugs—and back out into the light as he heads up to Mayfair. Funny how things look instantly better without an elevated train rumbling over your head.

Time for care and feeding of his confidential informants.

Wildey has three active CIs—two solid ones and another who is kind of a fuckup, inherited from the old NFU-CS. Somehow, despite the scandal, the man had managed to keep his identity secret. And, oh yeah, he has Honors Girl, too. But she doesn't really count.

One of his solid CIs—a twenty-six-year-old prostitute named Megan Stefanich—promised to point him to a stash house up in the Northeast today. Wildey rousted her under the El one night, not really intending to bust her, just shoo her in somewhere warm for the night, but they struck up a weird kind of friendship. For a while there, she was pointing out shit for free—"bad actors" to keep an eye on. Now she points things out in exchange for money. The going rate: $20 for each buy, anywhere between $150 and $250 for each bust, and $100 extra for each gun recovered at the scene. Wildey knows it all goes in her arm, but better that money come from him than some freak with a diseased dick. She talks about a friend in Florida or some such shit, but Wildey knows she'll never go anywhere. Her kind never does.

CI #69 clearly wants breakfast out of Wildey, because she asked to meet at the Red Robin Diner up in Mayfair. Parking is tight. Wildey arrives and there's no sign of the CI. The place is crowded, but they're not going to talk business here anyway. No, this is about getting a hot meal into her. Then they'll talk when they get back into the car. Wildey takes a table near the windows so he can keep an eye on Frankford Avenue. The waitress looks at him. Wildey doesn't drink coffee, so he orders two boxes of cereal and a carton of milk. By the time he's finished the second box, it's 7:51, and still no sign of his CI. What the hell? By 8:02 Wildey is making his way back to Frankford. Maybe she overslept.

Knocks on the front door get him nothing. Strange. This is not like her to miss an appointment. For a junkie, she's strangely punctual.

He knocks again. A neighbor a few doors down pokes her head out, sees Wildey, quick ducks her head back inside. Morning to you, too, ma'am.

Wildey knows he should split. Plenty of shit to do today otherwise. But he was hoping to spend the day staking out that stash house and working Honors Girl via the cell phone. It's Saturday already. Fuck, he should have taken that bet with Kaz. He would have been ten bucks richer.

But as he turns to leave, something stops him. This doesn't feel right. Wildey is stuck with the awful image of his CI up in this house, blue, with a needle sticking out of her arm. Winding his way through the weed-choked alleys, he hops the fence into the backyard and sees the back door has been popped open. Fuck. He reaches for his gun and makes his way in, clearing the place room by room—not that it's a big place—but finds nothing out of the ordinary. At least, it's no different from the last time he was here. The only thing new is a letter to his CI from that friend in Florida. So she is real, huh. Talking about the sun and the sand and the malls down there. Maybe she'll get out after all. Maybe she's already split.

No, that isn't it. She splits without clearing the slate, she knows her handler will come after her. So where is she?

NOVEMBER 30

Still no word from Tammy or D. That's what I should write on the cover of this secret journal. "No Word from Bestie or My Drug Dealing Non-Boyfriend."

What drives me crazy about Tammy is the one-way relationship we seem to have. Whenever she's in crisis mode, I'm the one dropping everything to give her a hand or give her a ride or pull the hair back out of her face. The one time—ONE TIME—I'm truly fucked? It's all apologetic texts and crickets.

As for D....man, whatever.

Now I'm not even hearing from Wildey. No texts since 2:13 a.m. I don't get it. He was up my butt sideways for Thanksgiving and Black Friday and now there's nothing but crickets?

I'm trying to finish my papers, Mom, I swear, but I can't focus.

I can't understand a word of *Naked Lunch*. Except for the drug talk. That, shockingly, I get.

FOX CHASE

SUNDAY, DECEMBER 1

Kevin Holland is not quite sure what to do with himself.

Thanksgiving weekend tradition for the past eight years or so has been to pile the kids in the car at the crack of dawn on Black Friday and get the fuck out of Dodge. Kevin's parents were gone, but there was the annoying contingent of aunts and uncles and cousins still in the area who expected visits, something that Kevin couldn't bring himself to do. Too much weird family shit, too many accusing eyes, and he was tired of explaining or apologizing or justifying his life choices. So he created the annual Turkey Day Getaway. At the crack of dawn on Black Friday, he and Laura would pile the kids in the car with enough books and clothes to last them for a few days and just drive. The destination really didn't matter, as long as it was someplace with a little bit of history and a clean hotel. Cleveland, Ohio. Portsmouth, New Hampshire. Huntingdon, West Virginia. Annapolis, Maryland. No shopping, no tourist bullshit, just some quiet family hang time. The kids liked the change of scenery, and Kevin liked that he had a handy excuse for extended family. Oops, sorry, yeah, you know us, always on the road. Last year's getaway had been put on hold because of their college trip to California for Sarie; there wasn't enough money to do both. And now this year Kevin just didn't see the point without Laura.

So Kevin goes to see what Marty's up to. As usual, the boy is on his handheld device. Said devices were the source of much debate in the Holland home the previous year, with Laura firmly against them (for many good reasons) and Kevin cautiously advocating for them (remembering his own parents' steadfast denial of anything fun or cool that every other kid at school already possessed). But when it was clear that Laura was sick, and it was serious, she relented. Smart phones were to be the big Christmas gift that year—she figured the kids would need something to distract them during the grueling year of treatment ahead, long hours in waiting rooms, long hours alone. And surprise, hey, the kids received their devices on Christmas and lost their mother the very next day. Marty didn't touch his device until February, but when he did, and discovered some game about mining, he never looked back. It was a bit of a fight to get him to put the damned thing down, but Kevin figured there were worse things he could be doing.

"Hey, you up for the game?"

Marty looks up. "Sure."

"Right on. But try to keep it down to five or six beers, okay? Tomorrow's a school day."

"You too."

Kevin stares at his son, wondering if the kid has taken a shot there or if he was just being overly sensitive. Marty's eyes flick right back to his mining game, so...yeah. Probably didn't mean anything by it. Doesn't change the fact that the shot would have been perfectly reasonable. He's already gone through a case of Yuengling this weekend, and it's only Sunday. He would have to make a run for a few sixes before the game.

Kevin was an Eagles fan but only by default. When you're born in Philadelphia they hand you a birth certificate along with some green and white face paint and a giant foam finger. His cop-father (also a Martin, and boy did he regret saddling his son with that name) lived for the games, drinking steadily during each. Didn't matter if the Birds were winning or losing—he'd pound cans of MGD to celebrate the former and console himself during the latter. Kevin was thirteen when his father let him have his first sip, which made him stupid for at least an hour. And he liked it. That first cold crisp sip contained the DNA for his entire adult life, right up to this minute. So fuck it, as Martin Holland would say. Crack open a cold one.

Sarie is downstairs in the den, working on a paper. She seems to always be writing a paper, ever since college commenced late August. Kevin never did the college thing and feels a little lost advising her, relying on his counseling-speak whenever she seems stressed.

"Sarie Canary—you want to take a break in a couple of hours, watch the game with me and Mart?"

She turns around slowly, an apologetic look already on her face. "I wish. But there's so much due this week..."

"Hey, a couple of hours won't hurt. If you promise not to turn me in to the authorities, we could even have a beer together."

"And then I'd be zonked out for the rest of the night."

"Come on, you had a few at the party, right?"

"Honestly, no. Just one. Barely." She squints. "You're testing me, aren't you?"

Kevin forces himself to laugh. "Yeah, you know me."

Good God. Kevin's applying peer pressure to his teenaged daughter. What the fuck is wrong with him? Let her work. Let her be the first (of two) Hollands to graduate from college. Go upstairs, old man, and crack your beer and watch your Birds. Take your mind off the fact that the phone hasn't rung and you're in limbo until it does.

Diggit File/MI6 Building/Torture Room 6

Sarie receives texts but then almost immediately erases them before I have a chance to look

Sarie's burner hasn't gone off since late Friday night—do drug dealers have days off?

Dad is drinking a lot.

Nobody's seen CI #69. Wildey spends most of Sunday scouring Frankford, as well as nearby Mayfair and Wissinoming and finally, in desperation, the Tracks, thinking maybe the girl relapsed and decided that if she couldn't go to Florida maybe she'd hop back on the heroin highway. It's bright and cold out here but nothing besides the usual lost faces. Then something occurs to Wildey as he makes his way back to the house in Frankford.

There was no sign of forced entry in the front, but Wildey realizes he never checked the back door. He makes his way through the weedy alley, crunching on glass (and worse) underfoot. He counts down the houses until he reaches the fifth one in, then tries the fence. It opens. The latch has been pried out of the old wood and tossed a few feet away into the grass.

And there we go — back door jimmied, too. This is not proof. The Man in the Widener Building wouldn't necessarily buy this. But it wasn't good news, either.

Who came for you, Megan? You owe somebody money or a favor? If you did, why didn't you come to me for help? That was our deal.

As Wildey makes his way inside he's not sure what he dreads more — finding Megan's body or having to tell Kaz about this.

DECEMBER 1

While Dad and Marty watch the Eagles-Cards game upstairs, I'm down in the den suffering through a barely contained panic attack. Every time I hear Dad's shouts and the roar from the TV, I think it's a narcotics strike force bashing in our front door, guns blazing. I flinch so many times I start twitching even when there's no roar.

Whenever I'm really up against it — paper due, need to speed-read a book for an 8:00 a.m. exam — I exist on the razor-thin edge of total collapse. My blood feels like it's on fire. My goddamn left eye twitches (yeah, the left, no idea why it never hits the right). My stomach revolts. One day Dad saw me like this and said the best remedy was to stand up and just walk away. Or take a bus ride. Or a shower. I hate buses, and if I showered every time I felt stressed my fingertips would look like raisins. So instead I would go for a walk into the woods just beyond our backyard. Tammy and I used to sneak out at night and walk the bike paths, listening for the voices of adults. (Okay, I can admit this now, Mom—but Tammy also used to hope that those potential "adults" would be drinking beer or smoking weed so we could party. I was secretly relieved the opportunity never arose.) I loved walking in the fall the most, the brittle crunch of dead leaves beneath my sneakers, breathing in the cold yet strangely humid air.

Maybe I should go into the woods and just keep on walking. Find the creek and follow it down to the river. Or the opposite direction, out into the western suburbs and keep going all the way to sunny California. Wildey can't force me to say anything if I'm just gone, can he?

Gave it some thought. But I couldn't do that to Dad and Marty.

Okay…so. I have to snitch on a drug dealer. One who is not D. But he's the only person I know who sells drugs.

I can't give him up.

Right?

About an hour later, as night falls in the Pennypack Woods, knowing that the next time the sun comes up it's deadline time, and there's a good chance I'm going to know what it's like to feel handcuffs around my wrists and hear a Miranda warning, I come to what I believe is a sensible decision. I'm going to go back home and tell my dad everything. Everything but D.'s name. I'll say he's just a guy I met at the party who needed a ride to his friend's house. I'll say he doesn't even go to school there, but he was cute and I gave him a ride and then all this crazy shit happened. I'll say he gave me a false name. Then I'll find a lawyer and put this behind me. Because I didn't do anything wrong.

But this desperate plan vanishes when I step out of the woods and see D. standing there in my backyard.

You ever see someone out of context and it completely freaks you out? This is what's happening to me right now. He's wearing a hoodie, both hands stuffed in the pockets. He's changed his pants, trading the bright red chinos for brown corduroy. There's an overnight bag slung over his shoulder as if he's just stepped off a bus. Which he probably has. He looks more disheveled than usual, but it's not exactly a bad look for him. Makes you want to tuck in his shirt, smooth out his hair, and give him a hug. Damn it, you'd think I'd be over this schoolgirl shit, given how much trouble I'm in thanks to his lame ass. But apparently not.

D. nods in my direction.

—Hey.

I wonder what he's got in those pockets. How well do I know this guy, anyway? Bang bang bang, that's to make sure you don't rat me, kid. If I am smart I should scream for Dad or run back in the woods. Instead dumbass me says:

—Hey.

D. shuffles his feet.

—Can I talk to you?

A quick scan of the second-floor windows—is there a Dad-shaped silhouette in one of them? No. Not yet.

—How did you find my house?

—Honors directory. Seriously, is there somewhere private we can go?

I turn my head all the way around and check the windows, the back door. Dad can't hear this. Not a freakin' *syllable* of this. I grab a fistful of D.'s hoodie, which looks and smells brand-new, pull him into the woods. We go down the trail about an eighth of a mile up to a break in the creek, where the water rushes over a ledge, creating some white noise. There's a concrete slab that used to be the foundation of something. After all these years, I still have no idea, but it's as familiar to me as our back deck. We sit on that.

D. looks at me.

—You okay?

—Yeah.

—I didn't hear from you all weekend. I was getting really worried.

—I don't have your number.

He blinks, confused, as if he assumes that every young lady at school has his cell tattooed on her wrist or something.

—Thought you'd, you know, reach out to me.

—I was thinking the same thing. You found my address in the honors directory. Pretty sure my home phone number is there, too.

—I didn't want to call in case you were…

He trails off but I can fill in the dots.

—What happened to you Wednesday night? Did the cops question you?

—Yeah.

—What did you tell them?

—Nothing.

—Oh thank Christ. They just let you go, then?

—Sort of.

D. squints.

—What do you mean sort of?

I say nothing.

—Fuck. They flipped you, didn't they.

I can't even look at him. Busted, so quickly. Is this a record? Do I just ooze *eau de snitch* now?

—How did you know?

—You're free. And obviously your dad doesn't know. I'm sure as hell they didn't just let you go, not with what I had in the car.

D. gets in my face, the way you do when you want to lock eyes with a puppy you're training. We're close enough to kiss. Or for him to tell me to roll over.

—Tell me what happened.

I take a breath, then look down at the frozen grass.

—I'm confidential informant number one three seven.

—Fuck.

—Yeah.

Silence for a while.

—If it makes you feel any better, I'm fucked double hard. Triple, quadruple hard.

—You're not the one wearing a snitch jacket. The police don't even know you exist.

—Do you know how much stuff was in my jacket, Sarie? Do you know how much money I owe?

—Looked like a lot of pills, that's for sure. You supplying the whole town of Wilkes-Barre, PA, or what?

—Do you have any idea what Chuckie's going to do to me if I don't bring back a pile of cash for it?

—Do you know how many years in fucking prison I'm facing? Because of *your* drug run? Five! Minimum! Either I give you up or I'm going away.

—They're not gonna do that.

—They seemed pretty serious about it.

—Sarie, they are not gonna do that.

We say nothing. Then he rewinds. Chuckie. The whole Friends of Chuckie park-for-free thing. So at least that part wasn't made up.

—Chuckie's the name of your drug dealer?

—Yeah. It's not his real name, nobody knows his real name, but he calls himself Chuckie Morphine.

Pretty sure my jaw falls open right about here.

—You work for a drug dealer who calls himself Chuckie Morphine?

D. explains:

Nobody knows his real name, as drug dealers tend to keep those secret. D. tells me he met Mr. Morphine through a friend (wouldn't say who), heard that he specialized in selling to college kids—especially ones who were too afraid to venture to ghetto hoods for their drugs. D. went from scoring from Mr. Morphine to taking some extra for his friends, then selling to friends, then selling for real. D. opened up shop over the summer break, taking trips down to campus—under the guise of an independent project—to re-up his supply to sell to friends back home. Apparently upstate PA doesn't have someone like Chuckie Morphine or anything close to the quality of his product. Especially when it comes to pharmaceuticals.

This past Thanksgiving weekend was supposed to be a major sales event. Five grand worth of three different kinds of pills:

1. Mollies = MDMA, commonly known as ecstasy
2. Oxy = OxyContin, painkillers
3. Suboxones = meant to get you off Oxys; people like it for the smooth, controlled high; called "stop signs" because of the shape

Presumably great for partying and then dealing with the hangover the next day. I don't know. I've never done any of this shit, except for a fake half-hit from a bong. And even that's new—thanks to D.

As we sit in the woods I process all of this. It's hard to reconcile the sloppy-cute boy next to me with all of this drug intrigue.

—Why do you do this? Is it the lifestyle? A discount on the product?

—Yeah, the lifestyle. Look at me, living large.

—Seriously, why go through all of this shit, taking so much risk?

You're an honors student! You're supposed to be studying hard so you can get a good job when you graduate and—

—For fuck's sake, Sarie…what year are you living in? Do you really believe the lie they've been selling us since we were kids? Play by these rules and you'll be rich and famous and pretty and smart and all of that other bullshit?

—That's not a reason.

—Sarie, come the fuck on. The game is rigged and every generation has it worse than the one before. Yeah, I'm an honors student who made the mistake of reading too much. Our parents were supposed to change things and whoa, big surprise, they fucked that up. Just like their parents did. Just like their parents did, and so on.

—Why drugs, though?

—The money, Sarie. I do it for the money. Just like everybody else.

—Do you need money that bad?

—If I don't have two grand in the bursar's office by next week, I'll be thrown out of St. Jude's.

—What about your parents?

D. sighs.

—Mom assumes Dad's paying tuition, but she's currently not speaking to Dad. Meanwhile, Dad assumes Mom is taking care of it, and currently not speaking to Mom. I don't want to talk to either of those two assholes, so I'm taking care of it myself the only way I can. I'm a good dealer, Sarie. Smart. Careful.

—Then how come Wildey pulled me over Wednesday night?

—I've been thinking about that. I don't think it was about me or you. I think this is all about Chuckie. Because that night he was acting all weird. He called me during the party—I guess this was around eleven. Pick up the shit tonight or don't pick it up at all, he tells me. Now, I'd gone through a lot of trouble to arrange a ride to his place Thanksgiving morning, and then a ride up to Tenth and Filbert so I could catch the Martz line back to my mom's. I told Chuckie all this. Chuckie agreed to this. Then all of a sudden he calls me, says he has holiday plans out of town—all the shit has to move tonight. Take it or leave it, bro.

—Which is why you suddenly wanted to go down to Pat's.

—I'm sorry, Sarie. I really am. I never wanted to drag you into this. I thought it was just a ride. And I wanted some time alone with you.

—Well, look, you got your wish twice. Enjoy now before you're visiting me in prison.

The agonized look on his face tells me I'm being a dick. He knows he screwed me. I don't have to keep reminding him.

I reach out, give his hand a small squeeze.

—I get the whole parent thing, I really do. Sometimes I think my dad and I just talk around each other, you know? Or we keep circling around the same thing over and over again—how much it sucks that my mom is gone.

—I didn't know about your mom. I'm sorry.

There I go, being an even BIGGER dick. I give his hand another squeeze, tell him it's okay, really. After a long, awkward moment of silence—no offense, Mom, but it's hard to follow talk of the deceased with anything but—D. turns back to more pressing matters.

—Do the cops actually think you're dealing?

—No, I don't think so. The one cop saw you. He keeps trying to get me to give you up. Next time you go on a run, by the way, leave your red pants at home. That's all he talks about.

—So what did you tell them?

—I swear, nothing.

—No, I know that. But I'm just wondering what kind of story you told them. Why you were down there, all that.

—I told Wildey I went for a drive.

—Wilder?

—The cop. Will-dee. That's his name.

We sit in silence. It's now dark. Somewhere out there, most people are having a perfectly reasonable Sunday evening dinner, not a care in the world. After a while D. asks:

—So what are you supposed to do?

—Find a drug dealer for him by 9:00 a.m. tomorrow. You don't happen to, ha-ha, know any drug dealers, do you?

Then D. looks at me funny.

Transcript of text messages between Officer Benjamin F. Wildey and CI #137, 12-1, 11:12–11:15

WILDEY: Tomorrow's the day

CI #137: Where have you been?

WILDEY: Busy. Cop stuff. So you ready? Or you just want to tell me now, make it easier?

CI #137: Not over the phone

WILDEY: You got something for me?

CI #137: Let's meet tomorrow

WILDEY: Outstanding

CI #137: Where?

DEALING

PORT RICHMOND

Monday, December 2

Wildey sets the meet for an old-school diner on Aramingo Avenue, near Ontario. Place has been around forever, nothing has been modernized. Tiny flecks of the hash browns you scoop up with your fork today were probably part of a potato originally served to your grandpop back in the day. Wildey likes the diner for its sense of history. Plus, it's cheap. Five bucks buys you an outsized meal.

He originally proposed 9:00 a.m., but Honors Girl groused about the idea of missing her 8:30 philosophy class. Shit, Wildey thinks. She's not going to have to worry about class if he slaps the cuffs on her.

Because that's the next step. Not that he wants to arrest this schoolgirl, but if she keeps stonewalling, then Wildey really has no choice. They'll put her in a room, she'll lawyer up, and the lawyer will realize he can make this go away if the girl cooperates. But none of that drama has to play out if she gives up the boyfriend's name. That's what Wildey wants to stress to her this morning.

Kaz is betting ($20) that Honors Girl won't do it. "Uh-uh, too stubborn." Kaz is of the opinion that Wildey should slap the cuffs on her right away and bring her in. Scare her straight. But Wildey told her he had another approach in mind. Another way to scare her. Kaz told him, "Whatever, go with God." The last word sounding like *got*.

97

So Wildey is waiting in a booth a good ten minutes early, his body filling the bench seat. Wildey is all neck and shoulders, which comes in handy when dealing some dopehead smoking wet on the street. With Honors Girl, however, Wildey finds himself wishing he didn't look like a monster. She needs to see him as her salvation, her lifeline.

Honors Girl arrives earlier than expected and is church-quiet as she slides into the booth, reluctant to make eye contact. She's taller, skinnier, and prettier than Wildey remembers.

"Go ahead, order something," Wildey says. "The omelets are pretty good here. Scrapple, too."

"No, thanks," she says in a quiet voice. "I'm not hungry."

"Come on. I don't want to sit here, chowing down, with you just staring at me. Makes me seem rude. Can't we break bread together?"

"Officer, I...listen, I don't know how to do this. I don't know what—"

Wildey sees the hysterics building and doesn't want it to go there. Not yet. So he waves a hand and shakes his head.

"Take it easy. Take a deep breath, honey. We're just talking about breakfast here."

This seems to do the trick. When she makes eye contact again, she takes a deep breath before continuing.

"Officer..."

"Come on, call me Ben. And let's order."

Some of the old heads at the counter turn around in their stools to look at them. Yep, just your average linebacker-sized narcotics detective and his tall white-girl snitch.

"Okay...*Ben*." She says it like the name doesn't quite want to come out of her mouth. But then the waitress appears, ruining the vibe. Wildey eases back into the vinyl seat, exhaling through his nose.

The waitress looks like she's been serving one eternal shift since around 1978. Wildey orders two boxes of Lucky Charms, a carton of 2 percent milk. Honors Girl orders oatmeal and a small fruit bowl. "No coffee?" she asks them. Wildey assures her, no, no coffee. The waitress clearly disapproves. Who comes to a diner without ordering coffee? It's just not done. She wearily writes down the order like she's translating Latin and shuffles away. Honors Girl glances at Wildey for a fraction of a second before turning her attention to the surface of the table. Pastel boomerangs. Flying all over.

"So how was your Thanksgiving?"

Honors Girl looks up, blinks. "What?"

"I had my great-auntie over. How about you? Dinner with the whole family, aunts, cousins, and all that?"

"No. Just three of us."

"Yeah? Why's that?"

Honors Girl shrugs.

"So who's the three—you, your dad, and ...?"

"My younger brother. Marty."

"You two close?"

Honors Girl shrugs again, keeps her eyes on the table. Christ. You'd think Wildey was asking her to spill the deepest, darkest secrets of her entire family. He realizes this isn't working. She's shutting down. He needs her to relax, to see him as one of the good guys.

"I don't have much family left either. Auntie M. is pretty much it, to be honest with you. Did I tell you I come from a long line of cops?"

Their order arrives. Wildey drowns his cereal in milk, filling the bowl almost to the edge. "Yeah, my great-grandpops was one of the first black cops in the city. Worked during the Prohibition days, cleaning up the town. You ever been to Chinatown, down in Center City? That used to be the big vice district, the Tenderloin, and that's where my grandpops worked. And my grandpops was also a cop, mostly in North Philly. Killed in the line of duty before I was born. Wish I could have met him."

"What about your dad?"

"Huh?"

"Was he a cop, too?"

Wildey crunches his cereal as he considers the question. "No. Musician." Partly true, but best to leave it at that.

"What did he play?"

"Not enough gigs. And before you ask, no, I don't play anything. Unless you count a gun as a musical instrument."

Wildey means it as a joke, but it has the opposite effect on Honors Girl. Her face goes all permafrost.

"Officer Wildey, can I ask you a question?"

"Sure. Go ahead." He scoops up a towering spoonful of Lucky Charms.

"How often do confidential informants get killed?"

Wildey almost spits pink hearts, yellow moons, orange stars, and green clovers all over the tabletop. "Huh?" he mumbles through a mouthful of half-chewed cereal.

Honors Girl goes digging in her shoulder bag and pulls out a newspaper clipping, then slides it across the table. Wildey doesn't even have to look at the headline, though. A double murder from today's *Daily News* reports: 2 DEAD, 3 WOUNDED IN OVERNIGHT SHOOTINGS. One is nothing. Usual *fuck-me-no-fuck-you* stuff, played out on a front stoop at the tail end of a holiday weekend. But the other, the shotgun murder of a thirty-year-old black man near Second and Somerset, is something else. It went down just a few blocks away from Wildey's house. And word around the NFU-CS was that the vic was somebody's snitch. The reporter hinted in this direction as much as he could without flat-out saying it.

"Why do you think this guy was a CI?"

"The reporter says so."

"No," Wildey says. "I read that same story, and it says 'allegedly.' Which I can tell you is a bunch of nonsense."

Another lie to join the one about his father, but he doesn't need to freak her out. He certainly doesn't need to tell her about Megan Stefanich. In fact, he needs to do the exact opposite. Which is why he decides to cut breakfast short and get to the point already. He's got a secret weapon in mind.

"Come on. I want to show you something."

DECEMBER 2

So earlier today Wildey takes me to the Tracks, an abandoned railway in the heart of the Badlands. I don't tell him I already know about the Badlands. Everyone in Philly does, more or less. Since Dad doesn't drive, we'd sometimes take the El downtown during the holidays, especially when you wanted us kids out of your hair. The view from the El starts out not-so-great and gets worse from there, until you come up in the middle of I-95 and you can see the reassuring safety of the Ben Franklin Bridge and the downtown skyscrapers. I'd look through the windows at the abandoned factories and houses and ask my dad what had happened here. Was there a fire? Yeah, he replied. You could say that. But I never stepped off the El for a closer look. Never drove through it, either. Dad didn't even have to warn me.

Wildey points.

—They call this area the Tracks.

—Why? Because of junkie track marks?

—No. Because it's an old set of train tracks.

People buy their drugs on the corners, then take it to the tracks—a mile-long stretch of commercial railway that almost nobody uses anymore. Wildey tells me nobody wants to admit this, but the PD has pretty much given up on this area. He says that people can do whatever the fuck they want out here.

—Seriously?

—I worked this neighborhood for five years.

—Why didn't you do anything about it?

Wildey takes a long pause before replying.

—It's not that simple.

—Why not? You see people doing drugs, can't you just arrest them?

—Am I supposed to arrest everybody on a street corner who looks like they're high? Look around.

I look around. The city streets look like a film set for a zombie movie, and a bunch of sleepy extras are stumbling around waiting for someone to tell them what to do. Everybody looks high.

—Not even eight in the morning and you got people with their first fix under their belts and already looking for more. Tell me who I should arrest. That guy? That girl over there, who looks about your age? Now let me show you something else.

We take a sharp right off Kensington, out of the shadow of the El, onto a street bordering a park. If Kensington Avenue is a necklace, then this park is the diamond hanging from it.

—See this park? What do you see?

—Grass. Statues. Walkways.

—What don't you see?

—I don't know.

—I'll tell you what you don't see. You don't see needles everywhere. You don't see junkies lounging on benches. You don't see guys selling works or Subs. Know why you don't see any of that stuff? Because a group of us spent a full year taking back this park. Yeah, just this one little piece of land, and it took everything we had—constant arrests, foot patrols, coordinating with neighbors who were tired of hiding behind their doors and barred-up windows. And for now, it's sticking. Come back here around three, when schools let out, and you'll actually see kids playing here, and their parents won't be worrying about whether they're going to step on a needle or get touched by some junkie. This is our DMZ. But this is just one patch of ground in the Badlands. And the Badlands, Honors Girl…the Badlands is big.

We continue driving around the borders of the park—McPherson Square, according to a sign. You squint, and it's sort of nice. But then we pull back under the El and a gloom descends. This is not a street you want to walk in the daylight, let alone after dark.

—Why are you showing me this?

—Because your boyfriend is on a train, and he's headed down these tracks. So are all of his customers. I've seen it again, and again, and again. You think because you live in a nice neighborhood and you have parents who say they love you, none of this can happen to you. Think again. These streets are full of people just like you, and just like your boyfriend. They get off the El, walk down those steps, and the next thing they know, two years have gone by and they're just trapped.

—I can assure you, Officer Wildey, I'm never coming down here.

—Yeah?

And screeeeeeech, Wildey pulls the car to a halt, right under the shadow of the El.

—Come on.

—What?

—Follow me.

—Is it safe?

Wildey just laughs.

—Come on.

He leads me up Gurney Street, toward a cyclone fence that has been ripped from its frame. Before I can say *uh-uh, no fucking way*, he's ducking under the fence and waving me forward, and then he disappears into weeds as tall as basketball players. I look at the ground and see the syringes, the fast-food wrappers, the broken bottles. I wonder about my bag, still in Wildey's car. Did he even lock the doors?

—Come on, Honors Girl. Otherwise you're gonna be late for class.

Every step I'm crunching on something. I'm angry. Wildey doesn't have to do this. If he'd just let me talk…

But then I realize, no. Better for him to take the lead. He wants to wind me up? Let him.

THE TRACKS

MONDAY, DECEMBER 2

Aimee Manion, 23, is a junkie. She stepped off the Somerset El platform two years ago and never quite made it back home. Wildey remembers her from earlier this year when he chatted her up during one of her more lucid moments, tried to find out where her parents might be, if he could help her home. She said home wasn't an option. Wildey followed up on the address on her license; she was right. Aimee looks a lot closer to death than the last time Wildey saw her, which was what—March? April? Eyes sunk deeper into her face, sneer more pronounced. Not that she knows she's making that expression. She's nodded off into that opiate dreamworld she visits six, seven times a day.

"Honors Girl, meet Aimee. Pretty sure she used to be an honor student, too."

No idea if this is true. She mentioned something about Catholic school at one point—or a uniform.

"Aimee, say hi. What's that, Aimee? You can't say hi because you're out of your fucking mind on Big H? Gee, Aimee, that's rude."

"She needs a hospital," Honors Girl says. "We can't just leave her here."

"What hospital's going to take her? They don't want to deal with her either. And she'd fight you, too. Believe me, that's the last place she wants to go. Isn't that right, Aimee? Y'all nice and happy here, aren't you?"

Sarie looks away.

"Want to know how she got here? Somebody like your boyfriend started selling her Oxys. She's okay at first, because she's got a job, and she can afford a few. Then she needs more. Then she's out of money, and then the prices on the Oxys go up. She can't just stop, so she hears about how to save money and get an even bigger high."

Again, no idea if any of this is true. Aimee wasn't exactly forthcoming about the road that brought her to the Tracks. But it was probably true enough.

"And that's heroin. And the honors student who grew up afraid of vaccinations is suddenly shooting up between her fingers and toes, doing whatever she can to keep scoring."

"I don't take pills," Honors Girl says.

"Not yet," Wildey says. "Even if you don't, you honestly want to protect some guy who'd send people here?"

Sarie says nothing.

"How long you two been going out? Long enough that you feel this need to protect him?"

More silence.

"You told me you didn't want him," Sarie says. "You want the people above him."

Wildey blinks. "That's right."

"What happens to him?"

"Same thing that happened to you. If he's willing to help us, it can go real easy for him."

"Can we go back to the car now?"

"Sure, Honors Girl. Say bye-bye, Aimee."

Back inside the warmth of the car, Wildey puts the key in the ignition but hesitates before turning it. This is the moment. If this little field trip didn't work, then nothing would. Time for Honors Girl to do her part.

"So . . . what do you have for me?"

Honors Girl takes a breath of cold air, then finally, at long last, says: "His name is Ryan Koolhaas."

D. and I came up with the plan last night, Mom. Well, it was mostly his idea. I was joking when I asked him if he knew any drug dealers and he gave me a funny look.

—What is it?

D.'s eyes light up.

—How about we give your Officer Will-dee someone else.

—What do you mean? Rat someone out for real?

D. tells me the name of this guy he knows who deals stuff on campus. No, not a competitor, he insists. Just some asshole who is creepy and kind of rapey and should have been smacked down a long time ago.

—Are you serious? You want me to dime on somebody I don't even know?

—Would you rather know them first? Trust me, the guy's an asshole, he totally deserves it.

—No no no. That's horrible. We can't!

—He's perfect, is what he is.

—The cop's going to know he's not you.

—I don't think so. I bolted pretty quick.

—Yeah, you in your oh-so-stealth red chinos. You seriously want me to just rat out this poor guy instead? Doesn't that violate some code in the international brotherhood of drug dealers or something?

—Like you said, you don't know him. What's the difference? You give him the name, the cop does his thing, and we can forget this whole thing ever happened.

I'm thinking no fucking way—it's an incredibly shitty thing to do to someone. But then again, I have to give Wildey something tomorrow morning, or…god knows what was going to happen next.

You're not going to be very proud of me, Mom.

"Ryan Koolhaas. That's his name?"

Sarie nods.

"Spell it."

She does. Wildey writes it down. "So just to be clear, this was the guy in the car with you last Wednesday night?" Honors Girl stays quiet, staring out of the windshield like she's afraid to overcommit herself.

"Look, you're offering him up. What difference does it make? Tell me how you know him."

"I don't. Not really."

"So I saw a total stranger get out of your car on Ninth Street."

"You asked me to find you a dealer. That's what I did. Why do you need to know more?"

"Fine, we'll take it slow," Wildey says. "So this guy deals on campus, though, right? And gets his shit from Ninth Street?"

D. briefs me. I take notes. This is one of my weird skills: Once I write it down, it's etched in my memory. I can read the same paragraph a half-dozen times and pick up the general idea, but not much in the way of specifics. But if I write it down I've got every word. A pen and paper is like a data entry system for my brain.

Ryan Koolhaas

21

St. Jude's Townhouses, D3

(215) 419-2108

Sells pot, Addys (Adderall), Percs, some coke, or so D. has heard

$5 a pill unless it's finals week, raises the prices to 10 or 15

"I have no idea where he gets his drugs."

"You ever see him pick up a package from Ninth Street before? You take him on a run some other time?" Sarie pauses, then shakes her head quickly.

"What else does he sell?"

"That's all I know for sure."

"Then how do you explain all that shit I found in your car?"

Sarie gives him a wide-eyed shrug, like, fuck if I know, Officer. Wildey glances out at the Avenue. More people out now. Guys selling works and Subs. Same scene as it was months ago. Same scene as it will always be, unless he cleans it up someday. Maybe it starts with this girl right here. Or maybe she's feeding him a line of bullshit just to save her own ass.

"If this is real, I'm going to need you to make a buy."

"Buy what?"

Wildey sighs. "Look, I'm going to give you money, and you're going to buy drugs from your friend Ryan Koolhaas. Unless that would be weird, because he's your boyfriend or something."

DECEMBER 2 (later)

Ryan Koolhaas is not my boyfriend.

But the way his eyes light up when he sees me, you know he's thinking it might be a possibility. At least for a couple of hours.

And in that moment I recognize him. Close-cropped curly dark hair, lopsided perma-grin, raptor nose, and tall—crazy tall. Even taller than D. Koolhaas is a senior, but he was in my freshman Intro to Psych class last semester. Probably skipped it early on and realized he had to make it up if he wanted to graduate. It's clear that Koolhaas only vaguely recognizes me.

—Hey. You're…

—Sarie.

—Yeah, Sarie, cool. Hey, let me sign you in.

Koolhaas turns to the security guard and reaches his long fingers through the opening in the bulletproof glass to pinch a sign-in slip. He writes quick, like he's accepting a takeout delivery. That is the way the townhouses work. Access only to the seniors who live there or their guests. Like me.

—C'mon.

I step up to the turnstile, hear a sharp click, push my hip against the rotating bar, and follow Koolhaas—it helps to think of him as just Koolhaas, my target, not Ryan or my classmate from Intro to Psych—back down the concrete pathway to his front door.

What I expect to see: bongs, stained carpets, two guys playing nonstop World of Warcraft, the aroma of fried grease and marijuana and cheese.

What I actually see: a clean, quiet living room that smells like someone vacuumed it recently. There are vacuum trails and everything.

—I'm upstairs. I've got a single.

He bounds up the steps. I guess I'm following him. The entire townhouse feels dead quiet. Sure, it's a Tuesday, but it's also 7 p.m.

—Where are your roommates?

—Don't worry, nobody's home.

Meanwhile I'm worried, but not for the reasons he thinks I may be worried.

Koolhaas's room turns out to be just as neat and clean. What is up with drug dealers today? It occurs to me that maybe this guy isn't a drug dealer, that D. fucked it up somehow. Which will be supremely awkward when I try to make a buy, not to mention make me the worst confidential informant in the world. D. wouldn't do that to me, would he? Just give me a random name, or the name of someone he hates?

Sure enough, though, Koolhaas digs out a shower caddy with a lid, puts it on his bed, then taps the space next to him on the bed.

—You said you wanted Addys, right?

—Yep.

—Let me ask you something. I know it's going to sound weird.

—Okay...

He's going to ask me if I'm a cop. I've seen it on shows a bajillion times. I'm going to swear I'm not a cop, then boom, we do the deal. Instead Koolhaas turns to face me so that our knees almost touch.

—Look, you're probably stressed out with finals and everything, and I know your friends probably told you that a few Addys will keep you awake and hyper-focused. But there's something else you can do.

—What?

Koolhaas scoots back a few inches.

—Here. Put your head in my lap. Let me show you.

I'm pretty sure I give him a genuine double take here. Put my face...in his lap?

Koolhaas sees my hesitation. He's puzzled for a second before he smirks.

—No, no. I'm not talking about that. Okay, turn around. Come on, trust me. I'm a good Catholic boy.

Yeah. Who just so happens to deal drugs out of his townhouse complex named for an obscure saint, sure. But then he's guiding me by the shoulders and turning me around and then I feel his fingers on my back and then I realize: Holy shit, this guy is checking me for a wire.

"Do I wear a wire?" Honors Girl asks.

Wildey looks at her. "What, you going up against Tony Montana? No, you don't wear a wire. You just go in there, you buy some drugs with the money I give you, then you come out. Boom. Possession with intent to distribute."

She looks relieved at first, but then squints like she's confused. "That's it? Really? This is the big sting operation?"

"Look," Wildey says, sighing, "all I need is proof that this guy is selling drugs. I'll take it from there."

"How much do I have to buy?"

"Whatever. Just a few pills will do it, to be honest, but if you can get more, go for it. I don't want to spook him. Like I said before, he's not who I'm after. I get him, I make him take me up the ladder."

"Then why not just go after him directly?"

"If only it were that easy, Honors Girl. Here's the money. Go buy some drugs."

Turns out he's not checking me for a wire. He's massaging my shoulders. Like, for real.

—All-natural stress relief. Pretty great, huh?

Koolhaas speaks in soft and reassuring tones. Meanwhile his bony fingers dig into my body like he's trying to find a hidden microchip fused to my shoulder blades or something. Jesus. What's proper etiquette when setting up a drug dealer? Do you allow him to knead your shoulders and neck for a few minutes? Do you cut it short and insist on making the transaction as intended? At what point is it polite to tell him to fuck off?

I turn and offer up my only defense: a shy smile.

—That feels good, but you're going to put me to sleep doing that.

Koolhaas smiles like, Duh, that was kind of the point. Or at least make you want to lie down on the bed.

—Anyway, the Addys aren't just for me. It's for a friend of mine, too. We're in the honors program and really need to crank out some papers.

—The honors triple, huh? I should have known. I think I supply most of your class. Guess you heard about me from one of them, huh?

—Yeah.

D. had coached me on this point: If I called Ryan Koolhaas and he asked how I'd heard about him, I was supposed to just say something like, Oh just around. Be elusive; Koolhaas won't press it. When I called, sure enough, Koolhaas didn't ask. At the time.

—Who was it? I should give them a little extra for the referral.

Shit. Not only do I have no idea that half of my honors triple is popping Addys like Pez, but I have no idea who to name.

—She didn't want me to say. She's shy.

Koolhaas looks at me for a second, deadpan, then breaks into a wide grin.

—I know who you're talking about. No worries.

Now I'm *really* wondering who it is. Those cheating assholes, jacking up on Adderall and cranking out papers while I'm trying to do it the old-fashioned way! I feel like a ballplayer who's the last one to find out everybody else has been 'roidin' it up.

—Okay, down to business.

Koolhaas flips open his plastic shower caddy, revealing Ziploc bags half-filled with pills. I ask how much. He tells me $5 a pill, but he can do seven for $25. I ask for $100 worth—what Wildey gave me for the buy—and Koolhaas makes it an even thirty. I hand over the cash, five twenties. Koolhaas hands me thirty Addys in my own little bag. My first-ever drug purchase. It's all kinda anticlimactic.

Now comes the tough part.

"There's one thing—he lives in the townhouses."

Wildey stares at Sarie. "Yeah?"

"They're on campus, and you can only get in if someone signs you in."

"So how am I supposed to arrest him after you make the buy?"

"I have no idea. You're the detective!"

Wildey rubs his chin. "You've got to get him outside."

"Any ideas?"

"Hey, you're the honors student."

So what I settle on is this: the usual damsel in distress/chivalry bullshit. I ask him if he'd walk me to my car, because, you know, it's late and stuff, and I couldn't find a parking spot in the student lot, so I'm up a few blocks on Olney. He looks dickhurt, he thought we were going to hang or something. I remind him I've got something like five papers to write in four days (truth), and I'd love to hang out with him sometime (not the truth), and he says maybe this weekend, and I say, sure, cringing inside, because I know he's probably not going to be on campus this weekend.

Anyway, it works. Koolhaas walks me out. We cut across the student lot next to the library—where I told Dad I'd be this evening—out onto Olney Avenue.

I use the burner to text Wildey: ON MY WAY. Koolhaas peeks over at my phone, being a snoop.

—Boyfriend?

—Dad. He's kind of a pain in the ass, keeping track of my every movement.

—Oh man I hear ya.

I'm going to feel like such a huge throbbing dick in just a few seconds.

Make that one single second. Because we're not a few steps onto Olney—public property—when we see Wildey walking toward us. Badge hanging from his thick neck. You can't miss him.

—Ryan Koolhaas?

He bellows in this deep voice that even startles me, even though I knew he'd be there, and I know exactly what he is about to do.

—Yeah?

Koolhaas is startled, too, probably for a half second thinking both of us are about to get mugged…that is, until he sees the shiny silver badge. Ryan Koolhaas may not be an honors student, but he puts it all together in record time. First-time buyer, cop shows up. His eyes go wide with fury.

—You fucking bitch!

That last word is already trailing off as Koolhaas bolts back toward the townhouses. But Officer Wildey is ready this time, and there's no street-splattered cheesesteak standing in his way. He takes three long strides and body-checks Koolhaas into the nearest vehicle, which is somebody's SUV. The impact is so hard the car rocks on its suspension. I'm surprised the glass doesn't shatter. In a blur of motion Wildey suddenly has Koolhaas's arms behind his back.

—Who's the bitch now?

After a sharp cry of pain, Koolhaas ignores Wildey and tries to turn his head around to face me, yelling.

—YOU CUNT, YOU FUCKING CUNT, I'M GOING TO FUCK YOU UP!

—Shut the fuck up.

Wildey tells me to go back to my car and wait. I take one last look at Ryan Koolhaas, the guy I just offered up to the Philadelphia Police Department like a fatted calf. His eyes are closed now because he's trying to squeeze off the tears. I suppose a back rub is out of the question now.

NFU-CS HEADQUARTERS

MONDAY, DECEMBER 2

Wildey sticks Koolhaas in the birdcage for the interrogation. The buy is good, the Addys are real, but something bugs him about this whole thing.

For starters, word is that Chuckie Morphine is dealing Oxys, not Addys. He found Oxys in Honors Girl's car. Also, this white boy in the birdcage looks nothing like the white boy he chased up and over the fence in South Philly. Could be him—it was late, and dark, and Wildey had been up for twenty-two hours straight. Still, Wildey's gut is telling him no. So who is this guy?

"Tell me about Ninth Street," Wildey says.

"I didn't do anything wrong."

"Yes, you did, Ryan, and you know it. But I don't really care about you. What I care about is Ninth Street."

"So why don't you go there!"

"Christ."

Round and round they go until finally Koolhaas asks for a lawyer, and Wildey sighs and tells him that calling a lawyer is really the worst move here. He doesn't deny him the lawyer; he merely continues talking, hoping that Koolhaas will change his mind. Koolhaas does not. Kaz says it's fine. A lawyer might actually speed things up.

A lawyer does not.

Because the lawyer is this slick guy Kaz knows from years back—

a real player around town. Guy smells like he's just rolled here from a Rittenhouse Square cocktail lounge, in fact. Slick Guy and the Loot spar a little. Soon Wildey gets the idea that Slick Guy once asked Kaz out, and Kaz told him to fuck off, and Slick Guy never got over it. He's all familiar with the Loot, asking about this one or that one. And then he finally brings out the nuke by asking about her ex, Rem Mahoney, which really gets to the Loot. You can tell by the way her eyes dim like someone's flipped a dimmer switch on the back of her skull. So Slick Guy drags things out and it's morning by the time they reach an agreement.

Which is this: total free pass for the college kid if he reveals his supplier and cooperates fully, including future buys to set up said supplier.

Kaz asks Wildey in private: "How do you feel about this?"

Wildey says: "If his supplier is Ninth Street, then it's completely worth it."

"I hear a *but* in there."

"But I don't know if my CI has done me a solid here. Something about this doesn't feel right."

Kaz considers this. "Even if it's not Ninth Street, he might turn us onto another supplier."

"True."

"You call it."

"Let's do it," Wildey says, his gut screaming DON'T.

Wildey should have listened to his gut. Because in the room Slick Guy is smiling like he's negotiated the free pass of a lifetime. Even Kaz doesn't like how much the guy is beaming. Which is saying something, because it's almost seven in the morning, and nobody in this room has slept in a full day.

"We all okay?" Wildey asks. "Okay. Good. Here we are, for the record: Where do you buy your drugs, Ryan?"

Slick Guy nods. "Go ahead. It's okay."

"Via Maris," Ryan mumbles.

"Via who?" Wildey asks.

"Via Maris, man. On the deep web."

Wildey is perplexed. So is Kaz. Is this another dealer, after all? Someone going by the handle "Via Maris"? And what does "deep web" mean? Is that some kind of new cartel slang?

"Where's this Via Maris?"

"I can't tell you."

"Are you aware of the deal we just made?"

Slick Guy raises a neatly manicured hand. "Hold on, Officer. Let my client finish."

"I can't *tell* you," Ryan continues. "I have to show you."

"You don't know the address?"

"I do, but it wouldn't do *you* any good."

Wildey and Kaz look at each other. *The fuck?* Either they've been up too many hours straight or this kid is willfully fucking with them.

"My client would like the use of a laptop," Slick Guy says.

Soon as the kid starts typing, Wildey realizes he's completely fucked. Via Maris isn't the name of a dealer. It's a website, named for a Bronze Age trade route that ran from Egypt to what is now Iran, Iraq, and Israel. (Slick Guy gives all of this background, beaming like a fuckhead, as if he's delivering his doctoral dissertation or something.) It's completely anonymous, if you know how to find its address on the "deep web," which means you can only access it if you have anonymizing software, which more or less renders you invisible and untraceable. ("In theory, anyway," Slick Guy says.) You pay with bitcoins, equally untraceable ("in theory!") currency. You drop whatever you want into the shopping cart, and FedEx delivers it within twenty-four to forty-eight hours, depending on what you want.

"You can get anything on here—isn't it incredible?" Slick Guy continues. "I couldn't believe it, either. I mean, *anything.* MDMA from

Holland, high-end weed, fish-scale coke, whatever. You can even order a stack of prescription pads."

"Fuck," Kaz says, getting it.

"I mean, it's horrible," Slick Guy says. "But at the same time—man, technology, right?"

"You're buying this shit online?" Wildey asks, putting it together about a second after his boss.

"Fuck," she repeats.

"And as per our agreement," Slick Guy says, "my client would like to fully cooperate with your investigation by making a purchase. However, as you can see, this is no longer an option."

Slick Guy turns the laptop around so Kaz and Wildey can see the screen, which has a bright red border and is full of law enforcement seals and badges from a host of agencies—FBI, Justice Department, DEA, Homeland Security, and the IRS.

THIS HIDDEN SITE HAS BEEN SEIZED

In accordance with a seizure warrant obtained by the United States Attorney's Office for the Southern District of New York and issued pursuant to 18 U.S.C. § 983(j) by the United States District Court for the Southern District of New York

"Apparently the Feds shut down Via Maris last month, so..."

"Fuck," Wildey says again.

"...so my client is free to go, am I right? I mean, it is a school day."

I'm still shaking. I tell myself it's going to be okay, that this is over. On the drive home to Fox Chase, my stomach doing somersaults, I text Dad to let him know that I'm done at the library and will be home in twenty minutes. I resist the urge to ask if he needs anything on the way home—like, say, milk, bread, Adderall, weed? Yeah, I'm a scream. I want to vomit. Instead I text D. CALL ME. Then I follow up with a text to Tammy: HEY, COFFEE? IT'S IMPORTANT. I slide my real phone into my jacket pocket and check my burner phone. Thankfully, nothing from Wildey. Maybe I'll actually get the chance to work on my papers tonight. I half-wish I still had those Addys, but of course, I had to surrender them to Wildey in the parking lot, Ryan Koolhaas calling me a cunt until Wildey told him to shut the fuck up.

(Sorry for the language, Mom. But you know…)

Did Dad see me shaking just now? I tell him I was exhausted and just wanted to shower and get back to writing my papers. And I went upstairs and did shower, hottest shower I could stand, hoping it would calm me down. It didn't.

I'm still shaking because I know I'm not a regular CI. With most CIs, the police give you money to buy drugs. You buy the drugs. You tell the police you bought the drugs. The police arrest the guy who sold you the drugs. All the while you're protected by this cloak of anonymity.

Except in this case, Ryan Koolhaas knows exactly who I am. And whenever he's back on campus, he's probably going to want to follow up on his promise to fuck me up.

I tell Wildey this, hours before I'm going to make the buy, but he tells me not to worry. Ryan Koolhaas will be too busy with troubles of his own to bother with me.

But that's only because Wildey thinks that Ryan Koolhaas was in my car last Wednesday night and is tight with some dealer named Chuckie. And maybe he is, but I doubt D. would screw over someone in his own organization (listen to me, Jesus). I just want this whole mess gone.

Ryan Koolhaas.

I can still feel his fingers digging into my shoulders.

Marty creeps down the stairs leading to the den. He's not sure what he expects to see. Sarie didn't say much at all when she came back from the campus library (allegedly), telling Dad she needed to shower to wake up and then get back to writing her papers, all of which were due this week. Marty waited until she'd been downstairs for a while, supposedly at work on those papers, before he ventured down.

To his surprise, though, Sarie was at the desk, writing furiously.

"Hey."

Sarie jumps, spins round, her hand covering her work. "Jesus, Marty!"

"Sorry. I just wanted to see if you wanted—"

"You can't do that to people! And thanks, you just crashed my train of thought. Goddamnit."

"I just wanted to see if you wanted any hot chocolate. To help you study."

"Aren't you supposed to be in bed?"

"Dad didn't say anything. So...marshmallows? Whipped cream? I think we have both."

Marty expects his sister's eyes to soften a little, because, you know, he's trying to be helpful. Who doesn't want hot chocolate, especially if they're going to be pulling a late-nighter?

"You want to help? Why don't you leave me the fuck alone!"

Sarie might as well have slapped Marty. Dad's foul mouth is one thing—that's part of his weird charm, and a game between the two. But Sarie doesn't curse. Not at him. *Never.*

Marty turns without a word and heads for the stairs. Dad catches a fleeting glimpse of his red T-shirt. "Hey I thought you were already in bed."

"Good night," he mumbles, hoping Dad takes this at face value and doesn't summon him back. He doesn't want to have to explain the stupid tears in his eyes.

Upstairs he flicks on his iPod, retreats to the MI6 building, Torture Room 6, and thumbs:

Sarie is not herself
Is she taking drugs???
Need to look through her stuff to make sure
Why doesn't Dad see this?

THE FELONY

DECEMBER 3

Mom:

Today feels like the first normal day since forever.

Normal means:

Honors classes, library research, a hurried lunch, more classes, a few hours at my work-study in the bursar's office, then home to make dinner and start my paper-writing in earnest. Yes, everything feels like it's all due at once. I cannot afford a single moment off. But this is all blessedly normal. These kinds of deadlines I can deal with. Even the burner stayed quiet all day.

I wonder if this is all over.

I'll be a happy girl when I can pop the battery out of the burner and crack the fucking thing in half like they do on TV.

I'm downstairs in the den with my laptop and a pile of books listening to one of Dad's Cure albums—*Pornography*—on cassette, which makes for good working music. The imperfect cassette tape makes it all the better. You never caught me but when I was little I was always digging through Dad's closet and pulling out crap I didn't recognize until he explained it to me. I spent the majority of one summer with Tammy just screwing around with Dad's old digital voice recorder, pretending we were interviewer and celebrity. (Tammy was the celeb, of course, and made certain former Disney child stars seem like Girl Scouts. Thank God you never listened to these things, Mom.) VCR tapes were another source of endless

amusement, especially when we realized that Dad had a function-
ing player buried in the garage. But this treasure trove was too
good to be believed. I've been listening to these mix tapes and cas-
settes all semester.

By midnight I'm five pages into my philosophy paper and there
is a knocking on the back window. My subconscious registers it before I do. Of course that would be D.

I open the door with my eyes wide, hoping he takes the hint.
Dad—upstairs. Me—working. What the fuck are YOU doing here?

He refuses to step inside. Instead he wordlessly gestures, follow me.

Dad is no doubt still awake upstairs. I heard him moving around
just fifteen minutes ago, probably pulling another beer from the
fridge. He's a night owl, like me. Our floorboards creak like mad. I
can't just leave.

But D. is practically begging me in mime. *Pornography* is still
playing, and Dad doesn't always come downstairs to say good
night—he usually passes out on his own, quietly. D. is so insistent I
really don't have a choice. Besides, I want to talk to him, too. Tell
him this whole thing is (probably) over, he can fucking unclench. A
few steps into Pennypack Woods, he finally speaks.

—You can't text me like that. That cop is probably monitoring
your calls on your real phone.

—I don't think so. Look, it's all over. He arrested that kid and I
think I'm off the hook.

—Do you really want to take that chance?

I have nothing to say, because he's right. Instead I change the
subject.

—How did you get here?

—Public transportation. Which is real fun this time of night, going through freakin' North Philly.

I bite my tongue before *poor baby* slips out.

—If it's so dangerous for us to be in contact, why are you here?

D. takes a deep breath, then looks away.

—Look, Ryan Koolhaas wasn't the big deal I thought he was.

—What do you mean? Do you think Wildey won't be satisfied? You said he was perfect.

—That's what I thought. I heard he was supplying Addys all over campus, had a great connection—some fucking guy who could get, like, anything. I thought it would be payday. But he's got jack shit, pretty much. And I'm screwed, Sarie. I'm really, really fucking screwed.

I'm still not following him. All of this is about D. not being screwed.

—What do you mean? I didn't say anything to the cops.

—It's not that.

—What then?

—I owe Chuckie Morphine two grand by Friday or he's going to fuck me up.

—What?

—Yeah. I thought he was going to be cool and all, but…

—Wait.

—What?

—What does this have to do with Ryan Koolhaas?

—He didn't have shit.

And then I got it. D.'s big plan was ripping off Ryan Koolhaas. I don't know if I should punch D. in his stupid throat or go call Wildey right now and turn his stupid ass in. But foremost on my mind, oddly, is not any of this.

—You're such an asshole!

—What? Like you didn't know the deal?

No. I didn't know the deal.

FOX CHASE

TUESDAY, DECEMBER 3

Has Wildey ever been to this part of the Northeast? He's not sure. None of it looks familiar.

Nice, though. It's all homes. Lots of single, semidetached homes. Trees, decent cars. They call Fox Chase a middle-class city neighborhood, but to Wildey's eye it might as well be the suburbs. Wildey's own neighborhood used to be full of homes, too—homes within walking distance to factories, so close you could walk home to have lunch, if you wanted. But the factories closed, and people upgraded. Moved out here, where you needed a car to get to work. Just like in the burbs.

This is where Honors Girl lives.

All day Wildey wrestled with himself over what to do with his tall, dark-haired CI. He'd been exhausted after the long night of waiting, and utterly beaten after Slick Guy pretty much handed them their asses. He'd driven home in a daze and crashed for a few hours. When he woke, he wavered between anger and confusion. How could he let her play him like that? Did she know about this deep-web shit the whole time? Probably. He was sure she fingered Ryan Koolhaas knowing it would lead nowhere. Which led to him wanting to arrest her right away, busting into one of her honors classes if he had to.

But Kaz talked him down off that ledge. She wasn't off the CI hook until they said she was off. This was no victory for her. She was still in their pocket.

She was still the link to Chuckie Morphine.

Wildey realized his mistake. He'd made some assumptions about her.

Time to find out where you live, Honors Girl.

*   *   *

We sit in the chilly silence of the park. I don't know what to say. Neither does D. You can hear the urgent rush of creek and pretty much nothing else. We're within city limits but we might as well be sitting at the edge of the world. That's what it feels like, anyway.

—So you have three days to give Chuckie Morphine the Drug Dealer his two grand.

—Yeah.

—Can't you tell Chuckie the truth? That the cops caught you leaving his place, confiscated your stuff? I mean, it's his fault Wildey followed us. Obviously Wildey was onto him. Which means that's, like, on him, right?

—Chuckie's not the kind of guy who likes people pointing fingers at him. I'm a big boy. I take the shit, it's my responsibility. No exceptions. And the last thing I want to do is tell him about you—that you've been flipped. He wouldn't like that at all, no matter who you are.

—What does that mean?

—Never mind.

—Well, he's not the only one. Our old friend Ryan Koolhaas called me a cunt and told me that he was going to, quote, fuck me up. Should I be worried?

—He comes anywhere near you, I'll break his arms.

Which is actually kind of sweet, in a totally messed-up way. D. sighs, puts his hands on my shoulders, then touches his forehead to mine.

—God, I'm so fried.

I let him stay there for a few seconds before pulling away. The temptation to find out what his lips taste like is almost as strong as my simmering rage at this whole situation.

—Yeah, I have a philosophy paper to finish.

—I guess a ride back to campus is out of the question?

Wow. A ride got me in this much trouble. What would a second ride do—put me on the FBI's Ten Most Wanted list?

—I…can't. I'm sorry.

D. gives my house the once-over.

—Is your dad home? I mean, he's not out in California for business again, is he?

I choke back a laugh and tell D. that Chuckie Morphine would be the least of his worries if Kevin Holland found a strange dude crashing in his basement. Which is a good thing, because after D. shuffles off all dickhurt and I slip back into the den, Dad is waiting for me. My heart slams to a dead stop.

—Pornography?

There's a tipsy, bemused smile on his face. He's holding the scratched and scuffed Cure cassette tape in his hands.

—Yeah, I found it in one of the containers. Hope you don't mind.

—Where were you just now?

—Stepped outside to clear my head, take a breath of fresh air. This paper is kicking my butt.

Dad nods as if he understands, but the truth is he's never spent a day in college. He puts the cassette case back on the table but continues to stand there, staring at the case that holds the other tapes I pulled out tonight. Wonder if he's having a high school flashback. You told me that when Kevin Holland was a younger man he found himself in a lot of trouble— drinking, drugs, messing neighbors' shit up—that ended with his parents tossing his ass out of the house in 1989. These tapes were the sound track to those times. Maybe I shouldn't have them out.

—I can put those away if you want.

—No, no. It's just funny you're listening to them. I thought I was hearing things upstairs. Haven't listened to this one in decades. But I still know every song.

Dad turns and makes his way to the stairs, but pauses on the first step and turns to face me.

—Grab your boyfriend there off the corner and tell him he can crash on the couch upstairs. It's way too late for him to be taking the bus back to campus.

Again: My heart slams to a stop. Busted. My mouth is barely open to start a confused denial when Dad raises a hand to stop me.

—I saw him from the upstairs window. You don't have to sneak around, okay? Just let me know what's going on.

—I will. I'm sorry, Dad. I just—

—Go ahead after him. It's cold outside.

We have one of those silent moments, Dad and I, the kind we haven't had in nearly a year. Our eyes lock and I tell him: I hear you, thank you for not being a jerk about this, I swear it's nothing, you can trust me. And his eyes say: I know. I'm paying attention again, Sarie. I promise I'm going to keep paying attention.

Then something on my makeshift desk buzzes. A cell phone on vibrate. The burner Wildey gave me.

Fuck fuck fuck.

Dad's already headed back upstairs, but he hears the buzz against wood. To my ear it's as loud as a chainsaw rev.

—That's probably him. You can tell him not to worry, I'll keep my gun locked away.

The moment Dad's out of sight I push aside the three-book pyramid I made to hide the burner. I drop it into a jacket pocket, pull on the jacket, then run outside, hoping to catch D. in time. I technically have five minutes to get back in touch with Wildey. That should be

131

enough time. But the phone buzzes again. It's not a text. He's calling. I can't not answer.

—Hello?

—C-minus, Honors Girl.

Shit.

I don't need this right now, I don't need this at all.

I'm basically running up the street now, the burner to my ear, squinting to see if D. or his ugly green backpack is anywhere in sight. The nearest bus stop is a few blocks down on Rhawn. At this time of night, though, they probably run once every twenty-three days. Another reason I'm thankful for your Civic, Mom.

—This guy you gave me, Koolhaas, he's no good.

—What?

—No good, which means it's not good for you.

—I'm sorry?

—What did you do—just throw me the first punk who came to mind so that you could protect your boyfriend?

I'm only half-processing the words. I pull my jacket tighter around myself as I hurry down the block. Long legs mean long strides. The going is slippery, though. The sidewalk is littered with wet, cold leaves.

—Where are you headed in such a hurry, anyway?

I freeze midstep. Up the block, a car high-beams me twice.

While on the phone, Wildey tries to keep the frustration out of his voice.

And then what to his wondering eyes should appear but his own CI, moving briskly up the block. Huh. Where you speeding off to this time of night, miss? He considers just telling her he has to split, hanging up, then maybe following her, seeing where she's headed this time of night. But he doesn't like his chances out here. It's a quiet block. She'd see the car pulling out. And following her on foot isn't smart, either. Neighbors in a white hood like this tend to notice a man of Wildey's size and complexion moving swiftly behind a young woman.

She's closer to Wildey now and looks distracted, eyes darting all over the place.

"Where are you headed in such a hurry, anyway?" Wildey asks.

Sarie stops moving. He flicks the high beams at her twice.

"See me? Come on, let's talk for a minute. I won't keep you long. I know it's a school night."

How long has Wildey been parked on my street? Did he see D.? Shit, maybe he's already in cuffs and tucked away in the backseat, and Wildey's simply luring me closer to arrest me, too. Two-for-one sale: dumb fucking college students.

When I open the passenger door I'm relieved that there's no sign of D. inside. Unfortunately, there's still Wildey to deal with. He leans over and waves me in, making me feel vaguely hookerish. Red-faced, I lower myself into the seat and my knees bang on the glove box.

Please, don't let Dad take this moment to look outside to check on me to make sure I picked up D. Good luck explaining that one.

—How you doin', Honors Girl?

—Tired.

—Going for a walk to wake yourself up?

—Yeah.

—Nice neighborhood. You know, I don't spend much time up here in Fox Chase. Why do they call it that, anyway?

—From the Inn.

—The what now?

—The Fox Chase Inn. It was built here in 1705, I tell him. Hunters from what is now Center City, Philadelphia, would travel up here to hunt foxes through the nearby woods.

Wildey leans back in his seat. Awestruck by my brilliance, no doubt.

—Foxes, huh? How do you know that?

—I wrote a report for high school.

—Foxes.

Wildey gazes out of his windshield at the duplexes and sidewalks and streetlights.

—Huh. Three hundred years ago. City was a much different place then. Hell, I guess it was different months ago, you look at it a certain way.

Now I'm pretty much at the edge of my seat, trying to will myself to stay calm. Calm and polite. Do not piss him off. Do not tip your hand...

—Sorry for asking, Officer Wildey, but...

—Ben. I told you to call me Ben. You keep mispronouncing my name and it's just going to piss me off. It's will-dee, for the record. But for real, call me Ben.

—What are you doing here? In my neighborhood? I thought this whole thing was supposed to be kept secret!

—Easy, easy. Can I ask you something?

I close my mouth and lean back into the seat. Of course he can ask. He can ask anything he wants, can't he.

—You think you're smart, don't you?

The way he spits out the question makes me whip my head around.

—W-what?

—Ryan Koolhaas is no good to me.

—You keep saying that, but I don't understand. I did exactly what you wanted. I found you a drug dealer. Which means I'm done.

—No. You're pretty far from done.

Wildey turns his big body around to face me. He's got that tractor-beam cop glare going.

—Koolhaas is nobody. And he's sure as hell not the cheesesteak-eatin' sprinter I chased through the park last week.

I say nothing. Wildey sighs.

—Let me put my cards on the table. I'll tell you the same thing I would tell a judge. Last Wednesday night, around midnight, I was watching the house of an alleged midlevel narcotics dealer. I'm watching, and I see this silver Honda Civic pulling up to the usual spot—up near the corner, where the valet guy lets all of this dealer's customers idle for a bit. This guy in red pants, about twenty or twenty-one, I'm guessing, green backpack slung over his shoulder, launches himself out of the passenger seat, goes up to the house, knocks three times, door opens. But he wasn't alone. There was someone driving.

Now Wildey looks down at his thin reporter's-style notebook.

—Female, maybe eighteen or nineteen, I'm guessing at the time, but hey, some people are blessed with youthful looks. Hair up in a ponytail. I write down the plate number, but I can't run a search, since I don't have a laptop in the car.

Then he shows me the page. Scrawled at the bottom: DRK-1066.

—Recognize it?

I say nothing, but of course it's my plate.

—Anyway, I'm sitting there watching. I've been watching this house for a while and getting tired of it.

I'm getting tired of hearing things I already know. So I go on the offensive.

—Why can't you just go up and knock on the door? I mean, you're an undercover cop. Can't you just go up and make a buy yourself?

—That's not how this guy works. It's referrals only. I knock, they not so politely tell me to go fuck myself. That's not the way you take down a dealer like this. What you do is, you find somebody who works for them, then you recruit them.

—Like you recruited me.

—Exactly.

—So why follow us?

—Truth be told, because of you.

—What?

—You didn't fit. Most of the guys who roll up into that place look like they're in the game. You didn't. If you're an amateur, I figure your boyfriend there is an amateur, too. Otherwise he wouldn't have brought you along. Plus there was that green backpack. I had a good feeling about that. So I followed you.

—Hoping to pull us over.

—Absolutely.

Wildey rubs his chin slowly, feeling his stubble.

—This Chuckie guy is serious bad news, Sarie. I wouldn't be spending so much time on this if I thought otherwise.

—How bad?

Wildey lets a smile slip for a millisecond before resuming his grim cop face. There's an opportunity here. A good fright goes a long way.

"I can't talk about an open case," he continues. "But if I were you and your boyfriend, I'd stay as far away from that house on Ninth Street as possible. I've seen what he's done to people."

Wildey leans in.

"Nothing's going to happen to your boyfriend, Sarie. I promise you. He talks to me, I can protect him. I make the charges go away."

"I have to go back," Sarie says. "I have a paper to finish."

"This is not going to go away," Wildey says. "I'm not going to go away."

* * *

Marty is half-asleep when he hears a car door slam. He fumbles over to his bedroom window, tripping over piles of his own shoes and clothes, then rubs away some condensation with the sleeve of his shirt. Down on the street is his sister, climbing out of a car he doesn't recognize. She hurries back up to their house. The car glides down the street, but Marty's vantage point is bad; he can't make out the plate.

This is not good.

One thing Marty detests above all else is being treated like a little kid. Even before Mom died his parents regarded him as the baby of the house, unable to handle "grown-up" topics like Sarie could. And after Mom was gone, it became even worse. Now he's the poor kid without a mom who needs constant looking after. It's annoying.

Sarie was different. She never talked down to him or assumed he couldn't handle something. That is, until Mom got sick, and Sarie kept it from him. He was angry for a long time about that. She, of all people, should have known better. And when it happened, it was a bigger shock than it should have been. Marty was completely blindsided.

Now Sarie had a secret of her own. And it involved a mystery guy in a busted-up-looking sedan. A boyfriend? Maybe. But Dad wasn't the overbearing break-their-legs type. If it was a boyfriend, and Sarie didn't want Dad meeting him, then he must be some kind of serious jerk.

But no, this isn't boyfriend drama. Sarie's involved in something bad and Dad's apparently zoned out again and Marty Holland refuses to be blindsided again.

DECEMBER 4

This morning, looking at D.'s messy hair and jeans he probably slept in, I wonder what would have happened last night if Wildey hadn't shown up. Maybe I would have caught up with D., dragged him back to my house, introduced him to Dad, sneaked a quick kiss good night before heading upstairs. Maybe we would have agreed on a smart course of action.

Of course, that's not what happened. Because instead we're freezing our asses off near Independence Square and I'm telling D. what I have in mind.

D. doesn't react the way I thought he would.

—What? That's insane! No way. Don't worry. I'll figure something out.

—How? You have until, like, tonight.

He averts his gaze, swallows.

—Actually I have until, like, right now, because I have to catch a bus upstate in two hours.

The air is freezing, but that doesn't stop hundreds of tourists, Asian mostly, from milling around Independence Hall, snapping digital pics and waiting for the next bus departure. My hands are already numb because I forgot to bring gloves.

We're being super-careful about meeting in person after Wildey's surprise visit to my neighborhood last night. I have to assume he might be lurking at any given moment. I can practically hear him now: Oh so THIS is the boyfriend, as he stands up from behind a shrub on the quad, handcuffs in hand. So no more meetings at my house, and I can never go to D.'s house.

D. comes up with the idea to set up phony Twitter accounts to communicate. Wildey would have to be psychic to intercept, right? We agree to meet at the Liberty Bell. His idea. He's such a tourist.

Now that we're walking around the Bell pavilion, it all feels so weird.

—Why here?

—I mapped it out online. This is pretty much right between my next two stops: Chuckie's place and the bus station.

I do the math in my head. It doesn't add up.

—Wait. Chuckie's place is down in South Philly. The bus station's like six blocks away. How is this in the middle?

D. looks at me, hesitating, then decides to open his mouth anyway.

—Chuckie's place moves around, week to week. Sometimes every few days.

—He has that many places?

D. shakes his head, gives a grim smile.

—You have no idea.

—How do you know where to go? I mean, does he call you or something?

Again D. hesitates, like he's a fucking cold war spy hating to give away his secrets.

—We have another way of communicating. It's all safe, no one can listen in.

—You're on Twitter with him.

—No, it's not Twitter.

I decide to drop it for now. Why do I even want to know about this stuff, anyway? Feels like the more I know, the worse the situation gets. Wildey would probably be able to sniff it on me. "You know something new, don'tcha, Honors Girl." Fuck that. Except that I kinda DO want to know. How could I not? D.'s wrapped up in this world I've been sucked into—isn't it natural to be curious about how it works? Knowing more means I'm protecting myself. Maybe even D.

—I'd better go. I just wanted to let you know where I'd be so you didn't worry.

—I'm even more worried now.

—Why?

I bug my eyes out at him. Duh!

—That's sweet of you, but seriously, I'll be fine.

—Look, can't you ask this Chuckie guy for an extension?

—What, like with a paper in class? It doesn't work that way. Dealers will always front you product as long as you pay them back on time. If I ask for more time, he'll know something's up, I won't get any more product. Without that, I have no hope of paying Chuckie back. Or the school. I might as well start running now.

—Shit.

—Yeah. I do seem to be buried in it, don't I?

We continue in silence until we reach the old slave quarters exhibit at the corner of Sixth and Market. I look both ways before crossing. D. seems lost in his own head. After we're safely on the other side of Market Street I tell him.

—No. You're not.

The idea hit me the moment I opened my eyes this morning. I could steal two grand from the student organization I co-founded.

The thought surprised me. Last night I was racking my brain for other ways to come up with $2,000—a loan from my dad (but no, he's still dealing with Mom's cancer treatment bills, he doesn't have it), a new student loan (nope, Dad would find out), a personal bank loan (with what as collateral?). I went to bed obsessing over it, and in the morning the answer was waiting for me.

A felony.

Yes an honest-to-God felony. I looked up the code in the school library, just to be sure:

(a.1) Felony of the third degree.—Except as provided in subsection (a), theft constitutes a felony of the third degree if the amount involved equals or exceeds $2,000, or if the property stolen is an automobile, airplane, motorcycle, motorboat, or other motor-propelled vehicle, or in the case of theft by receiving stolen property, if the receiver is in the business of buying or selling stolen property.

Two grand. The exact amount D. needs to avoid being mauled by a drug dealer with a ridiculous name. It's almost as if Pennsylvania code knows this, and is fucking with me.

I could try to rationalize things by saying I'm merely borrowing two grand, but the truth is, it's straight-up stealing. The money from this theft goes to D., who will take it to Chuckie Morphine to satisfy his debt. D. will receive more pills to sell. He'll ask for a larger package than usual. Over the next two days, D. will hustle like fuck to move them, making enough to satisfy his debt to the university by Friday and pay me back before anyone knows the money is missing.

This is stealing, isn't it?

I take the envelope from my jacket and hand it to D. A puzzled look remains glued to his face until he thumbs open the flap and sees the bills inside.

—Whoa.

—Two grand worth of whoa.

—Where's this from? Did you borrow this from your dad?

—Don't worry about it.

—C'mon, I have to know. What did you do?

—You have your secrets, I have mine.

D. doesn't know what to say. He looks at the envelope, then me, then the envelope again. The gratitude is practically oozing out of his pores. But, surprise, surprise, he's not done asking for favors.

—I need you to do one more thing.

—Wait…what?

—Make a date with Wildey.

—Why would I do that?

—Because he knows most dealers re-up on a weekly basis. I got my package last Wednesday, so he'll probably be watching the house. What if he recognizes me?

—Shit. So you need me to draw him away from his surveillance.

—Yeah. If you don't mind?

There's an awkward silence. We need to separate, because things are moving fast now, what with the felony and the imminent drug pickup and distracting the narcotics cop, which probably falls under the category of aiding and abetting, right? But I also want to linger with him. I wish we were just a girl and a guy who met at a party and we could just go and do normal stuff in the city, nothing hanging over our heads. Maybe it can be that way soon.

I reach out and grab D.'s arm, sort of my lame prelude to a hug. He doesn't get it. D. just looks at me.

—What?

—Do you like doing this?

—Doing what? Taking a bus upstate?

—You know what I mean.

—Yeah, I know. But I told you. I need the money for tuition.

—I've been thinking about that. There are other ways to make money.

—Are there?

—Umm…yeah. There are.

—You ever hear about Cindy Schraff?

—Who? Are you changing the subject?

D. shakes his head.

—Cindy Schraff was an honors student, graduated last year, so I guess you wouldn't have known her. Four point

oh—yeah, even with the honors triple—activities out the
ass, volunteers, the whole thing. Pretty much the perfect
student. She doesn't want to go on to law school or medical school or dick around with graduate school. She just
wants to graduate, get a job, move into her own place.
Home sucks, but who cares, because she's worked hard to
earn her own way out. Cindy graduates, sends out a billion resumes, scores a few interviews, but nothing. Like,
for months on end. Her student loans are due, and if you
default on those, you can't erase that with bankruptcy.
Her parents are no help. They're of the opinion that she
did this to herself, and nobody helped them out back in
college. She keeps plugging away, spending more money
on these leadership and job seminars, hires a headhunter,
everything. But nobody's hiring. You know what she did
next?

    —She started dealing Oxys.

    —No. She killed herself.

    Okay, I feel like a total asshole now.

    —Did you know her?

    —Yeah. A little. My point is, the game is hopelessly rigged.
You can do all of the so-called right things and what will it get
you? Ask Cindy.

    —I'll see what I can do.

PORT RICHMOND

Wildey pulls paper packets of fake sugar from the rectangular glass
container and spreads them out on the diner tabletop, still not believing he's doing this. He gestures to the sugar.

    "Okay, this is the product."

Honors Girl tells him hold on, hold on, then goes digging into her bag. She pulls out a robin's-egg-blue exam book and a black pen.

"What are you doing?"

"Taking notes."

"Notes? For what?"

"It's how I learn. I write it down, it goes in my head and stays there. Trick I learned in high school."

Huh. Honors Girl is the real thing, that's for sure. He was surprised when she texted him an hour ago—he didn't recognize the number at first. For the past week, Wildey has been on *her* ass, not the other way around. Maybe the week's worth of pressure is about to pay off. Maybe the ultimatum last night did the trick. Who knows. But when he called back, Honors Girl said in this whispery voice, *How can you tell somebody's a dealer? I mean, for sure?* And there you go. Caving in. Looking at her boyfriend with a new set of eyes. Kaz was right about her cracking. It had just been a matter of time. Wildey told her to meet at the Aramingo Diner—which was becoming their place, he supposed—in one hour.

This time she showed up hungry. Not that she orders real food. Instead it's just a garden salad, olive oil vinaigrette, and, weirdly, a bowl of oatmeal and honey. "You don't want some real food?" he asked. "This is real food," she countered. Wildey's not hungry. He ordered a coffee and they got down to business.

The business of drug dealing.

"How do you know how to find a dealer?" Sarie asks. "They could be anyone."

"Heh," Wildey says. "Now you understand why they pay me the big bucks."

"That's not what I mean."

"I'm not worried so much about dealers as what dealers can do for me, because the only way to do this job is to go up the ladder."

"The ladder?"

Which is when Wildey gets the idea to illustrate the whole works for her, starting with sugar packets as the product.

"The product?" she asks.

"You know, Oxys, Percocet, heroin, whatever," Wildey says, realizing he might be talking a bit too loud. A couple of civilians' heads are turning now. Black guy, white girl at a table, talking drugs.

"Got it," she says, oblivious. Honors Girl scribbles it down, God bless her. The tip of her tongue pokes out of her mouth and everything.

"It's a complex network. You don't have guys jumping off a boat somewhere and roaming the streets selling shit," he says, almost in a whisper now. "The product passes through many, many hands before it ends up with your average street dealer." He glances at the table, then slides an ancient ketchup bottle next to the plastic sugar container. "This ketchup is your Drug Lord. The guy in charge of everything. He gets the product direct from the source—South America, Mexico, Afghanistan, wherever. But a lot of the stuff here in town comes from Mexico, through California."

Sarie glances up, glances down, writes furiously.

Wildey can't help himself. He likes having an audience. He's feeling inspired. He grabs a sticky grape jelly tub from a small plastic rack of them. Then takes an apricot jelly tub, too. What the hell. He loads the sugar on top of the jelly tubs.

"These are your international smugglers. Drug Lord hires these guys to transport the product into the country. They're real good at it, too. Say it's coke. Their guys are sneaking five hundred tons of shit into the country every year."

Wildey slides the drug-smuggling jelly tubs across the tabletop toward . . . what now, what can he use . . .

Mustard bottle. One of those fat, squat ones. Yeah, that was right on.

"This is your kingpin. He's in the U.S., overseeing the shit on this end."

Sarie writes.

Wildey positions the plastic salt and pepper shakers next to the mustard. "Here's the next level down, the domestic distributors. They take the shit from the kingpin, they process it, cut it, whatever, then send it on to their dealers."

Sarie looks up from her notes expectantly. Wildey scans the table. What's left? Next to his coffee cup are four empty creamer tubs, paper tops all peeled back. Yeah, they would work. He gathers them up and drops them in front of Honors Girl.

"Now these are your dealers. The guys out there slinging it to their customers. They're nobody special. They're the guys behind the counter at fuckin' McDonald's. Expendable, replaceable."

And to illustrate the point, Wildey swipes his paw across the table, knocking the creamer tubs so they slam up against the Formica partition.

"Your boyfriend? He's a creamer tub. I truly do not give a high holy fuck about him."

"You only want to use him to get to the next level," she says. "The salt and pepper shakers."

"Yeah. Making cases against salt-and-pepper motherfuckers is what gets me up in the morning. Even better if I can take down enough of them to get me a mustard bottle. Big fat wide-mouthed one. That's my real goal."

Honors Girl writes it all down, leaving Wildey feeling like he needs to give a summary statement.

"All this, right here on this table? What you're sitting in front of? This is a seven-hundred-fifty-billion-dollar game. That's billion with a *b*. And I'm just a brother making sixty grand a year trying to throw a wrench into it."

She nods, puts her pen down, takes a bite of her salad. Chews thoughtfully, like there's a lot tumbling around in her head right now. "What happens to the creamer tub once you use him up?"

Wildey smiles. "Depends. But in this particular case, the creamer tub in question will be fine if he gives up his salt-and-pepper guy. You have my word on that."

Sarie chews more salad.

Wildey continues. "Let me tell you what usually happens to creamers. Either we catch them, or they end up dead. I'm talking the *vast* majority, Sarie. Doesn't work any other way unless they cop a deal. Your boyfriend's white, right?"

Sarie continues chewing, glancing down at her rabbit food. She's not going to answer this one. No. Not yet.

"I'll assume that's yes. Maybe he's got slightly better chances. But he's also more likely to be dipping into his own product if he isn't already. White boys do love their pills. Soon, you've got judgment lapses all over the place. For instance, you get your innocent girlfriend to drive you down to his salt-and-pepper shaker and then leave her holding the bag. If he's doing that kind of shit, he's already circling the drain, you know what I mean?"

Sarie continues chewing. Washes things down with a gulp of ice water.

"Which means you'd be doing him a huge f—— "

Honors Girl's cell goes off—a text or something. As she digs it out of her bag, Wildey tries to take a casual peek, but the glare from the diner lights makes it impossible.

"Who's that?"

Sarie looks up at him. "My dad. He's wondering if I'm going to be home for dinner."

"What, with all that salad you've been wolfing down?"

Then it comes: a real smile from Honors Girl. Wildey is floored. When his CI smiles, she looks like a completely different person.

"So," Wildey says, feeling emboldened, "anything you want to tell me?"

The smile fades just as quickly as it appeared, and a look of worry creeps back in. That's it, Honors Girl. You should be worried. Let's help your boyfriend—together. Kid talks tonight and Wildey can be preparing his end run on Chuckie by morning. I'll buy you all the salad you can eat. You know it's the right thing to do. You're smart. So come on, do it.

"Give me forty-eight hours," Sarie tells him, surprising Wildey for the second time in one day.

DECEMBER 4

Mom: You can't say I'm not learning anything. This afternoon I got a crash course in the drug trade, courtesy of Wildey. He had no idea I was just stalling for time, keeping him talking, asking him questions, giving him the I'm Totally Into What You're Saying look. (Though it was interesting, to be honest.) But halfway through, my real cell buzzes; I can feel it through my bag. I pull it out, check the screen, praying that Wildey is too busy with his creamer cups and mustard bottle to glance down.

Because it's a message from D.:

—I'm out.

Wildey tilts his head toward the phone.

—Who's that?

I lie and say it's Dad.

—He's wondering if I'm going to be home for dinner.

—What, with all that salad you've been wolfing down?

I look up at him and force a big smile. Wildey smiles, too, and I feel like I can breathe for the first time in a week. I quietly slide the phone back into my messenger bag. The coast is clear; in a few minutes D. will be on a Martz bus headed upstate, where he can hopefully turn a couple of bags of pills—*product*, she reminded herself—into four grand profit. And now it's up to me to find someone else to offer up in D.'s place. And I can do this. If I can crank out some bullshit paper on the French Revolution in eight hours, I can definitely find a drug dealer in Philadelphia.

Sarie is showering, which means she's headed out somewhere. Marty Holland knows this is strange for a school night. If anything, Sarie stays later at school to do some library research but then comes home, makes/eats a quick supper, and goes down to the den to work. Sometimes Marty would bring a book down to the den, ask Sarie about a word or phrase he'd pretend he didn't know, just to make sure she was okay. She never even goes out to hang with Tammy anymore. (Which is a shame, because Tammy was always cool to him, even though he knows she's probably just being kind to a dork for karma's sake.) Ever since starting college in September, Sarie never goes back out at night. So where is she going now?

Is Dad going to question her? Unlikely. He's in the living room watching an old eighties action movie, drinking his fourth bottle of Yuengling (judging from the three empties in the recycling bin). He asked Marty to join him, maybe they could even make some popcorn, but Marty passed. Not his kind of thing. Didn't anyone realize this was a school night?

Marty holds his ear to the wall to confirm the water is still running, then quickly takes Sarie's keys from the plastic hook on the fridge and darts outside. The gunfire and explosions from the living room cover up all sounds, which is nice. Confident now, Marty makes his way to the Civic, opens the door, keys the ignition to power up the vehicle, notes the odometer reading, turns off the car.

But this is just a backup measure, because now he has a new way to figure out where Sarie's headed. Marty ordered it online over the weekend, and it had arrived today: $18.95 scored him a first-generation sQuare, a non-GPS, Bluetooth-powered tracking device. Normal

Bluetooth range is only 100 feet, so unless Marty was only tracking Sarie halfway down the block, the little white plastic chip would be useless. But instead sQuare's designers came up with a pretty clever idea: crowd-sourcing the search. The moment your sQuare enters the 100-foot range of another sQuare user, you're notified in your app. The big limitation, of course, is that sQuares aren't going to be everywhere yet. But a bunch of early adopters and crowd-source funders snapped up the first wave, so Marty was hopeful that there were enough in Philadelphia to give him at least a rough idea of where Sarie might be.

Question now is: Where to put it? Marty doesn't want to bury it in the glove box (which Sarie keeps organized and neat anyway) and cut off from any potential sQuare hits. The outer edges of the Civic would be best. Short of mounting it on the dashboard, where could it go? This is when Marty glances up and notices the oversized St. Christopher's medallion clipped to the visor. Mom bought that the day they bought the Civic. She was Catholic and superstitious and refused to drive the car without one. Dad, who was a recovering Catholic, drove her straight to a St. Jude's shop and bought her the biggest he could find. Which was fortunate because the sQuare would fit snugly beneath it, hidden away.

As Marty touches the medallion he thinks about Mom, and thinks she'd be frowning at him right now, which is the worst possible thing he can imagine. His lip trembles and he bites down on it. Don't be a baby. Your sister doesn't need a baby brother; she needs someone watching out for her.

There. Snapped into place. Completely invisible, and wedged in tight. The metal shouldn't interfere at all with the Bluetooth signal, and the low-energy battery is supposed to last nearly a year.

"Sorry, St. Christopher," Marty says, just in case. "Don't hold this against Sarie."

St. Christopher, if listening, does not reply.

Marty steps out of the car, closes the driver's door as quietly as he can, then darts back up to the house. He opens the door and immediately hears the reassuring sounds of shouts and gunfire. But Sarie's in the kitchen, in a robe, hair wrapped up in a towel, making a cup of tea. She turns and notices Marty immediately.

"Where were you?"

Marty still has his sister's keys in his hand, which he now hides behind his back, praying they don't jingle.

"Thought I heard something outside," he says, the lie tumbling from his mouth almost automatically. "Are you going somewhere?"

Sarie turns away to face the counter again. "Yeah, I'm going to study with Tammy for a while."

"Tammy? Really?"

"Yes. Really. Tammy. What's up with you?"

"Does Dad know?"

Sarie turns back around with a strange look on her face. "Yeah, he knows. Why wouldn't he?"

"You know...Dad doesn't always pay attention. Just wanted to make sure he knew where you'd be so he didn't wake me up at midnight asking about you."

That comes out a little more aggro than Marty intended. Sarie looks a little wounded before she turns her attention back to her tea. Another concussive explosion echoes from the living room. Boom. Fail.

But at least now Marty knows where his sister is *supposed* to be. Tammy Pleece lives over in Rydal, roughly three miles away. If the sQuare pinged anywhere else in the city, Marty would know instantly. The odometer would tell the story, too, although Sarie could also lie about that and say that she and Tammy just hit a coffee shop somewhere in Abington or wherever.

Now Marty sits down at the kitchen table and pretends to thumb through today's *Daily News* while waiting Sarie out. He had to replace her keys on the side of the fridge before she left, but he wasn't too worried. She still had to blow-dry her hair and get dressed and do all of that girl stuff. So Marty squeezes the keys tight so they won't make a sound and looks at stories about people getting shot all over the city. Two in a playground in a neighborhood called Fairhill (which Marty had never heard of). Another, outside a bar on Lancaster Avenue near Powelton Village (which Marty knew, thanks to a true crime book called *The Unicorn's Secret,* which he'd read this past summer). And there were still no leads in an alleged drug house massacre in Rhawn-hurst, which was disturbingly close. Out in the living room a male voice makes a wisecrack Marty can't quite hear, followed by the rapid-fire cracks of a pistol and then another wisecrack. Sarie finishes making her tea and walks out of the kitchen without a word. Marty hangs the keys on the side of the fridge and goes up to his room to finish his math homework and wait. It is going to be a long night.

GIRLS

DECEMBER 4 (later)

Tonight: drug research, attempt one.

Before I regale you with my tale of hard-hitting, on-the-streets research…well, you know me, Mom. I am what people will politely refer to as an introvert. Large crowds are fine just as long as I can lose myself in them and no one tries to talk to me. So the idea of injecting myself into a large crowd to find out where one might score drugs…yeah.

I did have a lead, though. During one of my sporadic interweb frenzy-searches I found a story about this so-called junkie Bonnie and Clyde who went on a heroin-and-coke-fueled rampage through Camden and Philly. I remembered everyone at school talking about it last March, giggling and passing around their phones to watch some YouTube clip where a police car was smacking into a long series of parked cars. I didn't pay much attention at the time, so today I looked it up online. And damn…"Clyde" was a twenty-four-year-old day laborer from the suburbs, "Bonnie" was his twenty-three-year-old fiancée. In the before pictures they look like a happy couple—all smiles, heads leaning against each other, delirious with life. He's lean and muscular, with close-cropped hair and the handsome looks to pull it off. She's fresh-faced and busty, with perfect white teeth we all wish we had. That was the before.

After three days of bingeing on heroin, they decide to drive to Camden to cop some more. They're pulled over on suspicion of

155

buying narcotics, because, duh, why else would they be in Camden? Later they told police that they were intending to quit—they had a baby at home, after all—but wanted to go "out with a bang." Professor Chaykin is always telling us to avoid clichés like "all hell broke loose," but…all hell broke loose. Bonnie and Clyde decide it's a good idea to steal the Camden cop's car. Which they do, taking it over the Ben Franklin Bridge before they're pulled over again, by the Philly PD, at which point you'd think the story would be over. As YouTube can attest, you'd be wrong. With Clyde in cuffs, Bonnie decides it would be a good idea to steal the Philly PD's car—maybe she's trying to steal a cop car from every department in the Delaware Valley?—and hauls off into Fishtown, where she smacks into a bunch of parked cars before screeching to a halt. The cops manage to put some cuffs on her, and the next day, hundreds of thousands of people are busy cracking jokes and passing around the YouTube clip of her final moments of freedom.

No, Mom, don't worry, I'm not going to Camden to try to set up a street dealer. Nor am I going to embark on a two-state crime spree in two stolen police cars. Reading their background stories, however, revealed that they were big on the Northern Liberties drug scene, copping in hipster lounges and brewpubs. Especially places with live music. Exactly the kind of place I could get into, thanks to the fake ID from Tammy.

The trick tonight is going to be dressing up so that I look casual enough for a hangout with Tammy, then dolling it up in the car on the way. Dad won't pay too much attention to what I'm wearing—he rarely does, and I never give him reason to. Marty's been acting weird, though, interested in my comings and goings more than usual.

Wish me luck, Mom. If there are any patron saints of canaries, let them know the deal.

Text exchange between Kevin Holland and daughter Sarie:

HOLLAND: Hey, kiddo, it's getting late. You on your way home?

HOLLAND: Come on, Sarie, you know the rule let me hear from you.

HOLLAND: I'm calling . . .

SARIE: I'm here, Dad! Home soon.

WILDEY: Honors girl, give me an update

WILDEY: Five minutes are almost up . . .

CI #137: hang on

CI #137: can't text now

CI #137: working on something for you

WILDEY: What?

WILDEY: Update me when u can

WILDEY: It's getting late

WILDEY: I'm not going away. You know that, right?

DECEMBER 5 (very, very, very late)

Oh god.

   Mom, that was so fucking stupid.

   Don't even ask.

[-] crycrybribri 6 points 2 hours ago

   Obvious narc girl last night. Cops keep getting younger and

   younger huh

   [–] 2 boxer man 1 hour ago

   shit I think I talked to her too she kept asking where to find

   pancakes and syrup! stupid bitch

   ferrill215 1 point 1 hour ago

   someone should have made her breakfast

ridonkdonk 1 point 1 hour ago

   KILL ALL SNITCHES

cerealkilla 31 points 10 hours ago

   anybody got a pic of this girl? She at least hot?

BEAR CREEK, PA

THURSDAY, DECEMBER 5

Drew "D." Pike is twenty years old, a junior honors student at a small Catholic college taking in at least sixty grand a year as a small but successful narcotics dealer, and his mother still puts him at the little kids' table.

The "kids" in the extended, invented family that Mom gathered around herself in the wake of the divorce run from ages seven to twenty-two—Drew being the second oldest of the lot. Didn't matter. The party always divides itself into two distinct camps: those who could drink openly and those who had to hide it. Mom and her friends call it the "non-Family," after some lame-ass clique they formed back in high school.

The Charade is fascinating to behold. To hear Mom tell it, Drew had such a great time over Thanksgiving weekend that he wanted to come back home for a few days. The kid just craved more of her home cooking, she said. So why don't we gather at my place and have an impromptu party? Bring the kids! Sure, it's a Thursday, but so what?

Home cooking his ass. If Mom is so concerned about making a "home-cooked meal," why is she ordering six pizzas from the worst restaurant in all of Luzerne County and cracking open the first of many (many, many) bottles of cheap red?

No, the real reason for this impromptu party was simple. Last week

Drew didn't have any drugs. This week, he does. And Mom's friends need their fix.

You should have seen the looks on their faces last week, when the non-Family was gathered for Thanksgiving. First was the utter surprise. *Oh. . . . Really?* Quickly followed by faux-concern: *Is everything all right at school, Drew? If you need to talk to someone . . .* And finally, the blatant fishing for details on a possible re-up: *Are you going to be home again before Christmas?*

If Drew hadn't been so fucking terrified about what might happen to him, he would have enjoyed their weird little moments of desperation.

Now, though, the non-Family is in the mood to party. And to spend money to get them through until the holidays (*When you'll be home again, right, honey?*). Drew sells through his package in more or less an hour, after which he sneaks out back with Courtney, the twenty-two-year-old kids' table exile, bottle of wine tucked under his arm.

Out back Drew takes a long pull of the warm cheap stuff then passes it to Courtney, who does the same before coughing and asking for an Oxy. Drew thinks about asking her to pay for it—Christ, she's been freeloading all summer and fall—but decides this is ultimately a dick move.

Two kittens come bounding out from behind a shrub. The bigger one is completely white, with a gray swipe across the top of her head, as if she'd head-butted some wet paint. The small one is gray-blue and his hind legs work harder than his front, creating the effect of an eighteen-wheeler fishtailing on an icy road. Courtney points and laughs at the cats. Drew's phone buzzes.

I'm imagining D. on some desperate and shabby street corner of Wilkes-Barre, PA, hawking his pills to a rotating cast of blue-collar circus freaks. Earlier today I did a little Googling on his hometown, and, yeah, apparently shit's real bad up there. Lots of gun violence, home invasions, corruption out the ass. Makes Philly seem idyllic. So imagine my surprise when I call D. and hear not the chaotic ur-ban drama of some poor coal-mining town gone to hell but some girl giggling.

—Awww, look how cute! Look at that one, D.! He looks like he's broken!

—Hello?

I hold my breath for a few seconds.

—Hello?

—Hey.

—Who is this?

Who me? Shit, I'm nobody, man. Just some dumb tall bitch with a car who stole two grand for you. A million withering answers to that question come to mind. Instead I give him the silence.

—Sarie?

—Yeah, hey. What's up.

—Not much. I mean, all is good on this front. I took care of ev-erything. I'll have your stuff by Saturday morning, latest.

Takes me a minute to realize that "stuff" means "the two grand." He's already sold through everything? Damn, W-B must be harder up than I thought.

What's up? he asks, like he wants to hurry me off the phone. The picture becomes crystal clear. D.'s worked off his obligation to me, so we're all good. In his eyes, at least. Conveniently forgetting that I have to serve up a piping-hot drug dealer to Wildey in about twenty-four hours. Granted, a self-imposed deadline, but if I hadn't set my own clock Wildey would have remained firmly lodged up my ass. At the very least, the deadline bought me two days of leave-me-the-fuck-alone.

—Nothing. Good-bye.

—Wait, wait. I can tell something's wrong. So what is it?

I hesitate, then realize I'm only screwing myself over if I hang up on him.

—I tried finding a drug dealer last night.

—You what? Please tell me you weren't driving around street corners in North Philly all night. That isn't what that cop wants.

—No. I went to some dumb hipster bar and—

—And did what? Asked complete strangers if they knew any drug dealers?

Part of me wants to hang up again, let D. go back to his upstate girlfriend and get stoned or whatever. But again, I'd be fucking myself over. Before I let D. sail out of my life, I need his help.

—So how do I do it?

—Do what?

—Find a dealer. One who's not you.

He sighs.

—Wildey's not letting up on you, is he?

—No. And he's not going to, either. He saw you that night. He knows you exist. So his next step is going to be throwing my ass in jail, and…well, know what? Don't worry about it. Have a good time with your mom. If you leave the stuff at your place I'll come pick it up over the weekend and—

—Hang on.

—Why?

—Here's what you do…

And D. tells me what to do, how to act, what to say…basically, how not to come off as a big fucking narc.

Tonight I'll have my chance to see if it works or if D. is full of shit.

"That your girlfriend?" Courtney asks. "If so, I think she's pissed. You should tell her nothing's going on with us. It's okay."

Drew assures her she's not and Courtney hears the implication in his voice: *And you're not either.* Well, duh. Courtney and Drew messed around over the summer, two adult exiles from the kids' table, but for Drew it was all about the proximity and the convenience. One-stop pill shopping with benefits—an occasional break from her nowhere job at the Wyoming Valley Mall and whatever other guys she was fucking around with. Drew's mom of course saw big romance in all this, believing that Courtney might just be the bait to lure her son back to the valley for good. Mrs. Pike was always complaining about all the kids fleeing town, which was kind of like complaining about all of the woodland creatures fleeing a forest fire, but whatever. Meanwhile, Courtney's mom was visibly pained every time Drew's mom brought it up. Perhaps because earlier in the summer Drew had to deal with the clumsy, drunken—what did the oldsters call it? passes?—of Courtney's mom while copping her Oxys.

"She's just one of your customers, then?"

"Who?"

"The girl on the phone. Sarie." She draws out the name in a slightly mocking way: *sare-eeeee.*

"No."

"Totally your girlfriend," she says, teasing out the word and smirking.

"No," Drew tells her. "She's just a sweet girl doing me a huge favor."

DECEMBER 5 (late)

Okay, Mom, much better tonight.

Khyber Pass—South Second Street, Old City. I flash my bulletproof ID at a fat guy in a Sturgis Motorcycle Rally T-shirt perched on a creaky metal stool and head straight for the only open seat at the bar, where I order a Yuengling. I'm carded again, then served. I take a sip and wait. I don't go looking for parties. I wait for the parties to find me.

Lo and behold, they do.

I'm approached, like, six times in the span of an hour. Some dude in a shaggy haircut says he lives nearby, a bunch of his pals are going to play some Xbox, do I want to come along and play. I ask what he has back at his place. He looks at me.

—Uh…an Xbox?

—No, I'm good.

There's more of this, and I won't bore you with details, but mostly it's guys trying to get my number or ask me to do shots or go somewhere else. When drug talk does come up, I take D.'s advice and take it easy, let them do most of the talking, then I start bragging about this amazing weed I used to get all of the time. The past tense of that remark makes them curious. "Used to?" What happened to it? Because no matter what you're smoking, you're always on the lookout for something better.

D. told me the secret was not to flat-out lie. You have to mix up some of your real life in there to make it all convincing. This turns out to be excellent advice and surprisingly easy to follow.

I tell them the mini-story I practiced in my head: My boyfriend was a small-time dealer with an awesome supply, but then I caught him cheating on me and I dumped his sorry ass. Which I regret, because now it's hard to find shit as good as the shit he had. "I should have just let him keep banging that skank." (I had to practice saying that line without giggling.) What made it easier was imagining D. as the fictional dealer boyfriend and Tammy as the wayward skank. Totally unfair to Tammy, I know, but it put a face in my head, which was key to selling the story. Hey, it's her fault for not texting me back.

Nine times out of ten this story led to commiseration, but no real leads. But the tenth time…

—So who was this great connection?

—My dick ex-boyfriend.

—Seriously? Why's he a dick?

—Because one day I called him and I can fucking hear her in the background, giggling. He denies the whole thing, but it's not like I've gone deaf, you know? Anyway, I tell him to fuck off. And then he tells me to fuck off. Which means I'm cut off.

—That really sucks. It was pretty good, huh?

—You have no idea.

—Well…

—Well what?

—Heh. You're not a narc, are you? I mean, you have to tell me if you're a narc or something, don't you? By law?

I look at him, dead serious.

—You're under arrest.

—Heh-heh.

—No, I'm serious. Up against the wall, punk. Don't make me call for backup!

—Heh-heh-heh, that's funny. You're really funny.

—I'm, like, BFFs with the narcotics squad.

—Hey, what's your name?

So we go on from there, until the guy reveals that, yeah, he has this amazing source for pills, screw your boyfriend, we should be partners. I tell him this all sounds aces, what do we do now? Where do we go? He scribbles on a napkin, folds it, puts it in my hand, tells me to meet here tomorrow morning at 9:00 a.m. and not to shower or eat anything after midnight.

I'll explain more tomorrow.

DECEMBER 6 (morning)

Well, Mom, what sounded so good last night feels a little crazy in the cold light of day. This morning I'm going to do possibly one of the stupidest things I've ever done: sit on a freezing bench in North Philly waiting for a stranger I met in a bar.

If this is my last entry, know that I was probably killed by said stranger.

No, I don't know his name, other than "Bobby Ryall." He showed me his student ID, but, you know, these things can be faked.

If this goes well, by Friday night I should be off the hook. Bobby's lead is promising. Especially after the article I read over the weekend. Then again, by Friday night I could be <u>dead.</u> Problem solved, either way.

TEMPLE UNIVERSITY

FRIDAY, DECEMBER 6

Bobby Ryall's <u>dead</u> sure she's not gonna show.

When she *does* show, Bobby's sure she'll refuse to let him into her car.

And when she *does* let him into her car, he starts to wonder if he's maybe picked up the wrong girl. Maybe she's one of those Latino grifter types, and she's going to pull a knife or a gun or even a can of Mace, pointing it right at his eyes, demanding all his money. (She *is* taller than him.) And when she finds out he really doesn't have much in the way of money, she'll probably unload the full can right in his face, push him out of the car, then laugh all the way back to the barrio.

So when she *doesn't* do any of that and asks where they're headed, Bobby relaxes a little bit.

Bobby Ryall's been working up his nerve to pull this scam for a few weeks now, ever since he heard about the clinic over in University City. Sounded too good to be true (which meant it usually was). But his own connections had dried up—okay, not so much dried up as gotten seriously fucking expensive. And he didn't want to have to start going to the hood and shit. So when he heard all he needed was a young girl in her twenties, preferably in a brown shade, Bobby decided to give it a try. Only problem: He didn't know any young ladies of color. Just wasn't his thing, you know.

But this girl last night—Bobby was still stunned. She was pretty and all, but definitely Mex-looking. When Bobby nodded and said "hey," he expected her to open her mouth and sound like Rosie Perez or something. But no! She was quiet-spoken, with no traceable accent. Brain in her head, too, with clever banter and shit. Could this be the one? And then she talked about "partying" and he knew, yes, this was the one.

She even had her own car! Much better than taking the subway and the El over there.

Question now: Will she go through with it, or freak out when she realizes what Bobby Ryall has in mind?

Bobby directs me through some really sketchy-looking neighbor-hoods. He told me not to dress too neatly, not to shower, and not to eat anything after midnight. Does this mean we're headed to a crack house?

This would be bad for a number of reasons, not least of all: a) it's a crack house and b) Wildey doesn't want a crack house. He can find plenty of those. He probably lives next door to one.

But Bobby promised me a "connection," foolproof, safe as can be.

When the directions bring me toward Center City, with the giant City Hall tower coming at us, I feel a little better. When we turn right and start heading out to West Philly, not so much.

—Where are we going?

—Okay, listen…

—I'm listening.

—There's this doctor over near Drexel University. You know Drexel?

—I know Drexel. Who's this doctor? Is he a professor?

—No, a doctor for ladies. You know, female stuff. But he's not a perv or anything. He's like a grandpa. A great-grandpa, in fact. I saw this picture online. He just likes to help underprivileged girls and stuff.

—Help them with what?

—Oxys and shit. We're going to go in there, you're going to ask to see the doctor. I'll slip the receptionist a little something, and the doctor will look at you and hook you up with a prescription. He does this all the time. You go to a CVS or whatever and we're all set.

—Wait, wait. Look at me? What do you mean?

But I know exactly what he means. Suddenly this is worse than a crack house.

—No way.

—Look, I heard he hardly checks anybody. He's old, it's a formality.

I pull over, right on JFK Boulevard. We're on that part of the road that stretches over the Schuylkill River. In front of us looms Thirtieth Street Station, where Danny Glover once killed that guy in that movie with the Amish kid. Not the best omen.

—I'm sorry, I'm not going to do that.

—What's the big deal?

—Let's go to some drug dealer and have him look at your genitals.

—If that's all it took, I would. Believe me. Look, it's not like that. Girls who go there love the guy. He's apparently some local hero, a women's rights activist and shit. You can look him up.

—A real hero, huh.

—Just tell him you're sore and he'll hook you up. No hassles.

We split the prescription. I'll even front the fee. And when you see it's not creepy, you can come back every couple of weeks. We can keep this going for as long as we want.

Not if I have my good friend Ben Wildey bust this hero's ass after I make a buy. But I don't tell him that.

Bobby's spiel, though, makes me wonder what I'm doing. Is this guy truly some women's rights hero? And I'm going to narc on him and send him to prison? In place of D., who's probably upstate right now doing a gynecological exam of his own?

—Come on. Just try it. If he tries anything strange, I'll be right outside in the waiting room. But he's not going to try anything strange.

—Okay.

CI #137: You around this a.m.?
WILDEY: What you got Honors Girl?
CI #137: Can you get out to Drexel University real quick?
WILDEY: Tell me where
CI #137: Hang on

I hate waiting rooms.

Everybody does, I know that. But especially after what happened to you last year. Waiting rooms are merely places where you spend hours staring at the walls, waiting for them to tell you how bad things are going to get. And it's always worse than you thought.

This one is even worse. Yeah, it looks like an inner-city women's clinic. Lots of strollers, crying kids. But also a lot of young girls who have that casual junkie look about them. I try not to be judgmental, but seriously. They're not as bad as the people I saw near the Tracks, but they're clearly on their way there, or somewhere like it.

I take the forms from the unsmiling receptionist, a mannish-looking woman with the largest glasses I've ever seen perched on a human face. Fuck, forms. Forgot about that part. I'm going to have to put my real name and address and such on them. If Wildey does raid this place, hopefully he can pull this and destroy it. I don't want my pediatrician (yeah, Mom, I'm still seeing Dr. Dovaz) wondering why I was prescribed OxyContin in some dumpy clinic.

There aren't two seats together, so Bobby sits across the room from me, smiling like a kid. Jesus.

I watch other "boyfriends" wait for their "girlfriends." Ordinarily I wouldn't think anything of it, but now that I'm here with my "boyfriend" it's all suspicious. There's even one boyfriend waiting for at least four different "girlfriends" to be ushered back into the doctor's office. I wonder if D. would wait with me here, if I had a real appointment.

From time to time Wildey texts me on the burner and I tell him to hang on. He's impatient. I should have waited to text him. Because this is taking forever. I'm missing three classes as it is—the first classes I've ever missed. In my life. I keep telling myself it'll be worth it because soon it'll be over.

At long last, I'm called back.

The receptionist, Letitia, tells me to go to Room 3 and undress. I don't look back at Bobby for fear that he's going to give me a thumbs-up or something.

—Wait, honey.

Letitia points at my bag.

—You can't bring that back there.

—Why not? It's just books.

—Leave it out here.

—But I want to keep it with me.

—You want me to cancel your appointment? Leave it with your boyfriend.

Before I know it, Bobby's up and holding out his hand. Shit. Wasn't anticipating this. I reach inside my bag and thumb the power button on the burner to turn it off. Last thing I need is Bobby here intercepting a grouchy text from Wildey. Bobby smiles at me.

—Don't worry, honey. I've got it.

So it's "honey" now. Never mind that this is some drug seeker I picked up in a fucking bar. I tell myself that it'll be okay. He wants the Oxys more than the contents of my bag.

—Okay. Thanks.

—It's all good.

I go back to Room 3 but do not undress. If the doctor forces the issue and I get this creepy rapey vibe, I'll bolt, I swear. But surprisingly, when the thin wooden door creaks open, I see that Dr. Roosevelt Hill is pretty much just as advertised. He's a gray-haired old white guy, timid smile on his face. I have no memories of any of my grandparents, of course. But if I did, they might look like this guy.

—Hi, sweetie. Can you get undressed for me?

—Why? My back just hurts.

—Well, I need to take a look at you nonetheless.

—Can't you just look at my back?

Dr. Hill puts his cold hand on my forearm.

—You want me to help you, don't you?

So I have to go through with this. It's either this, or leave and admit defeat to Wildey. I'd have to call a lawyer and watch my entire future float away and disappear. What's a little nakedness? The doctor excuses himself, and when he knocks a few minutes later, my clothes are folded neatly on a chair and I'm wearing a flimsy fabric gown that's way too short. I assume the position and try to tune out reality as he does the usual explorations.

—Do you think you're pregnant?

—Uh...no? My back just hurts.

—Mmmm-hmmmm.

Is it me, or does his touch...linger? Why isn't there a nurse here? Whenever I've had an exam like this before, in a legit doctor's place, there was always a nurse in the room. They should ask if I want a nurse in the room. He didn't even ask!

—My back really hurts.

—Hmmm. You should try Motrin.

—I have, Dr. Hill. But it doesn't even touch it.

He stares off into the distance, shaking his head. I'm losing him. I didn't come all this way and get naked and felt up by an old dude just to walk away with nothing. His hand is still on me.

—Well, then.

To my surprise, Dr. Hill rolls away then goes to a desk in the corner and begins to scribble.

—Take this to Letitia. And don't forget to pay her in cash.

Bobby Ryall watches her as she emerges from the back, shy smile on her face. She gives Letitia the slip of paper the doc gave her. Letitia holds out her hand, waiting for the cash. She looks over at him, widens her eyes a tiny bit. Oh. Right. Bobby walks up to the counter, feeling like an asshole chump, and slides two twenties at the receptionist. Letitia takes it, puts one twenty in one envelope and another in the pocket of her scrubs. Finally she gives Sarie another slip in return—the actual prescription, he guesses. He wants to bolt, but he's come this far. He can't walk out of this situation empty-handed and forty dollars lighter.

But, man, he was right after all. He picked up the wrong girl.

The texts on her phone made that perfectly clear.

Letitia answers her cell. Before she has the chance to say anything, a young voice says: "Hey, someone might be coming for you."

She recognizes the voice. Not by name, but by recent memory. One of the boyfriends in here not too long ago. The guy holding the girl's books.

"Who is this?"

"Just consider me a concerned friend, okay?"

"You were just in here, weren't you?"

Click.

Wildey can't believe this. He and his CI are arguing over where to meet. He tells her somewhere on Drexel's campus would be easiest. Pick a bench, he'll be there. School's in session, plenty of kids milling around everywhere. Best place possible to meet. What's the problem? But of course Honors Girl has a problem. What if someone spots the two of them together? She can't be outed. Not after what she's read about.

"Who's going to see us?"

"Jesus, anybody could!"

"Why are we meeting all the way out there, anyway?"

"It's important. I promise, I'm not wasting your time."

Wildey thinks he has it figured out. Her boyfriend, Big Red, attends a different school. Maybe they're not as close as Wildey assumed. Maybe she needed to get him out into the open to find a vulnerability. If this is the case, extra points for Honors Girl. She's finally come to her senses. Still, it would be a supreme pain in the ass to go out to West Philly... for what could be another Ryan Koolhaas–type disaster.

Honors Girl finally agrees to a meeting place—her own Honda Civic, parked on the next-to-top floor of a garage off Market Street right on the fringes of the Penn campus. Wildey sees her right away, pulls into the next spot, looks over at her Civic, then realizes that's not going to exactly be a comfortable fit. He waves her over. Honors Girl's shoulders slump—this is not what she wanted. But Wildey stays put.

After a minute she climbs out of her car, thumbing the lock—as if someone's going to boost it while they're sitting one space over. He notices she has a white plastic CVS bag in her hands as she climbs into the seat.

"What's that?" Wildey asks.

Honors Girl hands him the bag. "OxyContin, I believe."

Wildey opens the bag, sees the prescription bottle, looks at the label. Her own name's on it. The count says 50. Wildey gives it a shake. No way there's 50 in there.

"Where's the other half?"

"I had to give it to my contact."

"Your contact? What are you talking about? Where is the motherfucker?"

"He left. But he's not the target, though. It's the doctor!"

"Slow down, slow down."

Honors Girl slows down and starts talking. This whole thing is not what Wildey was expecting. At all. But as she explains step-by-step, Wildey has to admit: This sounds like something. And not another Ryan Koolhaas Klusterfuck. The pills in the bottle are real. The doctor's name, Roosevelt Hill, is on the label. She didn't just pull these out of her ass. He stops her every so often to clarify a point or a detail, but no...this is something. Not Chuckie Morphine, but Wildey is willing to put a pin in that for now.

"I'm going to have to check this out," he tells her.

"Well, duh. But this is good, right? I mean, this is what you wanted?"

Wildey stares at her for a second. "You know this isn't what I wanted."

"I promised I'd find you a drug dealer. Someone dealing OxyContin. Which I did. Right?"

"So what—I'm supposed to go and arrest CVS?"

"But...you know this is more than just...seriously?"

She looks like she's about to blow a gasket. It's almost fun to watch. At least he knows she didn't pop one of those Oxys. She's too pent-up.

"Relax, Honors Girl. I'm going to check this out, see what's what."

"I can't go back in there," she says. "I mean, I was just—"

"I'm going in myself to take a look. If everything's like you said, I'm going to talk to my lieutenant about the next steps. This could be big, this could be nothing. Maybe he prescribed you those things on a fluke."

"That's not what my contact says. He says that—"

"Yeah, yeah, I know what you said your contact said. Doesn't do me a damn bit of good unless we observe it. We might need to build a case."

"We?"

"Yeah. We might have you go in again, keep making buys for us."

She slumps into the seat, head back, her skinny body appearing to deflate. Wildey almost—*almost*—feels bad for her. He reaches out, touches her shoulder.

"Hey. Give me a hand."

She looks at him.

"With what?"

Turns out Wildey has a bag he keeps in the trunk of whatever car he's using. I swear this is a different make and model than the shitbox we were driving around in this past Monday. Old shirts, caps, gloves, scarves, hoodies, whatever. He calls it his disguise bag. He wants to look like whoever would be in that waiting room.

— You need to be about a hundred pounds lighter.

— Is that a crack about my weight?

— No! But I'm saying, you don't look like a junkie.

— What do I look like?

A three-hundred-pound suck on my life, I want to say. But I don't know if that'll come off as mean, and I feel like I've already started digging myself a hole with that weight comment.

—Forget it. Just go in there pretending you're looking for your girlfriend or wife or something. There are lots of guys in there. You can probably sit for a while without anybody raising an eyebrow.

Wildey chuckles. I wonder if I should be insulted.

—What? What's wrong with that?

—Nothing.

—Then…what?

—It's just that you'd make a pretty good cop. You ever consider changing your major to criminal justice?

—Uh, no?

—Never mind.

The moment the big guy in the dark gray hoodie and ratty baseball cap steps into the waiting room, Letitia Braly knows he's the one.

"Can I help you?"

"Yo, just looking for my girlfriend."

Even if she hadn't received that strange phone call, warning her, she'd like to believe alarm bells would have gone off anyway. The hoodie and cap don't look right. Like he doesn't wear them every day. She can tell by the body language.

This is why Dr. Hill hired her almost five years ago, to be the gate-keeper that he couldn't be anymore. Not at his age. Plus, with their new sideline, the Good Doctor needed an enforcer posted out front. He paid for the training and license and everything. Dr. Hill assured her it would never come to this, that there were good people in this neighborhood. But Letitia knew this area better than that. Word had a way of spreading. Sooner or later, this was bound to happen.

She kept the Glock clipped under her desk, within easy reach.

"I'm sorry, but you're going to have to wait outside."

The Big Guy turns and sweeps his hand through the air, as if to point out the number of empty seats available. "Can't I wait in here?"

"This room is for patients only. Now please step outside."

"Those dudes over there patients? Thought this was a place for ladies."

"Please..."

"Yeah, yeah, hold on..."

Letitia watches as his hand goes into the pocket of that hoodie. There's a bulge there.

So many people shot in this city because they don't know it's coming. Letitia swore to never, ever be one of those people.

Which is why she pulls the Glock now, raises it over the counter, and begins to squeeze the trigger.

Of the many things Wildey thought might happen today, getting shot in the face wasn't one of them.

As it turns out, that doesn't happen.

But fuck—it sure comes close.

The receptionist, apparently some kind of Dirty Harriet, squeezes off a shot that goes a little high and wide and lands with a *thuh-chunk* in the drywall behind him. The people in the chairs scream and start to scramble. Wildey drops to the floor and rolls up against the underside of the reception area, betting (praying) that she won't shoot through the wood blind.

"Police officer!" he shouts, pulling his own piece. "Drop your weapon!"

Wildey thinks he hears Dirty Harriet curse. Though it's tough because of the sudden din in the waiting room—people cursing, praying, crying.

"Drop that fucking gun!" he shouts. "Now!"

Behind the reception area, a door thumps open. Hinges squeak.

Damnit, she's running for it.

Wildey rolls, then scrambles to his feet. Kicks open the door leading into the receptionist area, kicks open the second door, leading to a hallway lined with exam rooms. Where did she go? Wildey's been in gun situations before. Never been in a jam inside a building, though, and in such close quarters. Feels like he's doing battle inside a fucking cereal box, with these flimsy dirty walls and flakeboard doors. Any second a bullet could come slicing through and nail him.

But there's nothing in the exam rooms, as he clears them. Nothing in what he presumes is Dr. Hill's office—including Dr. Hill. As Wildey moves deep into the building, he starts to see the bones of the place. This whole medical suite was built up in what used to be a small grocery store. There are still meat cases and, more importantly, two swinging metal doors leading to a cooler. The doors are still swinging slightly. Wildey feels like he has no choice. If they're running scared, they're up to some shady shit. This could be the break he needs. He goes in.

A few seconds later, Wildey wishes he hadn't.

After what feels like five or six forevers, Wildey calls my burner.

—Go home, Honors Girl.

—What happened?

—I'll catch up with you later. But for now just go home. Don't talk to anybody. Just wait for me to call. Don't watch the news, and if you do, don't say or think anything until we talk.

—Seriously? You're going to leave me hanging like that? What happened?

—Yeah. Seriously. I gotta go.

Whatever. I hang up and drive back to campus, even though the classes I've missed are long over. But I have to be back here, because I have to turn on my cell phone. And just in case Dad's tracking my iPhone, I can't be popping up in University City. I'm supposed to be in class.

When my phone comes to life, I see that he's called four times and left three voicemail messages.

"HOUSE OF MEDICAL HORRORS" FOUND NEAR UNIVERSITY CITY

Dr. Roosevelt Hill Sought for Questioning
Anonymous Tip Leads Police to "Something Out of a Nightmare"

Wildey doesn't even know which body parts are supposed to be which. They float in amber fluid, little flecks of skin and what appears to be... seasoning? No, couldn't be, Wildey thinks. A deep voice bounces him out of his reverie. "Officer—your superior wants to talk to you." The homicide dick hands the phone over to Wildey.

"Loot."

"Jesus Christ, Wild Child—what did you step into?"

He isn't sure if she sounds incensed or bemused. Kaz's ordinary speaking voice sounds a little like both.

"You're not going to believe this. Not entirely sure I believe it."

"I don't. But I want you to listen to our friends from homicide and let them take it from here."

"Why? This is ours!"

"Wildey, I'd say the body parts of a dozen missing girls trumps the little Oxy ring you were investigating."

The Roosevelt Hill case would soon become Philadelphia legend. Dozens of articles, three books, and a cable movie would be based on it. But it would not become *their* legend. In fact, NFU-CS wouldn't be mentioned at all. They weren't in it for the glory; they were in it for

the busts. That's the point, she reminded him. They're the secret inves-
tigative arm that tees up the ball so the strike teams can swing the bat.
Wildey's involvement will be little more than a "tip to the police."

"You want glory, you're in the wrong business," Kaz says.

Wildey watches the floating body parts for a while, wondering about
the girls they belonged to, wondering what other kind of fucked-up
shit was in closets and basements and back rooms all over town.

Don't watch the news, Wildey warns me. Of course that practically
guarantees that I am going to watch the news. The story begins to
break online around 3:00 in the afternoon. "Horror in University
City." At first I don't realize this is the same case—my case. But
then the name practically leaps from my laptop screen and slams
into my chest: Dr. Roosevelt Hill. The nice old drug-dealing man
who saw me naked this morning. Whose touch lingered just long
enough.

Apparently he likes to look at naked lady parts. So much so that
he keeps them in big jars in the old cooler room behind his medical
offices.

As I watch, I go numb all over. What was going through the
doctor's mind as he was looking at me? Why did he ask if I was
pregnant? All I can manage is some muttered profanity, over and
over again, repeated like a mantra.

—Holy shit holy shit holy shit…

—What?

I spin around. It's Marty, standing on the stairs leading down to
the den.

—Nothing.

I start to close my laptop, but quick as lightning he's across the
room, and he reaches out to stop me.

—You don't have to do that. I've already seen it. That's crazy, isn't it? It's like that Gary Heidnik case. Only this is worse because he's like a doctor!

—How do you know about Gary Heidnik?

—Duh. Everybody knows about him.

Marty has a point. And he's right, this is worse than Gary Heidnik, because Gary Heidnik never saw me naked. It all hits me even harder now. Today could have turned out so, so different. Marty leans over me, scrolling down to read more details. I push away from the desk feeling like I want to throw up.

Please, Wildey, tell me you got rid of my forms. Please tell me you ditched that prescription bottle with my name and Dr. Psycho's name on the label. Please tell me I'm not going to be dragged into this mess.

And if you are, please don't call during family movie night.

That's why Dad was calling today—to make sure I didn't have any plans this evening. With my luck, Dad's probably rented *Silence of the Lambs*.

When Wildey steps into the classroom at NFU-CS, everyone is applauding. Half of the applause is in mockery. Wildey tells them to go fuck themselves and reports directly to Kaz's office. She has some Billy Joel tune on her ancient boom box but flicks it off when he steps into the room. "You wanted to see me?"

"Sit down, Ben."

Uh-oh. "Ben" and not "Wild Child." This is not going to be good.

"I didn't want to do this over the phone, for obvious reasons. But I need you to tell me how you found your way into this Roosevelt Hill thing. Because I don't remember you bringing this up before in any of our meetings. You know how this office works. Everything goes through me. Everything."

"I know, Loot. But it all happened kind of fast. You're not going to believe this."

She suggests that Officer Wildey try her.

"This one came from CI one thirty-seven. She set the whole thing up."

"The honors student? The little girl you had in here last week?"

They don't use her real name on purpose.

"Yeah."

"How did *she* find it? She's supposed to be your in with Chuckie Morphine, right?"

"Yeah."

"So do you think she's involved with Dr. Hill, too?"

"No. Not at all. I think she's so desperate to protect her boyfriend that she went out and did some actual investigating. She turned him up on her own, hoping that it'll get her off the hook for the other thing. I know, it's fucked up, right? Who would have thought it?"

Kaz stares at him, which makes him feel like another shoe is about to drop. Right on his head.

"What? What is it?"

"I'm glad your newest CI is working out for you. Because you're down to two."

Kaz slides a manila file folder across her desk.

SNITCHES GET STITCHES

FOX CHASE

DECEMBER 6

Twenty minutes into the movie (the first *Mission: Impossible,* the Brian De Palma one, which Kevin figures Marty will dig since he's into spies and shit), Kevin hears the unmistakable *ffffhhhhrrrrrr* of a cell phone set on vibrate. This, after the admonition that this was family movie night, and that meant their attention should be focused on the single screen in front of them, not any of their smaller screens. He can only assume it's Marty's phone. Marty seems disappointed in the movie, maybe even bored by it. Maybe he should have started with the fourth one, worked their way backwards. Kevin looks over at Marty, who's sitting on the floor.

"Okay, seriously, guys, put them away."

"What?" Marty asks.

"Seriously, don't make me take them."

"My phone's recharging, Dad."

Kevin turns to Sarie. "That's not yours, is it?"

"No."

"Maybe it's your phone, Dad."

"No, I turned it off." Or did he? "Crap, hang on." Tom Cruise freezes. Kevin moves toward the kitchen, where his phone is recharging, too. Sarie takes the opportunity to run to the downstairs bath-

185

room, leaving Marty on the floor alone, plate of half-eaten pizza in his hand, knowing that it wasn't his phone, or Dad's phone. It was Sarie's *other* phone.

Wildey: I need to meet with you tonight
CI #137: I can't! No way, seriously
Wildey: This is important, it's about the case
CI #137: There's no way. My dad made a big deal about us being home tonight and I can't leave without him freaking out.
Wildey: You'll think of something. Meet me at the doughnut place in 30
CI #137: No!
Wildey: Don't make me come knocking for you H Girl

So I'm in the bathroom erasing the message history and repeating the word fuck in my mind over and over. "You'll think of something." Fuck you, Officer Wildey. Fuck. You. I press the edge of the burner phone to my head as I struggle to come up with some reason, any reason, to leave the house in twenty-five minutes. What excuse would Dad buy? Nothing school-related. Already played that card a lot for the past week. Tonight's Friday, and there's nothing school-related that could be THAT urgent.

"You'll think of something." I can hear his mocking voice in my head, even though it was just a text message.

And then, I do.

BEAR CREEK, PA

Drew Pike explains it to her again, for a third time, but she's still too drunk and zoned out to fully understand. Why is she doing this? Who is this girl again? Can I just have another glass of wine so I can pass out in peace? Drew tells her: No, no wine. "Do me this favor." What favor. "You need to call this number like you're crying, like you're really upset." I am really upset. Upset that you're being an asshole. "C'mon, Courtney." Okay, okay, what do you want me to do again? "Call this number and ask for Sarie." Who? "Sarie." *Sare-eeee*, again. She's your girlfriend, then. "No, she's not." So why are you doing this? "Please just call."

Their moms are upstairs, drunk and loud. Oh my God, so fucking loud. They're listening to some kind of stupid swing Christmas music, some dough-faced crooner they all love, and they're joking and singing along and being old and stupid, so it's not as if they're going to hear.

"Come on," Drew says, handing her the house phone.

"Why can't I use your cell? What if your mom picks up the other line?"

"She won't."

Courtney takes the phone, unsure suddenly, drunk enough to do something like this but just sober enough to realize that maybe she's making a poor decision because she's mostly drunk. But Drew is good at talking her into all kinds of things. She puts the phone to her ear and starts to babble in her best fake-crying incoherent voice:

"Mr. Holland, is Sarie there, please, I need to talk to her right away . . ."

The phone rings. Dad sighs, hits the pause button again. Tom Cruise again freezes midaction. I watch Dad walk to the kitchen to pick up the house phone and catch Marty looking at me.

— What?

— Nothing.

— Why are you looking at me like that?

— I'm not, geez.

I hear Dad in the kitchen:

— Who is this again?

Oh boy. It's on. I silently thank D. for doing this, even though in my book he's not even remotely off the hook. I just hope his upstate girlfriend can sell it without overselling it.

—Hold on, honey. Are you sure there's nothing I can do? You sound really upset. Just take a deep breath, okay?

Marty's listening, too, and there's a quizzical look on his face as he tries to figure out: a) who could be calling the landline on a Friday night and b) why Dad is trying to counsel him/her.

—You sure? Okay. But you know I'm always here. You can always call me, anytime. Okay? I'll go get her.

When Dad reappears, I have to act surprised that it's Tammy on the phone, sounding really upset but wanting to talk to me. I'm hyper-aware of Marty staring at me, too, no doubt judging my (probably shaky) performance. He knows that it's weird that "Tammy" would be calling the house phone and not my cell phone. But I can always say that Tammy tried my cell first, got nothing, then called the house line. Of course, I have no proof that Tammy tried my cell. Which reminds me that I'm going to have to reach Tammy for real, as soon as possible, to get her to go along with this story, just in case Dad follows up with her (being Mr. Super Counselor and all). Fuck, this is all so complicated. Fuck you, Officer Wildey. Seriously.

I pick up the phone in the kitchen.

—You okay, Tammy?

Of course it's not Tammy on the other end. It's not even the upstate girlfriend anymore. It's D. himself.

—Everything okay? Did it work?

—We're just watching a movie, no big deal, tell me what's wrong.

—What? Oh. Got it. You can't talk. Well, whatever's going on, I hope it's nothing too crazy. Is that cop still bothering you?

—Yeah.

—Fuck. I'm really sorry, Sarie.

—Yeah, I know. I know.

—I should just fucking turn myself in. Make a deal with him.

—No. Don't do that. You know you can't.

—I know it's not fair to you, and I swear, I will figure out some way to make this right.

—Okay. Give me five minutes and I'll pick you up.

—What? Oh. Right. Where are you going, anyway?

—See you soon.

—Text me and let me know where you're going, okay? I'm worried about y——

I hang up. Take a deep, cleansing breath. Live the lie. You were just talking to Tammy, and she's upset over a boy, always a boy (you know Tammy), and needs to be talked down off the ledge, so you're going to do what you always did senior year—meet for coffee and talk it through. Did Dad remember those days? You certainly do, Mom. You used to talk about a friend of yours who sounded a lot like Tammy.

So I explain the situation to Dad, that Tammy really needs me now, and Dad admits that she did sound upset, that he's never heard her sound like that before. (Biting my tongue here.) Marty's giving me the goose eye, but that doesn't matter right now. What matters is that I have about two minutes to make it to the fucking doughnut shop before Wildey gets his panties in a bunch.

Wildey is parked outside the Holland home. He's been watching it for a few hours now, just the cold howl of the wind pushing around tree branches, leaves, trash to keep him company. Waiting for her to appear. Hoping nobody else is watching, too.

The porch light comes on and the front door opens. Honors Girl walks toward her car. Unlocks it. Slides behind the wheel. All without incident.

Was he just being paranoid? Maybe. But when two of your CIs die within the same week, you have a right to take a few precautions.

She parks at the doughnut shop and looks around, seemingly annoyed that he isn't there yet. Wildey takes his time, though, checking the area to make sure they don't have any interested parties following. Then he decides that maybe a brightly lit doughnut shop isn't the best place to meet after all. He pulls over and picks up his cell.

WILDEY: Leave your car there and step outside I'll pick you up
CI #137: Where are you?
WILDEY: Going to be pulling over on Pine Road in 30 sec
CI #137: kk

We go driving around the neighborhood. He asks me where he should go and I tell him up Pine Road is probably the best—it's not very crowded this time of night.

—Told you that you'd figure it out. You're good under pressure.

I almost say it out loud: Fuck you, Officer Wildey. Instead I sink back into the passenger seat in a vain attempt to hide myself away.

—Anyway, I'm guessing you probably watched the news. You really stumbled into something huge, Honors Girl. The whole department's going crazy.

—Is this your way of saying…thank you?

—Didn't do me much good, personally. This stopped being a drug case the moment I saw body parts. You think anybody's going to care about the pills? That'd be like nailing Jack the Ripper for jaywalking.

—Gee, sorry about that. Next time I'll make sure to find a dealer who isn't also a serial killer.

Wildey glances over at me, eyebrow raised, either in annoyance or admiration, hard to tell which.

* * *

Sarie seems insulted at Wildey for questioning her professionalism. She pouts and stares out the windshield at the cold, dark road ahead. What, did he insult her by saying she didn't look like a junkie? Besides, he's just trying to protect her. Then again, she does have a point. On the surface, this mysterious connection guy seems like no big deal. Just some drug seeker who heard a rumor and found a way to play it out.

What troubles Wildey—and what he can't tell Sarie—is that he needs to know exactly *how* she found him. How did his green-as-they-come CI (who isn't even a CI for real) stumble into something like this? Pure luck? Is she some kind of detective-savant beneath that good girl exterior?

Pretty unlikely. Much more probable that somebody's targeting her. Like someone clearly targeted his other CIs.

Wildey says, "Tell me how you found him."

Sarie huffs. "You told me I needed to find a drug dealer. So I went out and found one. Again."

"But how?"

"By asking around? By doing some research? How else do you think I found him? I went to places where people my age go to meet other people who might have drugs. We got talking. He mentioned this great connection he had. I followed it up. It's called research."

"What the fuck you talking about, research? You telling me you've been going out nights, hunting for drug dealers in your spare time?"

Sarie turns and gives him a gaze that could melt steel. Wildey doesn't have to look. He can feel the side of his face burning.

"Isn't that what a confidential informant is supposed to do? Go out and do research and report back with the hope that maybe, just maybe someday she'll come up with the magical piece of intelligence that will get her off the fucking hook instead of being harassed day and night?"

Wildey pulls the car over, violently and without warning. Good thing they're both wearing seat belts. Honors Girl lets out a small cry of shock.

Headlights from a passing car wash over them. The car seems to slow a bit, its driver rubbernecking. Wildey slowly exhales, readjusting his grip on the wheel. The car resumes speed and continues down Pine Road.

"I'm sorry," he says after a few moments of silence.

"I've been thinking about something, Wildey. You told me that you wanted to go after the salt and pepper shakers and the mustard tubs."

It takes Wildey a few long moments to realize what the fuck Honors Girl is talking about. The diner table. The salt and pepper as distributors, the mustard as kingpins. "Yeah. What about it?"

"You and the rest of the police are focused on taking them out, even though the minute you take one out, another one pops up in his place. Like, instantly."

"Who says that happens?"

"I'm doing research. It happens all the time. Are you really going to sit there and deny it?"

"So we're just supposed to leave the kingpins alone? Let their empire grow until nobody can touch them, with the whole PD and the government in their pocket? Then we're like Mexico. You ever been to Mexico? It ain't nice."

"Of course," she says. "But wouldn't it be much smarter if all of the money and power of the police and the government were focused on another part of that system?"

"I told you, going after the low-level dealers is useless. You wanna talk about weeds popping up...shit, I could spend all day crushing fuckin' creamers and they'd ship more in by the boxful."

"I'm not talking about them."

"What, then?"

"What about the people sitting down at the table?"

Wildey blinks, uncomprehending. "Huh?"

"The users, Wildey. What if you took all that money spent hunting down dealers and kingpins and used it to help the users? Jobs, training programs, rehab. That's the one thing in the system that can't be replaced. The customers. You take away the user and the whole thing collapses."

"Huh. Wow. Never thought of that, Honors Girl. Hey, wait—junk food is bad for you, too! All we have to do is talk billions and billions of people out of going to McDonald's for a Quarter Pounder."

"Joke all you want, but you know it's the truth."

"And I know it'll never happen, not on the scale you're talking about. I don't care what grants or rehab or bullshit do-gooder shit you got, people want to get their drugs on. Too many people are wired with the self-destruct button, you know what I mean? Ask yourself—why aren't you hooked on the Oxys? I'll tell you why. Because you've got a future. Not everybody's that lucky."

"It doesn't have to be that way. Our government spends over fifty billion dollars every year on the drug war. Imagine if you divided that up among addicts—"

"Yeah, they'd go out and buy one fuck of a lot of drugs, that's what would happen."

Honors Girl sighs. Wildey almost feels bad.

"Look, you're asking good questions. I asked myself more or less the same things when I first started out. But it's not about saving the world. It's about keeping this city from tearing itself apart. It's stopping scumbags like Chuckie fuckin' Morphine from profiting from the weak and turning whole neighborhoods into war zones. If I can drop the right kingpin, the boot comes off my neighborhood long enough to do all that good shit you're talking about. Right now, I just don't see it. Sorry," he says again, then flips the left turn signal, checks to make sure nobody's coming, and executes an illegal U-turn.

Wildey pulls into the doughnut shop parking lot but grabs Honor Girl's arm before she can reach the door handle.

"Look," he says, "don't do any more research."

"So we're done?"

"No. We're not done. Just stand by until further notice."

"What does that even mean? Can I at least get rid of this stupid burner phone?"

"No! I need to talk to my lieutenant, see where we are with the investigation."

"Whatever."

"Go ahead and get in your car. I'll follow you home to make sure you get back okay."

"Why?"

"Because even though you think I'm some kind of dick, I'm actually a gentleman?"

"That's nice. But I've got to stay here for a while."

"Why?"

"Because of the lie you made me tell my dad."

Wildey nods. Yeah, he deserved that one.

"Don't stay out too late," he says quietly. "And text me when you go back home."

"Why?"

"I wish you'd stop asking me why all the time."

"I wish you'd leave me alone."

He probably deserved that one, too.

"Night, Honors Girl."

Wildey doesn't leave, of course. He can't leave her all alone, defenseless, where anybody can pretty much take a run at her—not with the two dealers she's brought down and whatever forces are at work taking out all Wildey's CIs. So he pulls around the block and parks on a side street with a view of the insanely well-lit doughnut shop. Honors Girl, true to her word, sits alone in a booth, sipping a coffee out of a paper container. She looks up to glance at every customer who walks in. Not long, maybe a second. Which reminds Wildey to check the perimeter again, make sure no hostiles are moving in.

Maybe half an hour later she has a text exchange. Not on her burner phone. Her real phone. He can tell by the shape of it. The burner's a piece of shit. Daddy probably bought her an iPhone. Who are you talking to? That mysterious boyfriend of yours? What kind of an excuse did you give your father, anyway? Who does he think you're meeting?

Then the exchange ends and Sarie Holland smiles briefly. Catches herself in the act and quickly changes her expression back to bored concern. But it was there. Someone made her happy, if only for a few seconds. Who?

But then she puts down her iPhone and her face falls.

"What am I doing to you," Wildey mutters to himself. He pulls out of Fox Chase and takes the long way back to the Badlands.

So I'm thinking up the fake conversation I've supposedly just had with Tammy when I pull up to the house to see Dad out in front, hunched down, sweeping up something with a dustpan and broom.

—What happened?

—Somebody threw a bottle at the house, screamed something, then raced away in a car.

—You're kidding.

—At first we thought it was the movie, but…no. Not kidding.

—What did he scream?

—Well, that's the weird thing. I thought it sounded something like Eff You Sarie.

—What?

Dad gives me one of those classic Dad looks. Eyes that lock on and refuse to let go. I haven't seen one of those in a long time. Not since eighth grade.

—Something you're not telling me, honey? Somebody giving you a hard time?

Oh, Dad, if you only knew. Want to go punch a big cop in the face for me, tell him to leave your daughter alone?

—No, I swear.

After an uncomfortably long time, as if scanning my eyes for a possible lie, Dad continues to sweep up the glass.

—You'd better go in. I'll finish up here.

As I pass, I quickly glance down to check the broken glass to see if there's a label. But that doesn't matter. I know who threw the bottle. The same guy I threw in jail earlier this week. Guess he's out. And he knows my home address.

THE ROUNDHOUSE

The commissioner is not pleased.

"How many?" he asks.

His would-be drug czar tells him: "Five since Thanksgiving."

Katrina Mahoney doesn't give a shit about what any man thinks about her—except perhaps the commissioner. He's an old-school Philly cop who worked his way up from beats in the worst districts in North and West Philly to the top spot in the then-burgeoning narcotics squad in the late sixties, followed by two decades working homicide and organized crime. He was the ballsiest commissioner since Frank Rizzo himself, and that was saying a lot. Mahoney wanted nothing more than to impress him, and she was painfully aware she was doing the exact opposite.

The commissioner gave her a disarming smile. "Katrina, when you asked for this job, you told me your experimental system would be airtight. Did you not?"

Lieutenant Mahoney nods.

The commissioner stares off into the space over her head for a moment, as if seeking guidance from above. Then his iron gaze falls back on Mahoney. "Do you know what Fiorello La Guardia said about narcotics cops? This was back in the 1940s, mind you, long before the meth explosion in the sixties. La Guardia said that you could give a thousand cops to fight narcotics dealers, but then I'd need a thousand more cops to watch *them*. Do you understand what I'm saying?"

"I do, sir."

"So what the fuck is going on?"

"We have a rat. I'm actively working to flush it out."

"See now, that's the thing, Katrina," the commissioner says. "You told me your system would negate the possibility of a rat. That only you and I would be privy to your complete list of CIs and counter-CIs. So what you're suggesting here is that one of us is the rat."

"Commissioner, I have the situation..."

"Is that what you suspect? Tell me now, and be honest. Do you believe that I've somehow exposed your operations? Maybe bragged to a pal over too many drinks at Palm? Told a mistress? Wrote a note on the men's room wall?"

"No, Commissioner."

"Well, then. If this is your fervent belief, then there is no other conclusion than that you're the one dropping the ball. That you're compromising this operation."

"I want this resolved within the week," the commissioner tells her. "I want you to find out who's disappearing your CIs. I do not want any more CIs disappeared. Do you understand me?"

"Yes, Commissioner."

"And I want one of those big busts you promised me would be coming weekly."

The lieutenant's eyes narrow; her lips tighten. "We were instrumental in providing intelligence for the raids this past Monday..."

"That was last Monday. What do you have for me this Monday?"

The commissioner pauses to look around his office. "Remember, Katrina," he finally says. "Play with rats and you end up with bubonic plague."

RETURNING CITIZEN

WASHINGTON AVENUE

SATURDAY, DECEMBER 7

Ringo can't believe it. He's actually happy to be riding a SEPTA bus.

SEPTA, short for Southeastern Pennsylvania Transportation Authority. Who would have thought he'd miss that mouthful? But after a decade and change out in Buttfuck, Kansas, hawking used cars to Maw and Paw Sixpack—who'd always, *always,* fuckin' comment on how much he looks and sounds like one of those wiseguys they see on the TV (Never just "TV," always "the tv")—Ringo's glad to be back in a city that does not give a shit, populated with people who mind their own business.

His return is a little precarious, they say. He can't risk being pulled over, so no driving. The bus would have to do. It's an interesting way to see his city, he'll say that much.

Twenty years ago, Richie "Ringo" Gloriosa had been a loyal soldier on the side of the D'Argenio family during the brutal D'Argenio-Perelli war of the early nineties. And soldier wasn't a euphemism; Ringo was the real deal. A few years before the war, he'd gotten into serious trouble with some Russian gangsters, uncut heroin, a stripper, and a shotgun; the D'Argenios thought it was best for Ringo to head off to finishing school in the U.S. military. At least until the heat died down, which it always does. Ringo returned with an entirely new skill set and a certain amount of fearlessness. Which served him well on the home front.

After the D'Argenio-Perelli war, the D'Argenios ended up indicted, dead or in Witness Protection; the Perellis took the throne until ten years ago, when the same thing more or less happened to them. This was the way it went down in Philly.

Now, against all good sense and reason, Ringo is back.

And working with a Perelli, go figure.

The girl—he'd like to call her Lisa Lisa—offered to pick him up, but Ringo insisted on public transportation. (Now he was saying it, too.) They were meeting at this Asian bar/restaurant thing right on Washington Avenue. The place always changed; tonight it's gonna be inside a private karaoke room. Just as long as nobody decided to sing. Ringo doesn't think he'd be able to handle that.

Working with two ex-cops, that was the other surprise. He didn't know either of them from back in the day. Hell, these guys were pups back in the day. The one they called Frankenstein was probably a toddler back in 1994, when Ringo was in his prime. And Bird looked like a youngster, too. What did the police department do to these guys to leave them so demoralized at such a young age? Ringo could only guess.

But the biggest shock of all was who put all this together in the first place. The person who tracked him down through the feds—one of the few alive who could do such a thing. Get outta here, was Ringo's first thought. *Of all people—really?*

This is why he loves this town. Philly, where you can always count on someone to do the absolutely wrong thing.

One of the first headlines Ringo saw when coming back to town just before Halloween was about a City Hall ordinance to stop calling ex-cons "ex-offenders." Instead, the mayor wanted to call them "returning citizens." Philly had about two hundred thousand "returning citizens" at any given time. Ringo: Returning Citizen. He liked the sound of that. Like he could expect a parade and a key to the city.

Of course, Ringo wasn't Richard "Ringo" Gloriosa anymore, either. He bought a new identity before his return, so now he was just some asshole named Matt Carlson.

The leader of this operation was using a fake name, too: El Jefe. But of course Ringo knows his real name, knows him by sight. The audaciousness of it all astounded him. At the very least, they were in for some interesting times.

Anyway, El Jefe was their contact, the one running this ongoing operation. He called them his Four Horsemen.

Two members of this hit team, the ex-cops, should know him by sight, too. But if they do, they're not letting on. Frankenstein—well, it's hard to read anything on his scarred-up face. When he turns his head and the shadows fall at just the right angle, you can almost see the handsome Latino Lothario (alleged!) he used to be. But mostly he's just a freak show of burns and scars and a right eye that bulges out a little bit. A shotgun to the face will do that to you.

Bird, meanwhile—Bird is just like his name. Jittery. Eyes flitting all around. Most black guys Ringo knows have that level of cool, and Bird's missing that. He's all exposed nerve, like he's about to lose it at any given moment.

Then there's Lisa Lisa—the assassin formerly known as Lisa Perelli. She wasn't really in the game ten years ago. But she's done a lot of growing up since then. Ringo only knows her by reputation—and a few salacious stories that even made their way out to Kansas. She's the one he worries about the most, because she's clearly not in it for the money. She just likes what they do.

And what they do is kill people and dump their bodies in a secret location down by the river, after an amusing torture interlude.

Just like the old days.

*　　*　　*

Ringo heard about a sweet body dump spot that opened up about ten years ago at Penn's Landing. It was supposed to be the foundation of a children's museum, but when funding was held up it became a kind of free-for-all for every underworld organization that had a dead body on its hands. What amused Ringo the most was the location. Almost nobody knew that when the area was first settled by colonists, that exact spot was where they dug out these caves to live in. When they got around to finally building real houses, the caves became these little subterranean dens of vice—gambling, boozing, whoring, smuggling. Pretty much the ongoing activities of the modern-day underworld. To think of all those dead bodies pretty much piled up above those old caves, and beneath the concrete foundation above...well, it made Ringo laugh. Philadelphia was hilarious if you knew the history.

Take their torture room—the brainchild of El Jefe.

To the modern observer, it was just this crappy abandoned warehouse right under the Ben Franklin Bridge, ringed by a Cyclone fence and located across the street from the Race Street Pier. The place had been empty for at least thirty years and smelled like it, too. But as a torture room, it was more than ideal. The constant noise from the bridge and the avenue drowned out even the heartiest of screams. If you needed a break, you could step outside for a smoke and enjoy a pretty decent view of the lights bouncing off the water.

But that's not what cracked Ringo up. When he looked up the property on the Internet (he's always curious about the history of things, mostly as a source of amusement), he discovered that the place had been built in September 1914 as "a rat receiving station." Seems back then there was a worry about European rats carrying all kinds of nasty plague shit to American waterfronts. So a bounty was offered: two cents per dead rat, five cents for live ones—and you used to be able to bring them to this very building to collect your reward. Ringo even found a poster online:

KILL THE RATS
And prevent the plague
TRAP THEM POISON THEM
RAT-PROOF YOUR BUILDINGS

Always good to see a building returned to its original use.

Part of him wanted to print it out and stick it on the wall inside the torture room, but Ringo didn't think El Jefe would appreciate it.

El Jefe brought the meeting inside the Cambodian karaoke bar to order.

"I've got two more names," he says. "So we're going to split up into two-man teams."

"What neighborhoods?"

"Let's get the teams straight first," El Jefe says. "You and Franken-stein take one, Lisa and Bird will take the other."

"Me and Lisa work better together," Ringo says, even though it's a lost cause, "if the target is somewhere south of downtown."

"Hey, I set the fucking teams here, and you'll go wherever I say you go. You got a problem with that, you can put your complaint in writing, then file it up your ass."

"I'm just saying," Ringo continues, "it's something to think about if you want to play to our strengths."

It's not just that Lisa and Ringo know South Philly. It's that Frankenstein and Bird are former cops, and Ringo's still not used to the idea of teaming up with a former pig to go dump a snitch. But El Jefe would just say that's the point. He wanted his teams to be coed, in a manner of speaking. Wops and pigs, playing nice together, keeping each other in check.

Ringo sighed. "What are the jobs? Do we at least get to pick those?"

"No."

Fortunately, El Jefe gives him and Frankenstein the one he would have wanted anyway. The target was a DJ at a nightclub up in Northern Liberties, and he walked home to his Fishtown pad after his gigs. It just would be a matter of scooping the idiot up off the streets, escorting him to one of their two torture pads (Ringo assumed the other team would need the other, so hopefully El Jefe would sort them out in advance—otherwise, it'd be embarrassing), then dumping the body in the secret location. Also pleasing to Ringo is that the target is a DJ; he hates those fuckers. He grew up listening to bands, real bands, at weddings and clubs and shit until the dorks with the record player and zero musical skills muscled into the scene. Ringo's dad was a semi-famous guitar player working the clubs in the old neighborhood. He retired from the business a bitter old man, priced out by those idiots with their record players. If you were to give Ringo a job killing DJs, man, he'd be happy the rest of his life.

But this whole operation isn't about killing DJs. It's about killing snitches, and to Ringo, that's the next best thing.

El Jefe keeps the big picture vague, but Ringo is a smart enough man to figure it out. If you want to push your way into a castle, first you grab the lookouts. You force them to tell you everything about the castle's defenses. Then you rip out their eyes.

Early. Real fucking early. That point where it's pretty clear that last night slipped away but it's not exactly morning yet, either.

Ringo just wants to get it on already.

The DJ guy took forever at the club. The set ended at 2:00 a.m., but he sat around for another hour drinking vodka tonics and snorting blow with some asshole buddies in the back of the club. Frankenstein had binoculars and could see the whole thing from the roof of a nearby house. Ringo was spread out on the cold, sticky roof, looking up at the stars. "What's the good word, Frankenstein?" Frankenstein coughs in a pointed way. Almost a *fuck you* behind his tightened fist.

"What?" Ringo asks.

"Look, I know you don't know, because we don't really know each other, but don't call me that, man."

"El Jefe calls you that."

"Yeah, but that's different."

"Because he's your boss."

"Yours, too."

"Nah. I swore to never have a boss ever again. I'm an independent contractor."

"Whatever, man."

"You should see yourself the same way, Frankenstein. Your days of skulking around the lab, doing someone else's bidding, they're long over."

"What the fuck are you talking about? And don't call me that."

Frankenstein doesn't know that politely asking Ringo to *not* call him something pretty much guaranteed that he would be Frankenstein all the time. From now on Ringo will go out of his way to use the name, even in circumstances where he might settle for the pronoun. Ringo knows he's perverse that way. But it amuses him.

"Sorry, Frankenstein."

"Come on, man . . . wait. He's coming out."

"You think I like being named after the lamest Beatle?"

"Then tell people to stop calling you that."

"Nah, I'm just fucking around. I love it. What are my other options? John? Paul? Fucking George? No thanks."

Frankenstein doesn't know how to reply to that, so instead he turns his attention back to the target. "Come on, let's climb down and get ready."

"Why don't you stay up here and take a nap, Frankenstein. I got this."

"What do you mean?"

Ringo doesn't answer; he shows Frankenstein what he means. The target is just a pale corpse with legs, stack of vinyl records tucked under a skinny arm, and Ringo is so tickled by the sight that he insists on doing the grab himself. Frankenstein protests; Ringo ignores him. He pulls the van up next to the DJ and honks the horn, which stops the DJ in his tracks. Ringo climbs out from behind the wheel—Frankenstein says, "Come on, man!"—walks around the front of the van—"Seriously what the fuck?"—and without a word punches the DJ in the face. BAM. The DJ folds like a table. Vinyl records go sliding out of their cardboard sleeves. Some lucky hipster is going to find this stuff later this morning. Frankenstein climbs out of the passenger seat and looks down at the DJ, who's coughing and trembling and moaning. Ringo yanks open the side door, scoops up the bones of the DJ, then hurls him into the van like a sack of potatoes. "See? You could have taken a snooze." Maybe it's the coke, but the DJ apparently enjoys a surge of adrenaline and goes flying out of the van, but Ringo does a quarter turn and slams a meaty fist directly into his center of gravity. BAM, again. Not hard—too hard and he'd crush the guy's rib cage—but hard enough to steal his air, temporarily stop his heart, and pretty much rob him of all ambition.

"Why?" he croaks as he drops to his knees.

Ringo looks at Frankenstein. Despite the scars, the guy has managed to screw up his face into an approximation of confusion. He turns his attention back to the DJ.

"Haven't you heard?" Ringo asks. "It's snitch season."

THE BADLANDS

SATURDAY, DECEMBER 7

Still no answer from CI #89. Wildey's been trying all morning, since 4:00 a.m., but nothing. CI #89 keeps weird hours, but he always got back to him within ten minutes. There's a sour feeling growing in Wildey's belly. First the disappearance of CI #69 and now this.

Wildey eats a quick bowl of cereal, dresses, climbs into his peep car, and drives down to the bar in Northern Liberties, where CI #89 works weekends. The bar is locked up tight, but Wildey knows that the bartender (and part owner) lives in an apartment above the place. Some rapid pounding on the door brings the bartender out.

"Who're you?"

"You remember me," he says. "We've met a few times already. With Dana."

Which was true. He'd met CI #89 a few times in the crowded bar. People assumed Wildey was a dealer. He liked people making that assumption, because it made him invisible and protected his informant.

The bartender nods, pursing his lips in understanding. "Oh yeah. Right. Sorry, man. I'm half-awake. What can I do for you?"

"I'm looking for Dana. Dana Cameron."

"He left last night around three."

Wildey gestures to him in a way that asks, Can we talk in private? The bartender, weary, looking like he's been up for the past seven days straight, nods. They convene in the guy's dirty kitchenette.

"Look," the bartender says, "if he owes you money, you're going to have to take it up with him. Dana's just a DJ here, not an employee."

"No, no. Nothing like that. I was supposed to hear from him first thing this morning."

"Yo, man, still *is* first thing this morning. He's probably asleep."

Wildey ignores that. "Did he say anything about taking a trip?"

The bartender shakes his head. "No. He's on tonight."

"Is he hooking up with anybody? Maybe he's crashing somewhere else?"

"Maybe, but he left alone. He was here late, like I said."

"Huh."

CI #89 is the source that tipped him off to Chuckie Morphine. Doesn't make sense that Chuckie would send someone to take him out. Chuckie, far as Wildey knew, didn't know his snitch. CI #89 was a scenester—a tall, cadaverous-looking white guy who probably looked like a suave punk vampire in the late eighties but had devolved into a pockmarked zombie in cheap sunglasses. CI #89 was Wildey's first official snitch. Back when he was still at the Twenty-fourth, Wildey would see Mr. Zombie Sunglasses stop by the Badlands for a bundle or two. Wildey rousted him, told him to stick to his own neighborhoods, at which point an indignant Zombie Sunglasses told him: "The whole city is my neighborhood, man." Which Wildey thought was kind of funny, but he still told him to get his white ass the fuck out of Dodge. The pouting Zombie Sunglasses wasn't going to leave it at that. He walked over to a bright green newspaper box, pulled out one of those free newsweeklies (the *City Press*), flipped a few pages, and showed Wildey a column. *Zombie's* column, as it turned out. He was a nightlife columnist. And his byline was "D.A. Cameron"—the initials stood for Dana Andrew. People, Wildey wanted to yell, do *not* give your son a girl's name—it will make him hit the streets to score for drugs to take away the pain of being named Dana. "I'm not scoring," his soon-to-be CI said. "I'm *soaking* up the streets." Wildey told him to go soak his head instead.

Still, when the job at NFU-CS opened up and Kaz encouraged them to cultivate well-placed CIs, Cameron was the first person Wildey tracked down. The timing was excellent; *City Press* had just scaled back its operations in August, leaving Zombie Sunglasses without a column. More importantly, without the $350 he made each week on the column. Wildey came up with a solution: $300 a week to be his CI. "Imagine you're writing the column for me," Wildey said, "and it's all about drug dealers." Zombie Sunglasses eagerly agreed, and seemed to have no moral quandary about ratting out his former party people. "Shit, they sold my ass out long ago. Fuck 'em." Wildey thought that was funny, too. He liked CI #89.

And now he's missing.

His next phone call is to Kaz.

FOX CHASE

Marty thinks a lot about the phone call, about the broken bottle that shattered their front window.

Marty checked caller ID not long after Sarie left Friday night and saw that the last number had a 570 area code. That was northeastern Pennsylvania. Sarie's friend Tammy Pleece lived five minutes away, not in upstate PA. Even if Tammy were upstate, how could she manage to make it down to Philly to meet for coffee fifteen minutes later? She couldn't. The caller was someone else. Someone who sounded enough like Tammy to convince Dad. (Marty conceded that to his twelve-year-old ear, all girls between the ages of fifteen and nineteen sounded pretty much the same.) Someone who lived upstate would most likely be a friend of Sarie's from school, but that was by no means a certainty.

Then the bottle against the side of the house. The explosion of glass in front had freaked both of them out. But it was the screamed threat after the bottle smash that worried Marty the most.

"Fuck you, Sarie Holland."

Marty needs to find out who hates his sister. Part of him would like to go to Dad, but he'd just clamp down tight, and Sarie would respond by keeping her distance, putting her at greater risk. No, first he has to understand what's going on, then bring Dad solid evidence.

DECEMBER 7 (early)

The upside of not being able to concentrate on studying for my final exams, Mom? I can always totally play the "get out of finals week" card by turning myself in to Wildey and getting arrested!

I kid.

(I think.)

D.'s left me seven Twitter DMs, two phone calls (on the house line, no less!), and even an email—the latter being him pretending to have a question about an honors program—like we're total strangers. As if Wildey is tapping my email. (Then again, maybe he is.)

I ignore them all. I know I'm being a child, but I have to focus on my work. Five exams this coming week, all of them requiring me to process and master huge swaths of information so that I can somehow fill blue books with essays that will prove to my professors that, yes, I have processed and mastered huge swaths of information.

Except I can't stop thinking about drugs.

There's more on the Dr. Hill bust today. Police rounded him and Letitia up overnight. Dr. Hill claims he knew nothing about the drug stuff—that was all Letitia's thing. Meanwhile, Letitia's claiming that she didn't know anything about Dr. Hill's weird medical shit, that she was just hustling some extra scripts to make ends meet. Uh-huh. Not according to the feds (or "sources close to the investigation," as the online stories have it), who claim that the Oxy ring was bigger and more widespread than anyone realized. Wildey should be fucking doing cartwheels right now. We did this. We stopped it. And we will receive none of the credit.

Why do I care?

I don't.

Not really.

The thing with me is, sometime when an idea takes hold it becomes impossible to shake. This is why I can't have a laptop open in front of me for very long, especially when I'm trying to study. It's a rabbit hole, I tells ya…and right now all I'm seeing is Wildey dressed up as a White Rabbit, beckoning me to LEARN MORE ABOUT THE EXCITING WORLD OF NARCOTICS!

And why wouldn't I? Sure beats Western Philosophy and The Greek Way and The Beats in American Literature and Psychology and Advanced Composition and everything else I'm supposed to be processing.

Maybe I should submit this journal as my Advanced Composition final exam. I have been writing up a storm…

Okay, back to work.

Kevin Holland spends a lot of time on this rainy Saturday morning near the front of the house, hoping against hope he'll catch the punk who tossed the bottle last night. Because you don't throw a bottle to hit a brick wall. You're hoping to smash a window, right? Last night the little idiot missed, so maybe he'll try again. Thank God you're not here for this, Laura. This would freak you out. But don't worry. I'm on it.

Never mind that this is the kind of dick punk move that a younger Kevin would have pulled (probably did pull) back in the day.

Ah, karma.

His attention is divided between the lack of activity on the street and the lack of activity on his phone. Sure, it's Saturday morning, but

Kevin was kind of hoping to hear from them yesterday. Discounting the holiday weekend, they had all week to decide. (Shit, he was actually hoping to hear from them last Monday, but decided to give them the week.) Should he call? No. Don't call. A car whizzes down the street going too fast for a residential area. Kevin's head whips around. The car disappears. He checks his phone again. Nothing.

And this more or less plays out and repeats all morning.

Until it doesn't.

There. Some tall guy in a hat, across the street, looking up at the house. No, not a guy. A college-aged kid in a fucking hat and red pants. Way to be stealth. Wait a minute, Kevin thinks. I recognize this guy! When Kevin goes outside to take a look, the kid in the red pants starts moving in the opposite direction. And by the time Kevin yells, "Hey asshole," he's already bolted up the block. By "you fucking asshole" he's already gone.

Okay, Mom, I confess: I haven't been studying. But this time it's not my fault. Dad's crazy-ass yelling snaps me out of the tiny bit of concentration I've mustered up. No idea what's going on until I run upstairs and see Dad hauling ass up our block, yelling YOU FUCKING ASSHOLE before slowing, panting, hands on his knees, struggling to catch his breath. What the hell? Marty's on the porch, too, and gives me a shrug. I race after him, and hear Marty following.

—Dad, you okay?

Dad, still hunched over, still panting.

—I want his name.

—Whose name?

—Your boyfriend. The guy who was here last Sunday night. Clearly the guy who doesn't want to meet me.

—I don't—

—Knock off the shit, Sarie. You know exactly who I mean. Did

you break up with him? Is that why he threw a bottle at our fuckin'
house last night?

Marty's jaw drops.

—Dad!

I put my hand on Dad's back to try to calm him down. Just like
you used to, Mom.

—What happened? Why are you asking me about him?

—He was just standing across the street, looking at the house.
Maybe thinking about throwing another bottle.

Oh no. Is it possible Ryan Koolhaas showed up again?

—What did he look like?

—Hat. Stupid fucking red pants.

—Dad!

Okay; phew. Not Koolhaas. I'm unable to stop myself from blurt-
ing out his name as a question.

Dad's eyes light up.

—Yes! Him!

Dad repeats the name, drawing out the single syllable and making it sound as sinister as possible. Like it's the foulest name ever
created. Like just speaking it makes my dad want to hurl.

—I want his last name, his number, his address, his parents'
names, everything. And then I'm going to kick his ass for being a
psycho to you.

—Dad, I assure you, D. did not throw the bottle. I told him what
happened. He's probably just stopping by to check on me.

—Then why did he just run up the street?

—Because you called him an asshole and chased him?

Dad sees my point. His panting eases up a bit. Meanwhile I feel
this second set of eyes boring into the side of my skull and realize
it's Marty, who has a weird expression on his face.

—What?

—Nothing!

Dad's breathing returns to normal middle-aged levels. He's tall and thin but clearly not in any kind of aerobic shape.

—Okay, Sarie, fine, your pal D. didn't throw the bottle. Then who did? You have another boyfriend lurking around?

—I'm not dating anyone. I would tell you, I promise.

Dad shakes his head quickly, like a boxer shaking off a jab. Then he stares off into the near distance, his shoulders sagging.

—Come on, let's get back into the house.

I try to go back to studying but can't help wondering why D. would show up in person like that. (In his red fucking pants, no less!)

My real phone buzzes. It's Tammy, confirming for tonight. One upside of the whole mess last night was that I called her, just to cover my tracks in case she ran into Dad or something crazy like that, and she sounded ridiculously overjoyed, like I was her long-lost sister, back from the dead. Totally thrilled to hear from me! God, it's been too long! Oh, so much to tell you! Let's meet tonight for dinner! Downtown! Do it up!

God, Mom, women are so fucking bizarre.

Still, it'll be good not to think about any of this stuff anymore. No Wildey, no D., no pills, no nothing. So I'm going to put my nose to the grindstone right now and earn the right to go out tonight.

Naked Lunch, I'm going to understand you if it kills me.

MAYFAIR

On the way up Harbison Avenue, Wildey spies a window cling decal on the rear panel window of a pickup that reads THIS TRUCK WAS MADE WITH WRENCHES NOT CHOPSTICKS. Hard to imagine Kaz hanging out in a place like this. But all Wildey knows is that with two CIs missing, it's best to go somewhere off campus. Kaz agreed and suggested a place called the Grey Lodge Pub on Frankford Avenue.

Kaz is already halfway through a pint of amber-colored beer when Wildey sits down. There is no one else on this floor, which is strange for this time of night on a Saturday night. Not even a bartender, even though there's a fully stocked bar up here.

"Want something?" she asks as he sits.

"Just a Diet Coke, thanks."

Kaz leans over, nods her head to someone Wildey can't see. He's about to turn around when Kaz leans forward. "You find your missing CIs yet? Hang on. Don't answer that just yet."

A tall pint glass of Diet Coke, jammed with ice and a fresh half-moon wedge of lemon, appears in front of Wildey.

"Thanks, Scoats," Kaz says.

"No problem, Kaz. Need anything else?"

Kaz shakes her head, and behind Wildey the footsteps recede. "I take it you're a regular here?" Wildey asks.

"Regular enough. This used to be my ex's favorite place, so it makes me happy to show up often so he doesn't feel welcome anymore. I especially make a point of showing up every Friday the thirteenth."

"To make his day extra unlucky?"

"No," she says, cracking a slight smile. "That's the day Scoats taps new firkins. He calls it Friday the Firkenteenth. You should see the crowds here. Anyway, my ex used to love coming here for Firkin Day, so I make it a point to deny him that joy as often as I can."

Wildey has no idea what a firkin is, or what the big deal about it might be. The takeaway, he guesses, is that Kaz really hates her ex enough to ruin his favorite joint for him. He sips his Diet Coke. The lemon in there smells good.

"You're stalling, which means, I take it, sixty-nine and eighty-nine are still missing."

"I haven't been able to turn them up yet, no."

"They're not the type to flake out, are they?" She pronounces it like a foreign word: *flaykout.* Takes Wildey a second to decipher it.

"No," Wildey admits. "They're pretty stable. Which is starting to freak me out. I mean, one? That's one thing. But two in the same week...am I missing something here? Did I do something wrong?"

Kaz lifts one eyebrow as she takes a sip of her beer. "What makes you think this is only happening to you?"

"Other CIs have gone missing?"

The Loot says nothing, but he can see the fury in her eyes, even as her face stays perfectly placid. Somehow she keeps the white-hot blinding chemical rage locked up behind those eyes. The alcohol is doing nothing to calm it.

"How many others?" Wildey asks.

Kaz shakes her head, and Wildey remembers: She won't reveal shit to no one, because she established this system to prevent situations just like this one. She once likened it to the seal of confession. Sins are between you, the priest, and God. In this case: the narcotics officer, his lieutenant, and the commissioner.

"Which brings us to the girl," Kaz says.

"What girl?"

"Your honors student."

"Shit," Wildey says, already half-standing.

"Hold on. Sit down."

"Loot, come on, this isn't—"

"Siddown!"

All Wildey can see is Honors Girl perched in the Formica booth in the sad, brightly lit doughnut shop, looking utterly lost, no idea how truly lost she is. Or what might be waiting in the dark for her. But Wildey lowers himself back onto the wooden chair and nods. He'll give the Loot another minute, at least. Storming off now wouldn't help anyone.

"The girl will be completely safe," she says.

"How do you know that?"

"Normally I play my cards close to the chest. But since this is your CI, it's better you know. Maybe it will put your mind at ease, I don't know."

"Uh-huh," Wildey says, feeling pretty much the opposite of *at ease.*

"I got it," Wildey says. "Old school. What does this have to do with one three seven?"

"She's not really one three seven."

"What?"

"There is no one three seven. It's an empty slot. I never entered your girl into the system."

"What? Why not?"

The Loot smiles. "Come on, Wild Child. Keep up. She's not a real CI. She's just your wedge into your Chuckie Morphine, am I correct? You want to pressure her to give up her boyfriend. He'll become your one three seven."

"Yeah, but she's more than that. Look at what happened yesterday. If it wasn't for all that Edgar Allan Poe shit, that would have been a great case for us. Hell, the sheer number of the scripts he was writing..."

"She has a talent for floating toward trouble, I give her that. Certain girls always do seem drawn to the bad boys, don't they? That doesn't make her a skilled informant."

"Loot, she's doing what we asked her to do."

"Never mind that." Now Kaz twists up her mouth into an expression that is somehow between a grimace and a sneer. "Your girl's had a free ride from you for over a week now. She's been good at playing you, hasn't she, Wild Child? Working so dutifully to please you—"

"Loot, it's *not* like that..."

"—without giving you what you actually want. Just like a woman, as Bob Dylan said. Never took you for a guy who likes a good cock tease."

"Nothing's going on."

"You're not making trips out to Fox Chase?"

Wildey's head is swimming. It's pretty much an open secret that the Loot has her own set of snitches watching the shop. Kaz's theory is that narcotics cops go crooked because there's the belief that they operate in a vacuum, that no one's watching. So on the first day, the word made it to Wildey: *You ever get that tingling feeling, like someone's watching you... well, you'll probably be right. It'll be the Loot.* Some of the rumors, probably based on her accent, had it that before coming to Philly she worked for Russia's GRU, military intelligence, and was merely implementing her homeland training on the mean streets of Philly. Still others cracked that the C in NFU-CS stood for commie. Kaz, to her credit, never admitted as much. But Wildey guesses she probably started the rumors herself. Whether or not she had a network of her own spies.

"I check on all my CIs," Wildey says.

"But then again, she's not a real CI, is she?"

"What are you saying? You want me to cut her loose?"

"No," Kaz says, pausing only to hoist the pint glass to her mouth and drain it. "The ride is over. Time to collect her ticket."

WILDEY: Look we gotta meet

CI #137: You said I was done for the weekend. I have exams this week! Like five of them

WILDEY: it's important

CI #137: I can't!

WILDEY: You will. Tonight 8 pm

CI #137: No

WILDEY: seriously?

CI #137: haven't I done enough? What else do you want from me?

WILDEY: Just meet me

CI #137: No
WILDEY: You want this to go the other way?
WILDEY: Hey
WILDEY: Answer me
CI #137: Jesus fine...where?

The meeting place turns out to be a bookstore. I'm surprised. Wildey doesn't seem like much of a reader. Maybe I should ask him about *Naked Lunch*.

Anyway, it's a huge, weird bookstore, big as a church or a movie theater, in the middle of a block on Richmond Street down the street from a Polish restaurant and a Polish supermarket. The sun's already down and the place looks dark, but Wildey assured me that it would be open, just go inside. So I go inside. There's no one in the front room, just piles of random books and boxes and a rusty newspaper honor box and framed posters stacked up against a wall. This can't be it, can it? I open another door, and boom, there's the store proper, which actually looks like a book junkie's den. There is an office off to the right, and inside is a dude in a brown-and-gray beard sitting next to a priest. Both are sipping whiskey out of small square glasses. They look up at me.

—I'm here for...Ben Wildey?

The bearded guy gestures to his right with his tumbler.

—He's in the back, hon. Go ahead.

Only when I step through another door, down a short hallway, do I realize that I am inside a former movie theater. The floor has been leveled, and thank God for that, otherwise the countless shelves of dusty tomes would go sliding right into a huge wall. I've never seen so many books in one place before.

—Amazing, isn't it?

Wildey's in the back, or what used to be the front, of the theater, where there's some worn furniture. He gestures for me to sit in a wooden chair. Meanwhile, he sits on a sofa directly across from me, fingers laced, leaning forward, all business.

—I found this place last year. You could browse for days in here. Anyway, it's the quietest place I know in town.

—It's also freezing. I think it's warmer outside.

—Hard to heat a space like this, I guess.

—So what do you want? I have plans tonight.

—Plans, huh? Anybody special? And will he be wearing red pants?

—I'm meeting my girlfriend.

—Girls' night out.

—Just dinner, not that it's any of your business.

We sit in silence for a while. The bookstore is cool (if not freezing) and all, but I have to meet Tammy in less than a half hour and I have no idea how crazy parking will be downtown (insane, probably). I worked hard today; I deserve this night off.

—So…?

—I'm up against the wall here, Honors Girl. I'm not saying you've not been working hard for me. But you're not doing what we asked. And what we need you to do is give us the man in the red pants.

—You didn't ask me for anything like that. You said, and I quote, go find me some drug dealers.

—Come the fuck on, Sarie. That's because you said you didn't know any drug dealers. Which I knew was a lie because you had one in your car last week! You were supposed to sweat it out, then turn him in. Simple as that. You weren't supposed to be doing all of this extra work.

—Look, I don't care what you say. I'm not telling you his name.

The moment the words slip out I see Wildey's eyes widen. A smile creeps onto his face. Whatever. I'm tired of the charade and there's no reason to keep it up anymore. I meant what I said. Put a gun to my head, put a knife to my throat, whatever, I'm not going to be a rat. Not anymore.

— So there is a him.

— We both know there is a him.

— This would have been a useful starting place a week and a half ago.

— I'm serious. I don't care what you do to me, I'm not going to do that to a friend.

— How good a friend? You think he wouldn't do the same to you to save his own skin? Hell, he practically is. What kind of a man is he, letting an innocent friend of his take the fall for him?

— I've got to go.

— I haven't made myself clear. It's over. By tomorrow morning my lieutenant wants somebody in cuffs, either you or your friend. If not, it's my job. I'm gone.

— Then come arrest me tomorrow morning. You know where I live. Anything else?

Wildey walks the stacks for a while, but no book titles register; they all look like a jumble of random letters. Out in front, the proprietor, Greg, offers him an Irish whiskey, but Wildey declines. He rarely drinks, and now is not the time to start a habit.

Kaz didn't threaten his job, but he knows that's what's on the line. You don't lose two CIs in one week. Shit, you don't lose *any*. And maybe Kaz is right. Maybe he let this college girl play him. It's all just a waste, though. Waste of her future, waste of her talent. Why is she forcing him to do this?

Wildey climbs back into his car and heads down to Fishtown to start another long night of searching for people who might already be dead.

223

Tammy knows I'm vegan, so she asks me to meet her at a swank new place called Grayne near Washington Square. (Which is so Tammy. Like you used to say, Mom: Her ass is always writing checks she can't cash.) Anyway, Grayne: everything locally sourced, sustainable, and they don't let you forget it. The prices all end in periods—the hallmark of a classy joint. Though at $19 for a plate of beans I would've used exclamation points.

Anyway, Tammy seems happy to be out so I am, too. She's wearing more makeup than I remember her ever wearing, and she keeps looking around the dining room as if a more important guest is supposed to join us any second. Her eyes don't stop moving. I look at her and smile, trying to calm her with the force of my eyes.

—So...finally...

—Yeah, I know, it's been totally crazy! But I'm so glad you called me last night. Even if it was just because you needed an alibi.

—I've been trying to reach you for a while.

—I know, I know...

—You look amazing, Tammy.

—Aww, thanks. B.T. dubs, I'm going by Tamara now.

B.T. dubs = Tammyspeak for "by the way." The dubs stands in for the w. Don't ask. She's been doing bodily harm to the English language since we were in ninth grade. Amazing that I'm still able to translate.

—Really? Tamara?

—Yeah, you know, Tammy just sounds like...I don't know, high school. We're beyond that, you know?

Do you remember when I first met Tammy—sorry, Tuh-MARR-uh—freshman year of high school? Back then she was going by "T." I started calling her "T.T." which she hated/secretly loved. That evolved into "Double T." By the time she had her first boyfriend, however, Double T. was dead and "Tammy" was born. Thankfully she didn't insist on spelling it with an *i*. Whenever she reinvents herself it's always because of a guy.

—Okay, so who is he.

—What?

—Come on, give.

Tammy breaks into a smile. We can't lie to each other.

—Okay, so, he's older. Like, a lot older.

—Scandal! What is he, twenty-five?

—Not exactly.

Tammy tries to play coy, but I dig the details out of her like a seasoned pro. And as it turns out, my BFF is dating a baby-raper. The guy is forty-FUCKING-three years old! Not married (allegedly). But she swears, no.

—Forty-fucking-three.

—His name is Peter.

She says it proudly, like it's a brand name worth owning. Wow, an Audi. Oooh, a Cuisinart. Ahhh, a Peter!

—Does this Peter have a last name?

—Yeah, but I really shouldn't say. Not yet. He's sort of well known around town. I'd never heard of him—God, don't tell him I said that. But he wants to keep things on the down low for now.

—Wow, that's great, Tammy. What's it like dating a man just a few short breaths from the grave?

—Fuck you.

But she smiles as she says it.

—Does he get the senior rate for both of you?

—Seriously, fuck. You. Hard. So how about you, Saint Serafina? Who you bumpin' uglies with these days?

Now I am nearly busting at the seams to tell Tammy about

the two men I'm juggling—the narcotics cop and the campus drug dealer. Both older men, too. (High-five, sista!) They text me, like, all the time, never let me get a moment's rest. Terribly jealous of each other, too. Older cop is dying to know who his younger rival is...and my dashing drug dealer wants me to stop being handled by my burnin' hunk of law enforcement. What's a girl to do? I can't give either of them up...

I peruse the menu.

—Nobody, really.

—Uh-huh. Nobody means somebody, you little slut. Fess up.

I'm saved by the appearance of the server, a slab of 100 percent grain-fed beef with a shade-grown haircut. He dotes on Tammy—sorry, Lady Tamara—and barely hears my order of $12! jasmine rice and $19! pinto beans. Tammy catches me, though.

—Hey, what's with the starving-art-chick food? We've gotta try some of these entrees. They're all over Eater and Foobooz.

—I'm just a rice-and-beans kind of girl. Also, in completely unrelated news, tuition is due next month.

—Don't be a silly bitch, this is on me.

—On you? How?

—I got a new job and I am flush. So order whatever you want.

I'm nonplussed—Tammy? A job? That pays real money? Nevertheless, she proceeds to order a mind! bogglingly! decadent! assortment of vegan food as well as a bottle of white wine that is roughly the cost of a decent set of tires for the Civic. Tammy assures me that it's all okay. Mr. Grain-Fed cards us both, but we have awesome IDs. Besides, he's clearly macking on Tammy. It's not as if he's carding us for real. He's probably just scanning her vitals.

Tammy turns her attention back to me.

—Okay, tell me about him. And don't bother denying, because I can tell there's a him.

The wine arrives and it is uncorked and poured and glasses are clinked and the first sip makes me dizzy. I'm thinking, I'm going to tell her. Confess it all right here. I've gotta tell somebody. I need to know I'm not going crazy...

—He's...complicated.

—Aren't they all.

—No, really. There's not even a him, never mind.

Tamara Pleece takes a sip of her organic wine, enjoys the head rush. She's been drinking a lot of wine lately. Her friend here—Sarie? She could really use the wine. She could use a lot of things.

Listen, okay: Tammy knows how hard her friend works. Sarie Holland: hardest-working bitch ever. Back at St. Antonia's, and probably going back to the womb. Never took a shortcut, never fudged something. It's what attracted her in the first place—you want a friend who had it together so you could be pulled along in her wake. Tamara knows she probably wouldn't have survived Saint A.'s without Sarie's help.

But tonight at dinner, hearing her fret over tuition money and ordering fucking rice and beans, Tamara wanted to scream: *You don't have to do this. You don't have to work so hard.*

Okay, if she's honest, Tamara is wrapped up in twin desires. The desire to help, to be the friend who fixes, and the desire to unload. Christ, how she's wanted to just freakin' tell someone already—someone who knew her before September and could give her a reality check, maybe even a good old-fashioned "what the fuck were you thinking"...no, not that. Tamara couldn't take that. Not from Sarie, her best friend since the first day of freshman year at St. Antonia's Catholic Preparatory School for Girls. Life's too good right now to have someone throw a bucket of cold water over it.

What *would* Sarie think? Tamara dreaded telling her but also so badly needed her to know. She took a fortifying swallow of amazing wine and came up with a strategy, right there at the table. A safe way to float the idea and see how Sarie would react.

"You still working that campus job?"

"Yeah, the bursar's office. Why? You need one, too? Don't know if there are any positions open, but I can—"

"No, hah. No. I had a job in mind for you, actually."

"For me? What kind of job?"

"You're gonna laugh, but I heard about this thing, and I was kind of kicking it around, too, and thought maybe it'd be something we could check out together."

"You want us to be assassins for hire. I like it. Maybe we can even dig out our St. A.'s uniforms. I'll bet clients would love that."

"You're such a silly bitch."

"It's the wine. I'm trying to estimate how much every sip is costing."

Tamara smiles, but inside she's running some calculations. Again with the money thing. Maybe she's giving her a subtle go-ahead to spill it.

"Have you ever heard of Amoroso dot com?"

The blank look on Sarie's face tells her: Nope, no idea. But then she squints; she's making a mental association. That's it. You've probably heard of it. Or seen the billboards or those goofy stories online . . .

"Wait a minute," Sarie says. "Are you talking about the Italian bakery? The one that makes the hoagie rolls?"

Tamara fights the temptation to bark with laughter—but then does anyway. The occupants of the neighboring tables at Grayne turn for a moment to check. No matter what it says on their driver's licenses, no matter what they're wearing, Tamara knows she's just outed herself as a teenager. Her cheeks burn hot.

"No," she says, finally collecting herself, "not the bakery."

Tamara Pleece explains that Amoroso.com is a website that introduces rich "Papas" with younger "Bellas." (The Italian romance thing is played up like crazy, which admittedly bothered Tamara at first, being a quarter wop.) This is *not* a prostitution thing, nor an escort service. Not *at all*. What you do, Tamara says, is that you just hang out with your Papa a couple of times a month—maybe go watch a show, or eat a fancy meal, or just snuggle up on a couch to watch a Blu-ray, but no sex, swear to God, this is not about sex, it's *companionship*. And in exchange your Papa takes care of you, buys your schoolbooks or helps with tuition, or maybe gives you some money for new clothes, that kind of thing. You don't have to do anything you don't want to, it's all super-friendly and legit and, you know, it would beat working at the accounting office at school or whatever you do...

Sarie is watching her the whole time, taking in every word until Tamara Pleece exhausts her train of thought and lapses into silence, waiting for her friend's reaction, and she can tell by the cold, dead look in Sarie's eyes that not only is this a job she'd never consider, but it's one that offends her in a fundamental way, so she's waiting for Sarie to say something so she can then say, "Got ya! Ha-ha, had you going there for a second, didn't it, you should have seen the look on your face, and—"

"So," Sarie says. "How long has this Peter been a client?"

So my bestie is a ho.

I wish there is a more polite way to say it, Mom, but there it is. Explains why she's been avoiding me since Halloween, which is probably around the time she started turning her tricks for treats—no, sorry, "favors" for schoolbooks and milk money or what-the-fuck-ever. Or maybe her pimp requires her to keep her phone free at all times, in case he gets horny and wants a quick hit of "companionship."

Why did I think I could tell her about my problem? This is Tammy

Pleece we're talking about. Nothing ever changes. Though I did think that maybe, for once, I'd get to be the one who could lean on her instead of the other way around.

The rest of the wildly expensive dinner is super-awkward. Long periods of silence punctuated by me going to the bathroom to check one of my two cell phones to read messages from D. that I ignore. Tammy, meanwhile, has a terminal case of sad face. Looking like I've sat here for the past thirty minutes screaming at her and calling her a whore. Which I haven't. But I'm also not about to give this thing my blessing. Tammy wants approval for something of which I could never approve.

Then again, who am I to judge? I'm a drug squad snitch. At least she's engaged in a criminal profession with a long and storied history.

It's awkward right up through the arrival of the check, with Tammy snapping it up and slipping a credit card into the 100 percent recycled cardboard slip holder and polishing off the last of the seriously expensive wine. It's not until we're out on the sidewalk that I break down. I don't need any more enemies. I don't need one more thing weighing on my conscience.

—You know, I'd really like to meet him.

Tammy, for the first time in a good forty-five minutes, brightens.

—Seriously? You would?

—Seriously. I'm sure he's a really nice guy.

—I know you probably have to go home and study, but…

—But what?

—Well, okay, this is weird, but…do you want to meet him right now?

SOCIETY HILL TOWERS

Part of Ringo knows this is a seriously bad idea, this whole *soiree* thing. But then again sometimes a proud Returning Citizen just needs to knock back with a vodka rocks and enjoy the company of some beautiful ladies from the old nabe, you know?

They're not whores, his old friend and associate cautioned him before he arrived. "Just know that. These are friendly girls, it's all legit. So no offering them a Franklin for a hummer." Like Ringo was going to show up with a roll of hundreds in one pants pocket and a bottle of Viagra in the other? He just wanted to have a drink or three and appreciate the view before he and Frankenstein headed out later tonight for another grab/torture/kill gig in the Rat Receiving Station and a dip into the Lobster Trap.

Ringo hovers in the corner, near the stereo. He has to remember what it's like, being at a real party. From the sound of it, so does his boss, because somebody's iPod is playing a rock block of the most depressing Frank Sinatra songs ever. Seriously. The playlist is three back-to-back sad-sack Frank albums—*In the Wee Small Hours, No One Cares,* and *All Alone.* Yeah, nothing better to get you in the mood...to slit your wrists. After a while D'Argenio sees him, nods, then makes his way across the room.

This moment has the potential to be extremely awkward. It's been a long time, lots of bad blood. El Jefe assured him everything would be fine, nobody has a beef with anybody, that D'Argenio personally requested him...but still. All Ringo can think about is the day he sat in that federal wooden box at Sixth and Market and pointed his finger at the smiling guy who's crossing the room and headed toward him right now.

There's only one way to defuse a moment like this. The old standby. Namely: women.

"Okay, so I have to know," Ringo says. "What do you mean by friendly girls? I don't know what that's supposed to mean. Not sure how to behave."

"Well...it's this service."

"So they're whores."

"No, that's just it. They're not whores. They're *companions*."

"Escorts, then?"

"No, you bagadoughnuts, it's legit. Christ on a crutch, you been out in Kansas way too long."

Ringo does a double take. Flashback to twenty years ago, with some fed telling him how rock-solid WitProtec is, how he'd have the entire U.S. government standing between him and those who would wish to cause him bodily harm. Flash back to a little more than a decade ago, watching the towers fall, Ringo thinking, Yeah, there's the U.S. government, protecting everybody. So maybe he couldn't be surprised that his former/current boss knew his address this whole time.

"Yeah," D'Argenio says, smiling. "I knew."

"How long?"

"Bitch," his former boss/current business associate says, with a huge smile on his face, "if I wanted your fat ass dead, you would have been dead back before they invented the Internet."

Well, color my fat ass surprised, thinks Ringo, as D'Argenio slips back into the party proper.

Ringo does some Stoli drinking, some ogling, some eavesdropping. Christ, with the number of times his old boss/new business associate tells people he's going legit, Ringo thinks he should have bought a giant party banner with the word LEGIT in huge red letters on it. The party is full of people he doesn't know. New business associates, D'Argenio explains. Getting off on the idea of doing business with a former (reformed!) gangster. Whatever. Ringo continues mingling, looking for any sign of these friendly girls. So far, no sign whatsoever. You can tell the working girls from the groupies. Ringo asks D'Argenio what the deal is. D'Argenio tells him relax, they'll be here soon. Just a couple of real friendly girls. You'll like them. Everybody's friendly.

When two teenagers walk into the party, Ringo realizes that D'Argenio has gone off the deep end.

One step into the room and I realize I am woefully under-dressed. Hell, in my jeans and black shimmery top, I was un-derdressed for Grayne. This is not just a laid-back gathering for some rich middle-aged people; this is a full-blown soiree. I grab Tammy's wrist.

—Who are all these people?

—Just some friends of Peter's. Look, I'll be right back. Go get a drink.

—Oh no. You're not ditching me that quick!

Double T/Tammy/Tamara rolls her eyes and smiles shyly.

—I'm not ditching you. Just going to say hi to Peter.

—Sure. Fine. Whatever.

Tammy throws an air kiss at me.

—Love ya!

I call after her:

—Ditcher!

Tammy turns the air kiss hand into a middle finger.

I stand around a few awkward moments that feel like a few awkward decades and then one of my two cell phones goes off. Naturally. I don't want to risk checking either in a room full of strangers—especially if it's Wildey on the burner again. What does a person with two cell phones look like, other than a drug dealer? This kind of swank crowd, I'll be tossed out onto the street in no time. Maybe even without the use of an elevator. So I oh-so-stealthily nudge a partially open door with my butt and back into what appears to be a darkened bedroom, do a quick glance over my shoulder—huge wardrobe dresser, empty bed, but otherwise clear—then dig into my shoulder bag.

The buzzing is coming from my legit phone. Turns out to be Dad, asking what time I'll be home. Fuck! Forgot to text him. I type:

—Still out with Tammy. Won't be out too late.

Five seconds later Dad responds:

—Isn't this finals week?

Please. I type:

—I studied so hard today my eyeballs are bleeding, Dad.

—I'll let you know if any old boyfriends show up to break more windows.

—HAH.

—Seriously, not too late. Drive safe.

—OK.

I slide my phone back into my bag, turn around, and lean up against the door to take a moment to breathe. For just a moment. What am I doing here, anyway? Making it up to Tammy? I guess so. So that's what I'll do. I'll say hello to her creepy older boyfriend/perv/fifty shades of NO FUCKING WAY guy and then split. Dad's right. This is, after all, finals week. I worked hard today, but I don't feel prepared at all. Besides, I might be getting arrested tomorrow morning, so I suppose I should get a good night's sleep…

—Hey. You seriously need to try this.

The voice—as calm and deep as it is—has me nearly jumping out of my skin.

—What the fuck?

I take an unbalanced step forward and see this guy who a moment before was obscured by a massive wardrobe/closet thing. He's sitting at a desk with an assortment of brightly colored pills spread out before him, looking like a kid who is determined to sample every single type of jelly bean in the bag. And poised next to the pills are a pad and pencil. He wheels back a few inches and gives me this broad smile.

—Hey.

—Sorry! I just want somewhere quiet to take a call—

The guy looks like a Main Line hipster. Preppy clothes—immaculate blue sweater pulled over a crisp button-down shirt, wrinkled old khakis. Sloppy pile of hair, neatly trimmed beard, glasses, a warm smile, and a jittery demeanor. He's like a bed that's half-made.

—Come on over. I'm serious—you should try some of this.

—Some of what?

Guy clearly is having his own personal party. He waves his hand, beckoning me.

—Christmas has come early. Come on and sample a present.

He means the drugs, Mom. He's basically saying, Come on and TRY SOME OF MY DRUGS. You know, the ones spread out all over the desktop like someone just knocked over a jellybean jar. I've never had it offered to me so blatantly before.

Ordinarily I would have marched out of the room and spent the elevator ride to the lobby smirking to myself, cheeks reddened, soul scandalized. But that was the me from two weeks ago. The new me has a piece of Wildey in my head, and that part is thinking:

Whoa. Now there's a fuckload of pills. Where did this guy get them? How can I use this?

Honestly, it's not even a conscious decision, which is the scary-in-retrospect part. I am having an out-of-body experience. I glide over toward the desk, lower the bag from my shoulder, perch myself on the edge of the king-sized bed that's closest to the desk, then smile back at the druggie with a virtual pharmacy spread out in front of him.

—Okay, I'll bite. What do you have there, Partyman?

Partyman smiles, displaying teeth like perfect white tombstones. The kind that come from blessed genetics or an excellent dental

235

regimen. Lucky prick. I don't smile often on purpose because of my too-large teeth.

—Pretty much anything you can think of.

—Tell me what you've got.

—Okay…well, here's the thing. I don't mean to be rude, but are you legal?

I lean forward and stage-whisper:

—Drugs aren't legal for anybody!

And make this clicky sound with my tongue as I give him the ol' index-finger pistol crack. Which makes him smile that fucking perfect smile again.

—No, for real. Because you look like a kid. How old are you?

—Twenty-one.

—And I'm Hunter S. Thompson. Perhaps you know my associate, Dr. Gonzo? Let me see your license.

—Let me see yours.

—Ladies first.

—Are you actually carding me before giving me a sample of one of your illegal pharmaceutical pleasures?

Partyman leans back in his chair and smiles.

—Law is such a wonderfully malleable construct, isn't it? Give it up, young'un.

I'm not sure what to do at this point. My ID is really good— Tammy and I lucked out with a guy making the rounds among the honors triple freshmen back in September. Not only was he a senior design major at Drexel, but he'd recently completed a zero-pay summer internship at the Pennsylvania DMV and had access to the templates, cameras, everything to forge a perfect license. (Guess he decided he was owed a little dough for a summer of hard work.) For five hundred dollars he could even change your actual DMV file so that if a state store employee swiped your card you'd still be golden. My blood wasn't that rich, nor was Tammy's. But somehow she talked him into the upgrade for free—on both of our cards. I've never had the balls to try it out in a state store, but I'm sure that file is the reason Wildey still thinks I'm twenty-one.

Anyway, I'm sure Partyman here doesn't have a handheld reader. But what if there's some kind of visible flaw, and this guy's a narc? Just handing him the license could be a huge mistake.

Luckily, Partyman folds his hand. Maybe he's eager to get back to his pill collection, maybe he was just fucking around/flirting with me.

—Okay, fine. But if I ask you out later, and you turn out to be seventeen years old or something, it'll be a devastating blow to my soul.

—I'll try to leave your soul intact.

I inch a little closer.

—So whaddya got, Partyman?

—I'm pretty much an everything guy myself. You see, I'm a tester.

—A what?

Partyman gestures to the desktop.

—I sample new product, give each pill a one to ten rating, along with some other notes. Or I run tests on it, make sure it isn't some kind of bullshit. Beats real work. Who are you here with?

—My friend. She's going out with…Peter?

—Well, then! We're practically family. I work with Peter. So you want to help me do a little market research?

Inside I'm squealing, but on the outside my face is a mask of utter disappointment (hopefully).

—Look, I'd really love to, but I only stopped in for a minute. I can't stay.

—I did see a look of worry on your face when you were texting a minute ago. Pressing business?

—I have somebody waiting for me at home.

—Somebody special?

—Yeah, sort of.

—My loss, even though you're jailbait. But hang on.

He turns his back to me and a few seconds later he's handing me a little Ziploc full of an assortment of pills. A doggie bag of totally-breaking-the-law.

—Now give me your phone.

—Why?

—Part of the deal.

I hesitate but then hand over my for-real phone. It's the one he saw me using. What am I going to do, give him the cheap-ass burner? He thumbs in a number and the iPhone in his desk comes to life, playing the chorus of Lou Reed's "Walk on the Wild Side." *Doo, doo-doo, doo, doo-doo-doo doo, doo-doo...*

—You've got my number. If you have occasion to try these, with or without that special someone at home, drop me a line, let me know.

—Okay.

I smile. He leans forward. I give him a quizzical expression. He sighs.

—Aren't you forgetting something?

—What?

—Um, maybe your name? Just so I'll know what to call you, besides the lovely high school senior who stumbled into this bedroom Saturday night.

—I'm not a high school senior.

—When guessing a lady's age, I always shoot a little low.

—Thanks, Partyman. What's your name, by the way?

He grins, making his beard look even fuller.

—Partyman.

—Then you can call me Joan.

—Enjoy, Joan.

I don't leave right away. I hang around the party for a while longer. Maybe I'm just not ready for this study break to be over. I meet the infamous Peter. He's kind of a dick. Checks out my chest, decides what I have doesn't require further investigation, returns his gaze back to Tammy's chest. I worry about my girl. I nurse a white wine. I think about the pills on the desk in the bedroom. I think about Partyman. His number's on my iPhone. He never comes out of the room. I leave.

CI #137: Hey are you up

WILDEY: Well look who it is

CI #137: Can you meet tomorrow morning

WILDEY: it is tomorrow morning

WILDEY: almost

CI #137: Can you or not? I've got something big for you

WILDEY: no more excuses

CI #137: seriously you're going to want to know this

WILDEY: I'm serious too

CI #137: how about 10 am up here somewhere? I have to sneak away

WILDEY: fine, tell me where

WILDEY: but please don't be fucking around with me

CI #137: I promise I'm not

Marty is curled up on the couch when Sarie returns home. Dad's given up—too many beers did him in—but Marty crept down here an hour ago to keep up the vigil. The back of the living room couch faces the door, so she can't see him. He listens to her lock the door, sigh, peel off her coat, drape it over the easy chair, then walk into the kitchen. The light snaps on. Marty realizes that for a moment she's forgotten the phones. He has to act now. She rarely allows her phone out of her sight, and Marty is convinced the clues he needs will be on them. Especially the cheap one.

Summoning his inner cat, he creeps over to Sarie's jacket, reaches in, feels around. It's her iPhone in this pocket. Crap. He tries the other, finds the cheap one, flips it open. The tiny light feels like it throws a mega-watt spotlight on his face and the entire darkened living room. He cups it while flipping to the little text message icon. Presses it.

Holy shitballs.

Marty's eyes are bugging out of his head. He didn't expect her to forget to clear the texts. Every time he's stolen a peek it's already been wiped. But here it is: an actual exchange.

how about 10 am up here somewhere? I have to sneak away

fine, tell me where

but please don't be fucking around with me

I promise I'm not

Marty thumbs up it for a second before remembering he doesn't have much time. Sarie's probably just making coffee or tea, preparing for more final exam cramming tonight. He fumbles for his iPod, hits the camera app, aims it . . . shit, wait! He forgot to turn down the volume. He does. Then he snaps two photos of the text exchange. He's just slipped the cheap phone back into her pocket and turned around when Sarie walks out of the kitchen.

"Marty? What are you doing up?"

Almost busted. He fakes a yawn. "Couldn't sleep."

"Jesus, it's after midnight, dude."

"You're up late, too."

"I'm not twelve years old."

"I don't have finals this week."

"Gah, you sound like Dad. *Go to bed.*"

Marty goes upstairs to his room, but he does not go to sleep. He's too busy thinking about tomorrow morning, 10:00 a.m. *Something big.*

DECEMBER 8

The last thing I expect to see this morning is D. sitting at the kitchen table across from Marty.

—Hey.

D., with his hair neatly combed (as best as he can), shirt tucked in, wearing pants that were probably even washed recently. Bright-eyed. Smiling. The perfect boyfriend, if only he were: a) perfect and b) my boyfriend.

I blink a few times to make sure I'm not still asleep or having a weird paranoid dream. Unfortunately, this is reality, and I happen to be wearing my dumpiest T-shirt over a pair of pajama bottoms. My hair is like a fright wig. Marty, meanwhile, has a stormy look on his face, as if to ask why this strange dude has to be at the break-fast table first thing in the morning.

—Uh, hey.

I whisper-mouth:

—What-the-fuck-are-you-doing-here-talk-quick.

Dad is moving sausages around a frying pan trying not to burn them. I don't believe he is succeeding; the smoke and grease woke me up. He turns around grinning like, ho hum, this is just a usual Sunday morning with some dude sitting at our table.

—Sarie Canary! I'm making some meat for the boys, but can I put some oatmeal on for you?

—I'm okay, Mr. Holland, seriously. Sarie and Marty here can have the sausages.

Marty gives D. a withering look.

—You don't know she's vegan?

241

D. nods as he processes this.

—I did not know that.

I try to prevent the situation from spiraling out of control.

—So…I really wasn't expecting you this morning, D. I thought we were meeting up later?

D. reaches into the pocket of his jacket, which is draped over the chair behind him, and pulls out a paperback book. He shows me the cover. All black except for the title *Naked Lunch,* which pops out of the darkness in a kind of 3-D effect.

—I brought you this.

—I already have a copy.

D.'s eyes plead with me. Come on, work with me here.

—I know, but like I told you, this copy has my annotations in it. Might help you with Chaykin's final. And it's not cheating, because you're allowed to discuss the novel with other students, and that's what we're going to do.

—Oh.

Marty reaches up for the book.

—Naked what? What's this about?

—Wait, chief…

D. tries to pull the book away, but Marty is too fast. He's also a little too clumsy. It slips out of his hands, bounces off the table, then lands on the kitchen floor, pages open. And out of its pages come a series of hundred-dollar bills that fan out everywhere. Marty's eyes bug. D.'s jaw drops. And by this point Dad, pan of sausages in hand, is looking down at all of the money on the floor, too.

—That's a lot of cash. Hope you're not going to try to bribe your professor.

—Oh shit, sorry!

D. launches out of the chair and sweeps up the money with his hands. Dad and Marty look at me, but I keep my focus on D.

—Forgot that was in there. I owe some tuition money…

—You pay your tuition in cash?

—Ha-ha, not usually, but Dad has a cash business and he just thought it would be easier, since it's kind of late and everything.

Needless to say, breakfast after that seems kind of strange. Apparently D. just knocked first thing this morning; Dad, who'd crashed out on the couch, stumbled to the door surprised to see the mystery man in his daughter's life. After what must have been a surreal conversation, in which D. assured my father that he did not throw a bottle at our house Friday night, Dad invited him to stay for breakfast. Which, you have to admit, Mom, is a total Kevin Holland move. Keep your enemies close, and all that. Wait to see if drug money comes tumbling out of paperback copies of incomprehensible Beat novels.

Much as I would like to stick around and savor the awkwardness, I have a meeting with Wildey in about twenty minutes.

—Hey, you wanted a ride to the train, right?

I kick D. under the table before he can ask, I did?

Out in the car we can finally speak freely. He gives me the two thousand dollars he borrowed, all in hundreds. I thank him coldly and head toward the SEPTA station.

—I don't understand why you're so mad at me.

—What are you doing here?

—I've never met someone who didn't want to be paid back.

—It could have waited until tomorrow.

—True, but there's something else.

—What?

D. plays with the knob on the glove box. God help me if he pulls a cassette tape out right now. I speed up a little, a not-so-subtle indication that his time is running out.

—Look, I've been up for the past two days straight thinking

about this. I hate that I got you mixed up in all of this, and I've been racking my brain trying to think of how to get you out of it. And then it came to me. I can't believe I didn't think of this sooner.

I raise my eyebrows. And…?

—I want you to meet Chuckie.

—Chuckie the violent drug dealer?

—He's not violent. Who told you that? He's a business dude. Christ, I think he's a grandfather. Look, once you meet him you'll understand. And he can help us get the cop off your back.

—What exactly will I understand?

—Look, you just have to meet him. Once you see him, you'll know what I'm talking about. I'll set it up.

Nothing like a last-minute save, just under the wire.

ROCKLEDGE, PA

The gray skies are pregnant with snow. Forecast says it's supposed to be just a lawn-and-car storm, not one of those milk-and-bread storms that send people scurrying to the Wawas, but Wildey's not so sure. Looks like it's about to really cut loose. He sits in one of his cars, idling in the cold doughnut shop parking lot, trying to keep warm. He doesn't do coffee but needs the caffeine, so he nurses a Diet Coke. Which doesn't do anything to keep him warm, but whatever. It's going to be that kind of morning. He doubts Honors Girl will put up a fight, but he knows for damn sure that she'll cry. And that'll be a really shitty start to his week. Wildey sips his Diet Coke, trying to gear himself up for the task at hand. Honors Girl arrives right on time, slides into the passenger seat.

"Surprised you wanted me out here, in your neck of the woods," Wildey says. "Just because you're on home turf doesn't mean I can't arrest you."

"You're not going to arrest me."

Wildey's eyebrows lift. *Yeah? You pretty sure of that?*

"In fact, after I tell you what I've found, you're going to want to kiss me."

Wildey looks at her, not sure of how to respond to that one.

"You guys might even want to give me a job," she says, beaming.

"Will you spit it out already?"

"I can get you Chuckie Morphine."

Wildey narrows his eyes. "What's the catch?"

"No catch."

"So you're finally giving up that lowlife friend of yours."

"I have a friend who's helping me, yes. But he's not your source, he's mine. You don't touch him, that's the deal. Instead I'm the one who makes contact for you. I'll help you land Chuckie."

Wildey asks her how she plans on doing that, and she gives him a withering stare like he's a fucking moron.

"By going undercover and buying drugs and getting it all on tape? I mean, is there another way to do it?"

"How do you know he'll talk business in front of you?"

"Don't worry. I can do it. But that's not all. I'm onto something else. Something big."

"Hang on, now. I don't care about anybody else right now. Let's keep our focus on Chuckie Morphine."

"So you don't want a mustard tub?"

Wildey finally allows a smile to creep onto his face. "Girl, you know I'm all about the mustard tubs."

"If I'm right, I can score you one of the biggest mustard tubs you've ever seen."

Wildey has to admit: This is not how he saw this morning playing out. Don't get him wrong; if even half this shit is true, it's an embarrassment of riches. But how's he gonna sell this to Kaz? The Loot was pretty dead-set on this whole someone-in-cuffs-by-Sunday-morning thing. Wildey eases back into the driver's seat, knowing he's going to regret this, knowing that even before he's finished sighing.

"Tell me about this mustard tub."

"I will. Just give me forty-eight hours."

There it is. The catch.

"Come on, you're killing me with these extensions, already! Your professors let you get away with this shit?"

"You know I'm good at this. I just need the time to do it right."

Wildey turns to face her and gives her a long, deep cop stare. Nothing in her eyes says she's playing him. She's actually excited. Look at her. Wrapped up in her cases. Wildey recognizes the look. He reaches out for her shoulder and she flinches.

"What are you doing?"

Her sudden movement freaks him out in return. *Was* he doing something? Just reassuring her, establishing trust, just like he does with all his CIs. With anyone he's trying to connect with. It's a normal human response, right? Instead, Wildey puts his hands back in his lap.

"Okay, Honors Girl."

"Okay what?"

"Let's talk about you wearing a wire."

MORPHINE

DECEMBER 8 (later)

Surprise snowstorm this afternoon, Mom. Three inches falling per hour. Nobody saw it coming. You'd love this storm, especially because it's a Sunday and nobody's out. Dad and Marty are watching the Eagles-Lions game upstairs, which is apparently wild because Dad is yelling a lot. I steal a glance every time I go to the kitchen to make myself another cup of tea. The grounds crew has to keep brushing the snow off the yard lines so that the players can see what they're doing. Some commentator says that Detroit has the advantage because their uniforms are white, but another says you can't underestimate the Birds on their home turf. I'm not a big football fan, as you know, but this game looks like it'd be fun to watch. (Even though the more beer Dad drinks, the louder he gets; even Marty seems annoyed.) Much as I'd like to blow off the afternoon, I have a lot of work to do. There is much to figure out.

The baggie of pills Partyman gave me is full of bright colors and perfect shapes. D. would probably love it. I still don't understand the allure of taking what is essentially medicine. Girls in high school had plenty of pills, and I was offered my fair share. They'd look at me like I was crazy when I turned them down. Everyone was using them — I wasn't being fair to myself if I didn't take them, blah, blah. Want to know what kept me away?

You, Mom.

I know back when you were still Laura Gutierrez you were an

addict. If you hadn't been, I wouldn't be alive right now. Your addiction brought you to Dad's clinic in San Diego, and that miserable experience somehow brought you two together, and boom, out of all that came me. (And later, of course, Marty.) So I should be thankful to drugs, right? Yay drugs, makin' the world go round.

But I think that your addiction is what eventually killed you. I thought about this the first time I saw you have a seizure. Growing up, I would hear nonstop about the terrors of overdosing, and it was exactly how I imagined it—eyes rolling back in their sockets, body contorted in unnatural ways, veins bulging to the point where I could easily imagine them exploding. Suddenly, you just weren't there. You were replaced by some alien being that possessed your body.

I know you didn't O.D. It was brain cancer. But sometimes I can't help but wonder if you were paying for some earlier sin in your life.

Our drug talks at the dinner table—starting when I was twelve and Marty was five (and pretty much clueless at first)—were weird. Beneath the scary stories, Dad would seem a bit wistful about the allegedly bad old days. What I did was wrong and you should never try drugs alone, Sarie, blah, blah, blah...but they were also kind of fun, I'm not gonna lie to you.

Your stories, however, were right out of Edgar freakin' Allan Poe. All darkness and being out of control and terrified every moment. You would get so excited you'd lapse into Spanish (which Marty and I would tease you about, sometimes mercilessly: Ay! Dios Mío!). Dad would listen to your stories with his jaw clenched tight, clearly pissed to be hearing them again. Bad memories all around, I get it. Yet you guys would trot out these stories on a regular basis, especially when Marty got older. I always thought it was clever, the two-pronged approach. And it worked. I've never popped so much as an Adderall.

Looking at these pills now, though...I have to wonder. Maybe they'd help me focus. I am, after all, leading a double life. Maybe they'd help me to keep everything straight in my head.

Nope. Can't do it. Still scared straight.

Mom, you should be proud. I guess children really do grow up to rebel against their parents.

NFU-CS HQ

The conversation isn't as hard as Wildey thought.

It's infinitely harder.

The furious look in Kaz's eyes makes Wildey think he's guilty of high treason or something. Why does he not have the girl in handcuffs right now? Does Wildey think she was kidding?

"No, Loot, I did not," Wildey says. "But hear me out. We gain little by taking her into custody right now. She's only a stepping-stone to her boyfriend, and for all we know the boyfriend could lawyer up and drag this thing into the New Year. *If* then."

Kaz watches him carefully. "Go on."

"But if we send her in with a wire, we hopscotch past all that and land right on Chuckie himself. We get him on a wire, he's done."

"This all depends on your girl," Kaz says. "Feels real shaky to me."

"Give her the time she needs to work. This is going to pay off big."

"It had better. Okay, I'll detail Sepanic and Streicher as your surveillance. When is this going to happen?"

"She's going to text me the moment she knows."

DECEMBER 9

I take my psychology exam, the most straightforward of my four finals this week—just regurgitating definitions, multiple choice, simple short essays. Which is good, because I have to drive downtown for an afternoon date with Partyman.

Yes, Mom, for research purposes. Nothing more. I swear. I think he's in his early thirties, which might be robbing the cradle for Tammy, but it's a bit too old for me.

Originally I asked Partyman to meet me for coffee. Partyman said screw that, let's have a drink, give that clearly fake ID of yours a run for its money. So I agreed to meet him for a drink. His suggestion is a bar at the top of the Bellevue Hotel. He's already there, perched in a little banquette next to a window. Partyman is wearing a suit with no tie and looks considerably more calm than he did Saturday night.

—Find it okay?

—Nice place.

—I love the view from up here. If you squint you can almost make out the city as it was a hundred years ago. Anyway, I'm surprised you called. Do you need a prom date?

He teases me along these lines for a while, we order drinks (Chardonnay for me, Stoli martini, two olives, for him), and, yes, I am carded, but the ID holds up, though Partyman goads the waiter to check again. No, really, check the date. We clink glasses.

—I'm going to come clean.

Partyman sips his Stoli and lifts his eyebrows as if to ask, Yes?

—I'm not really into the whole pill thing...

—But if someone offers you free drugs, hey, why not take them and pass them around to your friends, maybe make a few bucks? It's okay, I get it.

—No, it's not that. I was just...curious.

—What I'm curious about is why a beautiful young woman like you wanted to meet with scruffy old me.

—Yeah, you never did show me your ID.

—No, I didn't, did I?

He shows me his perfect white teeth again.

—Okay, the suspense is killing me. Why are we meeting?

So then I give him the line I've been working on all night when I should have been studying for my psychology final. I tell him that I have an inkling of what he does for a living (geez, what gave it away, all of the drugs on the desk in front of me, he says), and no judgments, man, to each his own. And I'm eager to learn more.

—You are.

—Yeah.

—Why?

Because I'm working on a research paper on the drug trade in Philadelphia and want something that no other honors student will have. What's that, he asks. I tell him, field reporting.

I have a sip of wine while Partyman processes this. It's cold and seems to go to my head immediately. I have no idea if he's going to buy the paper thing. Then again, why else would I be curious? On paper I'm the perfect honors student. And in a sense, I am telling the truth. I am doing research. Just not for a paper in the traditional sense.

—I wouldn't use your name, of course. You'd be completely anonymous.

After a long swallow that drains his Stoli completely, he signals for the waiter.

—What if, and no judgments here if this is the case...but what if you're a police snitch, and here I go, telling you all about what I do for a living?

In my gut I know that here's where I really have to sell it. He has to believe me—otherwise, it'll be one drink and he'll pat me on the head (or my ass) and send me on my way, little schoolgirl that I am.

—You think I'm a snitch?

—It's not beyond the realm of possibility. Maybe you are into pills and you got yourself busted and the only way out is to find the police a dealer. Happens all the time. Especially in this crazy town. Is that what happened to you?

—I'm not into pills. And I've never been arrested.

—I'm going to have another Stoli. They go down so, so easy. How about you?

And, yep, there it is: I've lost him. Even though there's no possible way he can know for sure that I'm a CI. Maybe he can just see it in my face. Maybe I'm that bad at this.

—Look, this whole thing came out wrong. I'm sorry I wasted your time. I'd better go.

I stand up to leave. He puts a hand on my arm.

—Hey, don't rush off. Let's have another round. I'm not ready to head back out into the cold, are you?

We have another round. I finish the rest of my wine (which is half the glass) in one gulp by the time the next arrives but already feel my brain all swimmy. Tomorrow's my twentieth-century history final, a huge multi-part essay series on the cold war and the red scare, and I'm not even remotely ready. I tell myself I'll be polite and have another wine to not piss off the kindly bearded drug dealer.

—I will say this, the police culture here is so incredibly fucked.

—You're not from here?

—Let's just say I visit a lot of cities. And Philly's something special, let me tell you. You know the one vital element to any thriving drug operation? A complicit police department.

—You're saying the cops are in on it.

—Don't they have to be? There's really no other way it works. If they're not outright bent, they report to someone who is. And if they're not, then they're enforcing policy that is created at the highest levels and has nothing to do with crime prevention.

—That's a pretty cynical worldview there, Partyman.

—I'd say it's pretty dead-on. But fine, even if you don't believe that, take a closer look at the cops in this city. You know how many the police commissioner has fired since he took the job five years ago?

—No idea.

—One hundred and thirty-four. Let that number sink in for a minute. Now, consider that nearly half of them have found their way back onto the force, thanks to police union arbitration. Not that I'm complaining, really. The crooked ones are desperate and easy to control. That's a boon to people in my profession.

—So, Mr. Partyman, do you have a bunch of cops in your pocket?

He smiles.

—Why? Do you want to bum one?

I return the smile and take a sip of my wine, even though I don't like it very much.

—Okay, so how do you explain all of the drug busts I've been reading about since I started this research paper? The police aren't sitting back and doing nothing.

—You mean those small-time busts, the five o'clock news photo op with bales of pot on a foldout table? You're reading the wrong stories. You might want to look at stories about a series of home invasions within the past month.

—Home invasions? Why?

—And pay special attention to the back chatter in the comments section. That's where people vent.

—Mind if I write this down?

—Why? I'm not telling you anything you won't be able to find on your own.

—Oh. Okay.

—You also might want to pay attention to all the missing people lately. People just don't vanish off the street for no reason. They're most likely confidential informants, which underscores the futility of narcotics investigations at the city level.

—How so?

—Considering the rate at which snitches disappear in Philadelphia, it stuns me that anybody would ever agree to be one.

After the college girl departs, the guy she calls Partyman orders another Stoli and requests a luncheon menu. He is not as old as he led "Joan" to believe, but he's lived long enough to know that people don't drop into your life for no reason. He hopes he's surmised the correct reason and told her what she needed to hear. Then he orders the sautéed Pennsylvania lake trout, with almonds, green beans, brown butter, and capers. He hums "Stir It Up" while he waits. God, he loves his job.

Online conversation from private chat room in Big Bust V: The West Coast Connection (CultureWerks Games, 2013). 12/9/13 10:31 p.m.

ciscoPIKE: so anything going on this week? could use a break from finals

chUKeeMORPHine: I'm sure something can be arranged brudda

ciscoPIKE: at the new place?

chUKeeMORPHine: okay yeah why don't you drop by Tues nite

ciscoPIKE: sounds good man. cool if I bring somebody?

chUKeeMORPHine: sure, as long as she has tits

ciscoPIKE: ha-ha yeah she does

ciscoPIKE: awesome

chUKeeMORPHine: hang on

chUKeeMORPHine: whats her name

ciscoPIKE: why do you need to know that

chUKeeMORPHine: You know I like to keep track of my guest list

ciscoPIKE: oh okay

chUKeeMORPHine: Also, for my Christmas card list

ciscoPIKE: ha-ha

chUKeeMORPHine: So...?

ciscoPIKE: Her name's Sarie Holland classmate of mine real sweet girl

chUKeeMORPHine: Another honor student eh? Well then I look forward to meeting her. Does she have an attractive mother?

ciscoPIKE: ha-ha

chUKeeMORPHine: peace brudda

ciscoPIKE: peace

Online conversation from private chat room in Big Bust V: The West Coast Connection (CultureWerks Games, 2013). 12/9/13 10:37 p.m.

chUKeeMORPHine: Yo keef

KeithBurns06: Hey

chUKeeMORPHine: we might have a little problem

KeithBurns06: what's that man?

chUKeeMORPHine: remember that rumor about some chick getting busted a few blocks away from us right before Thanksgiving

KeithBurns06: yeah?

chUKeeMORPHine: got a feeling she might be coming for a visit Tuesday night. We'll need the gear and some more guys

KeithBurns06: on it

chUKeeMORPHine: hit your usual sources too and see what the good word on the street is, see if she's somebody we need to worry about. Her name is

chUKeeMORPHine: Sarie Holland

KeithBurns06: absolutely

chUKeeMORPHine: either way once that bitch is stripped we'll know if she flipped

Text exchange between CI #137 and Andrew Pike. 12/9/13 10:49 p.m.

PIKE: Hey you up?

CI #137: Yep

PIKE: We're all set. Tues night at 9

CI #137: Great

PIKE: you're gonna see, there's nothing to worry about, we'll be able to fix this

CI #137: ok

CI #137: gotta go study now

PIKE: kk

PIKE: thinking about you

CI #137: me too

New clips cut and pasted into CI #137's handwritten "crime book" journal:

Man concocted kidnap story to cover a bad drug deal, cops say (12/9/13)

Police investigate Newbold home invasion (12/9/13)

D.A.'s office tosses 12 cases tied to disgraced cop (12/7/13)

2 suspects sought in NE Phila. home invasion (12/5/13)

Ex-officer convicted of tipping relative to drug probe (12/4/13)

Reports: 2 dead, 3 wounded in overnight shootings (12/2/13)

Closing arguments to get under way in Philadelphia police officer corruption trial (12/2/13)

Victim in N. Philly home invasion tells of terror, beating (12/2/13)

THE WATERFRONT

MONDAY, DECEMBER 9

As far as body dump sites go, the Lobster Trap is a pretty clever setup.

Best Ringo has seen in quite some time (not that he was dumping bodies in Nowhere, Kansas, but before that, back in the day). Head south down Delaware Avenue—yeah, Ringo knows it's called Columbus Boulevard now, but it'll always be Delaware Avenue in his heart—and all you see are big box chains, fast food places, a PA license center, a strip club, union halls, whatever. What you don't see are the rotting piers behind all that. A billion years ago, Ringo's grandfather worked on those piers as a dock walloper, heaving crates of pineapples or sacks of sugar or heavy train parts or whatever else came chugging up the river. Philly was a port town, and those piers fed thousands of families who lived in the neighborhoods surrounding them. But now those piers have either fallen into the river or stick out into the cold water, looking around like they're asking, *What the fuck did we do?* Some are fenced off, awaiting possible development.

Like *this* fenced-off pier—number 63.

Back in Ringo's grandpop's day, this was a train yard for the Baltimore & Ohio Railroad. All that's left now is a crumbling pier where trains used to be backed right up to the river's edge so goods could be loaded. The metal rails themselves had long been stripped away, but the track work remained, sort of, and had been overrun by weeds and trees and garbage and feral cats. Not that you can see any of this from Delaware Avenue. A huge retail store—one of the ones that this year is holding a fund drive to help their employees with holiday bills because they're too cheap to pay them a decent wage—blocks the view to the river. And yeah, there's allegedly security back there, but when security is barely making more than minimum wage, it's pretty easy to suddenly have security working for you.

Ringo and Frankenstein pull the white van into the parking spot that's farthest from the store, then load the stiff into a shopping cart. Better than dragging it down to the pier. They carry the stiff through a hole in the chain-link fence—somebody else did that, not them—and then walk it out onto the tracks. The breeze off the river is seriously cold. Ringo regrets not wearing an extra layer. Even poor Frankenstein looks like he's shivering, and Ringo didn't think that bastard could feel anything.

"How many you think we got down there?"

"What do you mean?" asks Frankenstein.

"Bodies, how many? I've kind of lost count at this point. Then you've got the stiff that Lisa and Bird are bringing down here. I'm just wondering how many dead bodies are floating beneath our feet."

"Why are you asking that, man? Why would you ask something like that?"

Ringo stares down through the slats into the dark, dark water. *Yo, show of hands, how many of you got chunks of concrete tied to your ankles? Come on, don't be shy, I know your hands are free.*

Thing is, he does wonder. Wonders how many bodies they're going to stick down into the river before this whole thing is over. How many rats can there be in one city, anyway? How many nickels can he make?

There's a moment when Frankenstein looks like he could just lift that piece. Lift it and point it at Ringo's face and squeeze the trigger like it's nothing, just to shut him up. But then he shakes it off, remembering himself, the paycheck, his boss.

"Come on let's get the fuck out of here," Frankenstein says.

"Be right there."

While Frankenstein has his back turned, Ringo takes the snub-nose

revolver from out of his tube sock and tucks it under the rails for possible future use. Hey, when someone as ugly as that eye-fucks you, you
need to keep your defense options open.

FOX CHASE

TUESDAY, DECEMBER 10

It's 8:00 a.m. and the snow is coming down in big, wet flakes. Marty
received the email alert two and a half hours earlier, even before the
first flake had dropped: All public and parochial schools are closed today. Which is the best news ever. That means nobody has to leave the
house today, which means nothing bad can happen to anyone. Maybe
Dad will let them bake cookies, put on a movie.

But no. Sarie's already in and out of the shower and getting dressed.

"Where are you going? School's canceled."

"Unfortunately, final exams somehow find a way to carry on," she
says, rushing past him.

Marty checks the street from his bedroom window. It's getting bad
out there fast, and the Civic's not exactly equipped for snow travel.
Now he's worried all over again. He plays around with Diggit for a few
minutes but then starts hearing a fight downstairs. Marty moves down
the staircase, perching himself halfway down to listen.

"If I don't go, I fail history!"

"I'll call your teacher. Give me his number."

"He's a *she*. But Dad, no, seriously, I'll be fine. I know how to drive
in the snow, I'm not like Mom. I keep it in second and pop it up into
first when I hit some hills."

"The news is telling people to stay off the roads unless it's an
emergency. Believe me, your professor will understand. She's probably
canceling it now—have you checked your email?"

"Jesus, Dad, are you really the only father in the world right now trying to talk his daughter out of taking a final?"

"You're not going out in this weather."

"I have to."

"No you don't."

"I'm not like you, Dad, I can actually fucking drive!"

After a few seconds the door slams like a shotgun. Marty hears his father say the f word under his breath a few times. Before his father has the chance to come back into the living room, Marty spins around and pads back up the stairs as quietly as he can and makes it to his bedroom window in time to see Sarie driving away. Her tires leave perfectly symmetrical tracks in the snow. She is a good driver, but it's not her driving that worries Marty. It's the rest of Philadelphia.

Something Dad said sticks in his mind. *Have you checked your email?* Sarie left before she could. So Marty goes back downstairs, sneaking past Dad (who's fuming in the kitchen, banging around dishes) and goes down to Sarie's desk in the den, where he opens her laptop. Her email app opens up, no password protection. Sure enough, there is an email from her history professor, Calkins. Weird thing is, it's from two hours ago. Marty clicks on it.

Whoa. Professor Calkins did postpone the exam, told everyone to stay safe out there, details on the rescheduled exam to follow. So where is Sarie headed?

It hasn't worked worth a damn since he put it in her car, but Marty tries activating the homing chip again. He doesn't want to worry Dad unless he knows for sure something's wrong.

DECEMBER 10

Living with the lie of the final exam means I have to pretend like I'm reporting to class to take the exam anyway. I sit in the library with

D.'s $4.99 beat-up paperback copy of *Naked Lunch,* trying to wrap my head around it. His scribbled annotations don't help much. For one thing, I can barely read them; his handwriting is that shitty. But it's also the story (if you could call it that). I find myself drifting away from the text and looking outside. The snow is really piling up on the streets. What if I'm stranded here in the campus library?

Dad texts me; I ignore it, as I'm supposed to be in the middle of a two-hour exam. I hit him back an hour later telling him I'm joining an honors program study group for the philosophy exam tomorrow. He asks if I'll be home for dinner. I tell him I'll let him know. (I know I won't.) The snow continues to fall as I continue to plow through the book. One line from *Naked Lunch* jumps out at me:

"A curse. Been in our family for generations. The Lees have always been perverts."

And there's one that D. underlined twice:

"Ever see a hot shot hit, kid? I saw the Gimp catch one in Philly. We rigged his room with a one-way whorehouse mirror and charged a sawski to watch it. He never got the needle out of his arm. They don't if the shot is right."

I have to admit the part about the talking asshole is pretty funny.

Then, four to six inches later, it's finally time to leave. I have a busy evening ahead of me.

Despite the raging storm, I somehow make it alive to NFU-CS, where I'm wired up. Wildey ushers me into his classroom/office. I resist the urge to ask him if his asshole talks.

Like everything else, it doesn't go the way I expect. For starters, there is no wire.

—What do you mean there's no wire?

—You watch too much cable TV, Honors Girl.

Wildey plucks something off his desk and shows me this tiny black circle, no bigger than a dime, pinched between his two meaty fingers. And now I understand why Wildey asked me to wear a button-down shirt, preferably one with dark plastic buttons. I thought that's because it would make it easier for him to tape a wire somewhere on my torso.

—Come here. Need to sew this onto your shirt.

—Wait. You don't have someone real who does this? Like a tech guy?

—We're a small unit.

—Do you even know how to sew?

—I'm a bachelor. I know how to sew.

There's a supremely awkward moment where I debate what would be easier/not quite as creepy—me, taking my shirt off so he can sew on the bug, or him, working with a needle in close proximity to my chest. The former seems way too stripteasy, so I go for the latter.

As Wildey sews the bug to her shirt he notices she's trembling—a fast, fevered tremor that he's only noticing now that his hands are just an inch from her body. She's like a hummingbird.

"You okay?"

"I'm fine. I just have a lot to do. It's finals week, and then there's this..."

"Just relax."

"I'm fine! I just have a lot of work to do and I'm really not sure about what exactly you want me to do!"

Wildey can almost hear the internal combustion engine rev up as she spits out the words.

"I used to do a lot of undercover work," Wildey says. "Buy and busts, you know, that kind of thing. I was nervous, too, at first. But then a buddy of mine told me about emptying the bucket."

She glances down at him, but Wildey keeps his focus on the bug and the needle and thread. He knows he has her attention now.

"The bucket?"

"Yeah, the bucket. The one we all carry around with us, full of our worries and doubts and fears. All that shit. So what my man told me to do was, before every undercover job, imagine that bucket in your hands. Count to three, slow as you can. Then dump it out."

"Dump the imaginary bucket."

"Yeah yeah, I know it sounds all new agey, but trust me, Honors Girl. This shit works. And don't worry. The bucket fills itself up again soon enough. But for the next ten, fifteen minutes, maybe even an hour, you've got nothing but an empty bucket. Nobody can touch you."

Wildey finishes up with the bug, then finally glances at her. She has this look on her face like, What the fuck are you talking about? But the funny thing is—that tremor, shaking her whole body? Not as strong. As if her nervous system downshifted to a lower gear.

"There. You're all set."

"Wait."

"What?"

"The button doesn't match."

"What do you mean?"

"Look at it! Anybody with half a brain will realize that one of these things does not look like the other."

"Nobody's going to be looking at your buttons. You're not exactly, uh, busting out in that department."

"Jerk."

Wildey spreads his hands like, well, you asked.

"You should have told me what you were planning! I could have matched it better. Shit, Wildey...they're going to spot it right away. And they're going to know what I'm doing there."

"There you go, pouring water into your own bucket."

"Fuck your bucket! I need to go home and find a sweater or something."

"Uh-uh. No time. You're set to pick up your, uh, contact in about fifteen minutes, right? Besides, I don't want another layer of clothes on top of the bug. I want to make sure I can hear *everything*."

I excuse myself, and Wildey asks where I'm going. I tell him the ladies' room. Which is actually a boys' room, as evidenced by a row of urinals along one wall. Whatever. A quick check in a fogged-over mirror confirms it. The button's like two sizes bigger than the others. Different shade of black, too.

Back in the classroom/office, I ask Wildey what he wants me to do. He leans back in his chair, clasps his big hands behind his head, and smiles.

—Empty your bucket.

—It'll be empty, okay? Enough with the bucket. What next?

—Next, get your boyfriend's contact man to talk business in front of you.

—I have a feeling I might be escorted out of the room before anyone discusses business.

—Then be all clingy with the boyfriend.

—What? Are you serious?

—Pretend like you don't give a fuck about what they're talking about. You're all about the boyfriend. You're thinking about being alone with him. Or maybe you're all impressed with him. Yeah, that's it. You love your Oxy, and you're impressed your man's such a player.

—Uh, I don't know about that. Why don't you just let me try it my way.

—Your way, huh. Okay, Honors Girl. Do it your way. Just keep 'em talking.

—Okay.

—One more thing, I'm gonna give you money. Buy some shit if you can. If the opportunity comes up.

— You want me to buy drugs?

— Yeah. I'm going to give you the money, you're going to give me the drugs later. That's how this works.

— Great.

— Buy a gun, too, if you can.

— What!?

— Okay, I'm messing around with you about that. But if it comes up...

— Why the hell would I buy a gun?

— A weapons charge on Chuckie would make my job a whole lot easier.

— Sure. A gun. Some drugs. Anything else? Want me to see if he has a suitcase nuke, maybe some ricin?

— The gun sure would be sweet.

And then he laughs and I tell him fuck you, which makes him laugh even harder.

FOX CHASE

TUESDAY, DECEMBER 10

Three sad beers in, Kevin Holland comes to the revelation that he's been completely dropping the ball when it comes to his firstborn child.

He wants to call Laura in Mexico City (even though he knows she's not there, it's just easier to pretend she is) and confess to her that he's been parenting on auto-pilot, assuming that everything is okay. Sarie was supposed to be the stable one, she's always been the stable one. In fact, when Sarie started at St. Jude's U., she treated it like high school — report for classes, drive straight home, do homework, do chores, go to bed, repeat process. Which struck Kevin as the wrong way to do it. Bizarre as it sounds, Kevin started fighting with Sarie over staying on campus longer, while she insisted on coming home. Was she just being petulant about not being able to go to UCLA? Who knows.

Now she's taking the opposite tack, staying out all hours doing God knows what (with that kid Drew—*had* to be that fucking no-good-news kid), and, ha-ha, joke's on you, Dad. Because you did this to your parents, too, didn't you? How does it feeeeeel, his inner Bob Dylan whines.

Well, Laura, I promise, swear to God, enough of this shit.

When she comes home Kevin's going to have that hard talk with her. That if she fucks up her grades now it's going to make transferring to UCLA all that more difficult. Yeah, he'll have to ruin the surprise (the possible job out in L.A. was by no means a sure thing but is looking good). Then again maybe the prospect will help snap things back into place. He cracks another can of Yuengling and perches on the couch, flipping channels, waiting for his daughter to text to let him know when she'll be home.

He falls asleep before she does.

DECEMBER 10 (later)

In the car, D. goes through the tapes in my glove box again, saying we need appropriate party music. I'm not thinking about parties. I'm thinking about the mismatched button on my shirt that's transmitting everything we say to Wildey's ears. When I picked up D. and he heaved himself into the passenger seat, I put a finger to his lips and widened my eyes. But he misunderstood and kissed my fingertip. I pulled my hand away and shook my head. What, he said, then I handed him a Post-it note I'd scribbled beforehand: DON'T SAY ANYTHING YOU DON'T WANT RECORDED. He looked at the note, looked at me, looked at the note, then made some frenzied, bug-eyed gesture at his chest that I assumed was the universal sign for, Oh fuck, you're wearing a wire? I said nothing, snatching the note from his hand and crushing it up into a tiny ball that I shoved deep into my jeans pocket.

So tonight on my to-do list:

1. Get Chuckie talking business
2. Buy Oxys
3. Buy a gun
4. Prepare for my 8:30 philosophy final

Wildey follows the Civic down icy Broad Street, careful to keep a few car lengths of distance. He loses sight of it half a dozen times between campus and City Hall. Okay, yeah, he'll admit it: Tailing somebody is not exactly one of his strengths. Wildey didn't learn how to drive a car until he was twenty-five — where he grew up, you didn't really need a car unless you were involved in the life. Five years later, he's still very like a new driver.

Not that he needs to follow Honors Girl so closely; he has the address. But what if this is a setup? And someone takes a run at her between campus and the address?

Funny how Honors Girl still won't admit to the existence of the boyfriend — even though there he is, in the passenger seat. He listens in, though they're not saying much that Wildey can understand.

Your dad has rad taste in music.

Yeah.

Holy shit, he has Jim Carroll. Catholic Boy.

Yeah?

Those are people who died, who died, all my friends, they died

. . .

You okay, Sarie?

Uh-huh. Just got a lot on my mind. Eight thirty exam tomorrow.

Who?

Curnow.

Oh man. But here's the trick with Curnow. He doesn't do this all the time, but sometimes he'll throw in a trick to see if you're paying attention. Make sure you skim all of the questions first before you answer any of them. You might see a question, like, "If you haven't made a mark in your blue book yet, just answer the last question and turn in your exam and enjoy the holidays."

Times like these, Wildey is very glad he never bothered with college. Sounds like a lot of mind fucking.

Oh, you're going to want to park off Front, near Ninety-five. Chuckie says it's impossible to find a spot anywhere near his street.

Okay.

...all my friends, and they died...

Damn. This means Wildey is going to have to trail them for five blocks without being spotted.

But that's okay, because he has backup this time—Kaz loaned him Streicher and Sepanic, a two-man surveillance detail from the NFU-CS. They're already in an unmarked van on the edge of Dickinson Square Park, just two blocks from the target house. Everything Wildey hears, they're hearing. Something goes wrong, they'll be able to call for backup while Wildey goes in.

Honors Girl parks under I-95 in a no-charge lot for a nearby movie theater. Luckily someone plowed most of it this afternoon, after the snow stopped falling. Wildey pulls his car into a spot on the opposite side and watches them. This is one of these slowly changing neighborhoods—oldheads call it South Philly, hipster-gentrifiers want to call it Pennsport. Here along Front and Second streets, you can see the progress. The tiny, cramped blocks are decked out with Christmas lights and tinsel and ornaments. But venture a few blocks west and things change rapidly. There are sharp boundaries within Philly neighborhoods. You may not be able to see them, but you can definitely feel them.

The target is 527 Vernon Street, a small brick row house in the middle of a block.

Get ready, Chuckie. We're coming for you.

I park the Civic and hear the roar of the highway above us. It's freezing, and there's a lot of snow and ice on the ground. Take the wrong step onto some black ice and you'd go down fast. I loop my arm through D.'s for stability. (Well, mostly for the stability.) We walk west on Vernon Street. Cute blocks, lots of lights and decorations. Then the phone in my pocket starts vibrating. My real phone. Probably Dad. But when I pull it out I see that it's actually Partyman, which is completely random. The text, though, sends a chill through my veins:

—Morphine knows.

What the hell? How does he even know Chuckie Morphine, let alone know what he (allegedly) knows? Shit shit shit…

D. nods at my phone.

—Who's that?

—Nobody.

—It was that cop, wasn't it? I don't mean to be paranoid, but we're going to have to handle this cop thing very care—

—Shut up, it was Tammy. Hang on.

How does Partyman even know where I am? How does he know Chuckie Morphine? Worry about that later. Focus on what I know: Partyman is involved in the local drug trade. He knows me. Somehow, he knows where I'm headed. Which means he knows things I don't know.

—C'mon.

—One second.

I text back: Knows what?

D. is practically dragging me by the arm.

—Seriously, Sarie, I don't want to be late.

We cross Second Street, passing a bar on the corner called Dugan's Den, which is the only sign of life out here tonight. I have about three blocks to make a decision. If I leave the wire on and Chuckie finds it, the two of us are fucked. If I remove the wire, then this whole thing will be for nothing. I glance behind us. Wildey is out there somewhere, following us. I could break away from D. right now and go running back, have Wildey get me the fuck out of here…

And then what, genius? What's your next move? Watch D. get busted, and then be forced to testify against him? This is your chance to make all of this right.

So I decide to leave the button where it is. Even though it clearly doesn't match. Wildey, you'd better be fucking right about this.

Partyman, you'd better text back quick. What does Morphine know?

We arrive at 527 and it's kind of a shithole, at least compared to the other houses on the block. The marble steps are stained and chipped, the tin trim on the top of the house is rusted and flaked, and the windows look fogged over. A big step down from Chuckie's previous place, I must say. Which bugs me. Why would he throw a party here? As if on cue, my real phone buzzes again. I look down at the message:

—He's going to check you for a wire.

The man Sarie Holland calls Partyman places his cell on the bar top and orders another Budweiser. Nothing on tap in this place, which is disappointing, so he sticks to bottles. Aside from a few modern-day Eagles and Phillies banners on the rafters, everything here has that frozen-in-time look. Otherwise, as they said in *The Apartment,* it's Dullsville. The paint is dull, the floorboards dull, the vinyl on the stools dull, the conversation dull, the drone of the TV dull. The only thing that shines is the bar top, polished to a high sheen by millions of elbows rubbing against it since the Great Depression. He loves it all. He thanks the bartender, Sherry, for the Bud, takes a long pull, then checks his phone. No reply.

What's he doing, exactly? Why does he care?

He could explain it to his superiors easily enough, he supposes. Following leads, testing the local waters, pushing one side to see what the other would do. Stirring it up. But there's a deeper truth, he realizes, one he'd never admit to his superiors.

He likes the girl. He doesn't want to see her end up with a bullet in her head and dumped into some ravine.

So when her name came up on the back chatter of Big Bust V (Christ, you'd be surprised how many dealers talked openly in those chat rooms, like they're all the first ones to think of that particular joke), he wrestled with his decision. Wrestled hard. Then he determined that a world without Sarie Holland would be a much more dull one.

He orders another Bud, cracks a joke with Sherry, asks her if they have some kind of menu. Sherry says she'll see what she can do.

—Heyyyyy! D-Train!

The moment I see him, I realize that D. isn't kidding. There is something very strange and familiar about Chuckie Morphine.

He turns out to be a seriously older dude (at least in his fifties) with slicked-back hair and a suit, standing in the middle of an empty living room surrounded by four gruff older dudes who could play any number of roles. Put hard hats on them and they'd be construction workers. Put blue shirts on them and they'd be cops. But now they're wearing leather jackets, boots, and jeans, so they look like bikers. And not the kind who are in the mood to party.

But what's strange is that Chuckie looks soooo fucking familiar....

—And this must be the lovely Sarie! So great to finally meet you.

—Hi.

D. nudges me on the shoulder and smiles.

—So? Does his face ring a bell?

I stare at D., my eyes pleading for help, because, yeah, he does look familiar, but I seriously can't place it. Before I can speculate, though, Chuckie waves his hands dismissively, then puts an index finger to his lips. D. blinks, confused.

—Proper greetings first, brother.

A biker guy with long, skunklike hair steps forward, small black gizmo in his hands. My gut sinks. Partyman was right. They're going to sweep for surveillance. And in a few seconds, that gizmo is going to go off when it comes near my fake, oversized, ill-matching button.

Wildey is huffing cold air, hanging by a thread, waiting for Honors Girl to speak. *Doesn't he look familiar?* the boyfriend said. And then...nothing. So wait—does Honors Girl know this guy after all?

Come on, somebody say or do *something*.

There's only one thing I can do: empty my bucket, just like Wildey taught me...and fill it back up with a little bit of crazy.

Chuckie must have seen me flinch, so he tries to reassure me this will all be over in a second, you understand, a guy like me has to be careful. I channel my inner excited puppy dog.

—Oh this is just like the movies! So fucking cool!

—Just a precaution, sweetie. You understand.

—Hang on, hang on! I know exactly what to do.

I smile and take a step back and start unbuttoning my shirt.

Pretty much every eye in the room—including D.'s—is fixed on me in total surprise. They can't believe what I'm doing. To be honest, I can't believe it, either.

—Sarie, what are you...

—Trust me, big guy. I know what I'm doing.

—Are you drunk?

One, two buttons, and when I reach the third, the mismatching bug, I do a playful little twirl on my heel.

There's the rustle of fabric, a loud brushing sound like someone's taken a broom to a microphone, then a few seconds before a hollow POP.

"No," Wildey says, out in the cold.

The wire is dead.

She killed the fucking wire!

Why?

Trust me, big guy, I know what I'm doing.

That was meant for him, wasn't it?

Fuck. What the hell is she doing? Wildey is at the corner of Fifth and Vernon, hanging near an abandoned beauty shop. About a dozen sun-faded portraits of Marilyn Monroe, snipped from fashion magazines, stare back at him. Fuck, he needs a closer look. Streicher and Sepanic check in almost immediately, telling Wildey what he already knows. The wire has gone dead.

I heel-smash the bug, popping it like a tick. I stumble a little, as if I'm a silly girl who's had a vodkatini or three, laughing to disguise the sound of the crunch. To me, the pop echoes throughout this empty living room. But they're too busy looking at my bra to notice. I hope. Chuckie Morphine locks eyes with me.

—Not that I didn't enjoy that show, but we're going to sweep you anyway. It's not like the movies, darling.

—Chuckie, man, you don't have to do this, Sarie's cool.

—I'm totally not wearing a wire! Well, maybe an underwire.

D. gawks at me like I'm insane. Perhaps I am—wearing a bra, a crushed police surveillance device under the heel of my shoe— joking around with a drug kingpin.

—Sweep 'em, Keith.

Keith, the maybe-biker with the frizzy skunk hair, sweeps us, lingering on my tits for some strange reason. After he's been cleared, D. stoops down to retrieve my shirt and gives me the puzzle-eyes as he hands it back.

—Here.

(Eyes all going: What the fuck was that?)

—Thanks.

(My eyes going: Trust me.)

In the end, Keith finds nothing interesting, not even noticing the broken button on the floor. Chuckie nods.

—Okay, Keith, good stuff, why don't you and Drop head outside and make sure our girl doesn't have an older brother waiting outside.

D. is insulted.

—Chuckie, man, for real? You don't have to do that.

The more I analyze the features of Mr. Morphine, the more the webs in my brain clear away. He is familiar and it's starting to kill me. So, so familiar. But from where? Maybe if I'd had more time, it would have come to me naturally. Instead Chuckie Morphine himself clues me in.

—So, you take my brother's final exam yet or what?

Wildey's about three houses away from 527 when the door opens and two thick-necked goons in leather jackets come tumbling out. The street is narrow. There are no places to run. If he bolts now they will catch him. Wildey is sure of that. The only thing to do is commit to his undercover role, like he's just another corner boy in a hoodie walking down the street. Wildey flicks his eyes up at the bikers—*Just walkin' here.* They glare back at him—*You'd better keep walkin'.* They fall in line behind him and unofficially escort him all the way to Sixth, where Wildey hangs a right. Damn it, Sarie, why did you kill the wire? Are you in trouble? Have they already done something to you?

Trust me, big guy.

D. smiles like a lunatic.

—See? I told you, once you met him, you'd understand!

And now I do.

"Chuckie Morphine" is actually Charles Chaykin...brother of Professor Edward Chaykin, my honors lit teacher. As well as D.'s honors lit teacher, from two years back. Chuckie is the "yuppie scum brother" Professor Chaykin refers to in class whenever he goes on a tear about the antimaterialistic Beat poets of the 1950s (his personal heroes). Makes sense and it doesn't make sense at the same time. I feel like my entire world just tilted a few degrees to the left.

—Come on back, kids. Let's talk about your little police problem.

Chuckie leads us back, along with two other biker dudes. Along the way D. explains, excitedly, like he's been bursting to tell me. The whole thing started at a holiday party for honors kids that Chaykin (the professor, not the kingpin) held at his house up in Mt. Airy after finals. (Presumably I'm to receive the same invitation after my lit final this Friday—that is, if his brother doesn't kill me tonight.) Toward the end of the night, after the crowd had thinned to almost nobody, Professor Chaykin offered a joint to D.; D. took him up on it. One thing led to another and soon D. was scoring from Professor Chaykin, for himself, then for friends, and then at another party the following summer Professor Chaykin introduced D. to his supplier—his brother.

I grab D.'s arm.

—You said nobody knew Chuckie Morphine's real name.

D. looks at me, half sheepish, half proud.

—I was protecting you.

The three of us sit around a foldout table in the kitchen. The two bikers take up posts at the doorway and a back exit, presumably leading to a tiny yard.

—Cozy, I know, but what can I do?

—I thought this was a party, Chuckie…

—Do you live here, Mr. Chaykin?

—Please, sweetie, call me Chuckie. Mr. Chaykin was my father, and thank fuck that perverted old sadist is buried in de cold, cold ground. Anyway, as to who lives in this domicile, nobody at the moment. So we have it all to ourselves for the time being. And no, Mr. P., I'm not exactly in the mood to party.

—Chuckie's in real estate. That's how he—

Chuckie raises a chiding eyebrow at D.

—You sure do like to narrate, don't you, D. What else did you tell your girlfriend, hmmm?

—Nothing, man! You know that.

—He hasn't told me anything, Mr. Chaykin.

—What do I have to do for you to call me Chuckie? Take off my shirt and tie, be less formal? Believe me, you don't want to see that spectacle. I was already fat and sagging the day you were born.

There's an awkward moment of silence as our eyes flit back and forth. Chuckie's eyes flit on fast-forward, like he's trying to take us both in, brain-scan us, analyze us.

—Okay, Serafina Holland, my man here tells me you're good people. But here's the weird thing, and maybe you can illuminate some things for us? We heard a rumor that some pretty young Latino girl was busted near Pat's Steaks on November 27 and subsequently began to work for the Philadelphia Police Department and—

—I'm not—

—Please don't interrupt me, sweetie, it's rude. I know you're working with the PPD. Tall, handsome, and stoned here told me as much. But you've been feeding them everybody but me.

D. turns red, won't look at me. Son of a bitch. He told Chuckie/Chaykin here that I was a CI! Why did he do that?

—D.? What the hell?

D. finally has a mea culpa look in his eye.

—Look, Chuckie can help us, I told you that. That means being completely honest and open with him about—

—You asshole!

—Sarie, seriously, this is the only way we can—

Chuckie tap-tap-taps the table with an oversized gold ring.

—Kids, you can fight later. What I want to know is more about this cop, what's his name, Wildey—

—Will-dee.

—I'm sorry?

—He pronounces it *will-dee.*

—Well, thank you for that, sweetie. It's always important to know the correct pronunciations of the names of people who wish to prosecute you. Did you know my surname should be pronounced SHAY-kin, as in, what's shakin', baby? But everyone does the hard chuh, drives me fuckin' bonkers. Which is why I go by my admittedly silly alias, which I came up with in Cabo back in eighty-nine...but that's another story. Back to Will-dee...see, once you point it out, I won't forget. Will-dee maintains his Gamera-sized hard-on for me and won't leave you alone, is that it?

—He's very interested in your business, yes.

—And you've told him as little as possible about my business, yes?

—She hasn't said a thing!

—Hey. Boychik. Shut the fuck up and let the girl answer.

I swallow and empty my bucket. No time for the cray-cray anymore. Now it is time to fill it with 100-proof sincerity.

—He's right. I haven't said a thing. I'm working for them but targeting other dealers. I'm doing all this to protect D.

The way D. looks at me when he hears those words—as if he's just clued into this fact for the very first time.

—Well, let's be sure about that.

And that's when the tools come out.

Wildey tells Streicher and Sepanic to maintain their positions. Honors Girl said to trust her, so that's what he's going to do. For now. That doesn't mean he can't move in for a closer look. The front is out, but the interesting thing about this little slice of South Philly is that alleyways run through the blocks. He finds one off Sixth. The concrete pathway is bowed, presumably so rain will wash away the dirt and grime, but it clearly hasn't rained in this alley for fifty years. Broken glass, syringes, cigarette butts, and broken plastic toys litter his path. Wildey steps past them the best he can and then turns a corner . . . right into a ratty wooden gate with a thick padlock on a hinge.

The skunk biker behind me grabs a fistful of my hair and yanks it back. Something cold and sharp touches my neck right below the left earlobe. The biker standing behind D. also grabs a fistful of his hair and jerks back, only he doesn't have a knife or ice pick or whatever. Instead he's holding a hammer, wrist slightly turned so that he'll be able to bring it up and give it a good THWOK at a moment's notice.

D. doesn't see this. He's too busy arguing with Chuckie.

—Chuckie…what the fuck…you said you could help us!

—D., my good friend, for the remainder of this conversation I'd very much like you to shut the fuck up. Now, Ms. Holland, I do apologize for the theatrics but this is business, and sadly, sometimes this is how one must conduct business.

—You don't have to threaten us!

—Everyone always says that. But the truth is, sweetie, I do. I really do. Just like you felt that you had to do that silly little striptease out there in a vain attempt to build trust between us. But, see, you didn't just reveal your pert little bosom to me. You revealed a great deal more. You revealed that you're not the wide-eyed innocent that D. thinks you are. And that worries me. So why don't you tell me what you're doing here, Ms. Holland?

I swallow, try to stay calm.

—Just like D. told you, we came here for help.

Chuckie Morphine nods. The fingers in my hair tighten to hold me still and I feel a jab in the side of my neck. I gasp because my skin processes it a second before I do. I've been stabbed. This guy stabbed me in the side of the neck. D. bucks in his seat.

—Chuckie you fucking asshole!

Blood trickles down my neck and around my clavicle. Every instinct tells me to twist my head away, but I can't. My hair is being held in an iron grip. Chuckie leans forward, locks eyes with me.

—Lie to me again and it goes all the way in.

In this moment, Mom, I know things will never be the same, that I will never be the same. Since I got (sort of) arrested I've been pretending, just playing a role, telling myself that none of this is permanent. That I can go back to the way things were. But there's no going back now. I suppose I've known that for a while. So I fill Wildey's proverbial bucket with a few gallons of I Don't Give A Fuck, the only thing I have left, and dive in.

Despite the hand in my hair and the pointy object at my throat, I narrow my eyes and lean forward a little. Just a fraction of an inch, but I want him to know I'm not afraid.

— You're afraid they're coming for you, aren't you, Chuckie?

His carefully composed face drops a little.

— Afraid? Afraid of who?

— I'm sure you've heard the stories about drug gangs getting hit by strike teams. And you're wondering if I'm the scout dog, sniffing you out, setting you up for an attack.

Chaykin laughs.

— Oh, D., where did you find this one? She's a scream! Wait; don't answer that. You're supposed to be shutting the fuck up. Okay, Ms. Thing…and I can't believe you're really going to make me ask the question…but are you the scout dog?

— No.

— But you are a confidential informant for the Philadelphia Police Department.

— Not anymore.

He laughs, but it quickly dies in his throat.

— I'm sorry, what?

— Because now I'm working for you.

The howl of laughter that rolls out of Chuckie's mouth fills the kitchen and startles all of us, including the guys holding the knives, which is not good. I briefly wonder what the fuck I think I'm doing. I have no secret weapon, no trick to play. I'm winging it. Chuckie's laughter dies down and he says softly, almost as if muttering to himself:

— Working for me, huh.

*   *   *

Ignore the searing pain in your knees, Wildey tells himself, as he lands on the opposite side of the gate, trying to keep as quiet as possible. Because you know it's going to hurt. You gain nothing by complaining. He crouches down, moving as swiftly as he can along the freezing alley, counting the backs of the houses, looking for 527. Your knees don't mean shit. Getting to her, keeping her safe . . . that's the only thing that matters now.

My eyes do not waver. I do not blink. I tell him what I can offer.

—Someone is moving into your market the hard way. I've been doing some research and am close to discovering their identities. I'm also privy to the inside movements of the narcotics field unit tracking you. I can help you work around them.

—How about you just tell me what you know, little girl, and I consider letting the two of you live.

—Give me five thousand dollars in operating cash and in three days I'll lay it all out for you.

—You're something special, aren't you.

—It's a small price for valuable intelligence.

—Why don't you get your tuition money from the police?

—Because I'm not working for them anymore. I'm working for you.

—You keep saying that. What could have possibly brought about this sudden change of allegiance? Perhaps the sharp object held at your neck by my associate Keith there?

I remember D.'s advice about how the best lies are built around a grain of truth.

—Look, the police have been riding me hard for weeks. They're completely incompetent and disorganized. And they can't protect me. Do you know how many confidential informants have died in the past month?

Chuckie looks at the thug behind me, then at the thug with the hammer, then at D.

—Okay, you can speak now. Is your girlfriend here bullshitting me?

D. shakes his head.

—No, Chuckie. This is why I brought her to you, man.

Chuckie looks at me.

—Three days and five grand buys me what, exactly?

Here's where I have to show Chuckie Morphine a little leg.

—The murders of those confidential informants is a concerted effort by a major player trying to dominate the local market, and the narcotics squad has no idea how. I'm in a unique position to uncover the leader of this group, and I will bring him to you, along with details of his operation.

—Really.

—I can also give you information straight from Lieutenant Katrina Mahoney's office.

—The Russkie would-be drug czar?

—My handler reports to her directly.

Chuckie makes a whistling O shape with his mouth.

Now comes the big moment. He's either going to believe me, or I'm going to know what it feels like to be shivved in the neck by a skunk biker.

Finally, after a small piece of forever...

—Well, then. If you can deliver all that, my dear, then you've got yourself a deal. With one stipulation of my own.

—What's that?

—Our friend D. here stays with us. You know, just to give you incentive to deliver.

—No. No, we can't do that…

D. turns his head toward me. As much as he can.

—No, that's a great idea. I stay here, and Sarie…you go do your thing. Seriously. I'll be fine.

His eyes try to convince me, but his face is terrified. Chaykin leans back in his chair.

—Yes, he'll be fine. We'll play Big Bust V. It'll be a party.

—D. has final exams to take!

Chaykin makes a big show of wearily swiveling in his chair so that he's facing D. He extends his arms in a pleading manner.

—Let me ask you, in this very moment, do you give one shit about your final exams?

—No.

Chuckie's eyes flick toward me.

—See, he doesn't care about his final exams. Anything else?

I have no choice but to concede the point. But I also can't leave this house with nothing.

—Your M.O. is to keep moving, which is smart. So I presume you're not going to be at this address much longer.

—Yeah, I like to keep moving. Don't want moss growing on my feet. Or under them. Or whatever.

—So how do I find you?

—I'll give you a safe cell number.

—No. I want an address.

—You want me to trust a police informant with an address?

—How many times do I have to tell you? I'm no longer an informant. I just quit.

—And that just inspires me with confidence! Look, I'll leave a presence here, so why don't you just come back here when you're ready. My guys will let me know you're here. Okay? Okay. Grand. Keith, will you get her a Band-Aid?

*　　*　　*

The puncture in my neck is not that deep and won't require stitches. One of those scare-the-shit-out-of-you wounds. I clean myself up with wet pieces of toilet paper in a cramped bathroom. There's no waste basket, so I save the bloodied little balls of pulp on the side of the sink as I clean up. Guess I can just flush them down the toilet, just like I've pretty much flushed my future away. I check my neck in the mirror and my reflection gives me this look like, What the fuck are you doing? Are you crazy? I continue to imagine my bucket being full of brave crazy, but I can feel it evaporating fast.

I finish up, toss the wad of gross paper into the toilet, push the handle, and hear a dull THUNK and the rattling of a broken chain. Great. You'd think a kingpin would keep a working toilet in the place, you know, for raids?

There's a timid knock-knock-knock at the door. Crap. I close the lid, press more toilet paper to my neck, then open the door. It's D. He slips into the bathroom with me.

—Are you okay?

—I'm fine. But I don't want to leave you here.

—Look, all that was because Chuckie doesn't know you. Hell, I'm not even sure I know you.

He smiles as he says this, but it's a nervous smile. He continues:

—I can make up my exams next week, whatever, I'll just email my professors. And I'll be fine here. He's not going to do anything to me.

—Did you happen to see the guy standing behind you? The one with the hammer?

D. dismisses this.

—Just tell me you can deliver what you promised, that you

weren't just serving up a huge steaming pile of bullshit back there. Because just like his brother, Chuckie has no patience for bullshit. He'll hurt us both.

—What I have is real. I'm coming back for you, D.

—I'll be fine. Really.

He reaches out and takes my hand. The one that isn't holding bloody wads of wet tissue. Then he flashes me this high-wattage smile that's just a little mischievous and gives my hand a squeeze.

—I'm just bummed I have to wait until Friday to see you again.

—And what if we don't?

—Don't what?

—Don't see each other again. Like, ever.

The bright smile fades a bit, and I can see a flicker of real worry in his eyes.

When he leans in close I wonder if he's going to kiss me again. I can feel his breath on my cheek. But I'll never find out because the door opens suddenly and there's Hammer Guy glaring at us, telling me it's time to go.

Without warning the lights go out; the party is over. Which means either this was the shortest party in the history of South Philadelphia or something horrible has just happened. Wildey scrambles down the alley and up over the gate again (*ignore the knees, ignore the knees*) and makes it to the corner of Sixth and Vernon just in time to see a black SUV pull up to 527. A middle-aged man in an overcoat (too far away to see any other details) and two burly bikers hustle inside. No Sarie, no boyfriend. By the time Wildey has his cell to his head, the SUV is peeling away. He gives Streicher and Sepanic the make and plates and tells them to follow the SUV no matter what. *Do not lose sight of it.* The moment the SUV turns the corner, Wildey bolts down the block to the front door. Please God, please, don't do this to me. He's about to smash the door in when S&S call—they're still in pursuit of the SUV, currently headed east on Dickinson. But when they blasted up Fifth they caught a glimpse of Wildey's CI walking east on Tasker.

"Alone?"

"Far as we could tell."

"Thanks, Streicher."

"It's Sepanic."

"Sorry. Always getting the two of you mixed up."

"That's funny, Wild Child."

Streicher's a woman; Sepanic's a dude.

But Wild Child isn't trying to be funny. He's distracted by the mix of relief and anger coursing through his nervous system. Relief he won't have to bust down this door to find his CI slaughtered inside. But also anger that she didn't call him the moment she made it out of the house. What was she thinking? What the hell is going on? That skinny punk with the red pants is probably laughing his ass off right now, isn't he.

Wildey's knees scream as he hauls ass back down Vernon, rounding the corner on Fifth and then heading up to Tasker to see if he can catch her in time. But either Honors Girl is also running or those long legs of hers have carried her a long long way, because she's nowhere in sight. He sends a text to her burner, but by the time he's reached his car there's no response. If you just went home, Serafina Holland, I don't care, I'm busting down your door and arresting you. Me and your Pops can have a good old talk about what you've been up to the past couple of weeks.

A few minutes up I-95 she texts:

MEET ME IN THE STACKS

Stacks—meaning the bookstore in Port Richmond. Rocketing up I-95, Wildey makes it there in seven minutes. The store is temporarily closed, though, and a note from the proprietor informs potential customers that he's attending evening Mass but will return soon.

Wildey finds Honors Girl around the back in the small muddy patch of earth between the store and the highway, sitting on a plastic milk crate. She flinches when Wildey turns the corner, then relaxes when she makes eye contact with him.

"Thought this place would be open."

"It would have been a lot warmer back in your car, where you were supposed to wait for me."

Wildey knows this isn't the time to pound on her, though. She has the wide-eyed look of someone who was nearly sideswiped by a delivery truck and is taking time to appreciate the little things in life, like breathing.

"I asked you to trust me," she says. "You heard me say that, right?"

"Trust only goes so far, Sarie. And right now it's running real thin between us. What the fuck was that back there? Why did you destroy the bug? Which, by the way, is really fuckin' expensive, I've got to tell you."

"Bee tee dubs," she mutters.

"What?"

"Nothing. Chuckie Morphine had a scanner. I had to think fast. Turns out there was no party. He was waiting there for me because he was all paranoid, thinking I was a rat. I had to ditch the bug."

Wildey exhales from his nose, making him look like a steaming bull. "You don't still have it, do you?"

Honors Girl gives him a look like, *duh.*

"No. But I did get this."

She pulls a bag of Oxys out of her coat pocket. Far more pills than the $500 Wildey gave her could have bought.

"Whoa."

"I'm working for him now."

Wildey beams. "I could kiss you. I mean, I'm still pissed off about the bug, but this is good. Real, real good."

Honors Girl just stares at him, perhaps unsure of what to say or weirded out by that whole "kiss you" comment. Where *did* that come from, anyway?

"Tell me everything that happened," Wildey says. "And I mean everything. Starting with Chuckie's real name."

"His name is Charles Chaykin. His day job is real estate. He's the brother of my literature professor."

"What?"

I give Wildey an abridged version of the events at Chuckie's house. I do not tell him that Chuckie knows I am a CI. I do not mention my deal with Chuckie. I do not reveal that D. is essentially a hostage right now. Instead I tell him everything I learned.

Almost everything.

"Chaykin sets up his operation in empty houses before they go on the market. That way he stays ahead of you guys at every turn. Chuckie might be at a certain address for a week, or maybe only a few hours. He handles a lot of property, almost all of it in South Philly, near the river. Mostly Queens Village and Pennsport."

"How do you know that?"

"I just looked it up on the Internet."

"Good, good," Wildey says. "But wait. If he keeps moving, how does he stay in touch with his dealers?"

"Some video game—Big Bust V. There's a series of chat rooms where you can invite certain players. Chuckie leaves messages there for his network of employees."

Wildey nods. Clever asshole. He's read about some dealers keeping in touch online. It's nearly impossible to trace, unless you somehow subpoena the multinational corporation behind the video game.

"But he's moving around more than ever now, paranoid as shit, because apparently there's a gang of cops out there ripping off drug dealers."

"He tell you that?"

"He did, but it only confirmed what I've been reading."

Wildey gives her a sidelong glance. "What do you mean, what you've been reading? There's nothing like that in the papers."

"Are you telling me it isn't true? Read the comments section behind those same articles. That's all people are talking about. So...?"

"Yeah, it's true."

"And how many CIs have disappeared in the past two weeks?"

Wildey can't even look her in the eye.

"Why didn't you tell me? Didn't you think that might be valuable information to share with me? You know, watch your back for a bunch of hired killers who might be coming for you?"

"Would you tell me, if our roles were reversed?"

"If our roles were reversed, I wouldn't be in this mess in the first place."

"You wouldn't have let me go, who you kidding, Honors Girl. You're more law and order than I am."

Cars rocket past on I-95. The wind feels colder by the minute.

"Do you know who's doing it?" Honors Girl asks.

"Between you and me?"

She again gives him the *duh?* look. Who else would she tell? Wildey grapples with the next part. He shouldn't say a word, and he knows it. But it doesn't feel like he's talking to an informant anymore. It's the damnedest thing. He feels like he's talking to a colleague.

"The Loot thinks we have a rat inside our own unit."

"Oh, that's just fucking great. I knew it! If you've read anything about informants, you'd know that this kind of thing happens all the time. Nobody can ever keep a secret. About anything. Ever!"

"Hey. Easy now. More than anybody else, you're protected."

"How's that?"

"Because Kaz never officially entered you in the system. Look, you know from the beginning that we never wanted you—we wanted your boyfriend. And we didn't really want him. We just wanted him long enough to get us to Chuckie, or Chaykin, or whatever the fuck his name is. And now thanks to you, we're on him."

"So I'm free to go?"

Wildey looks at her, dead serious for a moment, then cracks a smile. "That's a good one."

They sit in silence, watching the traffic go by. People headed down-town or up to the Northeast and beyond into Bucks County. People with no pressing worries other than what kind of food they want to order tonight or what movie to put on Netflix. People who speed by these neighborhoods without the slightest idea of what happens in them. Or even if they do, they don't give a shit, because they don't have to live in them.

"I think I can figure this out for you," Sarie Holland says quietly.

"Figure what out?"

"What's going on. Who's killing the CIs, who's ripping off drug dealers. The whole picture."

"That would be great," Wildey says. "You maybe want to clue me in?"

"I said *I can* figure it out for you. But I need more time. Give me forty-eight hours."

"You and your deadlines. They're going to get you into serious trou-ble someday."

DECEMBER 11

I missed my exam today. Slept right through it.

I don't care.

My supervisor from the bursar's office called and left me a

voicemail about an irregularity in one of the student organization accounts. Could I please call back or stop in at the office immediately...

(The $2,000, all in hundreds, is still in my backpack. Along with the $5,000 Chuckie Morphine gave me.)

I don't care.

Dad is pissed and even Marty's looking at me funny.

I can't afford to care about that right now, either.

Because D. is a hostage and I'm pretty much the only one who can save him. I can't tell Wildey, because I just know they'll fuck it up, and I can't risk D.'s life. Not without first giving Chuckie the dirt on the strike teams and springing D.

So fuck exams.

I need information.

And there's only one person in this game who knows more than I do.

Last time they classed it up; this time Partyman thinks they should go down into the alleys and gutters. McGillin's Old Ale House is the oldest continuously operating bar in Philadelphia, established in 1860, just two blocks from City Hall yet serving right through Prohibition, like they didn't hear the news about the Eighteenth Amendment. You have to admire an establishment like that. These are pieces of this city that Partyman cherishes—the places too stubborn to die.

Inside it looks like someone vomited Christmas all over the place—tinsel and lights and cherubic Santas and reindeer. It almost makes him nostalgic. Even though Partyman arrives early to everything, Serafina Holland has beat him here and is waiting for him at a table. Partyman nods, accepts a plastic-covered menu from a server, then takes a seat opposite her. Before he's even gotten the chance to sit down, she leans in close and opens fire.

"How did you know Chuckie Morphine would check me for a wire? How do you even know Chuckie Morphine at all? I thought you worked for Tammy's boyfriend!"

"No, it's safer to say I'm sort of a freelance operative. It's my job to keep an ear to the ground."

"So you know Chuckie?"

"I am indeed familiar with Mr. Chaykin and his operation."

Jesus, she mutters. Partyman scans the menu, settles on a roast beef sandwich with extra horseradish. Oh, and beer. A pitcher of the house ale.

"Can you tell me what kind of guy he is? Because as of a few hours ago I'm working for him."

"That's a very bad idea. He's not a nice man at all. You should have told me you were looking for a job. I could have given you a few leads."

"This is not what I want to hear."

"What *do* you want to hear? You're leading so many double lives you can't keep it straight anymore, can you?"

"What do you mean? You don't even know me."

"I know everything about you, Serafina Holland."

Her face falls.

"Didn't think you looked like a Joan."

"You're not a dealer. You're some kind of cop, aren't you? With the DEA or something?"

"Let's just leave it at *or something.*"

"Will you tell me your name? I don't even care if it's your real name. I'd just like to be able to call you a name."

"I like the name you gave me. Partyman. Makes me sound festive."

"So what else do you know about me?"

Partyman grins. "I know you're a seventeen-year-old honors student whose mother, Laura, died last year, derailing your plans to attend

UCLA. Your father, Kevin, is a drug and alcohol counselor, which may explain why you've pretty much lived the straight and narrow your whole life...until the past two weeks, for some reason."

"Fuck me."

"I'm sorry. I liked you, so I looked into you. I'm really good at looking into people. And your ID is good, but not foolproof. So watch it."

"Please don't arrest me. It's finals week."

Partyman laughs. "That's funny. That's seriously funny."

"Happy to be a source of amusement to you."

"Serafina, listen to me. This life is not for you. Go home. Talk to your father, tell him you really want to go to L.A. He'll make it happen for you, I know he will. It's not too late."

"It is too late. The water's up to my nose and I'm about to drown."

"What would help?"

"A bullet to my brain."

"I'm asking a serious question."

"Okay. Fine." She pauses to bite her lower lip...then blurts it out, hushed and excited at the same time: "You don't happen to know anyone who's kidnapping confidential informants all over town?" As if she expects to shock or stun him.

Instead, Partyman beams. "Shit, that's an easy one. Peter D'Argenio. Your friend's boyfriend. Though I understand that relationship is more Internet-based..."

"Wait, *what?* Don't you work for him?"

"Like I told you, I'm freelance. But as it so happens, we parted ways yesterday. I couldn't work with a man like that any longer."

"Why?"

"Because I found out he was taking CIs off the chessboard. That's just not a nice thing to do. It also exposes his operation in a very stupid way."

The girl looks like she's been smacked. It's almost adorable. It's as if she doesn't know what to say next, though Partyman can predict the exact words she'll say next: *Why are you telling me this?* And, lo:

"Why are you telling me this?"

"Because I know you'll do the right thing."

DECEMBER 11 (later)

I spend the rest of the afternoon wandering around the city, trying to sort it all out in my brain. I know I should have come home right away and started writing this all out, but I knew Dad would be waiting for me, and I didn't want to deal with him. Not before I had the chance to think. The city is fucking freezing, even though the sun is out. People keep bumping into me, pissing me off. Maybe it's me, my indecision. I'm so turned around I don't know which way I'm going. Do I run to Wildey with this? Do I run to Chuckie and let him deal with this? No, I do nothing. Nothing until I've had the chance to think…

When I finally arrive home, Dad is pissed. He pounces on me the moment I step in the door. I tell him I can't do this now, I've got too much on my mind. He says, can't do what, talk to your own father?

—Not now.

—What if I have something important to tell you?

—I don't care! Can't you just get off my back for one second?

—Sarie, what's wrong with you? When did you stop being able to talk to me?

—Oh, now you want to talk to me? Guess what, Dad, it's a little too late.

—What does that mean?

—Go have another beer. I have to study.

I slam the door and go down to my desk and cry.

DECEMBER 12 (early)

Here's what I know:

1. There's a leak in Wildey's narcotics unit
2. Someone is kidnapping (possibly killing) confidential informants
3. Someone is raiding drug houses, posing as cops. Most likely using information from the tortured confidential informants
4. If Partyman is to be believed, then Peter D'Argenio is the one behind all of this

(Can Partyman be believed? Why would he tell me this? What does he have to gain? Is he a bitter ex-employee with an axe to grind? Or a DEA agent? Or something else?)

5. All of which means D'Argenio is trying to move into the drug trade, and is working with the leak in Wildey's narcotics unit

What I need to know:

1. The name of the leak
2. Partyman's deal

I'm not going to find the answers sitting in this den
Even though it's late, I text Tammy
Then, Wildey

*   *   *

FOX CHASE

THURSDAY, DECEMBER 12

The man on the radio says today is set to be the coldest day of the year so far. All Marty knows is that it's pretty frosty in here, too. Dad doesn't say a word all morning, and when Sarie appears in the kitchen it's only for 1.5 seconds—the approximate time it takes her to cross the room and slam the door shut behind her without a word. Which is weird, because Marty knows Sarie doesn't have an exam today (at least according to the handwritten schedule stuck on the fridge with a Portsmouth, NH, magnet). Where's she going? Marty asks his father if something's wrong; he tells his son not to worry, to hurry up and get ready for school. Which is the answer he's come to expect.

Before he leaves for school Marty goes down to the den and pokes around Sarie's desk. Maybe she does have an exam today—or some study group thing? There are books and papers scattered all over the desktop. Lots of blue exam books, a lot of them empty. Sarie must swipe them by the armful. Marty opens what he thinks is a blank one, half-wondering if he should swipe one (might be fun to do some cartoons inside, surprise Sarie), but there's already writing inside.

> Here's what I know:
>
> 1. There's a leak in Wildey's narcotics unit
> 2. Someone is kidnapping (possibly killing) confidential informants
> 3. Someone is raiding drug houses, posing as cops. Most likely using information from the tortured

Marty barely has time to comprehend what he's reading before his dad yells, annoyed, telling him he's going to be late for school.

MOOSE AND SQUIRREL

PORT RICHMOND

THURSDAY, DECEMBER 12

It's scary, the way Honors Girl lays it all out for him.

She has a manila folder full of newspaper clips, handwritten notes (in her impeccably neat script). It's even highlighted. It takes a while for him to process it all, and after he catches on Wildey starts firing questions at her, trying to poke holes in her logic. She answers his questions using clips or notes, and when she doesn't have a clip or a note, she cites a "source close to the organization."

"You're gonna have to tell me more about this source," Wildey says. "That's a big piece of this."

"No," she says. "You protect your sources, I protect mine."

"I can't go to my Loot with a big fat ol' 'trust me.'"

"See, that's exactly my point."

Only when she walks him through it again does Wildey understand the full implications of what she's saying. It's pretty much the unthinkable. The ultimate betrayal.

"Either you sold out your own informants..."

Wildey gives her a stern look. "You know that's about the fuckin' last thing I would do..."

"...or she did."

She, meaning Lieutenant Katrina Mahoney. The head of the NFU-CS. The unofficial drug czarina of Philadelphia.

"No. That can't be."

"I hope not. But there's a way you can find out."

Honors Girl tells Wildey the way. It's big, it's bold, it's potentially crazy. But even Wildey has to agree it's the only move.

The waitress comes back to see if they still don't want coffee. Neither of them says anything; they're too lost in thought. The waitress gives up, shuffles away.

"You don't have to do this," Wildey says after a long while.

"Yes I do," she says. "You know I do."

Yeah, he knows she does, too.

Today is supposed to be a rare day off for his Loot, but Wildey calls her cell; she answers after the first ring. He suggests meeting at that Grey Lodge place, but Kaz tells him she can't leave home.

"Well, I can't do this on the phone."

Kaz sighs. "Fine, come to my fucking house, then."

SPRING GARDEN

The lieutenant is making cabbage and egg *pirozhki* when Wildey arrives. The front hall reeks of sulfur and boiled sweat, which her neighbors must love. Kaz lives in one of those huge brownstone mansions that have been carved up into apartments; hers is on the first floor, rear. Wildey knocks on the door. He hears the Loot yell, "Come on in," and he opens the door and makes his way down a long, skinny hall to the galley kitchen. Weird layout, but that's what you get when you carve up a mansion into ten apartments.

Also weird to see Kaz standing in front of her countertop wearing jeans, a long-sleeved V-neck T-shirt, barefoot, arms all speckled with white flour.

"Smells good," Wildey says.

"It's pirozhki," she says. She pronounces it *peeroshkee*. "For a family dinner this weekend."

"Ah. You going to see your family?"

"A couple of cousins are coming here, that's all."

"Just a couple?"

Kaz looks at him as if she's considering sharing something, then turns her attention back to kneading a mass of dough that looks too large for her hands to contain.

"My maiden name's Fieuchevsky," she says, as if that explains it all.

And then a moment later, Wildey recognizes the name. Russian gang family, had a huge war with the Italian mob about ten years ago. Wildey was still at the academy during the worst of it. Also made sense that Kaz would keep her ex-husband's name. Mahoney's a fine cop name. Fieuchevsky, not so much.

Kaz glances over and sees that Wildey gets it. "So yeah, some of my family is otherwise engaged this holiday season. Let me just wash this flour off my hands and we can talk. Want a beer, something?"

"No, I'm good."

"Go ahead into the living room."

Which was a big box. Big windows, protected with steel bars, looking out onto a small porch and concrete patio. A staircase leading down to the basement, which must be the bedroom. There is no railing around the stairs—just a rectangle cut into the floor, with wooden steps leading down. More creative space-making, he supposed. Nice and everything, and the neighborhood is pretty great, but Wildey wouldn't trade his busted-ass row house for this place, no way.

"This is coming from one thirty-seven," Wildey says.

"What, did she ask for another extension?"

"You're not going to like this."

"I don't like anything these days."

Wildey spells it out for her. Indeed, Honors Girl has found something insane. "I think she's onto our leak. A friend of hers has been dating Little Pete D'Argenio, and Little Pete's been bragging about taking over the city's drug scene."

"Goombahs like to brag," Kaz says.

"Well, this one's bragging about having police protection. Like he's untouchable. And then he goes on about how he's even snitch-proof. That if anyone dares snitch on him, they're basically walking around with an expiration date on their foreheads."

"That's a bit of a leap."

"There's more, and I can walk you through that later. But I came out here because time is tight. One thirty-seven got herself invited to a party that Little Pete is throwing later tonight. When he drinks, he brags. She wants to wear a wire, get some of that bragging on tape."

"Why's she doing this?"

"She wants out. She won't give up her boyfriend, so instead she's finding me someone else."

"You ready to give up on Chuckie Morphine?"

"No. Not by a long shot. But if one thirty-seven serves up a mobster who's about to start a drug empire who also has pull inside the department, you know, I'll consider us even."

"Christ on a bike," Kaz says, sighing. "I thought we were done with this shit. It's gotta be one of the other NFUs. I mean, right? Here's what you do. You get her to get him talking about the cop who's protecting him. I almost don't care about Little Fucking Pete. But I want to know who's so eager to sell us out. And swear to God, if it's someone in our unit, I'm going to take a cheese grater to his balls and post it on YouTube."

Man, Wildey thinks. You are a Fieuchevsky after all.

"So I have your okay?"

"Yes. But don't tell a soul. This stays with you and me."

"Understood."

"You okay running her by yourself?"

"It's just a party. I think she'll be okay."

Rembrandt "Rem" Mahoney fucking hates *pirozhki.* That's one of the things he doesn't miss. (There are plenty of others.) He can practically smell that awful cabbage and egg bullshit all the way out here in the Northeast. Just listening to her speak of it resurrects the awful odor in his nasal cavity. But Rem listens just the same.

And he can't stop listening.

He tells himself it started because he worried about her. Honest. And, okay, he missed her. She was an insufferable commie psycho most days. But when she eased up—most often thanks to a shot or five of that Ukrainian firewater—there was nobody else like her. No drug, no high, no beating, no vice, even came close. Ten years later he could conjure the taste of her mouth, tinged with vodka.

Rem started the whole surveillance thing small. Keeping tabs, really, to make sure she didn't end up in any kind of trouble. She was keeping his last name, so it was his duty to make sure she didn't drag it into the mud. She moved into that place on Green Street, chose an apartment in the back, so drive-bys wouldn't work. One night, after getting soused at a small sports bar on the corner of Twentieth and Green, Rem did something stupid yet life-changing. He hopped a six-foot wooden fence, stumbled into a cramped alley, then crept into her backward patio. Lights in the apartment were on. Wow. She was home. That was the night Rem became...well, okay, he'll admit it...kind of a pervert. But only for his ex! No civilians.

At first it was just peeping through her windows, trying to listen to her conversations, that sort of thing. Slowly it escalated. Before he could talk himself out of it, he was breaking into the basement—the property owner had carved out a corner of the basement to serve as the one bedroom for the apartment above, Katrina's apartment. The construction guys hadn't done the best job in the world; the drywall was on the thin side. The rest of the basement was dusty storage that smelled like raw mushrooms. But Rem could easily slip inside and lean up against the flimsy drywall and listen to her breathe. Or talk on the phone—always curt, clipped conversations. Rem dreaded/hoped for the night Katrina would bring home a lover. Had to happen, sooner or later. The ex was a hellspawn, but she was still hot.

Rem couldn't spend all of his time in his ex-wife's basement. His clothes were starting to smell funny. So he went to the police supply shop and got himself a basic surveillance setup. Drilled a tiny hole in the cheap drywall when he knew she was on duty. The rest was easy, and tumbled along. Bugging the basement soon turned into bugging the living room, and then the bathroom (yeah, Rem already admitted he was a perv, big deal, let's move on), and then her car. Then...and okay, yes, Rem Mahoney crossed a line here...her office. Then he ran a tap on her cell. Not through the PD, of course, but a fed he knew. Rem kind of hinted that his ex might have been a bit more cozy with the rest of her family in the Russian mob than she let on.

End result, oddly enough, is that Rem feels like he knew his ex better now than he did when they were married.

Including pretty much all of the identities of her two hundred snitches. He had to hand it to her, the strategy was clever. And it was so like Katrina to respond to a citywide snitch crisis by, guess what, yeah, signing up even more snitches. Snitches to sniff out major cases, snitches to make sure her team was on the up-and-up. Airtight.

So was this CI #137? Rem was sure he could break into her place later tonight when she was taking her evening shower and dig up the name himself, but time is of the essence here. Besides, he's willing to bet there's someone who'll know the snitch's name straightaway.

CANARY

Transcript of phone conversation between Captain Rembrandt "Rem" Mahoney and Peter D'Argenio

MAHONEY: It's me.

D'ARGENIO: Hey.

MAHONEY: You alone?

D'ARGENIO: Yeah.

MAHONEY: No you're not. You're with that college girl you've been banging.

D'ARGENIO: What are . . . wait wait, how do you know about that?

MAHONEY: There's a lot I know. Like how you've been shooting your fucking mouth off in front of girls, trying to impress them. Christ on a crutch, you fuck, this is how I caught your stupid ass back in 1996. Thought you would have learned something in finishing school.

D'ARGENIO: Slow down and explain what the fuck you're talking about, man.

MAHONEY: No, no, there's no time to explain. You're about ready to get our shit hung out in the open so shut the fuck up and you do some explaining. Who is this college chick?

D'ARGENIO: You want her name? For what?

MAHONEY: Yeah, I want her fucking name. And a couple of others, too. Whoever you were showboating for.

D'ARGENIO: I ain't braggin' in front of anyone, man.

MAHONEY: Fuck, just give me her fucking name, we have to start somewhere.

D'ARGENIO: Jesus . . . okay, not that it matters, because I don't tell anybody shit about our business, but her name is Tamara Pleece.

MAHONEY: Spell that.

D'ARGENIO: Which name?

MAHONEY: Both.

307

D'ARGENIO: T-A-M-A-R... I don't know if it's two Rs or what.

MAHONEY: Doesn't matter. Last name?

D'ARGENIO: I think it's P-L-E-E-C-E.

MAHONEY: You meet any of her friends?

D'ARGENIO: A couple, yeah.

MAHONEY: College kids, right.

D'ARGENIO: Some of them. Why?

MAHONEY: Give me some names. Every name you can remember. Even first names will do. Whatever.

D'ARGENIO: I don't know. I don't really pay attention when we're out. Tammy knows half the city.

MAHONEY: *(sighs)* Do you really want things to end right here because you're shy about giving me names?

D'ARGENIO: I just wish you'd give me the respect to tell me what the fuck this is all about.

MAHONEY: One of your girlfriend's gal pals is a snitch. I'm trying to find out which one it is.

D'ARGENIO: Fuck me.

MAHONEY: Uh-huh. Yeah. You and me both, if we don't figure out who it is.

D'ARGENIO: Shit, I think I know who it is. It's the one with all of the questions.

MAHONEY: What!?

D'ARGENIO: Keep it in your pants, Mahoney, I don't say shit. But she figured out who I was, so she was asking about my life. I asked what, are you writing a paper? And she tells me yeah, she is, in fact. It was kind of flattering.

MAHONEY: You stupid asshole. What did you tell her?

D'ARGENIO: Nothing about our business, swear to Christ!

MAHONEY: *(sighs)*

D'ARGENIO: Swear to Christ, Mahoney, not a word.

MAHONEY: What's her name? The curious one?

D'ARGENIO: Sally.

MAHONEY: Sally what?

D'ARGENIO: *(lengthy pause)* I don't know. But I can find out.

MAHONEY: Never mind. Call you back in 20.

Mahoney consults the best source in the world: Facebook.

Seriously, you'd be surprised how many people hang ridiculously incriminating shit out there in cyberspace. If he'd had Facebook back in the 1990s he could have doubled his arrests, easy. Bad guys can't resist bragging, and social media gives them the perfect opportunity.

It also is a blindingly easy way to come up with a perp's associates.

So a search on Tamara Pleece in Philadelphia gives her up straightaway—why hello there, blond darling—along with her circle of friends. Little Pete is right. She knows half the fucking city. But a lot of scrolling turns up exactly zero Sallies. Fuckin' Pete. Maybe she's not on Facebook, but that seems unlikely. The goombah probably just botched the name. So let's narrow it down. Sully? Last name Sullivan, maybe? Nah, only guys go by last names. Sally, Molly, Mary, Marie...

Then he sees it: Sarie Holland. Close enough to be promising.

Clicky-click and he's on her page. Which she hasn't updated since December of last year. And after that, a lot of condolence messages to her, none of them replied to. The girl's mom died, apparently. Sorry stuff.

But that's not the most interesting thing on her page. Instead it's a series of hate-posts from a dude named Ryan Koolhaas, all of them a profanity-laced variation on a single theme: SARIE HOLLAND IS A CUNT SNITCH.

"This sneaky bitch came to me for a couple of pills and the next thing I know I'm arrested and thrown out of school! Don't trust this frigid cunt! She's working off her own shit and taking down everyone she can."

Well, there we go.

Hello, mysterious confidential informant.

> MAHONEY: I found the girl.
>
> D'ARGENIO: Yeah?
>
> MAHONEY: You're going to need to take care of her.
>
> D'ARGENIO: *(lengthy pause)* Why me?
>
> MAHONEY: Because apparently she's coming with your friend Tammy to a party you're throwing tonight. And by the way, I'm hurt, dude. You didn't invite me.
>
> D'ARGENIO: Fuck.
>
> MAHONEY: So what you're going to do is cancel that party and throw a smaller, more intimate affair. Meanwhile, I'll follow up with my ex to make sure she doesn't have any other surprises in store for us.
>
> D'ARGENIO: Fuck. Alright. I'll let you know.
>
> MAHONEY: You do that.

The names Rem Mahoney and Peter "Little Pete" D'Argenio have already been linked in the media dozens of times. And with good reason: He was the one who busted him back in the naughty nineties—the era Mahoney now refers to as "the good old days." Because let's face it, Mahoney's city is going to hell.

So Mahoney made a side deal with the Italians, who wanted to come back strong. Better the wops than any of the other ethnic screwheads—especially the Mexican cartels. Bring some order back to this crazy city. Confine the junkies to Pill Hill, the Badlands, and let the mob run the rest...so Mahoney can run the mob himself. In Philadelphia, law enforcement isn't so much about busting gangs as *containing* them. No straight citizen cares when it's not happening in his or her part of the city. Life's rough in Killadelphia. You don't like it? Don't be a fucking junkie. Don't sell drugs. You'll be fine. Mahoney's family had a long history of tangling with the mob families over the years. They tend to be greedy and stupid and easily controlled. And Mahoney knows he's the cop who can control them and bring order back to the city. But not if this college girl fucks with it.

It won't be a big deal. In this town, CIs die all the time.

DECEMBER 12 (later)

Not much time to write, Mom, but let me just say this:

Everything comes down to what happens tonight. And everything feels like it's exploding around me. Dad's not talking to me (and I guess I can't blame him). Marty's looking at me like I'm the daughter of the Devil.

And then there's this text I just got. I don't recognize the number, but I know it's from Partyman:

—Whatever you're doing . . . don't.

Which really inspires confidence, doesn't it?

But I have to go through with tonight. What choice do I have? I've worked too hard to set this up.

Wish me luck.

I'M NOT DOWN

THE WATERFRONT

THURSDAY, DECEMBER 12

Ringo spends the afternoon getting the Rat Receiving Station all ready, hanging new plastic sheets, sweeping the concrete slab floor, making sure the industrial-sized drain is clear. The work goes quickly, leaving Ringo enough time to wonder: Who's the guest they're expecting? Usually it's him and Frankenstein (or Bird and Lisa) scooping up their rats right from the street. That was most of the fun, truth be told. But Little Pete said no, just wait there, I'm bringing the rat to you.

And apparently Frankenstein is sitting this one out, which makes Ringo wonder: Has ol' Franken-face turned traitor on them? Is he the surprise guest tonight?

Ringo ponders and sweeps, ponders and sweeps.

Night comes faster than I want it to.

I don't want to make the mistake of underdressing for the occasion (again), so I dig out the black cocktail-length dress I wore to an honors formal two months ago. (Mom, you would have really loved this dress.) It's not exactly appropriate for the time of year, but who cares—I'll be moving straight from warm car to overheated apartment in a matter of seconds.

Thing is, I can't get dressed at home without Dad asking a million questions. So I go to the only warm and reasonably safe place I can think of: the nearest Wawa bathroom.

This time, thank God, there's no wire hidden in my clothes. Wildey managed to get his hands on this pen with a radio transmitter hidden inside. (How very Jason Bourne.) If I start to think that somebody's about to check me for a wire, it will be a lot easier to ditch a pen than tear off a chunk of my dress—and one hell of a lot less suspicious. Not that Wildey would be happy if I tossed his fancy spy toy. Otherwise this whole thing will be for nothing.

The object of tonight's mission: party with Peter D'Argenio until he loosens up enough to possibly brag about his drug operations. Hell, he's blabbed all about them to Tammy, so I'm hoping he'll be in a boastful mood tonight—because Wildey will be there listening the whole time.

Text message exchange between CI #137 and Tamara Pleece, 12/12/13, 7:47 p.m.

PLEECE: Quick change of plans! Peter wants to show us this new nightclub space he's considering
PLEECE: Can you meet us there?
PLEECE: It'll be awesome
CI #137: kk where
PLEECE: Sweet here's the address

I dig the pen out of my purse and speak into it like it's a talk show microphone. I'll admit it, Mom: I feel kind of fucking cool.

—Okay, just got a text from Tammy. Change of meeting place. I'm headed to a building on Columbus Boulevard and Race, right under the Ben Franklin Bridge. It's the only building there, aside from a hotel. Got it? You said to keep talking, constant updates, so there you go. You got my back, partner?

*   *   *

Wildey does not receive this transmission; a full minute before the text message was sent from Tammy Pleece's cell phone, Captain Rem Mahoney remotely disabled CI #137's transmission and replaced it with one of his own. Such a thing is ridiculously easy. With access to his ex's computer and files, he can pretty much do anything.

All Wildey hears is the faint sound of a car engine, which he believes is his informant's Honda Civic, headed to the Society Hill Towers for a small apartment party.

I find a parking spot right across the street from the building near the Race Street Pier. Within seconds some valet dude comes bounding out of the front doors and crosses the street, dodging traffic, waving at me with Muppet arms. What's this now? I tuck the burner phone under my seat then talk to the pen one last time.

— Here we go. Wish me luck, Wildey.

I roll down the window just as Valet Guy reaches the car.

— Ms. Holland? Your friends are inside, they're expecting you. I'll park your car for you. You don't want to leave it out here unattended.

I'll admit it, I don't like giving up my keys, but what else am I supposed to do?

— Okay, you can park my car, but just be careful with her. She's temperamental.

Wildey, you with me? You get what I just did there?

Wildey has no idea what she just did there.

Tammy's creepy old boyfriend Peter opens the door with a big grin on his face.

—Hey, sweetheart, come on in!

I'm already shivering from the brief trot across the avenue. The wind chill off the river is seriously intense.

I scan the interior, which does not resemble a potential nightclub spot in the least. It looks like a big basement—dusty, damp, and dark. And despite its size, the space is weirdly claustrophobic. The door slams shut behind me. I flinch, which at least momentarily stops the shivers. This beefy dude in his fifties stands in the corner, one hand over the other like he's trying to get through the Procession of Faith with a hangover. He's wearing a military jacket and black gloves. D'Argenio locks the front doors and there's a dull, echoing snap as the latch slides home. No. This is not good.

—Uh, where's Tammy?

D'Argenio smiles.

—It's just you and me, babe. Well, you, me, and Ringo over there. I thought we'd spend some time getting to know each other. You know all about my business, and I don't know much about yours.

No no no...

—I'm sorry—I have to go...

—You just got here. You want a drink? Ringo, get her a drink.

The big guy standing in the corner smirks.

—Uh, unless you want me to run out for a six, I'd say we'd better skip the drinks.

D'Argenio shakes his head, smiling.

—Yeah. That's my fault. I should have said something before. Doesn't matter.

Wildey, please be hearing this and speeding to my rescue right away.

—I really, *really* have to go.

I do a side step, wondering if I can do an end run around D'Argenio and make it to the door before he does. Then I realize this would do no good, because the key to the locked door is in his pocket.

—Uh-uh.

D'Argenio mimics my side step, blocking my path.

—We have to talk, Sally.

Creep wants to threaten me and he doesn't even know my name.

—Get the fuck out of my way or I'll scream.

D'Argenio grins but the expression melts away the second his hands lunge out, reaching for my dress. I pull away, release the most piercing scream I can, and throw a wild punch at D'Argenio, which somehow catches him on the side of his face. No one's more surprised than me. His eyes water and he's momentarily stunned, as if he's asking himself, Did this bitch really just do that? But the big guy with the gloves moves fast and has me in a tight armlock a nanosecond later.

D'Argenio shakes his head, smiles.

—We were just talking. And there you go screaming and hitting. Scream all you want, Sally. The walls and ceiling are soundproof. I made sure. Even if anybody could hear you, they wouldn't do anything about it. You're not the first snitch we've invited here.

The moment he says the word "snitch," I know I'm screwed.

—Wildey! I'm inside the building at Columbus and Race! He's locked the front door!

I struggle to break free, but the big guy has all of his weight against me. I'd be better off trying to nudge a boulder.

D'Argenio chuckles as he pulls a black gun out of his pocket. My stomach turns to water.

—Wildey, huh? Is he your handler? Well, I guess we'd better make sure he hears.

D'Argenio takes a step back, puts his hands at the sides of his mouth, gun still in one of them, and bellows.

—Officer Wildey! Come quick! Your girl needs you! Wildey! What, are you deaf or something? Break down the door!

D'Argenio pauses, cupping a hand around his ear, as if listening intently.

—Huh. Guess he really can't hear us.

Then, to the boulder behind me:

—Hold her still.

My arm is twisted up behind my back so hard it takes my breath away. The pain is electric. D'Argenio tucks the gun away in the waist of his pants, then touches both sides of my belly gently, as if trying to calm a wild animal.

—Now let's find that wire.

What the fuck? Wildey's hearing nothing but engine. C'mon, Honors Girl, talk to me. I told you to keep the commentary going, even if you're stuck in traffic. Especially if you're stuck in traffic. Shouldn't have taken you this long to make it to the Towers.

Don't tell me you killed the wire again. He checks the gear but the bug is still live, transmitting perfectly.

The transmission from CI #137's pen, however, is going to Rem Mahoney, and God help him, he's both sickened and titillated by what he's hearing. (Maybe he is a perv for other people, too.) How far is this crazy wop gonna go?

D'Argenio lifts my dress over my knees, then up over my thighs. I jolt involuntarily. My arm is twisted up harder, giving me another sharp shock. D'Argenio checks out my legs, gives me this skeevy appreciative nod, lips pursed, before lifting the dress even higher. Oh God. Not this. Not fucking this.

—Huh. Kind of thought there'd be one of those old-school wires taped to your belly. Guess these days, with technology and shit, you could hide it pretty much anywhere. We're going to have to do a real TSA-style search, ain't we. Body cavities and everything.

The asshole's eyes leisurely tour my body, from hairpin to shoes, and I can't do a fucking thing about it.

—Looks like this is going to be a party after all, am I right, Ringo?

I speak quickly, hoping that this is all just a threat, that if I tell him where the wire is, he'll stop.

—It's in my purse! It's a pen!

The dress drops back down. D'Argenio smirks, grabs my purse from the floor, snaps it open. He finds my iPhone, looks it over, asks if it's one of those new 5Cs or whatever, but I'm too numb to speak. He shrugs, takes a few steps, drops my phone into a plastic bucket of water. Then he says the scariest words I've ever heard:

—You're not going to be needing that anymore.

D'Argenio makes a big show of dropping the contents of my purse one by one—gum, eyeliner, compact, minipads—one by one into the water bucket before finally pulling out the spy pen. He waves it around like a magic wand.

—There ain't nobody on the other end listening for you, sweet-heart. Cops sold you out.

He slides the pen into his own jacket pocket, pats it. Maybe he thinks he can pawn it or something. After a moment of delibera-tion, he reaches for my waist. I try to twist away.

—What are you doing?

D'Argenio says nothing, reaches again for my waist.

—Stop!

—What? Don't you know why you're in here? Tammy tells me you're a smart girl. I'm sure you've figured it out by now.

—I don't know anything.

—Am I asking you any questions?

—Please stop, I don't know what you want.

D'Argenio lowers his hands, sighs, smiles.

—We had a guy...this is going back fifteen, maybe twenty, years, when I was first starting to come up. Anyway, this guy was a rat, big fucking snitch, and we got him down into a place like this. Only it didn't go like this. It was a little more, uh, to the point. The guy walks in the door, realizes in an instant what's going on, but by that time it's too late. Four guys grab him, one limb each, and then a fifth guy chops his foot off. Yeah. Thwack.

D'Argenio slaps the flat of his right hand into the palm of his left.

—Guy can't believe it. Like he's just stepped into a horror movie or something. One of our guys gives him a tourniquet and drops him in the corner, and he's just going into shock and shit. Everybody just stares at him, and after a while he starts staring back, wondering what's next. Because something had to come next, right? Either some questions, or more chopping. But the five guys, they do nothing. Say nothing, do nothing. They just stare at the poor bastard, which drives him nuts. He's still bleeding, and he knows he's never leaving the room alive, and he can't help it. He starts gushing. Everything he told the feds, every sin he's ever committed, every time he whacked off. Like a final statement. Most effective interrogation session I ever saw. Yeah, I was one of those guys. But not with the axe. That kind of grossed me out, to tell you the truth. But it taught me a lesson. You make the right statement, and you don't even have to say a word. You know what I mean?

"Let her go, Richie. I'll take her."

Ringo has no idea what Little Pete is going to do next. Not as if they had a dress rehearsal for this shit, but fuck, Ringo didn't know this was less about digging up some intel and more about Little Pete getting his jollies. If this is turning into a rape...then no thanks. Kill her, fine, that's part of the game, and if the girl's got some kind of wire on her, then yeah, she's in the game. But why torture her first? Doesn't make any sense.

Grip released, the girl scrambles away, but D'Argenio catches her in his arms. "Come on now. This is gonna be fun."

Ringo isn't squeamish. In fact, Ringo and violence are longtime friends. There isn't a bone he hasn't broken, or has *had* broken. His jaw has been fractured twice, his skull and palate once each. He's been shot through the cheek and ear. Dislocated both wrists, an ankle, his clavicle, right knee. Lost a handful of adult teeth. He's had multiple leg fractures, internal injuries. Countless scars, bruises, and contusions. But this is nothing compared to what he's dished out. He first killed a person for money at age thirteen, and has done it countless times since. But this...

"All due respect," he says, "but do we want to do this?"

"Ringo, all due respect? Shut the fuck up."

The snitch looks up at D'Argenio. "Tammy really likes you. She can't stop talking about you."

"Yeah? I think that's the problem here," Little Pete says, backing her up until she bumps against a metal support beam. "Her talking too much. Not thinking enough."

"She calls you her Little Pete."

The boss blinks. "Come again?"

"That's what they call you—Little Pete, right? Tammy told me all about it."

"Told you about what."

"About how little you are."

Ooof, Ringo thinks. If this girl wants to die fast she's walking down the right path. Still, it's a bit of a surprise when his boss says, "Do her, Richie."

323

SOCIETY HILL TOWERS

Wildey marches to the front desk. He's in plainclothes (and black) so he gets the narrow eyes from the security guard until he says he's here for the party up on 30. At which point the guard grows even more suspicious. There is no party on 30, sir, you must have this information wrong. Wildey asks if there's a parking lot under the building—he's expecting a friend. The security guard points to a stairwell, happy to be rid of him. Wildey descends.

He won't find anything. CI #137's Honda Civic has been moved to another location many blocks away, keys chucked down a nearby sewer drain.

When it comes to snuffing somebody, Ringo doesn't believe in drawing things out. None of that *got-any-last-words* shit. Unless torture is on the agenda and you need to play some mind games, better to just go and do it without preamble or warning.

Of course, D'Argenio fucked up the element of surprise with that stupid *Do her, Richie* crap. Fucking idiot. The girl, now on full alert, twists away, spins around, and takes a few steps back, eyes darting around for options. Of which there are few. But now she's armed with a valuable piece of information. D'Argenio may have a gun, but he knows (and she knows) that he's not going to just shoot her. He'd rather his hired gun do the honors to avoid bloodying his own hands. Nice going there, boss.

"Don't you take another step, you stupid bitch," D'Argenio says. "Richie, c'mon!"

Ringo sees the futility but takes a step forward anyway, more out of duty than anything else. As expected, the girl takes another step back and snarls, "Stay away from me!"

The veins in D'Argenio's neck bulge. "What are you waiting for?"

Ringo gives him a look like, *You're fucking kidding me?* The girl takes another step back, closer to the wall. D'Argenio makes two impatient gestures with the gun. Over there. Kill her.

Ringo sighs. "Just give me the Glock."

"No. No gun. That's too easy. I want you to twist her fucking head off while I watch."

"You know she's gonna claw the shit out of me."

"You afraid of a little girl?"

"Fuck you!" the girl screams.

"Yeah...as a matter of fact, fuck you indeed," Ringo says. "*You're* not the one who's gonna leave all kinds of forensics over her. Gun makes it a whole lot easier."

Now it's D'Argenio's turn to sigh, shake his head. He puts his hand on the butt of the Glock. "Fine. Hurry up and get this shit over with." Ringo, relieved, takes a step forward to take the piece, but is astounded when there's a loud crack. Takes a minute for Ringo to put it together. The girl wasn't backing up because she was afraid. She was inching back toward the closest thing to a weapon in the room: a wooden mop. The same mop Ringo used on the floor a bunch of hours ago. The girl is tall and gangly but moves quickly; the mop handle cracks D'Argenio in the face. Hands fly up to his face and he staggers to the side, not quite in the direction Ringo predicts, forcing him to make an end run around him. By the time he does the girl has pulled another surprise: her hairpin. Which is real fucking sharp, and pressed near D'Argenio's jugular. She's behind D'Argenio now, and with the pin pulled out, her hair is long and wild and feral. She looks like she could do *anything*. The tip of the pin sinks into D'Argenio's neck. Blood comes bubbling out of the tiny puncture wound.

"Either of you move," she says, "and it goes all the way in."

"Richie," D'Argenio says through gritted teeth, "you fuck!"

Ringo watches Feral Snitch Girl carefully. She telegraphs her next move but there's really nothing he can do about it. Not without setting off a chain reaction that will end well for nobody.

As predicted, the girl reaches out to D'Argenio, pulls the Glock out of his pants, clocks him on the side of the neck with it, then pushes him hard into Ringo, who's ready to catch him. D'Argenio pushes him away, pressing fingers to his cut neck and a free hand to his now-aching head.

Now the Glock is her hands, pointed at them. It trembles in her hands, but she has a firm grip.

"You," she says. "Richie."

"My friends call me Ringo."

"Don't fuck around with me!"

Ringo is already showing his palms. "Take it easy, honey."

"Fucking kill her!" D'Argenio says. He's slurring. She cracked him good. Maybe she splattered a little bit of his brains against his skull. Maybe that will be an improvement.

"Reach into your boss's pocket, take out his keys, then toss them to me."

"You're dead, you fucking cunt!"

Ringo looks at D'Argenio for guidance while trying to keep a straight face. Fucking Little Pete. If he had been a normal fucking guy and walked the gun over to Ringo, or even met him halfway, this wouldn't be happening.

"Gimme the keys."

You can always tell by the eyes, and Ringo can tell: She'd definitely pull the trigger. Not because she's a stone-cold killer or anything like that. She's a frightened, wounded animal. If all she has to do to stay alive is squeeze the trigger, then you can be sure as shit she's going to pull the trigger.

"Give me the keys, Pete," Ringo says.

"No. No fucking way."

"You're either going to hand them to me or I'm going to knock you out and then take them out of your pocket. Come on. It's the right move."

Ringo hopes the look in *his* eyes tells D'Argenio he means it. D'Argenio mutters something about not fucking believing this. He digs in his pocket, slaps Ringo the keys.

"You ready?" Ringo asks the girl.

The girl nods. He tosses her the keys underhand. She catches them in her right hand. Probably had a daddy who used to throw a ball around with her in a backyard somewhere. Good on you, Pops. You may have just temporarily spared your daughter an ugly death in the Rat Receiving Station.

"Back up against the wall," she says. Some of the fear in her eyes has been replaced with hope.

"You even know how to use that thing?" D'Argenio asks.

"Want to find out?"

Then the girl moves toward the door, looking at them, looking at the door and inserting a key, looking back at them, looking at the door and turning the key.

D'Argenio sneers. "You're not going to last five minutes on the fuckin' streets once I put the word out!"

The girl flips the lock, then glances back at him. "Are you actually daring me to kill you?"

Ringo can't help it. He starts laughing. A big belly laugh. D'Argenio's so pissed Ringo can practically feel the heat radiating from his skin. The door slams shut. Fuckin' Little Pete, just like the bad old days. Ringo's laughing so hard that he doesn't hear D'Argenio pick up the mop, tuning in only when he snaps it over his knee and comes at him.

Mom, I am such a fucking fool. They played me. Been playing me, all this time.

The only two people who knew I was wearing a wire: Lieutenant Mahoney and Officer Wildey. No backup, no tech support, nothing. Just those two. So they either sent me to die or they ignored my cries for help. Neither is forgivable. I can no longer trust them.

D'Argenio was right. The cops sold me out.

So now I am hurrying down Second Street in nineteen-degree weather wearing nothing more than a thin-strap nylon cocktail dress. The wind whips my hair around my face and stings my cheeks. My feet hurt so bad, but I don't dare take my heels off. I have nowhere else to go but south, south, south on Second, to a small row house on Vernon Street—the only hope I have left.

Rem Mahoney can't believe this shit.

He'd been taking a leisurely drive through the streets of his neighborhood, Mayfair, listening to sounds of two goombahs torturing a snippy little college girl. You could hear real panic in her voice, which made it all the more exciting. He turned down the volume as he passed his mother's old house (out of respect, God bless you, Rosemarie), but when he turns it back up something has changed; the worm has turned.

Give me the keys, Pete.

No fucking way.

He almost slides into a series of parked cars on Robbins Avenue as he listens to the sound of that bratty little snitch getting the better of two hardened gangsters, then slip away into the fucking night.

Rem guns it down Harbison, heading for I-95, and gets Frankenstein on the line as he weaves around slow-moving cars, still not believing this shit.

No Honda Civic down here. No Honda Civic around the entire perimeter of the Society Hill Towers, in fact. Not his CI's make and model, anyway. Was she intercepted on the way? If so, how soon did it happen? And how?

You know damn well how, Benjamin Franklin Wildey. You're just afraid to think it, let alone say it out loud. Isn't that right? The only reason you agreed to this operation is because you thought there was no way she'd be dirty. You thought this would expose some other kind of leak, force somebody's hand...

Forgive me, Honors Girl. Oh please, *forgive me*...

After endless freezing blocks forever, clutching my purse close to my side, I reach Chuckie Morphine's little drug house. The lights are out; there's a strong chance the place is already abandoned. And I'll knock and no one will answer and I'll freeze to death out here.

But Chuckie promised...so I knock, timidly at first, and then I pound as hard as I can. Doesn't matter; my hands are so cold they feel like they're on fire.

To my astonishment, someone answers. It's Keith, the biker thug guy who punctured my neck. Only now he's lost the leather jacket in favor of a puffy parka and a pair of dad jeans.

—Oh, it's you.

—I n-need to see Ch-Chuckie.

My teeth chatter like a piano trill. I don't know if I'm hyperventilating because of my near-death experience or the walk. Either way, I'm a cold mess. Keith, with the skunk hair, just stares at me, unable to make up his mind. I take a step closer, hoping to feel just a little bit of the warmth inside.

—Please, it's fucking f-freezing out here.

—Chuckie's not here.

—He's going to want to hear what I have to say.

There's another decade of indecision until he finally says, yeah, okay, then steps out of the way. I have never been so glad to enter a house, even if it does belong to a drug kingpin. The place is unheated but feels to me like the dead center of a pizza oven. I rub my hands, purse tucked under my arm, as Keith makes a call to Chuckie.

—Uh-huh…Yeah, I'm right in the middle of that…Uh-huh…Just now…Yeah…You sure? She says she has something important for you to hear…Okay…Right on.

Keith looks at me with weariness in his eyes.

—He says whatever it is, you can tell me.

—No. That's not the deal. I tell him directly.

—He's not coming down here, and I'm not taking him to you.

—And I want to see D. first.

Keith sighs, which pisses me off. Like I'm some big inconvenience? What other pressing business does he have here, sitting in a dark, empty, unheated house in the middle of South fuckin' Philly?

—I'm not going anywhere until I do. And you can tell your boss that.

Keith's shoulders sag, as if he's the most put-upon drug underling ever. But there's a cold gleam in his eye, too.

—You want to see your boyfriend? I'll take you to see him.

—Good.

—Follow me.

—Wait, he's here?

I follow Keith down a set of wooden stairs into a basement, but a cold, hard ball of ice is forming in my guts. Part of me is starting to understand what I'm about to see—but the other part of me doesn't believe it. The part of me that is screaming at me WRONG MOVE WRONG MOVE WRONG MOVE. I reach into my purse and pull out the dull black gun I took from Peter D'Argenio.

*　　*　　*

Keith the biker reaches into his parka pocket for a chloroform-soaked rag he has tucked in a Ziploc bag. He used it earlier today, but it should still be good to go. And if not, then whatever, he'll just snap her neck.

But he wants her to see the mound in the corner of the basement covered in a tarp. She's supposed to be a smart girl; she'll probably figure out what's under it long before he'll have to lift the edge. And the moment the shock hits her, Keith will nail her with the rag, put her out, then take her out, just as Chuckie Morphine requested. Then later tonight it'll just be a matter of some cement work down here, two for the price of one.

A few steps down and I see it, in the middle of the basement floor: an icy-blue tarp covering something vaguely human-shaped. Oh God, let this be my imagination. Next to it are chunks of foundation concrete that were presumably chopped away to expose the dirt beneath. A sack of mortar mix, a mixing pan, and a trowel. Please don't let this be what I think it is...

I point the Glock at Keith, who's a few steps below me.

— What's under that tarp?

Keith stops, turns around, looks up, sees the gun, smiles.

— How about you put that thing down, honey.

— Tell me what's under there.

— I don't know. What do you think it is?

— Tell me or I'll shoot you right now, I swear to Christ!

Keith puts his hands up. There's a small plastic bag in his right hand with something wadded up inside. More of his plan becomes clear. Shit, he's not even trying to hide it.

— You didn't actually think Chuckie was gonna let you live, did you? He was playing around with you two, figuring maybe he'd score some info. But you were never gonna walk away from this. You have to know that, right?

—This is your last chance.

—I'll tell you one thing. Your boyfriend did the full-court press for you. Begging, pleading, offering to spend years working it off, all just to let you walk away. When that didn't work, he tried to split. And that's how he ended up down here.

—No.

—Yeah. And the same thing's gonna happen to you.

That last word is still coming out of Keith's mouth as he lunges up the stairs for me.

I squeeze the trigger. There's a click but nothing happens. Fuck! No, no, no, this can't be happening.

I stumble backwards. My ass hits the wooden edge of a step. Keith pounds up the stairs so hard I can feel them shaking. He's about to grab my arms when I scream and pull the trigger again. This time there's a loud bang. I'm not even aiming, but the front of Keith's face explodes.

His body tumbles backwards, down the stairs.

I wait until I'm sure he won't move ever again. Then I pull myself up, using the rail. I'm shivering so hard it's almost like I'm on the verge of an out-of-body experience, and any second my soul is going to be flung away like a kid from a carousel. Somehow I force my legs to cooperate. Down a step. Down a step. Down a step. I step over Keith's body and move closer to the tarp. The hole next to it isn't six feet, but deep enough. When I crouch down I'm surprised to see the dull black gun is still in my hand. I reach out with my other hand. The surface of the tarp is rough and cold.

I'm crying by the time I lift the edge and pull it back.

*   *   *

"We need to talk."

"How did the op go? Where's one thirty-seven?"

"That's why we need to talk."

"Spit it out, Wildey."

"You're gonna make me do this, aren't you. What's your end game, Loot? Or do you even have one?"

"Are you fucking high? Start making sense."

"Only two people knew about her. You told me that. I sure as shit didn't tell anybody. Which leaves you. It's been you, this whole time."

"Oh fuck . . . what happened to the girl?"

"You're going down, Loot. Next call I'm making is to your husband. You know. The one who heads up Internal Affairs?"

"Tell me what the fuck happened to the girl!?"

I am no longer Sarie Holland.

I am Confidential Informant #137.

Confidential Informant #137 walks through the snow-and-ice-covered streets of South Philly in numb shock. She doesn't remember leaving the house or the route she takes. Streets go by in a blur. She's not supposed to be here. She's supposed to be on a sunny California college campus, not in a neighborhood where people bury other people in basements. Even the weather conspires against you in a neighborhood like this—the narrow blocks, the biting wind, the broken street lamps. You could lose yourself forever in here. There is no escape. There is only temporary refuge.

So CI #137 takes it when she sees it. She wanders into a corner bar, Dugan's Den, which is only half full. She takes a stool. The bartender is a blonde with frizzy hair, probably a young grandmother,

333

still doing her makeup like it's the 1980s. Maybe CI #137 will be carded and kicked back out into the cold.

—What can I get ya, hon?

CI #137 orders a Diet Coke. The bartender nods, asks if she wants to see a menu. She declines, not even sure how she's going to pay for the soda. No purse, no phone, no car keys, no identification, no nothing. But it's good to be out of the cold, even for a few minutes.

One thing she knows: She can't go home. Because the death that is stalking her will follow her there, and she can't do that to her father and brother. So what now? What's your move, snitch? Call the police?

—Here you go, hon. Sure you don't want something to eat?

CI #137 shakes her head.

She keeps things basic. She soaks up the warmth of the bar. Listens to the Dr. Dog song blaring in the background. Takes tiny sips of Diet Coke, trying to make it last. The longer it lasts, the longer she can sit here, among the living. The guys in the bar steer clear, as if they can tell she's doomed by just looking at her. Every guy but one.

—Hey. Mind if I join you?

When CI #137 turns to see who's speaking, her body goes numb. Fuck, fuck, fuck, it's the guy from the mafia kill building—the thug who was supposed to "do her." Now he's sitting right next to her, within immediate strangling/stabbing/shooting range. Looks like CI #137 is not going to survive this neighborhood after all.

The stool groans as he eases his weight onto it.

—Hell of a night, huh.

CI #137 didn't get a good look at him in the kill room. Out there he was just the two-legged embodiment of bloody murder—your prototypical goon, thug, bruiser. But now sitting just a barstool away, his face in profile, she notices the nose, hooked like a hawk's. His eyes, though, are softer and kinder than she remembers. Maybe that's how Death works. Charms you a little before snatching away your soul.

CI #137 takes a sip of her soda and asks quietly, calmly:

—Are you going to kill me.

A statement more than a question.

—Are you actually daring me to kill you? Hah! Or whatever it was you said. Best line I've ever heard! Anyway, what are you drinking?

CI #137 tells him. The bruiser makes a sour face, then says we can't do that. The night they've had, they need a real drink, the best bourbon a place like this has to offer. Which turns out to be Wild Turkey, neat. He orders two, slides one over my way.

—How did you find me?

—Well, I know you didn't go straight to the cops, because after I strangled Little Pete to death, I sat there for a good long while, waiting for the law to show up.

—You…you killed him?

—Long story. No, actually, it's a short story. He was an asshole. Fuck him. Whatever. I'm over it. Back to you. Once I realized you didn't call the law, I figured you'd be out here somewhere. So I went looking for you.

CI #137 takes a moment (and another sip) while she digests this information. Something doesn't add up.

—So your random search of South Philly brought you to this bar?

—Well…no. I saw you truckin' down Two Street like your pants were on fire. I couldn't figure out how to stop you without you screaming or freaking out, and before I knew it you went into that house on Vernon Street. I thought about knocking, but then you came out looking like a zombie. So I followed you here. Figured you wouldn't freak out as much in a public place. And by the way, thank you for not freaking out in a public place.

CI #137 takes a sip of Diet Coke, ignores the booze. The bruiser knocks back his Wild Turkey, shrugs, then does hers and orders another. The rest of the bar ignores them. Probably figure it's some father-daughter shit and none of them want to get involved in something like that.

—So if you aren't going to kill me, why did you follow me?

—I'll explain that in a minute. But can I ask something first?

—What?

—Your name.

Confidential Informant #137 tells the bruiser her name, her real name, figuring, What does it matter now? She's been outed. The bruiser, in turn, shares his real name (Richie), as well as his nickname (Ringo) and its origin (his nose). She tells the bruiser he doesn't look like a Beatle at all. The bruiser seems to appreciate that. They agree to call each other by their birth names. Richie orders another Wild Turkey. CI #137 orders another Diet Coke and a bag of potato chips.

—Serafina...that really is a beautiful name, by the way...okay, here's what I'm guessing, and correct me if I'm wrong. But you're a snitch, right?

—I prefer canary.

Richie allows a sly smile to sneak out.

—Okay, Lady Canary. But you do have a deal with the cops, right? Don't answer. I'm gonna assume you do. In fact, I'm counting on it. Because, you know, killing a guy like Little Pete isn't something that's easily forgiven. I'm pretty much fucked sideways, and my only way out is through immunity. So I'm hoping you'll bring me to your cop. Let me make a deal, too. Maybe you'd put in a good word for me, how I helped you and stuff?

CI #137 knows there is no "deal" to be had. Wildey fucked her over, left me for dead. But the neighborhood is cruel and cold and CI #137 could very much use a friend.

Death can go fuck itself—CI #137 wants to live.

Strike that—I want to live.

I want to punish the motherfuckers who killed D.

I want to hurt the police for what they did to me.

And you can't do that dead.

I drain the rest of my Diet Coke and turn on my stool to face my new best friend.

—Are you hungry, Richie?

He smiles.

—Starving. But the food here is crap. C'mon, my truck's down the street.

"We got them."

"Them?"

"Ringo's with her. I've been telling you, Cap, there's something not right about that fuckin' wacko."

"Goddamn it."

Rem Mahoney already knows that Ringo betrayed them. He heard the sickening crunch of Pete D'Argenio's neck snapping over the wire, followed by a mocking whisper into the pen transmitter—*Yo, El Jefe! I quit. Have a nice Christmas!*—before the pen itself snapped, too. Transmission over.

The loss of D'Argenio is serious bad fucking news but not insurmountable. There are always other wiseguys. Maybe he was wrong to pick the D'Argenio clan anyway. Maybe the Perellis were the way to go. Fuckin' Little Pete; he should have followed his gut back in the

summer and gone with Lisa. At the time he thought it was a rare instance of his brain overruling his dick, but now he's thinking he should
have sided with the penis. Lisa is one ice-cold bitch; Rem will forever
question his attraction to dames of her kind. She'll make a fine second-
in-command.

But no, right now his immediate concern is *containment.* Two people
out there in his city breathing air right now have the ability to blow
up everything. Rem needs them to stop breathing.

"So...Cap?"

"Do it."

"We're gonna need to be a little audacious."

"You have my permission to be audacious."

Ringo insists on the Melrose Diner. Passyunk and Snyder, represent!
There is no other place; Ringo loves it here, dreamed about it all the
time in Kansas. His first meal back, he ate here and licked his fingers
clean afterward. So many good memories.

Now Ringo orders the Chicago steak with eggs, hash browns, and
cottage cheese on the side. The girl, Serafina, surprises him by ordering bacon and eggs, with extra bacon (emphasis on the bacon). She
kind of struck him as the watches-what-she-eats, vegetarian type. But
you go, girl—do your bacon. On top of that, Ringo tells the waitress
to keep the coffee coming like Beyoncé, hot and black. Serafina stares
at him. "What did you just say?" But she kind of cracks a smile and
he knows it's going to be okay. The kid had him worried for a while
there.

Before the food arrives, Ringo slides his cell phone across the table
to her.

"You can use my phone. Figure we'll be safe here, in a public place,
until we can arrange a meeting place."

"Meeting place with who?" Serafina asks.

"Look, I know how this whole thing works. Not sure who was handling you, but I know the Russian chick was in charge. I'm no dummy. I know that's how we were scoring our intel."

"So you're the one who's been killing the CIs," she says softly.

"Yeah, well, no. Not just me. Me and three other people. But I can hand them to your Russian lady on a silver platter, along with all the dirt she'd ever need on her lousy ex-husband. Never liked that prick."

Ringo stops talking as the coffee arrives. But he gives her the raised eyebrows that practically shout, *Well, whaddya think?*

"If this is your master plan, then we're both fucked. The Russian lady, as you call her, is crooked. So is my handler. They sent me to you *to be killed.*"

"No, I don't think so. It was her husband, the Internal Affairs guy. Apparently he has her apartment wired for sound, cameras out the ass, the whole thing, like that creepy movie with Sharon Stone and the Baldwin guy, not Alec, one of the other ones."

Serafina blinks, utterly befuddled. "What are you talking about?"

But she doesn't have the chance to hear Ringo's answer. Because a moment later she's too busy screaming.

Lisa and Frankenstein, both in hoodies and the kind of face masks you wear in cold weather or bank robberies, step inside the diner just as Ringo and CI #137's orders are coming out. They fall in so close behind the waitress that Frankenstein could reach around and grab a piece of bacon from the hot plate as it moves its way through space. The bacon smells good. Maybe after this is all over tonight they'll hit some other diner.

Lisa glances at him, nods. Frankenstein nods in return. Lisa body-checks the waitress forward. The tray and breakfast orders go airborne. Frankenstein pulls his guns from the hoodie, aims. The girl snitch at the table sees the waitress tumbling, the guns; she screams. Ringo reacts to her screams. He turns and whips the table away in the same fluid motion. Lisa has her guns out now, too. Ringo dives forward, probably trying to crawl over the poor girl in an attempt to escape. But there will be no escape. They're too close.

They open fire.

THE CANARY FLIES

BENEATH THE BEN FRANKLIN BRIDGE

THURSDAY, DECEMBER 12

"Wild Child."

"Loot."

Wildey has spent the past two hours driving all over the city looking for the Honda Civic, listening to the police band radio, and thinking about his finger over the nuke button. Because that call to Rem Mahoney would indeed be the end of Kaz's career. While he knows the leak was coming from her, Wildey has no solid proof. Before he pressed that button, he needed to be dead sure. And while he was all the way up in Olney (hoping to see that Civic somewhere on campus), a call came in: an anonymous tipster reporting something about a body being loaded into a truck under the Ben Franklin Bridge. The bridge wasn't that far away from the Society Hill Towers. Wildey couldn't rocket down Broad Street fast enough.

Apparently his soon-to-be-ex-supervisor heard the same call and thought the same thing, because she's standing on the fringes while the crime techs work the scene.

"What's going on?" Wildey asks, winding his way through the crowd. Cops, TV reporters, lookiloos. Then, lowering his voice to a fevered whisper: "Please tell me she isn't here."

"No, she's not. I want to show you something."

Wildey trails behind her as they walk into the public works building. But once Wildey steps into the room and sees all of the plastic and blood, his stomach feels like it's dropped to his shoes. No. Not her. Not in this room. Every surface is covered in clear plastic, as if somebody is preparing to do a paint job. But this isn't remodeling; this is an execution room.

"Jesus Christ."

"No bodies, just trace amounts of blood," she says. "You don't know her type, do you?"

Wildey admits he does not. "Anybody hear anything? Screams, whatever?"

"No. The walls are too thick, the roar of the bridge too loud. Perfect place to torture and kill someone, though, wouldn't you say? I think we've finally stumbled into the place where our CIs have been taken."

"Where *you* sent them," Wildey snaps.

Ooh, the hatred in her eyes. She doesn't bother to answer the allegation.

"I'm fairly sure," Kaz says, "your girl was here."

"How do you know that?"

Kaz walks over to a corner of the room where the techs have bagged every object in the room that isn't nailed down. Wildey follows. She crouches, picks up a plastic bag, shows it to Wildey. Inside is CI #137's bugged pen, snapped in half.

"Fuck me," he says, then looks beyond Kaz at the other bagged objects. A purse. A nail file. An iPhone. All of Sarie Holland's things.

"All of the puzzle pieces are here," she says. "It's just a matter of putting them together. Until then, Officer Wildey, you're relieved of duty. Don't go too far."

FOX CHASE

DECEMBER 13

Whatever Kevin Holland is doing, you can't exactly call it sleep. His body has downshifted into a low-wattage inactive mode as he stares sightlessly at the ceiling, waiting for his cheap plastic cell to make a noise. Come on, dumb phone. Do something.

Sleep is impossible, anyway. Laura always joked that when you become a parent, the first thing you lose is the ability to sleep soundly...for the rest of your life. Rest is not possible until your children are safe under the same roof, where you can check on them at any given moment. Hey there, kid, just making sure you're still breathing. Sorry, part of the job. Carry on.

Kevin hasn't heard from Sarie since 7:14 p.m., when she texted him she'd be at the campus library for a few hours getting a jump on her last final exam before Christmas break. Which Kevin didn't really believe. He knew she'd skipped one exam today (the professor, concerned, had called). What was another one? But you pick your battles.

Now he is fervently wishing he'd picked this one.

Kevin rises from the couch. Stretches his lean frame, trying to crack his own back. (It refuses.) Checks his cell again. (Nothing.) How early is too early to hit the panic button? He checks his cell again, checks the audio mute button just to be sure he didn't accidentally set it to silence. (Again, nothing.) He does something he never thought he'd do in this situation. He offers up a little prayer, mumbling it softly in case the angels require vocalization.

Laura, honey, if you're up there listening, give me a little sign. Yeah, I know you're laughing at me right now, because I'm probably worrying for nothing. Or maybe you're scowling at me because I've been an asshole dad since last Christmas. But in either case, let me know.

Give me one of those cracks to the forehead. Check in on our baby girl, okay? Please tell me nothing happened to her.

Kevin pads his way to the kitchen, pours himself a cup of water straight from the tap. Good old Schuylkill Punch. His gut is so tight he almost throws it back up into the sink. He should have eaten dinner tonight.

"Dad?"

The sound of Marty's voice startles the shit out of him. Kevin recovers before he turns around. "Hey, buddy."

"Waiting up for Sarie?"

"Yeah. But what are you doing up? Hope you're not trying to catch Santa Claus in the act. Because you're a few weeks early."

Marty rolls his eyes. Kevin is fairly confident he knows the score on Santa. Especially after last year's horrible Christmas.

"What are you doing up, Dad?"

"Just waiting for Sarie to get home."

"Oh. Can I have some hot chocolate, Dad?"

"Sure, buddy. Make me a cup of coffee, too, if you don't mind."

As Marty busies himself with the tea kettle and a big ceramic mug with LA JOLLA on the side, Kevin checks his phone again. Again, fucking nothing. After a moment of contemplation Kevin sends another text, practically begging, please, whatever it is, just let me know you're okay. He tells himself that if this whole thing is Sarie punishing him for his behavior this past year, then he won't be mad. He promises, swears to God, on his own life. Sure, he'll let Sarie know how cruel this all is, but he'll instantly forgive her. Just as long as she's okay. He can't lose her, not now.

It's quick, but Kevin catches it—that vaguely squirrely look in his son's eye. Like he knows something but doesn't want to rat out his sister. Admirable but wrong nonetheless.

"Martin."

"Uh...Dad?" Marty knows it's never good when his full name is invoked.

"Do you know where Sarie is? You won't get in trouble, I promise. Just tell me the truth."

"I don't know, Dad."

Martin's eyes seem to be telling the truth. So, okay. Maybe he doesn't know where his older sister is right now. But there was that moment, just a second ago, where Marty was clearly hiding something. Kevin tells himself to circle back to that, focus on the task at hand: pinning down Sarie's location ASAP.

"She's not answering. Or texting back. Maybe she lost her phone."

"What about Tammy?"

Truth was, Kevin has considered calling the Pleece home, but it was—Christ, after midnight. It was late, but not obscenely late. He could make that call later if it came to it. But there *was* somebody Kevin could call now. Someone who'd probably be awake. Kevin thumbed his phone until he found the contact, hit send. Two rings and he was connected.

"George—you up?"

"You know I'mmm always up. What up, golden boy?"

Kevin's high school friend George Ponus is a cop. Not a *real* cop, as Kevin likes to tease. George works in organizational administration or some such shit and hasn't strapped on a gun in fifteen years. Still, Ponus can get cop answers. He's also kind of a drunk and an insomniac. George tried AA but found himself preferring the counsel of the crowd at the Grey Lodge or the original Chickie's & Pete's instead.

Kev doesn't judge, doesn't try to convert him; Kev and Ponus go way way back. If you're lucky, you find the kind of friend who keeps you from death. And likewise, at odd times—an unspoken agreement that, yeah, sure, I've got your back. Kev and Ponus had shared this since they were both fifteen doing really stupid shit. Funny how Kev relied on his oldest friends when life made a hairpin turn into darkness. Funny how Kev is suddenly referring to himself as "Kev." He hasn't done that in twenty years.

Kevin can hear the din of the bar in the background. Which one was it? Grey Lodge or Chickie's? Both on the same block. Both within walking distance of Ponus's house.

"Okay, you're going to think this is crazy, but —"

Marty reaches over and hits the END button on his phone.

"Marty, what the hell?"

"No, dad," he says.

"No police. We can't."

I am playing dead.

My would-be killers were in a hurry, tossing my barely breathing body next to Richie's in the back of the flatbed, quickly covering both of us with a waterproof tarp before peeling away from the scene and a group of stunned diners with half-chewed food in their mouths.

The ride is violent and bumpy. I try hard not to think about the corpse pressing up against my left arm. The corpse who didn't like to be called Ringo. The corpse who was my only friend left in this city. I try not to focus on the fact that just a few minutes ago he was smiling, joking with me, eating a meal, talking about the Baldwin brothers.

I try to block out the noxious chemicals in plastic barrels back here that smell like the world's worst blend of ammonia and vinegar salad dressing.

Mostly, though, I try to block out the fact that I've been shot and am, for all I know, slowly bleeding to death.

The pain in my right bicep is agonizing. I swear I can feel the bullet worming around in there close to the bone. And every road bump and jolt drives it closer still. What's it going to feel like when it completes the journey?

I bite down on my lower lip and try to do something. Such as: figuring out where they might be taking us. The tarp ten inches above my face flaps violently in the cold night air. Truck tires whine on asphalt. That means I'm on a major road. Maybe I-95? That means we could be headed somewhere in Jersey, like the Pine Barrens. Or all the way up to Bucks County.

Violent shivers now begin to rack my body, and I order myself to pull my shit together. One stray elbow knocking the metal floor of the truck would make them pull over, peel back the tarp for a closer look. And maybe then I won't be so lucky holding my breath. There was so much blood splattered on me they didn't bother checking back at the diner, but they might now. Another bullet and I'd be done.

I tell myself: Focus. Listen for clues. You can figure your way out of this. You always do.

There are police sirens. Distant shouts. The hum of engines, wheels on asphalt. For a second I consider sticking my hand up out of the tarp and waving for help. But what good would that do? Chances are my would-be killers in the front of the truck would see it long before any other driver on the road.

Without warning my body does an involuntary jolt, my right elbow knocking metal with a deafening CLUNK.

Did I just fall asleep for a second? Or longer? Did they hear that knock?

The tires hum, the tarp flaps.

I squeeze my eyes tight and wait.

Wait…

Nothing. Then the biggest clue of all comes from about five thousand feet above the tarp—the high/low scream of a jet engine, cutting through the air before quickly receding. Maybe we're near the airport? If I can figure out where we're going, there's a chance I can steel myself ahead of time, then jackrabbit away, maybe outrun their bullets…

No, that's stupid. Running's not the answer. But neither is staying put. Because they're probably going to dump me somewhere deep where I won't be found, not ever. Can I fight them off? Please. I am skinny, covered in blood, terrified, freezing, and probably still in shock. It would not be a fair fight.

So run?

Try to fight anyway?

Continue to play dead?

Before I have the chance to decide, the truck squeals and comes to a slow rolling stop way before I expect it to.

Truck doors creak open. Someone coughs. The suspension rocks. Someone—I assume one of the killers from the diner—unties the tarp, flips it back. I suck in air, wondering if this is the last time I'll be able to do such a thing. I command my heart to slow the fuck down.

They pull Richie's body out. Guess they want the tough job over with first. His corpse is heavy, so it takes both of them. One of them nudges me aside and I have to bite my tongue to stop a trilling tremor that feels like it's about to explode from my nervous system and rack my entire body. I taste my own sweet and salty blood. Strangely, it tastes better than it should.

A lot sooner than I like, rough hands grab my legs. Someone takes a left wrist. I hold my breath and let every muscle go slack. My dress bunches up in the back as I'm pulled across the ribbed metal of the flatbed. Please don't look too hard at my chest. Please don't see me breathing.

All at once I'm weightless, hurled through the winter air, my stomach flipping, everything suspended, like the first time you do a cannonball into a pool.

But then the impact is brutal. This isn't a river. It's a boardwalk. Wooden planks. My tailbone explodes with pain as I quickly suck in air. Can I hold my breath long enough for them to be satisfied with their work and pull away?

There is more pounding on wooden planks a few feet away. My lungs are burning. I need to breathe, to run, to scream, to SOMETHING. I can do none of these things. Not until they're gone.

And then, without warning, once again, my body twitches—a spasm that knocks my elbow against the boards.

—Oh, fuck me. This bitch is still alive, man!

—Didn't you check?

—Didn't you?

—She's a girl, I thought you were going to check.

—What does being a girl have to do with it?

My eyes pop open. Now it's time for the other plan—the one where I run like hell. I roll over, but they're on me before I can stand, so I lash out with everything I've got—elbows and knees and clawed fingers and teeth. One of the killers, the dark-eyed woman, laughs at me, pushes me hard back down to the wooden planks.

—Easy now, honey, easy.

The male killer pulls his gun as the dark-haired bitch squats down to hold me in place. She's much stronger than she looks. I can't move. Even if I could, there is nowhere I could go.

—Don't miss this time, Frankie, okay?

—Fuck you.

I realize: These are the last words I'm going to hear.

*   *   *

"What do you mean, no police?"

"We can find Sarie on our own. If you call the cops it'll go on her permanent record."

"Marty, swear to God, you'd better tell me what you know . . ."

A few hours ago the tracer chip finally started working; there are multiple pings. God bless social media. Marty knows where his sister is! He has the chance to save the day! But he also knows he has to play this right, not tip his hand too much.

"Okay, I'm sorry, Dad, but Sarie swore me to secrecy. She went down to South Street tonight." Because that's where the tracer chip says her Honda Civic is parked: on Fourth, near South.

"Jesus fucking . . . Get your coat and gloves on. We're going to get Sarie now. I'll deal with you later."

"What do you mean? How can we get Sarie? You don't drive."

Marty's dad has never driven a car, not as long as he's been alive, but tonight is apparently the exception. And George Ponus is drunk enough to agree to lend his buddy Kevin Holland (via his half-awake wife) the keys to a 2007 Chevy Cavalier, parked in the driveway next door. Mrs. Ponus isn't as sure, but Kevin lays it on thick: I just need to pick up my daughter, thank you so much, we'll have the car right back to you.

"Dad, you sure you can do this?"

"Are you buckled in?"

"Yes."

The Cavalier rockets down their street. Marty checks his iPod. The tracer chip says that Sarie's car is still on Fourth Street.

As Frankie opens fire, I steel myself, will it with all of my might—DO NOT FUCKING FLINCH. If I'm going to die, I'm not going to do it flinching.

But the bullets don't touch me. That's because they're coming from behind me—and I'm not the target.

I watch Frankie twist and half-spin and drop.

And then the dark-haired woman holding me down does this sudden jerky head-snap thing, and her strong body goes soft, falling away from me.

The ride downtown feels like forever, even with little traffic at this time of night. Kevin and his two children live so far away from the city's center they're practically tipping over into the next county. It's a long slog all the way down Rhawn Street, followed by a trek down State Road—which has been a construction zone all year long. They keep rebuilding I-95, over and over and over again. Kevin swears it's been at least three times in his lifetime. Lanes disappear. Off- and on-ramps change position. Familiar landmarks vanish. The highway continues on.

How many times has he done this? How many times has he driven down an ancient version of I-95, into the heart of Philadelphia, looking for trouble? So different now. Christ, what he put his parents through.

Marty spots the Civic first—on Fourth Street, half a block up from South. Seeing the cold and empty car parked there is a hard fucking jab straight to Kevin's heart. This was confirmation; Sarie lied to him. What else has she been lying about? Kevin finds a spot across the street from the Civic. If Marty were older, Kevin would leave him in the Cavalier as a lookout, in case Sarie wandered back on her own. But smart as the boy is, he is in fact only twelve. No way is Kevin leaving his twelve-year-old son alone in a car a block away from the drunken chaos of South Street—he's already fucking up enough as a parent, thank you very much. *Let me get this straight, Mr. Holland, your daughter went missing so you abandoned your kid in a freezing locked car while you prowled bars looking for her?* Kevin pulls on his gloves, then tells Marty to do the same and follow him.

Marty's all wide-eyed. He's only seen South Street during the day.

Cheesesteak runs and such. At night, it's another story. Somewhere out in the darkness a guy screams, then laughs. Somewhere else, a glass bottle explodes against a wall. Father Holland and son hurry down Fourth Street, their footsteps echoing off the storefronts. Kevin jerks his arm up, checks his watch; it's five till two, the magic hour when all bars have to close up for the night. Fuck. They have a lot of ground to cover. The bars line the street from Front all the way to Ninth or Tenth. Sarie probably parked on Fourth because she was hitting a bar nearby.

"Where do you think she is, Dad?"

"Honestly, kid, I have no fucking clue."

"Dad!"

Marty hates when his father curses. Kevin doesn't even realize he's doing it half the time.

"Sorry. C'mon, let's head to the right. Stick close to me, okay?"

Kevin looks at the signs, the crowds, and the printed menus posted to the outside walls. So, Kevin Holland, what's your daughter's taste in bars?

A systematic search of a half-dozen of them yields nothing except stares and sidelong glances. A middle-aged guy, bald, with tattooed arms and his twelve-year-old kid tagging along? Sure, it's going to look a little weird.

Kevin's daughter is not hard to pick out of a crowd, being taller than most girls her age. Taller than most women, in fact. Her long, dark hair is frequently up, out of her face, held in place by her mother's silver hairpin. Kevin scans the drunken masses in each bar, looking for tall, dark hair, silver hairpin. But tonight, having her big underage night out on the town, she might be wearing it down. So Kevin also listens for her voice, cutting through the din. Parents' ears are forever tuned to their kids' voices.

And now South Street is shutting its collective doors, having expelled all of the stragglers, drunks, and lonely guys still hoping, in vain, to hook up with some living being with a pulse. If his daughter was here, she's since departed.

"Dad, why would Sarie come here?"

"Because that's what college kids do. College kids about to be grounded until their senior year."

"Maybe she went back to the car?"

At a loss for a better idea, Kevin nods. They double back, padding down the sidewalk, breathing frigid air, hoping for a piece of recognition. But the Civic is just as quiet and dead and cold as before. A PPA ticket flutters against the windshield as an icy wind blows in from the Delaware River just a few blocks away. So if she's not in a bar, where is she? Does she have a friend from school who lives down here somewhere? If she does, maybe Tammy knows. Might be time to make that call, after all . . .

"It's seriously freezing out here."

"I know, I know. Hold on a minute."

Kevin huffs, stamping his feet, trying to clear his head. Maybe it's time to get back into the car, crank the heat. At least then the boy won't freeze to death, and Kevin could drive around the neighborhood, hoping to spot Sarie. But on a cold night like this, why would she be wandering around outside? No. She'd be inside, where it was warm.

Maybe it *is* finally time to call Tammy. Fuck worrying about waking up the parents. They have it easy—their daughter is home safe with them. They can take his worried, paranoid call and go right back to sleep.

Kevin glances at the Civic across the street, stamps his feet again. Exhales cold air that looks like smoke.

"Uh, Dad? What are we doing?"

Kevin tosses Marty the keys. "Get inside, turn up the heat, and wait for me. Just want to check something out."

Marty doesn't need to be told twice. He's practically shivering as he climbs into the front passenger seat, no doubt figuring Dad is too preoccupied to bother hassling him into the backseat. Kevin meanwhile walks across the street to the Civic, looking both ways up and down Fourth. He crouches down, peers inside the vehicle, looking for…clues. Something *off*. Whatever.

But the interior of the Civic is spotless and tidy, just like her mother used to keep it. He squints harder, trying like hell to get the hard-core analytical part of his brain to kick on. Come on…*nothing, Sarie?* No notes to yourself? Not even a paper bag from a store, so that I can have some clue where you might have been during the past twelve hours?

He unlocks the Civic with the spare key fob he brought with him (thank God he remembered that, otherwise he'd be considering breaking into his own daughter's car) and sits behind the wheel. Kevin doesn't even have to adjust the seat, because Sarie is almost as tall as him. A quick check of the little compartments and cubbies and glove box reveals nothing. In the backseat is a change of clothes in an overnight bag. Guess she wanted to look nice for her big night out. Where did she change? Probably that fucking kid's place—Drew. Kevin glances over at Marty, who's huddled in the passenger seat of the Cavalier, warming his hands in front of the vents. He should wrap this up, relock the car, then call Tammy. Kevin gives a halfhearted feel under the driver's seat, and there it is.

A cell phone.

Thing is, it's not Sarie's cell phone. She received an iPhone for Christmas and adores the stupid thing—never lets it leave her side. So what is this? Kevin picks it up. It's a simple flip phone. No fancy touch screen. Plastic, something you could pick up for twenty bucks at a convenience store.

So of course Kevin flips it open. No recent calls, and only one text exchange:

Let me know when you're at the towers

And the response:

kk

And...nothing else. The rest of the phone had been cleared—or purchased just for that one exchange. What the fuck? Was this Sarie's, or did it belong to some friend of hers who forgot it in her car?

Only one way to find out. Kevin texts back:

hey

Kevin waits.

No response.

He thumbs the keypad:

you there?

Kevin waits, thinking that the person at the other end of the message could be with Sarie *right fucking now,* and this mini-parental nightmare could be over in a few seconds. Just text back, whoever you are. Come on.

There's no return text; this time the cell rings. Kevin fumbles it as he flips it open to answer.

"Hello? Who is this?"

There's huffing at the other end of the phone, almost a sigh...then a staccato beep.

"Who the fuck is this?" Kevin shouts, even though the call is already disconnected. He feels the urge to lash out at something, his hands practically shaking. He settles on the Civic's horn, pounding it with the flat of his fist. *BARRP!* Marty looks over from the Cavalier, a slightly panicked look on his face.

Wildey is on the fringes of the Badlands, driving in stone silence, when his phone receives a text. He checks the screen and can't believe it. It's from Honors Girl.

hey

He pulls his car over to the side of the street, scaring the shit out of some sleeping junkies. He's about to respond when there's another text:

you there?

Which gives him pause. That doesn't sound like Honors Girl. That sounds like someone who has (found?) her burner phone and is throwing up a test balloon. So instead of sending a text, he dials the number. Wildey's stomach sinks when a gruff male voice answers. "Hello. Who is this?" Shit. Wildey hits END.

All kinds of ruinous thoughts race through his head. Whoever grabbed Sarie took the burner. Maybe that same person (or people), are looking for him, too, and just tried to trick him into revealing his location. Shit, if Kaz *is* involved in the conspiracy, they would know he was headed home and could have people waiting for him.

Wildey sits in his car, listening to the El above him rumble down the tracks, wondering what he should do. Maybe Honors Girl is still out there, waiting for him to save her. Maybe there can be some kind of trade; his own life for the girl. He flips on the police radio again and instantly hears fevered chatter about a massacre down at the Melrose Diner — reports of two victims, one male, white, fifties, one female, eighteen or nineteen years old, Latino.

Forget amnesty. If Kevin finds the guy — and he just *knows* it's some guy — on the other end of that line, he's going to fucking annihilate him.

Sarie's going to be in trouble, too.

Kevin returns to his own car, but not before leaving a handwritten note on the ticket on the windshield:

Sarie this is Dad. Call me the minute you see this.

They drive around. There's an active crime scene under the Ben Franklin Bridge. Flashing cherries outside the four-story building, tape strewn everywhere, TV news vans blocking the streets.

Don't freak out. This is not her. This has nothing to do with her. Just because your daughter is missing and you see police lights doesn't mean something's happened to her . . .

There is nothing left to do but return home. They could drive up and down the streets all night, but the chances of spotting Sarie are pretty much nil. But he can't just stake out her car all night, either. Maybe if Kevin was alone, but not with poor Marty out here in the cold. No, the best thing is to go back home, let Marty go to bed, and wait by two phones now—Kevin's, and the cheap-ass one from Sarie's car. Tonight, sleep will not be an option.

Christ, is Ringo glad he hid that snub-nose beneath the tracks.

Because while Sarie Canary there was twisting around and screaming her lungs out—always a good play—Ringo was pulling his trembling, leaking, fucked-up carcass along the tracks, feeling the blood spurting out of a few holes but not caring. Reaching that piece was all that mattered. That, and pulling it from its hiding place. Rolling over. Performing one sit-up, yeah, just like in the military days, and more or less aiming at anything over the two-feet mark. Bang bang bang bang. Bodies went twisting in the darkness, stumbling on the tracks. Ringo feels like he's gonna puke from moving too much. The bodies drop. Bye-bye, Frankenstein. Good night, Lisa Lisa. The girl cries out in panic and horror one last time. Ringo's torso drops back down to the tracks and he mutters "ah shit" before he passes out.

When he jolts awake a few minutes (hours? days? years?) later, the girl is kneeling next to him and crying. Holding her right arm, which is covered in blood. "Hey," he tells her.

"Ohmygod," she says, and the tears stop. "You're alive."

"Think you're the only one who knows how to play dead?" Ringo asks. "Ah shit."

"I'll call nine one one..."

"Really not a good idea, honey," Ringo says. "Forget about me for a second. How about you? How's your arm there?"

"I got shot," she says quietly.

"You and me both. Come here and let me have a look."

However, when Ringo takes a good look and wipes away some of the blood—the girl flinches like he's touching her with a hot iron—he's happy to inform her that the bullet only grazed her skin. A bleeder, but nothing serious.

"I wasn't shot?" she says, almost disappointed.

"If you want bragging rights, I think you've got more than enough after tonight." Ringo coughs. It hurts. "Ah, shit."

They both watch the dark river flow down toward the Delaware, where it will eventually spill out into the ocean. Ringo thinks about just crawling off the edge of the pier and floating along with it. After a while, the cold would sink in deep, and he wouldn't feel anything anymore. On the other hand, he'd probably wash up in Delaware, and he always hated that fucking place.

Then there's the matter of this girl, who looks utterly and completely fucking lost. Ringo understands. He's been there. Shit, he thinks he's there now.

"Can you just go home or something?"

"I don't think so."

"You've got unfinished business, huh."

She nods.

"You know which cop did this to you—this handler you mentioned?"

She bites her lip thinking it over. But yeah. She knows.

"Okay, good. This gives you a purpose in life, and with that, honey, you can do anything. Know what your purpose is? Go and do worse to him. Far worse. Right now you've got the element of surprise. You're assumed dead. This won't last forever, but if you're smart I'd give it a day or so. Use that day."

"Okay."

"Sun's coming up in a few hours. You'd better get going. I wouldn't use that truck. That's probably how they found us, with that GPS shit. You know how to get where you're going?"

"I think so."

"Good."

"What about you?"

"Me? I'll be right as rain."

"Like hell you are—you were shot like five hundred times."

Ringo smiles, rubs his ample belly a little. "Yeah, but I'm well insulated."

Truth is, he has no idea how badly he's shot up. There's a lot of numbness in places that shouldn't be numb. Whatever. He'll figure it out later. Ringo feels strangely free, like he's hopscotched away from the jaws of death enough times to go pro. If the Grim Reaper were to claim him now, then it would strike him as perfectly fair.

"You know," Ringo says, "we should probably get out of here."

"I want to do something for you," the girl says abruptly.

Ringo, shot to hell so bad that when he smiles his teeth are streaked with blood, says, "Yeah?"

"There's a man who killed a friend of mine. He's a drug dealer with a goofy name. Chuckie Morphine. He has a boat down by Penn's Landing. If you're looking for a way out of the city, a boat's not a bad way to go."

Sometimes, Ringo thinks, gifts come in the most unexpected places. Now he had a purpose in life, too. He smiles. "This Chuckie Morphine guy, he a tough one?"

"You're tougher."

Ringo considers. Doesn't sound like a bad idea at all. But then some dormant strain of chivalry kicks in.

"What about you? Don't you want to escape on a boat, too?"

"No, Richie," she says. "I've got things to do on land."

I strip the black hoodie from the dark-haired killer. I'm thankful for the head shot: It left her hoodie in pretty much perfect condition. Yes, it's a dead woman's garment, but it's freezing out.

Just a few hours ago I would have never gone near a dead body, let alone touch one. But nothing can freak me out now. Nothing will ever freak me out again.

I take her boots, too. A little tight—her feet are shorter and wider—but that's okay. The tightness will keep me alert and awake.

Richie is going to take care of Chuckie.

Now it's my turn to go after the police.

Kevin glances over at his son's face every minute or so on the ride home. Deep thoughts going through the boy's mind, he can tell. Or maybe it's just worry. Or lack of sleep. It is...what, quarter after two in the morning? The streets are deserted, and the Cavalier is pulling into a space in front of their house when Marty finally turns to face him, looking as if he is about to cry.

"I have to show you something, Dad. But don't be mad." The way Marty says it makes Kevin's blood turn ice-cold. Kevin asks, almost yelling, what's he talking about, what the fuck is it? Marty says he can't tell him.

"I have to show you."

As Marty leads the way down to the den in the basement, Kevin's mind really starts having fun with him. What could his twelve-year-old son possibly show him? And why couldn't he have done it before? You know, when they were searching his older sister's abandoned vehicle? Marty leads him across the room to Sarie's desk and pulls out a stack of blue exam books. The kind college professors hand out for a test. At least six of them.

"What is this?"

"Just open it. I'm not supposed to know about them, and Sarie doesn't know I know about them. But maybe they can help."

Kevin repeats, *What is this?* but he's more mumbling the question to himself as he pulls the exam books from the Ziploc. He fans them out in his hands. They're all dated, and they feel like they're stuffed with other pieces of paper.

"What the hell *is* this?" Kevin asks again, but Marty urges him to just read it.

The first of the books is dated 11/27–11/30. Kevin searches the calendar in his head. Wasn't that the day before Thanksgiving? When he was in San Diego? Flying back on a red-eye that night so he could be with the kids first thing in the morning? Yeah, that made sense. That was the night Marty slept over at his friend Ethan's house, and Sarie went to a party on campus, promising to have no more than two beers over the course of the night. She'd picked him up the next morning at the airport, looking tired, but then again, so was Kevin.

Kevin flips open the front cover to the first page, which is filled with Sarie's clean, perfect handwriting. The first line:

Hi, Mom. So I got arrested last night. (Sort of.)

Kevin looks at Marty. "What is this? Did you know about this?"

"About what?"

"About Sarie getting arrested!"

"I had no idea."

Kevin scans his son's face. Maybe Marty's telling the truth. Maybe he knew about the hidden exam books, not what they contained.

For a moment, Kevin is utterly lost. He wants to absorb the contents instantaneously and know exactly what to do about his daughter's situation. But he doesn't even know the situation. He pulls the last book from the pile, the one where the cover date (12/11–) is open-ended. He flips to a random page near the end:

So tonight on my to-do list:

1. Get Chuckie talking business
2. Buy Oxys
3. Buy a gun
4. Prepare for my 8:30 philosophy final

None of these words make sense. Oxys, a gun? The part about the philosophy exam — now, that sounds like his daughter. The "Chuckie talking business" part, not so much. She's an honor student, the most conscientious person he knows. She's never handed in anything late, never accepted anything less than an A-minus. Exactly the opposite of the fuckup Kevin was back in high school.

But the stuff about the pills and the gun...a fucking gun? That seems like the words of an alien being that has taken possession of his daughter's body. Yet the words are in her unmistakable handwriting. Just a few hours ago, his baby girl went out into the city of Philadelphia to buy drugs and a weapon.

From whom? Why? What in the fucking hell was going on?

Kevin flips through the blue books, searching for a meaning to emerge from the flurry of notes, cutout headlines from newspaper articles (FEDS; 2 PHILLY POLICE OFFICERS ROBBED CONFIDENTIAL INFORMANT, DRUG DEALERS AND NARCOTICS COP SUBJECT OF 18

COMPLAINTS), scribbles on napkins. He sees a familiar name—Tammy. *Of course* she's involved in this.

He dials her cell.

Tammy's phone doesn't ring because it's been submerged in the Delaware River, along with the body of Peter "Little Pete" D'Argenio. Tammy Pleece has a decision to make, but right now she's too drunk to be making any good decisions. So she stares out over the city for a while. From her vantage point near the top of one of the Society Hill Towers, facing South Philly, all appears calm. Way too calm. Deadsville.

Just wait at the place, he told her. *I'll call you.*

Hours and hours ago.

Where could he be? Should she just sit here and wait for him?

Without her phone?

So she mixes herself another drink. There's plenty of expensive Russian vodka, plenty of fresh-squeezed orange juice. She adds ice and mixes the two together, measuring by taste. Tammy takes a sip and realizes she put in way too much vodka. The alcohol tastes so sharp it hurts her teeth. Peter once made her a dirty martini, which sounded fun in the abstract but made her want to barf. She's adding more orange juice when the door opens. It's one of Peter's employees—a guy she always sees around. But now he's wearing a valet uniform.

"Come on, you gotta go."

"I don't think I should drive."

"Then walk."

"You asshole! I'm going to have you fired."

"Yeah? Good luck. Now get out."

"I want my phone."

"Forget your phone. Just *go home.*"

Forget her phone? What the hell does that mean? This whole

night is confusing. They were supposed to be partying. Then out of nowhere Peter asks to borrow her phone "for just a few seconds, babe" and promptly disappears. *With the phone.* So when he calls a little later it's on the apartment landline, telling her the party's canceled for tonight, he has to take care of some business, but just wait at the place, I'll call you.

"I want to speak to Peter."

"Listen, nobody's speaking to Peter ever again. Forget you ever knew Peter. This is not your world. Go. The fuck. Home."

Drunk as Tammy might be, she finally gets it. Oh god does she get it. Oh god . . . Sarie.

FOX CHASE

"George," Kevin says, "me again."

"What's up, man? Tell me you didn't crash my car. . . . Ah, I'm just kidding, bro. You find Sarie?"

"Who do you know working narcotics?"

"What? I would think you'd know more of those guys than me."

"I'm looking for a specific guy. Ben Wildey. Just something that came up during a counseling session. It's important. You know him?"

"No. How about you tell me what this is about? Because you're not exactly making much sense."

"It's confidential."

"Like telling you personal shit about a cop isn't breaking some kind of confidentiality thing?"

"George, I'll tell you everything, but man, the clock is ticking. I need to find somebody who knows this guy."

There's silence on the line. Kevin can hear faint swallowing, which would be George, resuming drinking. The man claims to drink to fall asleep, but he never ends up sleeping.

"Who's he with? Which unit?"

"Something called Narcotics Field Unit-Central South. NFU-CS. What is that?"

"Shit, Kev."

"Don't do this to me, Ponus. I wouldn't ask if it weren't really important."

SOUTH PHILLY

Wildey flashes his badge, but it doesn't yield him much except the basics, which he already heard on the police band. An older white guy and a girl—who depending on the witness was thought to be either his daughter or an escort—shot multiple times by a pair of masked killers, one of whom might be female. The weird part: The killers took the bodies with them, dumping them into the back of a waiting truck (tomorrow the headline will read: DOUBLE MURDER TO GO) before peeling away into the night.

To dump the bodies, Wildey thinks.

Honors Girl was a big fan of to-do lists. Now Wildey compiles one of his own. Real short and nothing fancy:

1. Find her body and bring it home to her family.
2. Make Kaz Mahoney pay for what she's done.

FOX CHASE

Marty watches his father tremble and fidget and pace and curse under his breath, waiting for his cell phone to ring. So many questions race through Marty's brain, and he realizes that pretty soon he may not have the chance to ask them. Especially when Dad's friend George calls back.

Sometimes you just have to ask the question direct, see how your subject handles it. Marty has pieces of evidence—the immunity deal, the glamour photos—that he dug up out of those plastic containers. But he doesn't have the whole story.

"Dad, was Mom a drug dealer?"

His father's face falls. "No. *God,* no, Marty. Nothing like that at all. Where is this coming from?"

"But she testified against a cartel in 1995."

"How did you...? Jesus. Fuck. *Fuck.* Yeah, she did."

"So she was involved in the drug business."

"Not by her own choice." Kevin sighs. "Look, Marty, this is a long story and this isn't the time to—"

Marty snaps.

"Screw *you,* Dad! It's never the right time, because you think I'm too young to handle anything. Like Mom being sick with terminal brain cancer! When did you and Sarie decide to not tell me? Why did you wait until she was already dead before you told me?"

"We didn't want you to worry."

"Congrats, Dad. I didn't worry. Not until she was already dead, and now I worry all the time. Worry about what you're not telling me. About what Sarie's not telling me. What's next, huh? Well, I'm tired of that shit. I went looking for the answers myself. And I found them."

Dad looks like he's about to cry or explode. Marty's not sure which. What does it matter? He's not going to start telling the truth now, anyway. He swears, if he ever has children—and that's a big if, knowing the track record of this family—he'll never tell them a single lie. No matter how hard it is. He will only deal in truth. He won't put them through this. Ever.

"Your mother was not a drug dealer," his father says quietly. "What she was...was beautiful. Her parents were poor, but they scraped together enough money to enter her in a few pageants. She kept the family afloat for quite a while, appearing in those things. But then she was caught somewhere she shouldn't be, in some cartel business, and now they had something over her head, over her entire family's head. Cartels are like that. They don't care about who they're using or hurting. If you serve a function, they're going to use you. Anyway, she was forced to do things."

"Like muling?"

Kevin blinks, surprised to hear the word come out of his twelve-year-old son's mouth. But then again, he shouldn't be surprised.

"Yeah, muling." And worse. Forgive me, Laura. He wasn't supposed to know any of this. Guess this is punishment for The Fiction—having your face stomped into the curb of The Truth.

"So you rescued her from the cartel?" Marty asks, and Kevin is tempted to deliver more Fiction here. Yes, son, I rescued your mother from the evil drug cartel, gun in my hand, bowie knife strapped to my belt, smuggling her over the border with bullets flying over our heads. But that would dishonor her strength.

"She escaped and somehow found her way to the DEA. I met her in the retreat where I was working. The feds wanted her cleaned up so she could testify."

Marty catches on instantly. "She was on drugs?"

"Yes."

But then he tells his son that while his mother was born beautiful, she was like a zombie when they brought her in for treatment. That was the thing nobody understood. Wow, Kev, you lucked out, got yourself a Mexican beauty queen. He didn't fall in love with her because of her looks. It was her strength. She could survive anything.

"I was in complete awe," Kevin says.

"Then Sarie will be okay, too," Marty says, believing it for the first time.

SPRING GARDEN

Man, the ex looks like shit, thinks Rem Mahoney as he rubs his hands together, watches her. He's been out here for a couple hours now—where else is he supposed to go, with the entire world blowing up around him? No word from Frankenstein or Lisa confirming the body dump, news of the so-called Melrose Diner Massacre (seriously, folks, two people ain't a massacre) spreading everywhere, his man Bird apparently flying the coop...Mahoney thinks maybe his ex-wife is, shockingly enough, his last chance.

Look at her shuffle into her apartment. Hair looking like it hasn't seen shampoo since the previous weekend, bags under her eyes. You should take a nap, sweetie.

But no, no nap for Katrina. Just a cup of coffee, which sends her pacing around her place like a tiger down at the zoo. She's trying to figure out where it's all going wrong.

How about I come in and tell you.

A minute later Rem is knocking on her back door, and the ex panics and pulls her gun, so Rem ducks his smiling face into the window and waves. The look on her face: almost worth all of this effort. When she recovers, she wearily unlocks the back door and lets him in.

"Nice place."

Not that he hasn't prowled this place a thousand times already. But it's weird, actually being invited in. Weird, too, the way she sits on her couch and sighs as if she's been expecting him.

"That motherfucker Wildey called you, didn't he? Jesus, he didn't waste time."

Oh, this is too good!

"Yes, Wildey did call. We had a very interesting conversation. Oh yes."

"Don't listen to a word of his bullshit. He's the fucking leak in my department!"

"Actually, no, he's not."

"What? You can't think that I'm behind this! Look, Rem, whatever fucked-up shit there is between us, you know me, you know I couldn't possibly—"

Rem laughs. "Oh, Kaz, honey, you should see yourself. I'm really going to enjoy listening to this later."

Come on, sweetheart, you can do it. You can figure it out now, can't you? Because it won't be any fun if he has to spell it out for her. Judging by the expression on her face, yeah, she's getting it. Eyes darting all over her apartment, as if she'll somehow be gifted with fucking X-ray vision and see all the bugs Rem planted in the walls. That's right. You've totally got it now.

At their wedding, some asshole Russian disc jockey did this stupid thing where he forced Rem to sit in a chair while Kaz lifted his arm. *Ladies and gentlemen, take a good look, because this is the last time Rembrandt here will have the upper hand, har har har,* all her fucking Russian mob family laughing their asses off. Well, who has the upper hand now, my bride?

"Now, here's how we're going to proceed."

As it turns out, Kaz has her own ideas about how to proceed. She pulls her gun and aims it at her ex-husband.

I break into Wildey's home shortly after 5:00 a.m. The block looks abandoned at this hour.

If I'm going to have any prayer of staying alive and keeping Dad and Marty safe, I need proof. The proof has to be somewhere inside this house. Maybe it's stacks of cash, maybe it's another burner phone, maybe it's a bunch of files. I don't really have a plan other than gathering up whatever it is, carrying it down to the El, and taking it right to the D.A.'s office in the Widener Building. On my way here, stomping around in my too-tight boots and thin hoodie, I briefly considered going straight to the D.A., camping out in the doorway if I had to. But without proof, did I really have a prayer at untangling a massive police conspiracy?

Hence the need to break into Wildey's house.

It's the nicest one on the block, but that's not saying much. Like the one good tooth in a meth addict's smile. Most of them have been demolished, leaving muddy, weedy lots in their place. Others are still standing but with little more than old paint, grime, and a prayer keeping them up. On the sides of those surviving houses, you can see the phantom images of their former neighbors. Pink paint where a bathroom used to be. Pale green where a kitchen once stood. Then I notice an odd feature on the freestanding houses. Something that would be fine if this were a full block.

Wildey's car isn't out front or anywhere on the block. No doubt he's out there somewhere looking for me, making sure I'm really dead.

Still, I probably don't have much time.

The house has a neighbor on each side, but both of those buildings are obviously abandoned. I choose the one on the left and make my way through the empty living room, heading upstairs to the back bedroom, where I find a closet. I open the door, and a horrible smell punches me in the nose; something died here a long long time ago. But I hold my breath, step over the carcass (pigeon? squirrel?), and feel the back of the closet. Drywall. At some point these houses were connected by doors; instead of bricking them over, construction crews just put up a sheet of drywall.

Which I now kick through, using my would-be killer's boots.

The room on the other side—in Wildey's house now—is jammed with filing cabinets and plastic crates full of albums. Jesus, what a hoarder. This is going to make the search for proof a little tricky.

And I have no idea how much time I have left when I hear a voice to my right:

—Jesus Christ!

Wildey is in the door, slightly crouched, pointing a gun at me.

I scream and dive back toward the closet, pushing through old clothes in a frenzy, but I can't move fast enough. Rough hands grab me, pull me back out.

Wildey yells it over and over again, *I'm not gonna hurt you, I'm not gonna hurt you!*, hoping that it will sink in before some neighbor calls the police. Finally the words sink in and she stops fighting him. They move back into the back bedroom, which is where he keeps all of his dad's old shit. Wildey eases back onto a stack of crates while Sarie sits on the one open space on the floor, hugging her knees, staring at nothing in particular.

"I didn't think you'd be home. Didn't see your car."

"I use a lot of different cars. How the hell did you get in here?"

But she ignores the question.

"You said you'd be listening," she says quietly. "Where *were* you?"

"We were both set up. My lieutenant…she's crooked. She's going to pay for what she's done. You can help me do that."

"No."

"I know you've been through a living hell, Sarie, but listen to me, you don't have to be afraid anymore."

"No, that's not what I mean. Lieutenant Mahoney is not the one leaking the information. Her ex-husband was spying on her. Had her apartment bugged. He knew about all of your CIs. Gave their names to the mafia who are muscling into the drug market."

Wildey feels the onset of a crushing sensation in his chest.

"Ex-husband? You're telling me Captain Rem Mahoney, of Internal fucking Affairs, is behind this?"

"He's the one calling the shots, Peter D'Argenio was his second-in-command. D'Argenio's dead. You can find his body and the missing confidential informants down at Pier Sixty-three, under the abandoned tracks."

That crushing feeling only intensifies, like a fucking heart attack, but Wildey knows it's something else. "Fuck me," he says, standing up. "Don't move. Promise me you won't move until I get back!"

Sarie doesn't reply; she rests her head on her knees.

The moment the door slams shut, I start crying again.

For me, for Wildey, for Dad and Marty, for you, for this whole fucked-up situation.

But mostly I cry for Drew—his name was Drew Pike, and I think you would have liked him, Mom. We thought we could save each other, but we underestimated this city and its cruelty.

Wildey didn't set me up, but that's no real comfort. Because the danger's still out there.

There's only one play left, and it makes me sob even harder just thinking about it.

Wildey kicks in the back door—the wood around the knob splinters. He goes in, gun first. But there's no real need, because his lieutenant is already dead and her killer, Captain Rembrandt Mahoney, is hopelessly drunk and sobbing and mumbling, *I only wanted to see what she'd do, I just wanted to see what she'd do, just wanted to see her . . .* They're sitting together on the couch, Kaz with her head tilted to one side, Mahoney pressed up against her, like they'd just been watching TV. There are two bullet wounds in the lieutenant's chest and one in Mahoney's right arm.

Wildey calls it in and places Mahoney under arrest.

*   *   *

By the time Wildey returns home later that morning, he finds two notes. One, slid into his mail slot, is from Kevin Holland:

Officer Wildey, please contact me immediately. Phone number below. This is in regards to my daughter. If you do not contact me I will be forced to be in contact with your supervisor.
Sincerely,
Kevin Holland

The other is a note placed where Sarie had been sitting, held in place with the corner of an album crate.

Wildey,
I had to leave. You'll understand why soon enough. PLEASE:

1. Do not tell anyone I am alive
2. Keep the burner with the number I know
3. Destroy this note after you read it

I will explain later. Sorry I doubted you. Also, I took one of your burner phones and some clothes. It's cold out there.
#137

TRY ANOTHER WORLD

NORTH PHILADELPHIA

CHRISTMAS EVE

The memorial service is bullshit.

Not that it isn't nice or that the university hasn't put real effort into it (even the student choir showed up to the tiny chapel in the basement of College Hall). But Kevin Holland knows it is bullshit because a) his daughter is not dead, he just *knows* it, and no, this is not another case of The Fiction, and b) his daughter is not a criminal, even though this is how she's being presented.

The "official" story from the Philadelphia Police Department is that Serafina Holland was busted while transporting drugs for her boyfriend, Andrew Pike, and agreed to work as a confidential informant to avoid prosecution. Holland also embezzled $2,000 from the bursar's office to help Pike pay off a drug debt. However, Pike's dealer, real estate agent Charles Chaykin, became aware of Holland's status as a CI, and is believed to have ordered the murder of Andrew Pike, whose body was found in a stash house in Pennsport on Friday, December 13. Holland is missing and presumed dead. Chaykin is the prime suspect and is actively being sought by authorities.

Kevin knows this story is bullshit because of Sarie's journals.

So his daughter's memorial service, while touching, is simply part of one big Fiction.

Kevin scans the interior of the chapel. Wildey is here, bowing his head as the choir sings "Ave Maria." All of Sarie's professors are present, with the exception of Professor Chaykin, of course, who promptly resigned (and last Kevin heard was assaulted by persons unknown and is currently under police protection). To Kevin's left is Marty, whose strength and clear thinking through all of this still have him stunned. To his right is Tammy, who's been spending a lot of time at the Holland house lately. Maybe it's guilt, maybe she misses her friend; either way, Kevin is happy to have her around.

After the service, they walk back to guest parking. Wildey approaches.

"Hey."

"Any word?" Kevin asks.

"Nothing yet."

The day it all happened (Friday the thirteenth, no less) Wildey finally showed up at Kevin's house in person. Kevin grappled with the urge to pummel the shit out of the motherfucker, demand to know what he did with Sarie, why the fuck didn't he encourage her to come clean, to ask for help instead of taking this on by herself... but he kept his cool. Wildey, though apologetic, walked in armed with the "official" Philly PD story. Though instead of the "presumed dead" part, he insisted that Sarie was alive and would be located. He'd devote his days to finding her.

"Bullshit," Kevin said.

"Mr. Holland, I can't imagine what you must be feeling right now, but listen to me. Your daughter is the smartest, toughest, and most resourceful person I know and—"

"Yeah, I know. Which is why I'm calling you on your bullshit."

And then he showed him the stack of blue exam book journals.

"What's that?" Wildey asked quietly.

"Pretty much everything," Kevin replied.

After a moment of stunned silence, Wildey started grilling Kevin on how much of his investigation was in those blue exam books. Kevin gave Wildey enough to make him drop the official line.

"What I'm about to tell you has to stay between us," Wildey said.

Kevin told him, "We'll see about that."

Wildey shook his head. "No. Really. You're going to want it that way."

By the end of the conversation, Kevin felt like he'd been whacked upside the head with a sledgehammer. Sarie was gone because Sarie knew she had to stay gone. After all, you can't prosecute someone for murder when they're missing and presumed dead.

"This is insane . . . this is *fucking insane!*"

Wildey told him they both had their fingers on the trigger. Nobody, from the D.A. on up, wanted the truth about Captain Rem Mahoney's ties to organized crime—it would be a fatal blow to a city already reeling from dozens of police scandals. This, though, would be the nuke that could bring a department down. And Kevin sure as shit didn't want his daughter tried for murder—even though it was arguably self-defense, her prints were on that Glock, and her victim had no weapons.

"So where is she now? What is she going to do?"

"She told me she wants to make up for her sins," Wildey said, "and that she'd be in touch."

"Jesus . . ."

"Like I said, Mr. Holland, your daughter is the smartest, toughest, and most resourceful person I know."

That was eleven days ago. And now Wildey is saying there's still no word. *Laura, our daughter is somewhere out there, alone, this huge weight on her shoulders, and I can't do a fucking thing about it.*

"Happy holidays to you, Officer Wildey."

"You too, man."

FORT LAUDERDALE, SLIP F-18

Yo ho ho ho!

Now *this* is where Ringo should have landed after his long stint in Buttfuck, Kansas. Look at that sun sparkling off those pristine white cruisers! Look at all that money bobbing up and down on the clear blue water! Sure, fucking off to Florida is a cliché, but man, sometimes the clichés are that way for a reason. Florida, man, the Sunshine State, the Land of Good Living, also happens to be a fairly convenient way to flee the country, too. Especially if you have your own boat like this motherfucker here, this Charles Chaykin.

Everybody's looking for you, Chuck. But listen up: Your secret's safe. Because even with a couple of slugs in me, I had enough left in the tank to go have a little talk with your dorky brother. He didn't give you up right away. Only after a couple of minutes (and teeth). Oh, and don't worry about him talking to the police. I whispered in his ear a little and told him how that would be a seriously bad idea.

Ringo and Charles, aka Chuckie Morphine, need some quality time together.

Ringo won't kill him right away. That would be foolish. First of all, he needs somebody to teach him how to drive a boat this size. (Or do you pilot a boat? Steer a boat? Ringo reminds himself to ask.) And it'll be smarter to heave his tortured, broken corpse as far out into the ocean as possible. Forget the Lobster Trap; the Atlantic can't be beat when it comes to chump dumping.

Ringo boards the ship, which Chuckie has named KEEPIN' IT REAL (ESTATE). Fuck—this dude seriously needs to die for *that* alone.

Anyway, Merry Christmas, Serafina Holland.

"Yo ho ho ho!" Ringo calls out, as a courtesy.

FOX CHASE

A mutant canary knocks on the front door of the MI6 building.

Canaries? Marty didn't add any canaries to this level. He debates sending some of his mutant sheep up there to take care of his avian problem but then realizes something. *Holy shit. No way...*

His avatar makes it to the front door just in time to watch the canary fly away. But the bird has buried something in the front lawn. Marty's av marches over and digs it up.

There's a password-protected message: five digits. Marty ponders that one for a while before realizing there can only be one possibility. He thumbs: C-I-1-3-7.

HI MARTY. LOVE YOU. MERRY CHRISTMAS

Marty wants to scream with joy, but he's afraid he'll wake Dad and Tammy up. They'd both turned in, leaving Marty to leave out the cookies and milk (even though he totally knows the deal with that) and play a little Diggit before going to sleep.

On second thought, to hell with that. Marty runs to tell his father the news. He swears, no more secrets between them ever again.

DECEMBER 25

Dear Mom,
I wish I'd asked you more about Mexico when you were alive. It's truly beautiful here.

I won't be writing to you anymore; I hope you understand. But words on a page are very risky where I am now. (Going to burn this the moment I finish it, along with the rest of the pages, but I thought you wouldn't be able to hear this if I didn't write down the words. It's kind of our thing.) So much has happened over the last few weeks, and I can't possibly tell you everything except the highlights:

I am safe and gainfully employed and well fed and warm. Most importantly, I know that Dad and Marty will be safe from now on.

The guy who I referred to as Partyman before is looking after me. After I reached out to him on that horrible day, he got me out of Philly and found me this job. He says he's very impressed with how quickly I've adjusted. (I finally know his real name but don't want to risk writing it down, even once.) No, he's not an undercover cop or anything. He actually works for the cartels, traveling around, looking for new business opportunities. The cartel that employs him—well, us—is VERY interested in Philadelphia. Somehow he knew about my past, about you, and it turns out that you were involved with a cartel, so he sees me as a kind of good omen. But mostly, he says he likes how my brain works, and I'm sort of his protégé. In exchange, Partyman will see to it that Dad and Marty are kept safe. Nobody will touch them, so don't worry.

I learned more in the past two weeks than I have during thirteen and a half years of school. Does this say something about me, or about school? Maybe both? Do I take after you, or Dad? I guess that remains to be seen.

Did I mention I was warm? I never want to be cold again. I don't think my blood was meant for Philadelphia. I have more of you in me than I thought.

(I always wanted to go to California. Baja California counts, right?)

I am at peace with what I've done, what I must do, and who I am.

If you see Drew, tell him I'm sorry. He didn't deserve what happened to him, and I will love him forever for trying to save me.

No matter what you hear about me, no matter what I may do, know that I am trying to do the right thing, just like you and Dad taught me.

I love you,

Serafina

THE BADLANDS

CHRISTMAS

Lieutenant Benjamin Franklin Wildey tours the desperate streets of the Badlands. Busy, even on this oh-so-holy night. There will always be people looking to get their high on. Not that he's concerned with that right now. He's headed to pick up his Auntie M. for Christmas dinner. He thought about making something at home, but the hell with that. He's going to take her to a nice restaurant. There are a few open for people like them, people without big families. As much as possible, Wildey wants to enjoy the yuletide calm before the storm.

Narcotics Field Unit-Central South is no more. Having lasted just a little over six months, it will be expunged from the history of the department. Conceived in secret, it was buried in secret, in a shallow grave right beyond the land of Who Cares.

Tons of Mexican heroin about to flood the streets. The smaller ethnic gangs have either been forced out or have been compelled to fall in line. What Mahoney and D'Argenio were setting up would have been torn apart anyway. Unlike before, there is only going to be one supplier. One pipeline. Prices will fall, customers will flock. Then will come the stranglehold. There's going to be a drug war the likes of which this city has never seen.

Good thing Wildey, head of a completely new aboveboard narcotics unit, has a secret weapon in this war.

His burner buzzes. A message he's been waiting for all day finally arrives. It's his informant; she's all the way inside the cartel now.

It's going to be a good new year.

ACKNOWLEDGMENTS

Canary was inspired by dozens of true crime stories in Philadelphia and across the country, so let me tip my hat to the journalists working on the front lines, among them: George Anastasia, Emily Babay, William Bender, Mensah M. Dean, Jeff Deeney, Jenny DeHuff, Daniel Denvir, Dana DiFilippo, Sabrina Rubin Erdely, Mark Fazlollah, David Gambacorta, Dan Geringer, Barbara Laker, Samantha Melamed, Jason Nark, Mike Newall, Jeremy Roebuck, Wendy Ruderman, David Simon, Joseph A. Slobodzian, Allison Steele, Sarah Stillman, Steve Volk, Aubrey Whelan, Sam Wood, and Morgan Zalot. Also, Matthew Cooke's 2012 film *How to Make Money Selling Drugs* was an invaluable resource.

Special thanks to Lou Boxer for assisting me with location scouting, as well as an early read. And thanks to the good folks at CultureWorks Greater Philadelphia for providing me with a quiet place to write.

This bird wouldn't have flown without the Mulholland Books team: Joshua Kendall, Wes Miller, Garrett McGrath, Reagan Arthur, Michael Pietsch, Pam Brown, Morgan Moroney, Kate MacAloney, Jayne Yaffe Kemp, and Janet Byrne. And let me pass the spliff of

ACKNOWLEDGMENTS

thanks to the gang at Inkwell, especially David Hale Smith, Lizz Blaise, Alexis Hurley, and Richard Pine, as well as Lindsay Williams and Shari Smiley at The Gotham Group.

At its heart, *Canary* is a family story, and I couldn't have written it without *my* family. My wife, best friend, and first reader Meredith Swierczynski makes it all possible—you have no idea. My son, Parker, and daughter, Sarah, are sources of constant delight and inspiration, and I'm proud to have finally written a novel they can read without warping their delicate minds. (Too much.)

ABOUT THE AUTHOR

Duane Swierczynski is the author of several crime thrillers, including the Shamus Award–winning Charlie Hardie series (*Fun and Games, Hell and Gone, Point and Shoot*), which is being developed by Sony Pictures Television. He writes the monthly comic series Judge Dredd for IDW and X for Dark Horse, and has written various bestselling comics for Marvel, Dynamite, and DC. He has also collaborated with CSI creator Anthony E. Zuiker on the bestselling Level 26 trilogy. He lives in Philadelphia with his wife and children.

Enjoyed *Canary*?

Why not check out Duane Swierczynski's Charlie Hardie series?

Fun and Games
Hell and Gone
Point and Shoot

Charlie Hardie is a man down on his luck.
He's about to enter a world of trouble.

'Swierczynski steps on the gas early ... and doesn't let up'
Publishers Weekly

'An addictive action trilogy' *The Australian*

'Terrific' *Courier Mail*

'If non-stop, cool action sequences with fun characters are your thing,
you need to read some Swierczynski stories.'
Wired.com

'The most unusual thriller series in a long, long time.'
Booklist

'Like a Quentin Tarantino movie on speed' *CNN.com*

'Swierczynski is a much-needed breath of fresh air in
the book world ... a great storyteller.'
Michael Connelly

'Enough indestructible villains to satisfy a Die Hard fan'
Bloomberg

'A furiously paced tale that cries out to be filmed ... Great fun.'
Canberra Times

'Brilliant...one hell of a rollercoaster read. Mr Swierczynski
writes like Elmore Leonard on adrenaline and speed.'
New York Journal of Books

'More exciting than whatever you're reading
right now.' Ed Brubaker

MULHOLLAND
BOOKS
HODDER